The
Red Shore

William Shaw has been shortlisted for the CWA Gold Dagger and longlisted three times for the Theakston's Crime Novel of the Year. A regular at festivals, he organises crime fiction events in the UK and in south-west Ireland where he now lives. Before becoming a crime writer he was an award-winning journalist. *The Red Shore* is the first in a new series of crime thrillers set in Devon.

@william1shaw
/williamshawwriter
william1shaw

Also by William Shaw

Breen and Tozer series
A Song from Dead Lips
A House of Knives
A Book of Scars
Sympathy for the Devil

DS Alexandra Cupidi
Salt Lane
Deadland
Grave's End
The Trawlerman
The Wild Swimmers

Standalone novels
The Birdwatcher
Dead Rich
The Conspirators

WILLIAM SHAW

The Red Shore

HEMLOCK PRESS

Hemlock Press
An imprint of HarperCollins*Publishers*
1 London Bridge Street,
London SE1 9GF

www.harpercollins.co.uk

HarperCollins*Publishers*
Macken House, 39/40 Mayor Street Upper
Dublin 1, D01 C9W8, Ireland

Published in Great Britain by HarperCollins*Publishers* Ltd 2025

1

Copyright © William Shaw 2025

William Shaw asserts the moral right to be identified as the author of this work.

A catalogue copy of this book is available from the British Library.

ISBN: 9780008720407 (HB)
ISBN: 9780008720414 (TPB)

This novel is entirely a work of fiction. The names, characters and incidents portrayed in it are the work of the author's imagination. Any resemblance to actual persons, living or dead, events or localities is entirely coincidental.

Set in Sabon LT Std by HarperCollins*Publishers* India

Printed and bound in the UK using 100% Renewable Electricity by CPI Group (UK) Ltd

All rights reserved. No part of this text may be reproduced, transmitted, down-loaded, decompiled, reverse engineered, or stored in or introduced into any information storage and retrieval system, in any form or by any means, whether electronic or mechanical, without the express written permission of the publishers.

Without limiting the exclusive rights of any author, contributor or the publisher of this publication, any unauthorised use of this publication to train generative artificial intelligence (AI) technologies is expressly prohibited. HarperCollins also exercise their rights under Article 4(3) of the Digital Single Market Directive 2019/790 and expressly reserve this publication from the text and data mining exception.

MIX
Paper | Supporting responsible forestry
FSC
www.fsc.org
FSC™ C007454

This book contains FSC™ certified paper and other controlled sources to ensure responsible forest management.

For more information visit: www.harpercollins.co.uk/green

*In memory of Chris 'C.J.' Sansom,
with much gratitude*

The Red Shore

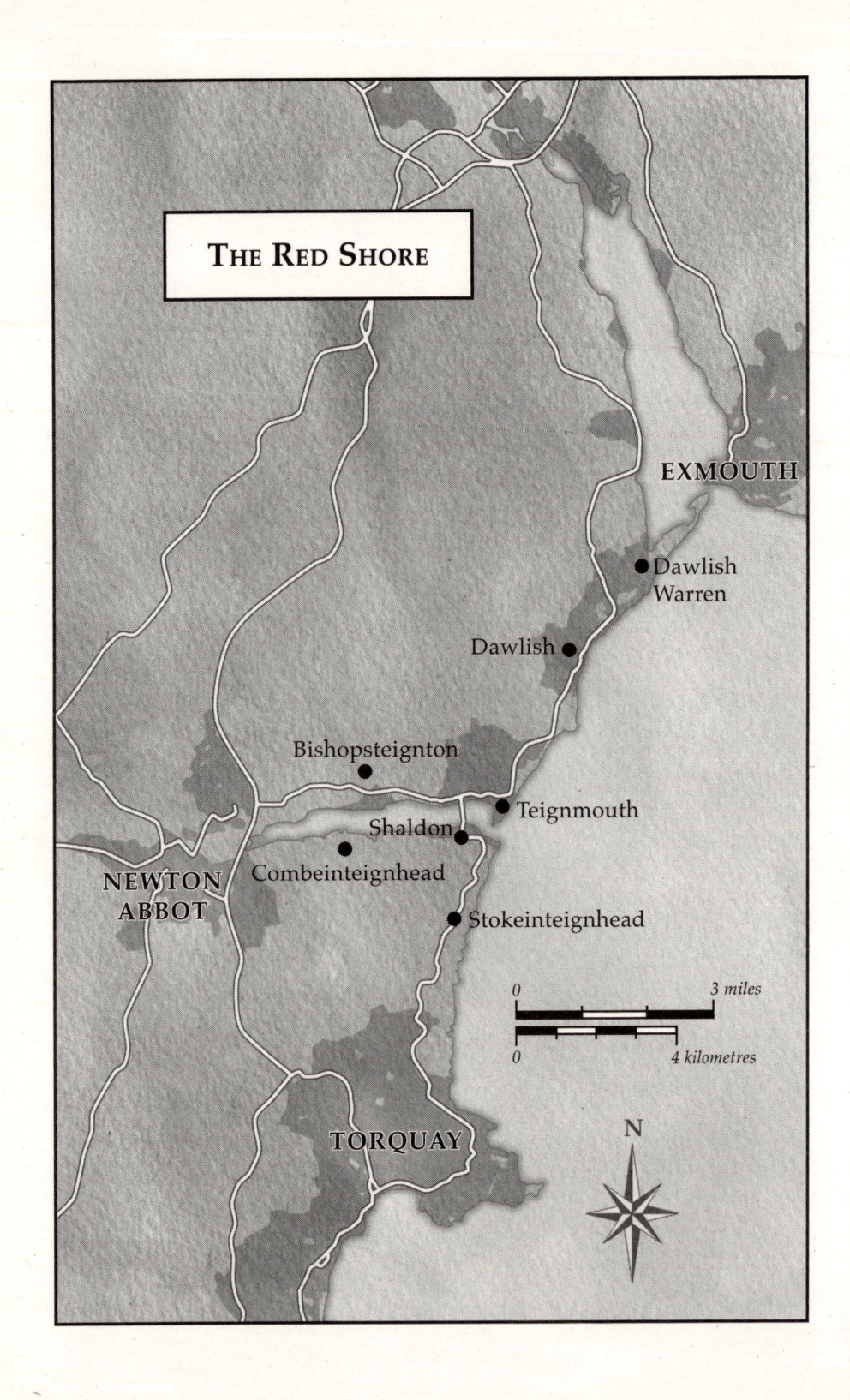

- Exmouth
- Dawlish Warren
- Dawlish
- Bishopsteignton
- Teignmouth
- Shaldon
- Combeinteignhead
- Stokeinteignhead
- Newton Abbot
- Torquay

0 — 3 miles
0 — 4 kilometres

N

Prologue

The boy wakes, scared. Something is wrong. It is all his fault.

'Mum?' he whispers into the night.

The bed he has woken in is rocking from side to side. Above him, voices howl: *Ooooooooo*.

In his night-foggy brain, still tangled in sleep, the boy realises he is not at home in the house on the red beach. He knows he is somewhere else, far away.

He is in the boat.

And then he remembers shouting at his mother and telling her he hated her for taking him out in the boat and for being so weird that everyone teases him at school.

Your mum is so fucking weird.

There is the water, slapping at the boat's sides: *blap blap blap blap*. *Oooooooo*, blows a ghostly wind through the mast's wires, a note that rises and falls in intensity.

He is nine. He has been on this boat often enough to know that it is not ghosts that make the eerie noise, but it might as well be.

He does not like this story. He should have been nicer to his mum. He should not have got angry. The boat should not be moving like this, tipping, pausing, then tipping back the other way – not feeling like it was ever going to stop.

'Mum,' he says out loud. 'I feel sick.'

There is no answer.

'I'm sorry, Mum,' he whispers, reaching out his left hand across the gap between their two bunks. The sheet where she would have been is empty and cold.

Mum is not there.

Of course. She must be sailing the boat.

The black is very black and that makes it harder to breathe. Nothing is steady. Everything is in motion. There is acid in his throat.

Blap blap blap blap. A little bit more awake now, he realises that water should not be slapping at the boat's sides like this. It is not the right noise. The right noise would be the creakiness of being at anchor, or the thump of sailing into waves, or the grumbling of the diesel engine. This is something different. The boat should not be moving this way, like a roly-poly toy clown. It doesn't feel right.

'Mum.' He sits up, feels instantly seasick. 'I'm scared.'

On the right side of his bunk is a curtained oval window. He pulls back the fabric and peers out, nose against cold glass. No lights; no stars. Just black.

Added to the noise of the water and the wind, his own breath. *Please don't cry. Please don't cry.*

When he tries to get out of the sleeping bag it's like someone is grabbing his legs. His feet are tangled in it. He tugs and tugs until finally one is free, then the other.

'Mum!'

He drops his legs over onto the unsteady floor, feels in the dark for the aluminium doorhandle, turns and pulls.

It does not move.

'Mum?'

He tugs at the door harder. He has been locked in.

'Mum!' Voice trembly now. 'I'm sorry, Mum. I didn't mean it.' Bangs now. 'Mum!'

Eventually fingers find the switch on the round light above the head of his bed and suddenly he is blinking in the brightness. There is no sign of his mother; no sign her bunk has been slept in.

'Mum, where are you?' he shouts.

Blap blap blap blap goes the water.

Oooooooo goes the wind, its note higher.

'Mum!' he screams, louder than he has ever screamed in his life, and he yanks at the handle as hard as he can but something is stopping the door from opening.

His mum is not sailing the boat, he realises. There is no one on the boat apart from him and his mother has gone.

And if he hadn't shouted at her this would all be different.

He peers at the narrow crack between the door and the frame and he can see nothing at all.

He is here, in the middle of the sea, all on his own and the night is dark and the boat is out of control. And now he is really cold and scared. His mother is gone, and it is all his fault.

In a small, dark room in London, a woman reads the Shipping Forecast into the BBC microphone. 'Portland, Plymouth,' she says, 'Southeast, 6 to 7 occasionally gale 8, squally showers, good becoming poor in showers.'

The weather in the Channel is worsening. Out in the sea, there is a boat. Its navigation lights should be on, but they are not. There is no sail hoisted. Hull side on against rising wind, the mast sways to and fro in a wide arc sweeping across the water. The keel creaks. The noise of the wind in the halyards is louder now. It is drifting, at the mercy of the south-easterly.

'Help me,' says the boy in the cabin, slipping onto the cold floor. 'Please help me. I'm alone.'

One

'Single. And happily so,' answered DS Eden Driscoll.

'No big ex?' teased Constable Lisa Ali.

'Shut up.'

'No kids?'

'With this job? Last thing on my mind is children.'

'Well, that's just one more challenge I'm going to have to overcome,' announced Lisa in a sing-song voice. 'I see us with two children. Girl and a boy.'

Eden could hear other coppers' laughter in his earpiece. The third day of sitting on the bench at Walthamstow Waterworks in East London, Constable Ali was obviously bored. Some people were just not cut out for undercover work.

'Are you lot enjoying this conversation?' whispered Eden.

'Loving it,' answered Lima One from his post in the unmarked van.

Constable Lisa Ali was five years his junior and she was taking the piss. Eden stood in the bird hide at the centre of the waterworks, a pair of binoculars round his neck, raising them occasionally to scan what he could see of the footpath behind the wall. Lisa was talking to Eden on the radio she was wearing under a headscarf. DS Eden Driscoll had laid the trap, and Constable Lisa Ali was the bait.

'We can call the boy Eden Junior if you like. Eden. That's an interesting name,' said Lisa.

'You reckon?' Eden whispered into his mike.

'Just that I've never met anyone called Eden before.'

'At least I did better than my sister. She's Apple.'

Lisa laughed, a good, hearty laugh.

'Not so loud,' cautioned Eden. 'You're not supposed to be happy.' Eden could hear Lima Three snorting too. 'Come on, guys. Keep it together.'

'He's not here,' answered Lisa. 'Three days and there's no one bloody here apart from you and me and the rest of the boys – and, while it's been nice, my bum is getting cold. He's not going to show.'

'We have two more hours,' pleaded Eden.

'He' was Ronan Pan, also known as Tony Markle and Tony Jalil, ex-partner of Hasina Hossein. Hasina Hossein was currently living under protection at a women's refuge miles from here after Ronan had threatened to kill her.

Lisa looked a lot like Hasina: tall, dark-eyed, round-faced and slight. It was why Eden had picked her. Eden had warned Lisa, Ronan was a very dangerous man who had coerced several women – including Hasina – into sex work and threatened to kill Hasina for leaving him.

Lisa had jumped at the chance. 'Are you kidding?' she had said. 'I could be sitting in a patrol car watching my sergeant pick his nose or I could actually do something to help catch a very bad man.'

The first time Hasina had tried to leave him Ronan had poured boiling water on her back. Working on the Major Incident Team, Eden had seen the half-healed skin for himself, pale white. There had been other women before Hasina too. Once, Ronan had sprayed a teenager's face with battery acid. Afterwards the girl had refused to testify against him because she was so afraid he would do it again.

'So you've never had an actual girlfriend?' asked Lisa.

'I didn't say that.'

'Oh, God. I think Diesel is pooing again. How much can a dog hold?'

Diesel was Ronan's American Bulldog, a beefy, big-jawed, stupid-looking animal. Hasina had taken the dog with her when she escaped. Apparently Ronan was as angry about that as he was about Hasina leaving.

After the assault, Ronan had vanished, just as he had done before. He appeared to have the keys to properties all over the East End, and no amount of intel would reveal his whereabouts. Eden had worked to win Hasina's confidence. He had promised to keep her safe.

It was the dog that had given Eden the idea. It was a pretty distinctive beast. They knew that Ronan had operated around Limehouse. He had spent a little time seeding rumours among the market workers on Commercial Road that Hasina – and Diesel – had been seen out here in Walthamstow. Hasina might have gone into hiding, but she would need to take the dog out for a walk every day. Eden had gone so far as to create a fake women's refuge at an address close to here. Every morning for the last three days, Lisa had walked Diesel from there to here, to the wildlife reserve that had been created in this disused Victorian water treatment works, waiting.

'Oh, bloody God!' exclaimed Lisa. 'It's a runny one. I am not going to clear that up. I bet you Hasina wouldn't. And I'm acting as her, right? Like, method. I probably hang the poo in trees if I do pick it up.'

'Voice. Down.'

'Oh, come on, Eden. Three days and no sign of him. He's not coming, is he?' complained Lisa.

The Detective Chief Inspector had okayed the budget, but only for a limited period. He had not been convinced. And now this was Saturday, day three of three, and they had come up with nothing. Operations like this cost money. It had all been Eden's idea, and it had been a waste of time, so far at least. Either Ronan had not picked up on the rumours Eden had tried to start, or he was not as angry about losing Hasina and the dog as Eden had calculated.

They had four pairs of eyes on the small park. There was an unmarked van parked off the Lea Bridge Road, another officer dressed as an angler on the footbridge over the Lea, and a fourth was concealed in brambles to the west. Time and money.

Today was Saturday too, which was more expensive. He only had the officers until 4 p.m.

'Seriously. You're a good-looking boy, Eden. Loads of the girls say so,' flirted Lisa.

'Thank you. You know this is all on tape, don't you?' said Eden. 'That's on public record now.'

'What about the rest of us?' Lima Four demanded.

'You're not single like Driscoll is, Billy,' said Lisa. 'Or as good-looking.'

Lima Four was DC Bailey, known as 'Bill'. Bill was an old hand at this kind of thing.

'Lima One,' a voice interrupted. 'Woman coming your way down main track.' Lima One was the van, parked by the main road. 'Birdwatcher, I think it's the one who came yesterday, by the look of it. Red coat. Scarf. Maybe you can strike up a little relationship, Eden, like Lisa says. She's got a lovely big pair of binoculars.'

'Hands off, bitch,' said Lisa. 'He's mine.'

'Come on, you lot,' said Eden. 'Last couple of hours. Keep it together. We have to concentrate.'

For a while, the mics went quiet. They sat in silence, waiting. Birds sang. A heron flew overhead, neck long, beak sharp.

Then Lisa's voice burst into Eden's earpiece. 'Oh, God!'

'What?' Eden lifted his binoculars, tense. But Lisa was still on her own, just hunched over her phone. There was no one else in sight.

'Anyone else seen this story, just come up on the news? The RNLI picked up a yacht floating in the Channel this morning. No one on deck,' Lisa continued. 'It looked abandoned, but when they boarded it they found a nine-year-old boy locked in one of the cabins. All on his own. His mother had been sailing it, apparently. But she vanished. They're doing an air and sea search for her. I guess she must have fallen overboard. Boy on his own, out there on the sea, shut in a cabin.'

'Poor kid,' said Lima One.

'Just imagine that,' said Lisa.

'Concentrate,' said Eden again.

'Breaks my heart,' said Lisa.

'Oi! Handsome,' interrupted a voice, speaking in a whisper. 'Man resembling the suspect approaching from my direction.'

'Say again?' said Eden.

It was Bill's voice. 'Man, on his own, coming across from the marshes. Fits the picture.'

'Serious?' breathed Lisa.

'Yes. Ten metres away from me now.'

'Shit.' Lisa was suddenly quiet.

They had all been issued with photographs, mostly culled from social media. The photos had never been of Ronan himself; he was camera shy. His was just a face glimpsed in the background of other people's photographs. They had clipped his fuzzy face from group shots. It was the best they could do. There was a photofit too, done by Hasina. But they knew for sure he was stocky. Hasina had reckoned around five-eight.

'Yep. I think it's him,' said the voice again. 'Short-arse.' The voice was DC Bailey's – Lima Four – stationed at the footbridge over the River Lea.

One of the reasons Eden had chosen this place was that there were only two ways of approaching the site without climbing over fences – from the main road to the north, where Lima One was stationed, and the Hackney Marshes to the south.

'He's past me. I'm following the suspect now,' whispered Bailey.

'Fuck, fuck, fuck,' muttered Lisa.

'Don't worry, Lisa,' Bailey assured her. 'I'm right behind him.'

Eden had a good view of Lisa, but not of the path leading towards her from the south. He scanned to the right to try and spot the man approaching.

'I got eyes on him too,' said a third voice. 'Looks good. Closing in.'

Eden looked around but could see nothing. From where he stood in the middle of the old waterworks, trees and scrub blocked his vision. Two men said the suspect was a good match. That was enough. Eden didn't want to risk Ronan getting anywhere near Lisa.

'Move,' he said into his mic. 'All officers.'

Abandoning his position, Eden jogged over to where he could get a better view of the land to the south. He lifted up his binoculars and scanned the vegetation, looking for movement.

There was the suspect, walking towards them, just a silhouette against the tree trunks. Eden broke into a run – not towards him, but towards Lisa, to make sure that he was between the suspect and her. There were two officers behind the man, closing in.

They had discussed in detail how they would detain Ronan. They needed to make sure they had Ronan surrounded before they let him know they were police. They didn't want to risk his getting away.

Lima One would be out of the van and running towards them. The other two were closing from the opposite side. Now he was in open ground, Eden could see the man wore a pale grey mac and black trainers. As soon as Eden saw that Bailey was behind the man, taser at the ready, Eden said quietly into his radio, 'Go!'

'Stop. Police!' called out Bailey.

The figure stopped, turned to see a man holding a warrant card in one hand and a taser in the other.

'Stop. Police. Get down on the ground,' ordered Bailey, voice loud and clear.

Instead, the man turned again and ran, lunging straight towards Eden – towards PC Ali – then darting to Eden's left.

Eden threw himself at him, but the man was quick. Eden only managed to grab his calf but it was enough. The man fell heavily onto the gravel path. He screamed.

Catching up with them, Bailey threw himself on top of the prone man, landing heavily.

'What the fuck?' squealed the man, kicking the leg Eden was holding.

'Ronan Pan,' Bailey panted, 'we are arresting you under Section 76 of the Serious Crime Act—'

'What you bloody on about?' Face down, the man was wriggling under the weight of them both.

'2015 . . .'

Eden was up on his knees, cuffs out. Lima One had arrived too, panting.

'You broke my bloody nose,' the man was complaining loudly.

But something was wrong, Eden realised. The man they had wrestled to the ground was talking in a Midlands accent. Eden had heard Ronan's voice on Hasina's voicemail. It didn't fit. 'Roll him over.'

But before they could do that Lisa screamed.

Two

Afterwards, in the Escape Bar, where the whole team had gathered to celebrate the arrest of Ronan Pan, Eden bought the first round, then the second.

Lisa was on Aperol Spritz. 'You can drink as much as you like of this stuff and it never makes you drunk,' she said. 'Apparently.'

'"You broke my bloody nose!"' Bailey was laughing, recounting the afternoon's events again to the officers and PCSOs who had joined them in the pub. 'Poor guy. He was fucking furious.'

It was like this on the rare days when the Major Investigation Team scored a success. Everyone was jubilant, drunk on the sense that they had done a dark job and that the world was better for it.

Eden handed Lisa the drink and led her away from the crowd towards an empty table in a quieter corner. It had been a busy evening, completing paperwork, conducting preliminary interviews. There had not been a chance to talk to her properly.

Lisa sat at the table, pulled the slice of orange from her drink and sucked on it.

'Are you sure you're OK?' Eden asked her.

'Bit shaky. I still got loads of adrenaline going round inside. It all happened so fast.'

'I'm sorry about what happened,' he said. 'It was my fault. I take full responsibility.'

'I mean, he didn't actually do anything to me.'

Ronan Pan been the one wearing a woman's red overcoat and headscarf. He was the one who had been carrying a pair of binoculars. Just as they had been watching out for him, it turned out he had been observing Lisa and the dog, Diesel.

'He could have, though. You must have been scared,' he said.

'I screamed pretty loud, didn't I?' She smiled lopsidedly, and for a second Eden thought she was going to cry.

'It certainly got our attention.'

She laughed, but she was looking at him more warily now. 'What about you?' she asked.

'What do you mean?'

'Are you OK?'

'Me?' Eden blinked. 'I'm fine. We got him, didn't we?'

'Yeah, we did, but that's not what I meant. I mean, I was scared, but you . . .'

'Me what?'

She took a gulp from her glass. 'Only you were hitting him pretty hard.'

Eden wasn't expecting that. 'Was I?'

When Lisa had screamed, Eden had leapt up – and off the legs of the man he had tackled. There wasn't much time to think.

When he turned, he saw that Ronan Pan had grabbed Diesel's lead but was staring at Lisa. 'Who the fuck—?' Ronan had exclaimed, realising that the woman holding the dog was not his ex-girlfriend.

He must have heard Eden running towards him. Looked up. Figured out in that moment that it was a trap. Ronan's mistake had been to hold onto the dog's lead, wrapping it round his wrist. When he had tried to run, Diesel hadn't. Maybe Diesel wasn't as stupid as he looked. Maybe he had liked Lisa more.

Eden was on him before Ronan could disentangle himself from the dog, colliding with the man, his head down, shoulder into his stomach, hitting so hard he knocked Ronan right off his feet.

'He was trying to get away,' said Eden.

Lisa nodded. She took another mouthful of her orange-coloured drink. 'Only he was already down when you began to hit him.'

Eden remembered now, the shock in his fist as it connected with Ronan's cheekbone. He looked down at his hand holding the glass. The knuckles were swollen. He tried to remember how many times he had hit him after the first time, kneeling on the man's chest.

She pursed her lips.

'I was worried he'd get up,' Eden said, though he was not sure that was true.

'Right.' Lisa dipped her finger into the glass. 'It was just quite a lot, that's all. I understand he's dangerous. But.'

He looked at her. 'And have you said that in your report? That I used excessive force?'

She shook her head. 'No.' She looked nervous though.

Eden had been in the Major Incident Team for three years. Domestic violence was a specialism. He loved the work. He loved helping vulnerable people. He had a mortgage on a nice cool flat. All that could vanish with a word to Professional Standards. 'You saw it,' Eden said. 'You should have put it in your report. If that's what you think happened, you should say so. You're a police officer. I wouldn't stop you.'

By the time the other two officers reached them, getting off the unfortunate man they had mistaken for Ronan, it was all over. Only Lisa had witnessed him punching Ronan.

'I was just a bit shocked, that's all,' she said. 'I mean, I'm not saying he didn't deserve it – the things he's done to women . . . I just didn't think you were that kind of bloke.'

'A man who hits people?'

She nodded. 'It wasn't just hitting him. You looked, I don't know . . .'

'Angry?'

She shook her head. 'Not really angry. Upset, I suppose. Confused. Sad, really. Yeah. So that's why I asked whether you're OK or not. What was all that about?'

He looked down at his lager. Though he had bought two rounds for the team, he'd hardly touched his own drink.

'Don't get me wrong,' Lisa said. 'I'm dead proud of what we did there. That whole thing was your idea and it worked. Yay for that. He's a terrible man.'

'But?'

'Yeah. But. So . . . are you OK?'

Before they could talk more, DI Sammy Kadakia – Eden's boss – was next to them, grinning. 'Hope I'm not interrupting?'

Immediately, both Lisa and Eden shook their heads.

'Wow. I really was interrupting something!' Kadakia laughed.

'No. No,' said Lisa. 'Nothing like that.'

'Woman of the hour.' Sammy addressed Lisa. 'We are

so grateful to you, Constable Ali. We couldn't have done it without you. Let me buy you a drink.'

She held up her glass. 'Aperol Spritz, please, boss. You can drink loads of them without getting drunk.'

'Right you are. Eden?'

Eden shook his head. He never really enjoyed long drinking sessions with his colleagues.

'Eden Driscoll,' said Sammy, putting his hand round Eden's shoulder at the bar, 'you did good. When I told Hasina Hossein that we had him in custody, she danced.' Grinning, he raised his palms, pushing them skywards, and did a little dance of his own. 'The SIO is taking all the credit, obviously.'

'Obviously,' said Eden.

It was half-ten, and Eden was just going to slip away home when one of the PSCOs approached him and said, 'That PC, Lisa. She's being sick in the bathroom. I think someone needs to take her home.'

Eden looked around. All the women had gone home apart from the PSCO, who was drunk herself. 'I have a babysitter to get home to,' the PSCO protested.

Outside in the cool May air, waiting for a taxi, Lisa said, 'I think someone must have put something in my drink.'

'Alcohol, probably,' answered Eden.

'Oh, yeah. Probably that too.'

Before letting them in the cab, the taxi driver looked at Lisa suspiciously. 'Is she OK?'

'She's fine,' said Eden. 'Just a tough day.'

Lisa lived on the fourth floor of a yellow-brick apartment block in Rotherhithe. Eden led her from the cab towards the front door. He had to use her key to open the door and then hold her up when the lift came.

It was a nice flat, if small, and it smelled of mandarin air-freshener. There was a bowl of fresh fruit on a table in the middle of the room and photos of smiling friends and relations crowded onto the shelves.

'I'm going to put you in your bedroom. Is that OK?'

'I'm so ashamed,' she said miserably.

It was only a one-bedroom flat, so it wasn't hard to guess which room it was. The bed hadn't been made. There was a white carpet on the floor and her pyjamas were lying on it.

'Shoes off,' he said. 'Just lie down and I'll get you a glass of water, then I'll let myself out.'

He found a bowl under the sink to put by her bed in case she was sick in the night. He was expecting her to be asleep by the time he returned with the water and the bowl, but she wasn't. She was still lying on the bed, fully clothed.

'I'm so sorry,' she slurred. Tears were running down her cheeks. 'I really am. I'm just so fucking embarrassed.'

'Happens to all of us. I'll leave you now. OK?'

'It's just so awfully sad,' she said quietly.

'What is?'

'That boy in the boat. Out on the sea. All on his own. It's just so sad.'

For a second he wondered what she was talking about, then he remembered the news she had been reading on her phone.

'Go to sleep, Lisa. I'll let myself out and post the key back through the letterbox.'

She rolled onto her side and curled up like a baby. 'I keep thinking, what would that have been like for that woman, falling overboard, knowing her child was still on the boat?'

Walking to the door, he turned out the light.

'Go to sleep now,' he said.

'Would you ever have kids, Eden?' she asked in the darkness.

'I'd be no good at that.'

'No,' she said. 'I don't think you would.'

He paused at the door. 'I'm sorry about hitting the man like that,' he said, backing out. 'I shouldn't have. Maybe I can explain.' But she was already snoring gently, so he locked the door behind himself, pushed the key through the letterbox and called another taxi to take him home.

The next morning he woke in his own bed, in his own flat in Manor House, his phone buzzing gently on the bedside table.

He picked up the mobile. It was just after seven, but he would be getting up soon anyway for a Park Run. It was Sunday morning. He wondered if it was Lisa Ali calling to apologise. Peering at the number, he didn't recognise it, so he ignored the call.

The phone buzzed again. This time it was a message.

Please call me at your earliest convenience. Mike Sweet, Devon and Cornwall Police.

He frowned. It would be something to do with work. Odd for him to be calling so early on a Sunday morning, though. Eden was awake now, so he went to the kitchen and made himself a coffee, pulled open the blinds onto a sunny May morning, and returned Mike Sweet of Devon and Cornwall Police's call.

'Detective Sergeant Eden Driscoll,' Eden said when the man answered.

'Oh. You're a police officer?' There was surprise in Sweet's voice.

'Yes.' Eden was puzzled now, too. He had assumed he was being called on police business.

'Are you the brother of Apple Driscoll?'

'Yes.' As a police officer he was suddenly aware of the role he was about to play in this conversation and he knew from experience that it was not a good one.

'I'm afraid I have some bad news,' the officer said. 'Your sister is missing.'

'What do you mean, missing?'

'I'm sorry to have to tell you that your sister disappeared from her sailing boat in Lyme Bay some time on Friday night. Though the search is ongoing, at this stage we have to assume that she may have drowned.'

He looked at the bubbles on the surface of his black coffee, trying to understand what he was hearing.

'Mr Driscoll? Are you still there?'

Three

Eden Driscoll had not spoken to his sister in twelve years and now she was missing. Worse. She was almost certainly dead.

He followed the satnav in a daze of misery and self-reproach for what felt like hours, until finally it told him to leave the dual carriageway and he found himself crossing a mile of heathland, dotted with scrubby pine trees, brown bracken and yellow-flowered gorse. The route descended into a high-hedged road that wound towards the Devon coast. Rounding a corner, a huge green tractor chugged in front of him, flashing orange lights. He slowed.

He had watched the news again on his phone before setting off. This time, with a shock, he had recognised the yacht. It was *Calliope*. They hadn't mentioned his sister by name; they would still be trying to get in touch with other relatives. He had wondered if there were any and who they might be. There had been a boy aboard the yacht. Eden hadn't known that Apple had a son.

The last time he had heard from Apple was when their mother died. She had written him a letter telling him their mother was ill, but it had taken too long to arrive and she had been dead by the time he read it. They had spoken briefly on the phone; she had tried to persuade Eden to return to Greece for the funeral. He had said he was too busy. The truth was he had not wanted to come back. They had not contacted each other since.

He had left the car radio on 5 Live in case there were updates about his sister, hoping she would be found alive somewhere in the Channel, but there was nothing. The story of the yacht was already yesterday's news.

In his rear-view mirror, he saw that cars had begun to queue behind him. He did not know these twisting roads, so he hung back, reluctant to attempt overtaking the tractor. It turned off, finally, then he rounded a bend and there, at the bottom of a steep hill below him, was the mouth of a large river.

On the far side rose a bulky red cliff, crowned with thick trees. Inside the narrow river mouth lay a curve of water, a wide estuary crossed by a long road bridge, anchored boats dotting the blue.

He was tired. He needed a coffee. It had taken him four hours to get here. He guessed it would take him at least another three to make it back to London this afternoon.

The roads became thinner still as he descended into the seaside town and neared the address Sweet had given him, until he finally turned into one that was barely wide enough to slide his Audi into. As he inched down it, cautious of his paintwork, the noise of a foghorn startled him. The unexpected bow of a large blue ship crossed the end of the street, absurdly massive against the tiny houses on either side of him. He had not expected a place like this to have docks.

He turned into a tiny cul-de-sac that ran behind two rows of houses, a hotch-potch of irregularly shaped yards and extensions on both sides. At the end of the street he got out, grateful to be still for a second, and looked around.

'You all right, mate? Lost?'

He looked up. At the other end of the cul-de-sac, a young man was hefting an outboard motor in one hand, making its weight look light.

Eden straightened. 'I'm OK, thanks.' The man, hair the colour of straw, arms tanned brown, nodded, continued on his way. Eden watched him disappear down towards the estuary.

Detective Sergeant Mike Sweet had told Eden to call him when he was at the address. He pulled his phone from his pocket. 'Five minutes,' the voice replied.

Eden checked the house number and looked around. It was not easy to make out which house was his sister's. According to the address Sweet had given him, his sister's house was number 14, but the numbers he could see only went up to 13.

He noticed an alleyway at the end of the narrow street, a dogleg that ran alongside an old stone wall. 'Hello?' he called out. No one answered, so he made his way down it. It led to the back of a small house that looked like it had been squeezed in between two larger neighbours.

To the right of the door was a small window. He put his forehead against the glass and peered in. His sister's kitchen was messy, washing-up piled in a sink below the window. On the opposite wall, a child's drawings – felt-tip dinosaurs and super-heroes.

'Eden Driscoll?'

He turned. Detective Sergeant Sweet was in his forties, a tall, big-bellied, broad-shouldered man who filled the alleyway. 'I'm so very sorry for your . . . situation,' he said awkwardly. Behind the police officer, peering around his bulk, was a woman. She was younger, with bleached Afro hair, blue dungarees, a bright green T-shirt and scuffed red Kickers.

'Anything?' Eden looked at Sweet.

'Oh, yeah.' The older man looked awkward. 'Unfortunately not. No news. The coastguard resumed the aerial search at sunrise but nothing so far.'

The woman behind Sweet pushed past, hand extended. 'Bisi Smith,' she said. 'From Devon County Council Child Protection.' Bisi had the look of someone auditioning to be a children's TV presenter. 'You must be devastated.'

'First thing is,' said Sweet, 'do we have your permission to enter the house?'

'My permission?'

Bisi stepped forward. 'I'm sorry. This must be very confusing for you. Your nephew, Finn, is with an emergency foster family right now. We'd like to get him some of his clothes, and some toys maybe. Things he feels familiar with.'

'And we need your permission for entry,' said Sweet.

He should have known this. Even if Sweet was an officer, he couldn't just go barging into a property without asking. 'Finn?' His brain seemed to be a beat behind everything that was happening. 'That's the boy?'

'Your nephew.' Bisi looked at him as if she was trying to figure out why he wouldn't know that already.

'Of course,' he said. 'Finn.'

'May we enter?' Sweet asked again.

'Yes. Go ahead.'

Sweet stepped forward and reached behind a downpipe to the right of the back door, pulled out a Yale key and slotted it into the lock. The policeman in Eden scolded his sister for being so careless. They had always been so different.

'You knew it was there?'

'Oh, yes,' said Sweet. 'Already found it.' He led them through the grubby kitchen into a tiny but cluttered living room, pictures, postcards and notes tacked haphazardly to the walls, which had been painted a hippy-ish maroon. A pair of glass doors on the far side dominated the room; they seemed to open straight onto sand outside.

The house appeared to have been built right on the beach. The sand wasn't pale, like the beaches he knew. It was a dark, brownish red.

'You probably want a minute to . . .' Sweet said hesitantly. 'You know. To yourself.'

The view through the glass doors was remarkable. A broad curve of estuary, thronged with moored boats. There was a piece of paper taped to the door. The afternoon light shone through it so Eden could read the message in reverse, in big red handwritten letters:

**Take your rubbish home
PLASTIC KILLS**

He tried the handle. The UPVC door was locked. He turned the key and opened the door.

The air smelled of salt and seaweed. He stepped outside onto the sand. In front of him was a large circle of water: the docks to the right, the bridge ahead, some houses on the opposite bank. He took a couple of steps towards the water, then looked back.

His sister's was part of a terrace of cottages built above the high-tide line, painted in chintzy pinks and blues and yellows. He realised he was standing on a spit of sand that seemed to extend from the higher ground behind the docks, right out to the mouth of the estuary. To the left there were thick-walled stone warehouses. To the right, more houses that gave way to a jumbled line of beach huts that decreased in size and eccentricity as they neared the end of the spit.

The tide was in, leaving only a few yards of sand in front of the house. What remained was crammed with small boats pulled up out of the water. Beyond, yachts and trawlers bobbed in a fast current. To Eden, the water seemed dangerously close.

'Tea, Mr Driscoll?'

The police officer was calling him. He went back inside.

'I'm putting the kettle on,' said Sweet from the kitchen.

'Long drive?' asked Bisi.

'Long enough.'

'Oh, dear God.' It was Sweet's voice again. 'There only seems to be oat milk.'

'Is there coffee?' Eden asked.

'No . . .there's every kind of herbal though. Lemon and ginseng. Elderflower.'

'How did you know how to find me?' Eden raised his voice so Sweet could hear him.

'Social workers tracked you down,' said Sweet. The sound of cupboard doors opening. 'Oh, dear lord. Turmeric chai.'

Standing beside him in the living room, Bisi spoke softly. 'We were looking for relations, obviously. We worked out the name of Apple's mum and dad, saw she had one brother. Not many Eden Driscolls around. Police tracked down a phone number in your name. Obviously if we'd had time, we'd have looked for an address book in here.' She looked around.

'It wouldn't have helped if you'd found one,' said Eden.

'Why?' Bisi looked puzzled.

Sergeant Sweet appeared around the door, interrupting before Eden could answer. 'I'll just go out and fetch a coffee from the pub, then. Only be a minute.' He paused. 'One thing first though.'

'What?' said Eden.

'Bit sensitive, I know. But if you're taking a look around, if you find anything like a note, you will pass it on, won't you?'

'A note?'

'Explaining your sister's state of mind,' said the sergeant.

Bisi was glaring at Sweet. Eden blinked. 'You think she killed herself?'

'Well,' said the older man, wrinkling his nose as he stood in the doorway. 'Don't want to sound insensitive, but obviously, you know . . . it's a possibility.'

Four

'Sorry about that,' said the social worker. 'Lovely man, but not the greatest social skills.'

'I know a lot of coppers like that.'

'Me too,' said Bisi.

He was finding small talk difficult. 'You a local?'

'Do I look like a local?' She laughed. 'From London. Like you.' So she had read up on him.

On the sand below them, the man he had seen earlier was tugging a canvas cover off a small boat of some kind. Eden twisted a key in the door and pulled it open. The air smelled of salt.

'The best view, isn't it?'

He turned.

'I would love to live in a house like this,' the social worker said. 'This view. I expect your sister must love it too.'

Present tense. She was more tactful than the copper, at least. He would hate to live in this house. Too small. Too old. He liked the rectangular modernity of his London apartment.

'I'm sure your nephew will be glad to see you.'

Eden looked at her. 'Will he?'

'A friendly face,' she said.

Eden had been driving all morning. He was feeling disoriented. 'Actually, I have never met him,' he said. 'In fact, I didn't even know he existed until this morning.'

'Oh.' The social worker pursed her lips. 'Oh,' she said again. 'Well. That complicates matters a little.'

Suddenly exhausted by everything, Eden stepped back and flopped down on a small couch that faced the open door. To the door's right was a small shelf with a couple of books; propped next to them was a painting of the Hindu god Ganesh, surrounded by half-burned candles. The small, messy room was the exact opposite of his modern, white-walled London apartment. 'You were hoping I would be able to take Finn off your hands without a fuss,' he said.

'God. I hope we're not as brutal as that.' Bisi propped herself on the arm of a low armchair opposite him. 'But obviously in your line of work you would know the score. It's an awful situation. Fortunately, as I told you, we found a carer for him last night. I mean, Mrs Sullivan's great, but it's not ideal. We were hoping there was a relative – somewhere safe he could go.'

'He was on the boat on his own?'

'Yes.'

'How awful.' Eden gazed down at his trainers. 'The truth of the matter is, I haven't seen my sister in a very long time.' He looked up, meeting Bisi's eye. 'Apple and me . . . we were not close. What about the boy's father?'

Bisi pursed her lips, then said, 'That's a bit of an issue. No record of him. Nothing on the birth certificate. We'll continue to look, obviously.' She watched him sympathetically. 'Do you mind if I ask you why you were not close with your sister?'

He knew now why she was taking such an interest in the details of his life. It was what social workers did. They had to assess the situation.

'Long story,' said Eden, gazing past her through the glass. 'My sister and I, we grew up in an abusive situation. Not sexual abuse – just a kind of neglect, really. I ran away. My sister chose to stay. She was the oldest. The more responsible one, I suppose. I don't think she ever forgave me for leaving.'

'It was just the two of you – and your parents?'

Eden nodded slowly. 'Our father died. I left not long after that. And then our mother went a while back.'

'I'm sorry.'

Above Ganesh were more of Finn's drawings. A pirate ship with a space rocket flying over it. A picture of a pig with a speech bubble coming out of its mouth that said, for no apparent reason, 'Kingsize Fart'.

Though he found his sister's clutter annoying, as a police officer who had been involved a great deal with domestic abuse, he always thought it was a good sign when you walked into a house full of children's drawings. The houses where you didn't see that always put him on alert. This made him a tiny bit happier. His sister had obviously been a much better mother than theirs had been.

'Finn must have other relations,' Eden said. 'I mean, I can't be the only one.'

'I'm sure he must.' Bisi nodded. 'We'll keep looking, and you never know.'

She obviously hoped so too. In just a couple of minutes he had demonstrated that he was not her ideal candidate to look after Finn.

Sweet returned with three takeaway coffees.

'I'd better go and pick up some of his belongings. He'll be happier in his own clothes,' said Bisi, standing. 'I'll leave you two to talk.' She took her paper cup and disappeared with it up a steep, narrow staircase.

'Find anything?' demanded Sweet.

Eden shook his head. He looked around the small living room. Among the mess of images and notices tacked to the walls hung a badly framed hippy-ish painting of a naked woman, pregnant, with a flame rising above her head. To its right was a school photograph of Finn in a white shirt, a big grin on his face. With shock, Eden recognised the photo Apple had pinned next to it.

In it, Apple and Eden were sitting on a rocky Mediterranean wall, their mother and father standing on either side of them. Mum, shyly squinting at the camera in the sunlight. Dad, bare-chested and tanned, his expression fierce. Eden had no photographs of himself as a boy.

The boy, Finn, looked so much like him. Maybe his sister had thought the same, and had deliberately pinned up the two images close together. He must have been about the same age as Finn when it was taken.

'How long was he alone for?' He pointed at the school photograph.

Sweet gave him a professionally sympathetic look. 'We don't know. He's not been that keen to talk about any of it. Understandably.'

'And he was locked in his cabin?'

The sergeant nodded. 'Maybe that makes sense when you're on a sailing boat with a young child. To keep him out of harm's way. Was she an experienced sailor?'

'The boat used to belong to my parents. I had no idea she still had it. You see, we haven't spoken for years.'

Sweet took the lid off his cup and blew on his coffee. 'That's not exactly what our social worker wanted to hear.'

'Imagine being on the boat on your own. Did he know his mother was gone?'

Sweet nodded. 'He was locked in the cabin crying when they found him. He'd been banging on the door, apparently. He's in a lot of shock, poor bloody kid. We were hoping you'd be able to help us communicate with him.'

A large white gull landed on the sand just outside the window, head cocked slightly to one side. It seemed to be peering in at them with its little black eye.

'I'm sorry,' Eden said. 'I don't think I'm going to be a lot of use to you.'

'The search for her is still on-going,' Sweet tried to reassure him. 'There may be a chance.' A kindly meant platitude.

The gull turned its head, looking at them with its other eye.

Eden took a sip from his coffee. It tasted thin and milky. 'What do you think happened?' he asked, looking down at the floor and noticing grains of dark sand in the cracks in the wood. He imagined a barefoot boy walking in from the beach.

Sweet said, 'She doesn't seem to have been wearing a harness. And it seems she may not have been wearing a life jacket, either.'

He nodded. 'And so you assume it was deliberate. That she jumped in the water knowing what she was doing?'

Sweet looked at him for a second and said, 'I mean. She might have just fallen overboard by accident, mightn't she? But . . . it's what people reckon. She wasn't always that well, if you understand what I'm saying?'

'I don't, no,' said Eden, irritated by the other officer's fumbling attempts at tact. 'You mean you think she was mentally ill?'

Sweet looked at his feet. 'I suppose. She had a few issues.'
'Did she?'
'We took her into custody once or twice. Nothing bad,' he added hastily. 'Just, you know . . . minor public-order stuff.'
'Like what?'
'Nothing really. And I'll need to take a toothbrush and maybe a hairbrush if there is one, if that's OK?'

Eden understood. The simplest and most reliable way to confirm the identity of a body, if they found one, was through DNA. Drowned people never looked pretty.

Just then Bisi reappeared, making her way down the stairs with two black carrier bags. She paused on the bottom step. 'Well, then. Would you like to meet your nephew?'

Five

Bisi from Child Protection parked her little car on a steep street outside a red-brick terraced house.

'Ready?' asked Bisi, hand on the door handle.

'You do understand that I have to be at work tomorrow? In London.'

'You do want to meet him, though, don't you?' said Bisi. 'He's your nephew.'

'Yes. Yes, of course I do.'

Bisi rang the bell. The front door was shiny and red, right at the pavement's edge. The woman who opened it was in her late fifties, wide, wearing a yellow top. Bisi greeted her warmly. They would have worked together a lot, guessed Eden: a child social worker and an emergency carer. 'This is the boy's uncle Eden,' explained Bisi. 'Though apparently they've never actually met before.'

'Oh,' said the woman – Mrs Sullivan. She eyed him up too, just as Bisi had earlier. 'Well, you'd better come in. Finn is in the garden.' She led them into a kitchen, where her husband was standing at the open back door watching a small dark-haired child kicking a football.

Eden looked out to the sunlit garden. The football was attached to the boy's ankle with a length of elastic. When he kicked it, the ball came back and he kicked it again, over and over, with no particular grace or skill.

Mr Sullivan called out to him, 'Try kicking it with the side of your foot, not just your toe. That's the way footballers do it.'

The boy ignored him, continuing to kick the ball with the front of his foot.

'How was last night?' asked Bisi.

'He had a nightmare,' said Mrs Sullivan, who was already filling a kettle. 'When I got to him he was standing up by the door, calling for his mum, poor little man. Cried a bit. He didn't sleep much, I don't think.'

At the sound of their voices, the boy turned. His pale face showed the darkness around his eyes. They were light blue, exactly like his sister's. Finn glanced at the adults with hostility, then turned away to kick the ball again.

'He's been doing it for half an hour,' Mr Sullivan informed them, without looking back at them.

'Finn?' called Mrs Sullivan. 'Come in, love. We have someone special we want you to meet.'

The thump of shoe against ball continued.

'Finn?' Bisi stood up, went outside and approached the boy, putting her arm around his shoulders. She leant down and spoke to him, her voice low, then returned to the kitchen.

The boy kicked the football a few more times then stopped and walked slowly to the kitchen doorway, football still tethered to his leg. Mr Sullivan stood back to let him come in.

'Finn,' said Bisi, 'I want you to meet your uncle Eden. Your mum's brother. He's come a long way to say hello to you.'

'Hello, Finn,' said Eden gently. 'I'm pleased to meet you.'

The boy nodded, but made no attempt to approach him, or answer him, or change his furious expression.

'I'm sorry we've not met before.'

Finn looked at him then addressed Bisi, 'How do I know he's my uncle?'

'Well, because he is,' she answered. 'He's your mother's brother.'

'Who says?' Finn turned and went back outside, dragging the ball behind him.

'Your teacher, Miss Killick, sends her love,' Bisi called after him. 'She says she's hoping you'll be back in school soon.'

Finn appeared not to hear. Kicked the ball a little harder.

'I'm sorry, Eden,' said Bisi. 'He's in shock, obviously. His world has just turned upside down.'

'Yes. It has.'

'Can we talk, Angela?' Bisi asked Mrs Sullivan. They left Finn kicking the ball and went to the front room, Mr Sullivan following with a pot of tea and a plate of biscuits.

Eden sat on a large L-shaped sofa in front of a TV screen. Tucked to one side was a plastic storage box full of toy cars, dolls and children's books.

'No surprise he's acting up a bit,' said Mrs Sullivan. 'Any child would be. His mum leaving him on his own.'

'We don't know exactly what happened,' observed Eden quietly.

Mrs Sullivan smiled thinly. 'Of course not. Not yet. The coastguard haven't found her, I suppose?'

Bisi shook her head. 'I'm thinking we may need you to have Finn for a few more days yet, Angela.'

Mrs Sullivan looked at Eden. 'You said Mr Driscoll here was going to take him.'

'I didn't say it was definite. I said it was a possibility. It turns out the situation is a little more complicated than we imagined. Mr Driscoll plans on returning to work tonight in London.'

Mrs Sullivan looked at Eden, eyebrows raised, then turned back to Bisi. 'I made it very clear that I could only look after him temporarily. My mother-in-law has an operation on Thursday, and she's up in Lancashire.'

'Of course. We'll have to find an alternative of some kind. But if you could manage for a day or two more.'

'It's not ideal,' complained Mrs Sullivan.

'Is he eating much?' asked Bisi.

She turned to Eden. 'He says he's a vegan.'

'Yes,' Eden said. 'I suppose he is. We were raised vegetarian, my sister and me. My father had very strong views about food.'

Eden had a sudden memory of the stewed beans their mother had used to cook for them in old caravans and camper vans, or in the cramped galleys of boats.

In Spain, when Eden was maybe twelve, he had hung around a group of local men fishing on a quay in some small port they were camping near. The men were friendly, offering him bread and digging out sweets from their pockets, giving him their fishing rods to hold, cheering when he caught a fish. Eden took the one he caught home with him: a long, thin fish with big round eyes. When he arrived back at the van there was nobody around so he had placed it in the frying pan, poured in a little oil, and tried to cook it, in the same way his mother fried aubergines. The fish had disintegrated, spewing out black innards, flesh flaking from strange green bones. When their father had arrived back from the building site he'd been working on to earn a little money, he had taken one look at the mess in the pan and grabbed it, angrily flinging the whole lot, pan included, over a rocky cliff, into the blue sea below.

'Has Finn talked about school at all?' Bisi was asking. 'Do you think he's missing it?'

'He doesn't say much of anything,' said Mrs Sullivan.

'I think it might be good for him, going to school,' said Bisi. 'He should be with his friends.'

Mrs Sullivan shook her head. 'They'll only be asking him questions all the time because everyone's seen it on the news.'

'What do you think?' Bisi turned towards Eden.

'Me?' said Eden. 'I really don't know.'

'The most important person in his life has disappeared,' said Bisi. 'At least if he was with his friends he would have some of his life back.'

Mrs Sullivan sighed and said, 'I mean, I can look after him here Monday and Tuesday, maybe even Wednesday, but after that it's going to be difficult. If he goes to school, I'll need a taxi to take him there and pick him up. We haven't got a car, you know.'

Eden left his un-drunk tea on the coffee table and stood. 'Where's the bathroom?'

'Top of the stairs.'

There was a small open window above the low cistern. From below came the mechanical *thump thump thump* of the boy kicking the ball. Looking down, Eden could see his dark hair flicking as he kicked the ball over and over. Even from there he could feel the boy's misery radiating out of him.

Finn kicked the ball hard. It bounced back at him fast and he missed it this time. He whacked at the ball again, this time furiously.

'Maybe I can try to take a few days off,' said Eden, back in the living room. 'Until we can sort out something more permanent.'

Six

Bisi drove Eden back to Apple's small house.

'Thank you for staying,' she said. 'I appreciate it.'

'Just to be straight, it can only be for this week,' he said. 'To help you until you find someone suitable for him. Do you know of a hotel I can get a room in?'

She glanced towards the end of the cul-de-sac they had pulled up in. 'Aren't you going to stay here?'

The thought hadn't occurred to him. He looked warily at his sister's little house. 'I suppose.'

It would give him a chance to look around, because he was beginning to realise that he needed to see if he could find anything that explained his sister's disappearance.

'This is a difficult question. I don't suppose you'd know if your sister had a will, then?' Bisi asked.

He turned back to her. 'We don't even know if she's dead yet.'

'Of course we don't. I'm sorry.' She looked contrite, but he was a police officer. He knew how unlikely it was anyone would find Apple alive and she had to put some kind of care framework around the boy. She would need to know what his sister had wanted.

'Mrs Sullivan, the foster carer—'

'Yes?'

'She seems to think that my sister had deliberately left Finn alone on the boat. So did Mike Sweet. Is that what you think? That she left him? That she committed suicide?'

'I'm afraid the police think that's a possibility. You need to know this. Your sister struggled sometimes. This isn't the first time we've met Finn.'

'What happened?'

'Your sister may still be alive, so – you know how it is – I can't discuss the details. She had some trouble with the police and she ended up in custody. Because she was the mother of a young boy, we became involved. And during that time there was a psychological assessment of her. Can I ask, did she have any issues with her mental health as a child?'

That time seemed impossibly long ago. 'I don't think so,' he said. 'Honestly? In my family, she was genuinely the only sane one.'

'OK. Well, that's good.' She raised her eyebrows. 'Now. If she didn't leave a will, you'll need to apply for a grant of letters of administration,' she said. 'I can help you with that.'

He nodded.

'And there is some other paperwork I need to go through with you. I'll come by in the morning. Is that OK?'

Alone in his sister's house, he took a little time to look around. Next to the candles on the little shelf in the living room there was a book called *Herbal Antibiotics* and another on stone circles alongside several dog-eared novels bought from charity shops, he guessed. There was no wi-fi router that he could find, no TV, no computer. Their father had despised televisions and computers. He had said they were for idiots.

A purple scarf lay draped around the bathroom mirror, and next to it a tiny cabinet was full of alternative remedies. Between the arnica tablets and evening primrose oil there was a packet of prescribed pills: a box of something called Lustral. He looked it up on his phone. It was a treatment for panic attacks and obsessive-compulsive disorder. That was a surprise. He knew so little about his sister.

Eden was exhausted again. The bed upstairs was made up. He should change the sheets, he supposed, but that felt a little like erasing his sister.

It was a warm spring afternoon. He opened the bedroom window to the noise of seagulls and children playing on the beach.

The tide was lower now. Boats that had been at anchor when he had arrived now lay on the river bed, cluttering the red sand and stones.

Apple's bedroom was small. A pair of green cotton trousers had been left on the floor, knickers still inside them. He looked around for a laundry basket but couldn't see one.

Apart from the bed the biggest piece of furniture in the room was a dark old wardrobe, so large that Eden wondered how anyone had managed to get it up the stairs. He opened the doors and below hangers crammed with clothes there was a yellow plastic trug full of dirty laundry, so he picked up the trousers and added them to the pile.

Apple's clothes were bright and various, the kind people found by chance in second-hand shops. There were three big fake-fur coats – one yellow – taking up a lot of the hanging space.

He put his hand between the coats, vaguely remembering a story he had been told once as a child, about a wardrobe that had been a doorway into another world. The back of his sister's wardrobe was solid wood. He withdrew the hand, feeling a little foolish.

Detective Sergeant Sweet had asked him to look out for a note, or for something that might explain his sister's disappearance. He didn't know where to begin.

Instead, he lay back on his sister's bed, numb. He had always intended to reach out to her, to try to make amends.

He closed his eyes.

When he woke, groggy and disorientated, it was almost dark. The smell of fried food drifted in through the open window. He was starving. He realised he had not eaten yet today.

The Ship Inn was a few yards away, a pub built next to a stone quay. The woman behind the bar looked at her watch and said they could do food if he ordered right away, so Eden picked a roast-pork sandwich and took a large glass of wine out onto the riverbank.

It was a grubby, crowded spot, with ashtrays and crisp packets stuffed into empty glasses on the picnic tables. A sign screwed to the table read: 'Only food and drink purchased at The Ship is to be consumed here.'

When the sandwich arrived, he had barely taken a bite from it when a voice said, 'Scuse me. Mind if we . . .?' A couple – both very young. She had a single dyed-blonde braid in her dark hair and was drinking a bottle of fruit cider. The boy had a pint of lager and his eyebrow was pierced.

Eden moved his glass to make room for them and wondered if she was old enough for that drink.

The couple were in mid-conversation as they shuffled onto the bench, side by side, the girl opposite Eden. 'I don't see what the big deal is,' the boy said. 'Your dad's working and your mum is out getting pissed somewhere.'

'Don't,' said the girl.

'True though.'

'I got college work to do anyway. I can't.'

Eden looked at his sandwich and thought of his sister in the cold Channel water. He picked it up and put it down again, unbitten.

'So?' the boy was saying, leaning across the table. 'She won't know. It'll be a shindig. Just this once. You and me. And the boys.'

The girl laughed nervously and tugged on her braid of hair.

'Seriously. Even if your mum gets home, she'll be too bladdered to notice you're not there.' The boy leaned forward.

'Don't say that about my mum,' the girl protested.

'Oh, mate. You know your mum is an absolute pisser when she's had a couple.'

The girl's eyes caught Eden's and he saw shame there.

'Get a few beers and smokes,' the boy was saying. 'Lovely job.'

'My dad would murder me,' the girl said.

'Your dad won't find out. Mate's got the sound system and he's going to take us round to Labrador, says he's got a genny. Gang of us going on the boat. A bit of puff. Tunes. Here comes the summer. Let's jump off the deep end for once.'

The smile left the girl's face. 'Don't say deep end.'

'Why not?'

'Not after what happened to that woman.'

Eden focused his eyes on his sandwich.

'You are so superstitious.' The boy leaned into her.

She shouldered him away. 'There's something really, I don't know . . . horrible about it.'

'Some people are just funny in the head like that,' said the boy.

'You shouldn't talk about it like that. It's disrespectful.'

Eden lived in a big city. This was a small town. Here everyone knew each other's business.

'Buddy?'

Eden looked up.

'Mind if we . . . ?' The boy was waving a packet of tobacco at him.

'Man's still eating, Davey,' the girl scolded.

'Only asking.'

'It's rude when people are eating.'

'I don't mind it,' protested the boy.

'Well, maybe he does.' The girl looked at Eden apologetically.

'Thank you,' said Eden quietly. 'I would rather you didn't.'

'No problem, bud,' said the boy loudly, but he set about rolling a cigarette on the wooden table in front of him all the same.

'I've got to be up early anyway,' the girl said. She was picking at a scab on her knuckle.

'Seriously?' The boy licked the paper and placed the rolled cigarette down in front of him. 'You need to have a little more fun.'

'And you think you're fun?'

The boy laughed and took a large gulp from his glass. 'Going to have a ciggie over there on the wall with Stubbsy. Coming?'

She didn't look enthusiastic. 'I'll keep our seats.'

'Suit yourself. Let me out, will you?'

When she sat back down again, the girl turned away, looking up the estuary.

'Did you know her?' Eden asked.

The girl turned towards Eden, startled. 'What?'

'The woman who was lost overboard two nights ago.'

The girl shook her head, curious. 'Why?'

'You were talking about her.'

'Just on the news. It was messed up. She was from right here, you know,' she said, pointing down at the row of cottages.

'Yes. I do.'

She frowned. 'You a journalist or something?'

He shook his head. 'No. I saw it on the news too, like everyone else.'

The girl nodded. 'She had a child and everything. Isn't that the most horrible part?' she said. 'I can't stop thinking about them.' And she turned away, looking upriver.

Eden pushed his plate away. He wasn't as hungry as he'd thought he was. He pulled out his phone and messaged Sammy Kadakia.

Sorry to message on a Sunday, boss. Going to need to stay here a couple more days. More complicated than I thought. Can I take some leave?

Sammy would understand. He was good like that. As if to prove the point, the DI texted back immediately. *Take as long as you need, pal. Thinking of you.*

Back next week, I promise, answered Eden. *Will need to do some work on the Ronan Pan case.*

He looked up from the screen. The girl was looking over towards the boy, smoking with his mates by the low wall above the beach. 'Don't let him put pressure on you to do anything you don't want to do,' said Eden.

'What?' Her nose wrinkled.

'That boy. If you don't want to go out drinking and whatever with him – that's fine.'

She flushed. 'Fuck off and mind your own beeswax,' she said and stood, picking up her half-drunk bottle of cider to join the boy, putting her arm around his shoulders.

The tide was coming in again now, floating the boats it had stranded. The sky behind was a deep, dark purple.

When Eden checked his phone again, his boss had messaged.

We will handle the Pan paperwork. Don't come back until ur ready.

He was ready now, he thought.

Seven

Eden lay awake that night in the unfamiliar bed, on sheets his sister had slept in. As the sky lightened, the birds feeding in the low-tide mud outside called to each other – strange, haunting noises. He must have fallen asleep at some point, because when he was woken by the louder yelling of herring gulls, the sun was bright, glaring through the blind.

He went to the window and was shocked to see the familiar white hull of a sailing boat, moored on a pontoon just off the beach.

He blinked. It was *Calliope*. She had not been there yesterday.

He grabbed his trousers.

Calliope had been their parents' yacht – their father's really. Apple and Eden had lived in that 32-foot boat for almost two years. Eden had hated it, and, looking at it, he realised he still did.

Clearly Apple had not felt the same way about it. Seeing it on the news bulletins, rolling in the waves, loose boom crossing from side to side across the cockpit as it drifted, had been one thing. Seeing it here, right outside the window, was another.

Calliope was old now. Rust streaks ran down the hull from the deck stanchions. The aluminium mast was grey with age.

He ran downstairs, out of the back door, onto the empty beach, shirt unbuttoned.

'Apple!' he shouted.

The boat was silent. The tide was coming in again. He raced towards the water's edge, trying to spot any sign of life on the boat. A sudden wave splashed water over his sockless feet, pouring into his unlaced leather shoes. 'Shit,' he said, laughing. His sister would find it funny, too, remembering the way she'd used to laugh at him when they were kids.

He needed to get a better view. Shoes squelching, he ran back up the beach and along to his right, onto an ancient stone quay that looked down onto the moored boat.

'Apple,' he shouted again. The docks were quiet. It must only be six or seven in the morning.

A man opening up a lock-up on the quayside looked at him quizzically, but said nothing.

With a start, Eden realised Apple could not be on board. The boat was obviously empty. He was being stupid. Someone else must have salvaged *Calliope*, waiting for the early high tide to bring her back, mooring her here while he slept.

Sitting on the granite dock, legs over the side, he checked his phone. It took a little while to find the news item on a local BBC news site, saying that the coastguard had called off the search for the woman missing in the Channel.

'You all right, bud?' called the man.

When Eden emerged from the shower back at the house, there was a new message on his phone from Bisi. *What about coffee? 9.30 a.m.? We have a lot to discuss.*

He was about to reply when the phone buzzed in his hand. This time it was DS Sweet.

'Don't tell me. You called to inform me they have called off the search,' Eden said before Sweet had had a chance to speak.

Pause. 'Oh. You already heard.'

'Yes,' Eden said. 'Because it's on the news.'

Sweet sounded contrite. 'I'm so sorry, Mr Driscoll. We were only told ourselves just now. Don't know how the news got to it first. You must be upset.'

Eden took a breath. 'It's OK. I know things like this happen.'

'Shouldn't though,' said Sweet.

'And the boat?'

'What about it?'

'I'm looking at it now. It's moored right outside my window.'

'Shit,' said Sweet. 'You're kidding me. You must think we're bumpkins.'

'It would have been nice to have a little warning.'

'Where is it? On the pontoon?'

'Yes.'

'Jesus. Sorry. I figure the lifeboat must have towed it in last night. They probably weren't thinking that you were going to see it. The boy hasn't seen it, has he?'

'No. He's with the foster carer.'

'Thank Christ. Poor lad doesn't need that. I'll get them to move it. Thing is, marine investigation officers need to be giving her a look-over to see if there's anything of interest.'

'What do you mean, "of interest"?'

'I guess they'll want to take a look at the boat's logbook, just in case there's anything in there. Check the gear to see if there are any signs of an accident. Standard stuff.'

Out on the estuary, a boat was hoisting brown canvas sails as it headed towards the river mouth. 'Can I take a look round her as well?'

'The boat?'

'Is there a reason why I can't?'

Sweet considered this for a second. 'I'll have to run it past my boss but I don't see why not. Just one other thing I wanted to mention, before you go.' Eden turned around and looked back at the house. 'Look, I know you probably don't think much of us right now,' Sweet was saying, 'but if you hear of anything the lad has said about the incident – anything at all that you might think is relevant – you will pass it on to us, won't you?'

The café was close by, in a little curve of road in the old fishing village. A bell rang as the door opened. Eden ordered coffee and picked up a local newspaper, thankfully a few days old.

He was on his second cup when the café door swung open and Bisi stepped in carrying a plastic shopping bag. 'Christ. Sorry I'm late,' she said. 'Have you ordered?' Bisi threw the bag onto an empty chair.

He held up his coffee. 'You said you had some papers for me to sign.'

'Give me a minute,' she said, and marched over to the counter to order. When she returned to the table, she pulled up a chair next to him and started to take out the documents for him.

'I'm going to be straight with you, Eden. As you're obviously all too aware, it's useful, you being here. All sorts of reasons. One, you're a relative. Well. You're the only relative we know of so far. Two, you're a police officer. It saves us a lot of messing around looking into whether you're a suitable person to look after Finn or not.'

She looked him in the eye. 'I think the best thing for him is to be back at school with his friends, to be back in his house, don't you? Now you've slept on it, I need to make clear what's going to happen next. Mrs Sullivan can only look after Finn for a few days and without her around he'll be sent up to Exeter or somewhere where they've got more capacity than here. Or further. Which means being separated from his friends and his home, and right now that's not what we want. Ideally he would stay in his house with a relation looking after him – just for the short-term at least.'

A woman at the next table was busy rubbing a coin on some scratch cards. Eden lowered his voice. 'What I do know is I'm not the man you want me to be. I've no experience at all with children.'

'If every parent had to have experience before they had kids there would be no kids,' said Bisi.

'I'm not a parent though. I'm sorry. I genuinely want to do the best for him. The best for him is not me.'

'I'm not going to lie to you, Mr Driscoll,' said Bisi. 'Even without a full assessment, it's a good guess that Finn is a deeply traumatised young boy. When I heard that Finn's uncle was a police officer, I thought, hallelujah – my job is going to be a lot simpler. Because you're a copper, it makes the bureaucracy very easy. We can do a viability check on you right now and you'll have your DBS check and personal records all at the ready because of what you do for a living. Then we can get a court order in the next day or two and they'll fall over themselves finding a way to let you look after Finn because of who you are, and that would be that. And even if he doesn't know you, you're family.' She gave him a hard stare. 'But it looks like you don't really want to be family. I'm not here to try and persuade you to do something you don't want to do. But if we can put him in your care temporarily, you can live with him at the house. At least for a few days while he adjusts he'll be at his own home, somewhere he can feel safe.' She attempted a thin smile. 'So I am asking you to do this. And, if you're not ultimately going to take responsibility for the child, fine.'

'If you're looking for someone more suitable than me, the bar is pretty low,' said Eden.

'Oh, I'm pretty sure I know the kind of person you are.' Bisi looked straight at him. 'You're not the first man I've met. And all I'm saying is that if you stay at least it'll buy us a little more time to assess Finn's needs and find something more permanent for him.'

Eight

The harbourmaster was waiting for them in a grey inflatable, bows beached in the sand, a little way from Apple's house. 'This is Apple Driscoll's brother,' explained Sweet as the harbourmaster held out an arm to help him clamber aboard.

'I'm very sorry about your sister,' the harbourmaster said. He was a wide-faced man with dark hair that blew across his forehead. 'Any news?'

Eden shook his head.

'They'll be doing their best,' the harbourmaster said. 'I'm sure of it.'

'Matter of fact, they called off the search last night,' said Sweet.

'Oh. Sorry to hear that,' said the harbourmaster, suddenly awkward. 'So, as you'll see, we've towed your sister's sailing boat a little further upriver, put her on a mooring near the bridge,' he explained. 'Out of the way, like.'

'I appreciate that.'

He guided Eden into the inflatable. 'Put these on,' he said, holding up a pair of buoyancy jackets, one for Eden, one for Sweet.

A light breeze blew the water into small waves. They sat in chairs, facing forwards in the boat while the harbourmaster steered into a current that pulled them upriver, past the docks with their big blue warehouses. There were no ships moored there today.

'There she is,' called the harbourmaster. He slowed the engines as they came alongside *Calliope*'s familiar hull. The halyards that held the mast steady were tinking gently against its aluminium. Eden had forgotten that noise; it was like hearing ghosts.

The harbourmaster slowed the boat and, with practised skill, leaned over the side to tie his painter onto the stern of the boat, then stepped on board and held out a hand again towards Eden.

It was strange, climbing into the *Calliope*'s cockpit for the first time in fifteen years. It was smaller than Eden remembered. In his memory, the ship's wheel had been wooden; this one was stainless steel, though it looked as ancient as the rest of the boat.

'You OK?' asked the harbourmaster as Sweet followed Eden onto the yacht.

'I haven't seen it close to since I was fifteen.'

While the harbourmaster made his way to the bow, ostensibly to check the boat's chain, Eden opened the cockpit door and gazed inside.

The galley was messier than it had ever been when his mother and father had had the boat. His father, ex-army, had always insisted on tidiness.

Now old pans and chipped cups were secured on shelves by frayed bungee cords. There was washing-up left in the sink. A couple of wine glasses, a couple of bowls. More of Finn's drawings were tacked to the wood, dozens of them, some in crayon, others in biro.

He wiped his eyes on his shirtsleeve. The galley opened up onto a small seating area. It had been a cramped home for four people. If you moved the table, the benches below became bunks; that was where his mother and father had slept if they were aboard. Beyond that was a dark wood wall with a single door in it. It opened into Apple and Eden's cabin. They had lain in narrow bunks that tapered as the boat narrowed its bows. There was a steel latch across the door that Eden was pretty sure had not been there when he was a boy. Maybe Apple had stored stuff in the forward cabin when the boat was moored here on the estuary.

'I don't understand it,' he said to Sweet. 'For a mother who has carefully pinned all these drawings around the walls, to lock her child up in a cabin and abandon him at sea . . .'

'This must be very hard for you,' Sweet said.

Eden opened the door to the fridge. It had been switched off but it still contained a carton of oat milk, some margarine, a pack of oily plant-based burgers and a half-empty bottle of white wine.

Next, he opened the cabinet below the sink and peered into the small bin on the back of the door. He could make out peelings from a carrot, onion skin and an empty tube of tomato puree. Apple had cooked a vegetable soup or a stew for them both, he guessed, the night she had locked her son in a cabin and disappeared.

He took everything except the wine out of the fridge and put them in the bin, then pulled out the bag. 'You don't mind me chucking all this?' He waved the bag at Sweet. 'Only they'll go off and stink the place out.'

'I guess,' answered the sergeant.

Eden pulled open drawers, but found nothing of interest in them, only cutlery, kitchen knives, packs of batteries and biros.

Abandoning the galley, Eden stepped forward and opened the door into the small cabin. From the look of it, Finn must have been asleep in the bunk on the starboard side on the night his mother disappeared. His sleeping bag was still there, unzipped, with a pair of orange headphones lying on the crumpled pillow. That was the same side as Eden had slept on. Apple had slept in the other bunk, feet towards the bow.

Sweet and the harbourmaster were in the cockpit now, talking. Eden turned to check they were not watching, closed the cabin door a fraction, then lifted up the foam mattress on Apple's bunk and pulled up the plywood sheet that lay below it, revealing a fresh-water tank below.

He knocked the tank. It rang with a hollow tone, which meant it was empty. Inching his fingers either side of the polythene, he grasped it and slowly eased it up to try to peer into the cavity below it.

'What are you doing in there?' Sweet asked.

Eden let go of the tank. It dropped back down with a light *thunk*. He replaced the board and the mattress.

'What were you looking for?' Eden turned to see Sweet standing right by the door, looking in.

'Nothing,' Eden replied evenly, wondering how long Sweet had been watching him. In the enclosed space, the rocking of the boat made him feel a little nauseous. He reached over and grabbed the orange headphones.

'OK if I take these too?' Eden asked. 'For the boy? He's probably missing them.'

Sweet stared at him for a second longer, frowning, then relaxed. 'Knock yourself out.'

Eden emerged into the sunlight of the cockpit holding them.

'All done?' the harbourmaster asked.

'Do you know what time my sister set out on Friday?'

'Sorry,' the harbourmaster apologised. 'I don't keep tabs on the movements of every vessel that moors here. Just too many of them.'

Sweet said, 'But Finn was in school on Friday, we checked, so it would have been that afternoon that they left. Some time after school.'

'Did she often go out at night?'

'Again, I wouldn't really know,' said the harbourmaster.

'But it would have been unusual for her to be out with a child at that time of night?'

'I'd say so, but like I said, I don't keep track. She was an unusual woman, your sister. No offence.'

'What do you mean?'

The harbourmaster looked embarrassed. 'Well. You know. She had strong views, let's put it that way. She didn't believe she should be paying mooring fees, for one. I used to have to chase her for them.'

'Because?'

'She didn't think anyone should own the sea.'

Eden couldn't help but smile. 'My father used to say the same thing. He always tried to get out of paying harbour fees to moor this boat.' Though that wasn't the only reason his father had often moored out of the way of other boats.

Eden looked around him. They were in a broad stretch of water with houses on both sides, the town to the north and a village to the south. 'Is there any way of finding out where she went?'

'Every vessel this size and larger is tracked by the AIS. Automatic Identification System. There are one or two companies who record the data,' the man answered. 'But you'd need to pay them a fee to access it.'

Sweet was watching Eden. 'Why would you want to know all that anyway?' he asked.

'I just want to understand what happened,' Eden answered.

The harbourmaster was untying the rope from the back of the boat, preparing to get back aboard the rib, and Sweet was securing the cabin door with a padlock, when Eden said, 'Wait.'

Sweet turned. 'What now?'

'The sink.'

'What?' Sweet said again.

'I just had a thought. Did you notice?'

'Did I notice what?'

'Take a look.'

Sweet took off the padlock again and peered inside and into the cabin.

'There are two wine glasses in the sink, not just one,' said Eden. 'Can you see?'

'So? She used two glasses instead of one.'

'Or there was someone else on the boat,' said Eden.

Sweet seemed to consider this for a minute. 'Seriously?'

'It's a possibility, isn't it?'

Sweet stood with the padlock in his hand. 'You do realise this is our investigation, don't you?'

'But if there was someone else on the boat, that would be important, wouldn't it? Will you do forensics on them?'

Sweet had the same expression on his face that he'd had when he'd been at the cabin door. 'Do you have any reason at all to believe this is anything more than a missing person investigation, Mr Driscoll?' Sweet asked, eyebrow raised. 'Because if you do, I think you need to share it with me.'

Holding the bag of rubbish in one hand, Eden stepped down into the harbourmaster's boat. 'Me? No,' he said. 'No, I don't.'

Nine

Bisi Smith stood impatiently on the beach, hands on hips, in her dungarees.

'Sorry to keep you waiting,' said Eden, stepping out of the boat, bin bag in his hand.

'I suppose you needed to see it,' she said. 'Your sister's boat.'

'Yes. I did.'

'So I've made a couple of calls. I will need to do a viability check.'

'Do I have a police record? Do I take drugs?'

'Exactly. Do you have any mental-health issues? Once we've done that, we can get the court order tomorrow afternoon for you to look after him back at his home. In the meantime, if that's all OK, I suggest I bring Finn back here for a little while later today – just an hour or two – just so he gets used to you. It's a big change for him.'

'The boy's coming to live with you here?' Sweet asked. 'That's great, right?'

'For a little while, maybe, until we get something more permanent,' said Eden.

'That's right,' added Bisi with a tight smile. 'Small steps.'

'I'm glad to hear it. Knew you'd step up.' Sweet nodded at the bag Eden was holding. 'Want me to chuck that in the bin over there?'

Eden turned. By the side of The Ship Inn stood a large black bin. 'Looks pretty full,' Eden answered. 'Don't worry. I'll chuck it at home.'

'So, this afternoon, just for a couple of hours. What do you say?' Bisi said.

They were both looking at him, waiting for an answer.

Eden was an officer who worked as part of a Major Incident Team. He dealt with violence and murder every day. In his world, people hurt each other, stole from each other, poured boiling water onto a lover's back, threw acid in teenagers' faces. He knew that, over time, being part of this affected how you saw the world. You saw darkness everywhere.

Most of the world was not like this. Most of the world was full of people who just got on with life in an ordinary way.

His sister had disappeared at sea. Maybe that's all there was.

When he had taken the bag of rubbish, it was with the intention of laying the contents of the bin bag out to examine each item separately, which was what crime scene investigators would do if this were a murder investigation. But it wasn't. He felt ridiculous. His sister was gone and he would never speak to her again or make it up to her, and he couldn't fix things by treating it as another investigation.

Instead, he dumped the bag on the kitchen floor next to the bin and went back outside.

With nothing better to do until it was time to meet his nephew, Eden thought he might as well take a look around the small seaside town that his sister had lived in. He locked up the cottage and made his way out of the back door, down the alley and found his way to the seafront.

Eden had not grown up in England. He didn't understand the national obsession with these Victorian seaside towns that always looked a little past their best. He didn't remember his own childhood fondly, but the sea there had usually been warm and always blue.

The Teignmouth seafront was an elegant white curve of houses, hotels and guest houses, some smart, others struggling, a mixture of Georgian and Victorian, alongside modern buildings that pretended unconvincingly to be a bit of both. There was a bowling lawn, and on it men and women dressed in cream, bending over, deep in concentration.

Though he had not yet had breakfast, he bought an ice cream cone from a stall by the pier. It was the seaside, so he chose a cone with a chocolate flake, because it seemed like the thing to do, and sat on the sea wall eating it, watching birds plunge into the fast-flowing water where the estuary joined the sea.

There was a small, plain-looking pier, jutting out into the sea. If one was in any doubt, it had the word 'PIER' written in large red letters above the entrance.

He had only licked the ice cream a few times before a gull snatched it from him – much of the vanilla landing with a soft plop at the bottom of the sea wall.

Eden laughed out loud.

A man walking a Yorkshire terrier laughed too and said, 'Saw you coming.'

Later, in a piazza built around a heavy-looking granite fountain, he ordered a coffee and a pastry, and watched as men with reddened skin walked in shorts and mismatched

T-shirts. Children played tag. A woman sat in a mobility scooter smoking a cigarette. The shops sold coloured plastic buckets and orange crab lines.

This was not one of those picture-postcard pretty villages that were dead in winter, though, he decided; this was a working town with a docks and a railway passing through it. There was something else here.

Wind flapped at the awning over his head. A squall of rain sent people scattering.

He had only been away from London since Friday but it felt like an age.

Finn sat silently all the way back from Mrs Sullivan's.

'I went to see Miss Killick from your school today Finn,' said Bisi. 'She sends her love.'

Eden and Finn sat in the back of Bisi's car while Bisi drove. Finn looked sideways, out of the car window at the rain falling.

'Miss Killick says you're excellent at maths, Finn. Were you good at maths, Eden?' she asked, trying to draw the pair of them into conversation.

'We were home schooled,' said Eden. 'My dad taught us maths. I never liked it much.'

'Oh.' Bisi paused at a roundabout.

Eden sensed Bisi's eyes in the rear-view mirror, observing them.

'Maths is easy,' said Finn.

'Really?' Eden frowned.

When they arrived into the small street at the back of the house Finn got straight out of the car, marched to the door and felt behind the down pipe. When he didn't find the key, the boy looked around, eyes wide.

Eden took it from his pocket and held it up. 'I have it. I

didn't think it was a good idea to leave it in such an obvious place. Anyone could find it.'

Finn snatched it from him angrily.

'Your uncle Eden was just looking after the place for you and your mum,' said Bisi gently.

Finn stepped up to the door with the key. In a second, he had put the key in the lock, opened it, then closed the door firmly behind him. They heard the Yale click.

'Bugger,' said Bisi. 'I shouldn't have let him do that, should I?'

Ten

They waited. After a while, Eden ran through the rain to a small newsagent to buy a packet of sweets. He returned with Haribos.

Bisi was still kneeling at the front door in a plastic rain mac, talking to Finn through the letter box.

'I know it's your house,' Bisi was saying gently, 'but we'd just like to come in and talk to you. Can you let us in?'

Eden couldn't hear any answer. 'Is he listening?' he asked.

'He told me to go away and leave him alone.'

Eden bent down towards the letter box. 'Would you like some sweets?'

After a brief pause, the boy's voice came through the letter box. 'I'm not supposed to take sweets from strangers.'

'He's not a stranger,' said Bisi. 'He's your uncle.'

'No, he isn't,' said Finn.

'Your uncle's sad too, you know,' said Bisi. 'Your mother was his big sister.'

There was a small pair of eyes at the letter box now. 'He doesn't look sad.'

'I am,' said Eden. 'I just don't show it.'

'It's getting wet out here, Finn,' said Bisi.

'Go away, then.'

'We can't leave you. You're a nine-year-old boy.'

'I don't mind.'

It was a stand-off. Eden knew he could probably break down the rear door, but that it would not be a good idea to.

Eventually Finn asked, 'What kind of sweets?'

Eden squatted down in front of the letter box and held up the packet. 'Haribos,' he said.

'They're made of cow,' said the boy.

'Really?' Eden looked at the packet. He checked. Finn was right. Fourth on the list of ingredients was gelatine.

'People who eat animals are horrible.'

'Maybe they just don't know as much as you do about what to eat,' said Bisi.

'Then they're stupid,' announced Finn.

It took forty minutes for Bisi to persuade Finn to open the door first to her, then to Eden.

Bisi looked through the cupboards in the tiny kitchen. 'What about some blackcurrant squash?'

'OK,' said Finn. 'Can I stay here now or do I have to go back to that woman's house?'

'Don't you like Angela?'

'No.'

'Would you like to stay here with your uncle Eden?'

Finn shook his head vigorously.

'That's the thing. Because he's your uncle, he's allowed to look after you here. If we find someone else to look after you, it will have to be in their house, not this one.'

Finn considered this. 'That's not fair. This is my house. Why can't I stay here?'

'You can. If your uncle stays here too – and if the court says it's OK for him to look after you.'

Finn went to the living room and sat on the small two-seater sofa. He picked up a red action figure and started playing with it.

'Well?' asked Bisi, following him with a glass of blackcurrant squash. 'Do you want to stay here with your uncle Eden for a couple of nights?'

Finn said nothing.

'OK. Take your time.' She disappeared back into the kitchen and returned with her shoulder bag. 'Oh, and Miss Killick gave me this,' she said, pulling out a large white envelope.

'What is it?'

Bisi smiled at him. 'Have a look.'

Finn took it, turned it over in his hands, looking at it. His name was on the front.

'Aren't you going to open it?'

He nodded and, after turning it over again, pulled at the paper on the back, tearing it slowly. On the front of the large card there was a drawing of a lion cub. Inside the printed message read 'Get well soon'.

'I am well,' protested Finn. 'It should say, I'm sorry your mum is probably dead.'

Bisi glanced at Eden. 'I expect it was the only card she could find.'

The message was surrounded by handwritten scrawls and notes. In a rounded, teacher's hand was 'We are all missing you Finn!' Around that, the names of other children in different coloured ink, some scratched, some carefully written. A few had drawn pink hearts and kisses in felt tip. One boy had drawn a biro cartoon of himself.

Finn studied it for a while, looking at each name one by one.

'I think it would be good for you, Finn,' said Bisi, 'seeing your friends again.'

Finn closed the card. 'They're not all really my friends. Only some of them. The rest are just pretending.'

'They're just trying to be nice, I suppose,' said Bisi.

'Maybe.'

'I was thinking you might want to go back to school tomorrow, too.'

Finn nodded. 'OK.'

'That's great. And then maybe your uncle could pick you up tomorrow, after school? And bring you back here again?'

'Can't I stay here now?'

'I'm sorry, love. Not today. We need a thing called a court order to allow Eden to look after you. We need a bit of time to get that.'

'So I have to go back to Angela?'

'Just for tonight. Tomorrow, if we get the right paperwork, you can stay here with your uncle. If you want.'

The boy nodded, twisting the arms of the action figure.

'What did Angela give you for lunch? Are you hungry?'

'Not really.'

'What if I make some oven chips anyway? That'll give you two a chance to get to know each other.'

The boy played silently with the action figure, putting it on the arm of the sofa then lifting it up into the air as if it were flying.

'Is that Iron Man?' asked Eden.

The boy shook his head.

'Hulkbuster,' continued Eden, contradicting himself. 'I should have known that. From *Age of Ultron*. The Hulk can't beat him. Have you seen the film?'

The boy gave a tiny nod.

'It's not as good as *Avengers Assemble*,' said Eden.

Again, another nod.

Eden sat down in the small armchair. He lowered his voice. 'I wanted to ask you, Finn: do you know what your mum was doing out in the sailing boat with you at night?'

Finn turned his head and looked at Eden, frowning, but didn't answer.

'You often went out at night with her, did you?'

The boy looked down at his toy again.

'Do you remember what you and your mum talked about on the boat? Was she happy, or sad?'

A sigh. 'Don't know.'

Bisi appeared at the kitchen door, giving Eden a warning look. She shook her head.

When she was back in the kitchen, Eden lowered his voice. 'When the coastguard officer found you, you were locked in your bedroom. Do you know why your mum locked the door? Had you done something? Maybe something she didn't like?'

Bisi was back at the door, watching them warily. 'Go easy on the boy,' she said.

'Was it to keep you safe?' Eden asked.

Eventually Finn looked up from his toy angrily. 'I don't want to talk about it!'

'I'm sorry,' Eden apologised. 'I didn't mean to upset you.'

'Leave the boy alone now,' cautioned Bisi quietly. 'We want him to feel safe here, don't we?'

The smell of cooking oven chips filled the room. 'Maybe we could watch *Avengers Assemble* together some day,' said Eden. 'Would you like that?'

Finn shrugged, wrinkled his nose. Eden remembered he had not seen a TV in the house.

'Would you like some of these chips?' asked Bisi. 'And

then I should probably take you back. We can bring you back here tomorrow, if you'd like that?'

'OK,' said Finn.

While she was filling the plates in the kitchen Eden moved to the two-seater sofa and sat down beside the boy.

'Can I ask you one more question, Finn?' Eden said quietly.

'I don't care.'

'Who was on the boat? You . . . and mum . . . nobody else?'

Finn stared at him and shook his head slowly. 'Why?'

'When you were in your cabin, you are sure you didn't hear anybody else apart from your mother?'

Finn shook his head slowly.

Bisi put her head around the door. 'What are you two talking about?' she asked, suspicious.

'Nothing,' said Finn quietly, still looking right at Eden. 'We weren't talking about anything, were we?'

Eleven

After Bisi took Finn back up to Mrs Sullivan's and Eden was alone again, he wandered up the road to an Indian restaurant he had seen and ordered a takeaway, and while they were preparing it bought a bottle of red wine from the Co-op.

He didn't normally drink during the week, but he was off work. This was different.

He took one of the dining chairs and sat by the open beach door, watching the drizzle on the water. A group of brightly coloured kayaks was working its way upriver, weaving between the moored boats.

By the time the streetlights on the bridge came on, he realised he had drunk over half the bottle and it was getting chilly. He closed the beach door, picked up his plate and took it to the kitchen, washed it under the tap, rinsed the takeaway containers and threw the paper lids into the bin. That was when he noticed the green bag of rubbish he had taken from *Calliope*.

He was tipping its contents into the bin when there was a loud bang on the beach door, startling him.

'Apple?' a woman's voice shouted.

Eden put down the bag and peered into the living room. There was a woman at the beach door, silhouetted against the harbour lights.

'Apple?' the woman shouted again, pounding on the door with the flat of her hand. 'Open the bloody door. It's me.'

The room was dark. When Eden opened the door, the woman gasped. 'Oh, I thought . . .'

She was in her thirties, had dyed blonde hair with long roots showing, and was wearing jeans and a plain T-shirt.

'Sorry,' said Eden. 'You thought Apple was back.' He checked his watch. It was after eleven.

'Who the fuck are you? And what are you doing in Apple's house?'

'I'm Eden. I'm her brother.'

The woman seemed to take a while to absorb this. 'Oh, Jesus,' she said eventually, a hint of a Devon accent in her voice. 'The policeman.'

Eden stared at her.

'She talked about you.'

'She did?'

'Can I come in? It's pissing down.'

He opened the door, stood back and she came in, shaking her head like a wet dog.

'I don't suppose you've heard anything?' she asked. 'Have they . . . ?' She stopped, catching sight of the glass. 'Sorry. Am I interrupting something?'

'You're a friend of my sister's?'

Then, without warning, she put her arms around him and gave him a hug. 'I'm so sorry for what happened. It's just so fucked-up.'

When she finally released him, he asked, 'Would you like a drink? There's only red.'

'Red's good.'

In the kitchen he poured a glass for her.

'See,' she said, following him, 'I heard they called off the search and that was awful, and then when I saw the light on I thought maybe the whole thing had been a giant mistake. I thought she was back. I hoped she was. Stupid of me.'

'And you are . . . ?'

'Shit. Sorry. Molly.' She took the wine, took a gulp and nodded. 'We do the gigs together,' she said.

'You went to concerts together?'

'No, no, no.' She put her hands in front of her and pretended to grasp a pair of oars. 'Gigs and Seine boats. Rowing boats. Rowing club.'

'Right. My sister rowed?'

'She grew up on boats, she always said. So I guess you did too?' And then Molly started to cry loudly, unembarrassedly, and the crying turned into a howl until Eden stepped forward, took the glass from her hand and put his arms around her this time and felt her sobbing slowly subside.

'Sorry,' she said eventually. 'I'm upset.'

'Actually, I wish I could do that,' he said.

'Can't you?'

'No.'

'Sometimes it's all you can do. You should try it. She's gone, hasn't she?'

A burst of rain hit the glass door. The knowledge that his sister was dead had been there in his chest, hot and heavy, ever since he'd heard the news on Saturday night. 'I think we've got to assume it.'

'Fuck,' said Molly. 'Fuck. Fuck. Fuck. Poor Finn.'

She sat in the small armchair; he returned to the sofa. He asked, 'You know her well, then?'

'Kind of. I suppose.'

'What is she like . . . was she like?'

'God. You really didn't know her?'

'Not really. Not since we were kids.'

She leaned forward, pushed hair from her forehead with the back of her hand. 'Well. I mean. She is great. I don't know. Mad. Totally mad. Loyal. If she says she'll do something, she'll do it. And very kind. She was good to me when I was messy, which I can be. But also very annoying, because if she got something into her head like the chem trails, she would be mad about it for weeks.'

'The chem trails?'

Molly rolled her eyes. 'She thought the 5G telephone masts cause Covid blah blah blah. And Covid was all about the government trying to control us. Chem trails. You know. The works. Hardcore Apple I used to call her. But she was like that and you just forgave her because she was so . . .'

'So . . . ?'

'So bloody lovely.' And she wept again.

Eden stood and went back into the kitchen, tore off a square of kitchen roll and returned to give it to her. 'All I've got,' he said.

'Sorry.' She held out her glass and he emptied the last of the bottle into it. There was just a dribble.

'No. It's good to hear about her.'

'You know. I used to take the piss out of her. She never minded. It wasn't all nuts. A lot of it was good. Everything she did was because she cared. She led a campaign to clean up plastic on the beach and loads of people joined in. She did a big thing about fly-tipping, especially people dumping old chemicals and fridges and shit like that and got into the papers about it. You forgave her all the madness because she had such a big heart and because it was just her and Finn against the world. And he's not the easiest child.'

'Isn't he?'

'Just shy. Thin-skinned. Deep, you know? Bit weird but weird is good.' She upended her glass and held it out again.

'Sorry. I'm out.'

'There's more in the cupboard under the stairs,' she told him.

'Is there?' He stood and unbolted the small tongue-and-groove door. The cupboard was crammed full of boots, beach toys, tools, coats and boxes, plus a blow-up mattress and pump. There were two bottles of cheap white on a high shelf next to a couple of bottles of spirits. 'Only white and it's not cold,' he said.

'There's ice in the freezer.' Molly stood and walked round to the kitchen. He followed her.

'Your sister keeps some tobacco in the drawer here.'

'She smoked?'

'Mind if I . . . ?'

Eden had never smoked. 'Go ahead.'

She reached into the kitchen drawer and pulled out a pack of Drum tobacco and some Rizlas.

'You said she could be dark sometimes?'

'It wasn't like she shoved it down your throat, but sometimes we'd have a drink and it would all come out. She had dark days. Our phones are tracking everything. Mossad have infiltrated the internet . . . Post-truth Apple. She thought it was pretty funny. But she pissed a few people off round here.'

He cracked ice out of a freezer tray and put a couple of blocks in both glasses. 'So how did you know her?'

'Boats. Me an' my brother own the boatyard on the other side of the bridge. We take her boat out of the water each winter and store it on our hard-standing.'

'How could she afford to keep a boat?'

'She couldn't, as you can see.' Molly waved her arm around the kitchen. 'Apple struggled a lot with money. She did a bit of care work when Finn was in school. I think she inherited a bit after your mum died but that was it, basically.'

'Right.' It was the last time they had spoken on the phone – after their mother's death. She was angry that he hadn't wanted to come to the funeral.

Opening the back door, Molly stood by it and lit her roll-up. 'And to be honest, after we became friends, I never really charged her much, which always ticked off my brother. So, win-win, you know?' She grinned a little lopsidedly, standing just inside the doorway. Then she wiped her eyes again. 'What about Finn? What's happened to him? Is he OK?' Her cigarette went out and she threw the stub into the kitchen bin and returned to the living room.

'He's with a foster carer at the moment.' Eden sat down facing her on the small sofa.

'Jesus. Poor mite. Going to need to sort that out. You look like her, you know?'

'So people always said. Do you have any idea who Finn's father is?'

She sat down beside him. 'Apple wanted a child, so she went out and got herself pregnant. She was happy enough not to have a father on the scene.'

Eden said, 'Yeah. Well, I get that.'

'Not a fan of your own father, then?'

'Not exactly, no.'

'Apple used to say he was a difficult man.'

'You might say that.'

It was a small sofa. They sat side by side, uncomfortably close. 'So. Tell me about yourself. Wife? Girlfriend?'

'No,' he said. 'And I'm not looking.'

She laughed. It was a good, deep laugh. 'Jesus. Fuck you.

"And I'm not looking!" Did you think I was asking you on a date or something?'

He reddened. 'No. Swear to God.'

She smiled at his discomfort. 'Don't mind me. All I was thinking was, you're going to have to look after the boy, aren't you? And there's no woman in your life. I mean. There's no one else but you to look after him, is there?'

'I'm not really cut out for that.'

He tried to imagine himself and Finn in his apartment in London. Besides, the hours he worked left no time for a child.

'Don't be ridiculous,' she said, contradicting him. 'Who else has he got? Listen. It's late. I got to skip.'

'Wait. I wanted to ask you something.'

She raised her eyebrows. 'Go on.'

'You don't think it's strange, do you, her just falling off the boat like that? With her child in the cabin?'

She looked at him for a second. 'I mean, sure it's strange. What are you trying to say?' She was rummaging in her bag for something.

'You don't think that someone else was involved, do you?'

She looked up from the bag. 'What do you mean, involved?'

'You said not everybody liked her.'

She had pulled out a packet of cigarette papers. 'God. You mean you think someone . . . ?'

'I'm a policeman. It's how I think.'

'I mean. That would be absolutely crazy, wouldn't it?' She stood, thinking. 'No. No, it couldn't be anything like that. Not around here.' She grabbed a pen from a mug on the shelf by the door and wrote her number on one of the cigarette papers then stuck it on the wall.

She turned and walked unsteadily away into the drizzle. 'Call me if you need anything,' she said over her shoulder.

And after she'd gone he took the wine glasses to the kitchen to wash them up. Only when he went to throw away the empty takeaway carton did he notice the small piece of notepaper on the kitchen floor, tucked under the swing bin.

He had not spotted it before. It was folded in half. There was a small shaving of potato peel stuck to it. The only potato peelings he had seen in the house had been in the green bag he had thrown away. He realised the paper must have been in the rubbish bag that had been on *Calliope*.

He leaned down to pick it up.

Twelve

The sheet of paper had been torn out of a notebook.

There were two things written on it in what looked like his sister's handwriting: '15W E14' and 'TVES'.

Both had been underlined three times.

Eden held the sheet up to the ceiling light to see if he could make out anything else on the paper but there was nothing but these two scribbles that he didn't understand. The first one seemed to be some kind of location, but he had no idea what the second was. When he Googled 'TVES' all he could come up with was the name of a Venezuela TV channel.

He was drunk, he realised. He had consumed most of a bottle of red wine, and a large glass of his sister's white. He should go to bed. Look at it in the morning. It might make more sense in the daylight.

He was still asleep when the doorbell rang.

'Mr Driscoll?'

Eden opened the back door a crack in his boxer shorts and a T-shirt, head still muzzy. DS Sweet stood there in an open-necked shirt, buttons straining at his belly.

'Apologies, mate. Can I come in, have a quick word?'

'Is there news?' Eden asked, thinking they might have found Apple – or her body.

'Sorry. No. I was just wondering if the lad had said anything about what happened on the boat.'

Eden looked at him for a second, then opened the door. 'Come in,' he said. 'Just give me a minute.' He went upstairs and grabbed a pair of trousers.

'How are things there with the Met these days?' Sweet called up the stairs as he was putting them on. 'You're not very popular up there, are you?'

The Metropolitan Police were in the headlines a lot these days, usually for all the wrong things. 'And they love you down here, do they?'

''Course they do. Adore us.' When Eden returned downstairs, Sweet had wedged himself into the small armchair. It looked even smaller with him in it. 'So. How was he?'

'Why are you asking?'

''Cause it's my job. And I'm curious. Like you.'

Eden was grateful. 'My theory about there being someone else on the boat? I asked him about that.'

'And what'd he say?'

'He said he didn't hear anything.'

'Well,' said Sweet. 'It was worth a try. Truth is, I was hoping that he'd say something that would make sense of what happened.'

'He may yet. I'm not sure he's telling me everything.'

'What do you mean?'

'I don't think he trusts me.'

'Stands to reason. You're with the Met, aren't you?'

Eden went to the dining table and picked up the torn-out page he had found last night. 'When I was throwing away the rubbish from the galley, I found this.'

He handed the paper to Sweet. Sweet took his reading glasses from his jacket pocket and peered at it, then said, '15W E14? What's that supposed to mean? Is it a place? Fifteen west? Fourteen degrees east?'

'That's what I thought,' said Eden. 'Only why not W15? Why 15W?'

'Yeah, well. Can I keep it?' Sweet asked, still looking at it.

'You might as well.'

Sweet wriggled in the chair, digging into his trouser pocket, and pulled out a plastic bag. He slipped the paper inside.

'And will you check the wine glasses for prints?'

Sweet grinned. ''Cause you'll think us all a bunch of yokels if we don't?'

'You'll have to work pretty hard to change that,' said Eden.

Sweet laughed, delighted at Eden's response. Sweet was an old-school copper who enjoyed old-school copper banter. 'As a matter of fact, going to head back out there this morning to bag them up.'

'Will you let me know?'

Sweet looked down at the bare wood floor between his feet. 'It's a little awkward,' he said with a half-smile. 'I mean, you understand that you're not part of this investigation, don't you?'

'Of course.'

'But do you? So even if I do find something out, I'm not supposed to share anything like that with you.'

Sweet was right, of course. If Apple's death was suspicious he would be treated as a relative, not a fellow police officer. There was a difference in what he was allowed to know. 'OK. I get it.'

Sweet scratched the back of his hand slowly. 'On that particular matter, I understand you've been talking to Molly Hawkins.'

Eden stared at Sweet. 'How did you know that?'

'Small town.'

'Are you watching the house?'

Sweet burst out laughing. 'God, no. Who do you think we are? Line of bloody Duty? It's just like I said. Molly Hawkins tells someone she's met you and five minutes later it's all around the houses. Everyone knows pretty much everyone round here.'

Eden checked his watch. 'It's only half past nine.'

'Exactly.' Sweet grinned.

'She came here last night when she saw the light was on. She's not a friend of mine, nor is she likely to be. She says she's a friend of my sister's. I've only met her the once and happy never to again. What of it?'

'Like I said, small town. And not everyone here is necessarily on your side, whatever they say. I wanted to ask you to take care what information you share with her.'

Eden squinted. 'What do you mean?'

Sweet rubbed his unshaven chin. 'Look, Eden. Copper to copper. I'm not saying that there is anything suspicious around your sister's death. You've raised that as a possibility. Obviously we'll look into that, right? It may well have been purely accidental. And I know it's hard for you, but it may well turn out that she took her own life. But if there's any room for doubt, even the slightest chink, this will be become an investigation into manslaughter, or worse. We don't want to get people round here speculating before we know anything. In a place like this, that runs out of control fast.'

'And . . . ?'

Sweet rubbed his palms together gently. 'Just be a bit careful of Molly. You didn't hear this from me, but her brother is known to us – to use a phrase.'

'Her brother?'

'Frankie Hawkins.'

Eden understood now. 'That's why you're really here, isn't it? You heard that she was here and next thing you're round knocking on the door.'

He nodded. 'Not just that. But yeah. I wanted you to be careful. You know your sister used to go out with Frankie, don't you?'

That was news. 'Did she?'

'Molly didn't actually mention that, then?'

'No. She didn't. So there's an existing investigation into Frankie Hawkins, is that what you're saying?'

'Can neither confirm nor deny . . .'

'Right. And you don't want me telling his sister your business?' Eden peered at the older police officer. 'Why? You think there is something that might connect the disappearance of my sister to Molly Hawkins – or her brother?'

'Steady on, now. Honestly? No, I don't. I just wanted to warn you off her. I would love to tell you all about it, copper-to-copper, but you know I can't.'

Eden stared at him.

'Because you seem like a nice bloke. A good copper.' Having said what he had to say, Sweet prised himself out of the armchair.

From the back door Eden watched Sweet reverse the unmarked car down the narrow road, swinging the rear round towards the beach, then putting it into a forward gear and disappearing onto the road ahead.

When he'd gone, Eden went to fetch a take-out coffee from the café.

'Any news of your sister?' asked a red-faced woman behind the counter.

'What?'

'You were in here yesterday. You're the missing girl's brother, aren't you?' she said and turned her back to knock coffee grounds out of the filter.

Sweet was right. Small town. He returned to the house with the coffee, took a folding chair from his sister's living room and set it up by the back door.

The river was busy. Tourists balanced unsteadily on sailboards. Toddlers ran naked into the water. A trawler chugged slowly against the outgoing tide.

He looked at the wall next to him where Molly had stuck her number, and took his phone from his pocket.

Thirteen

Eden had not expected to stay. He needed a change of clothes. Quickly abandoning the idea of looking locally, he drove to the nearest city, Exeter, and found a River Island, filling a basket with T-shirts and boxer shorts, two pairs of trousers, a zipped sweatshirt and a pair of trainers. This was not how he usually shopped. He liked to take his time, but he had grabbed what he could to see out the week.

By the end of the week, he promised himself he would be on his way home, but it was going to be a long week. An idea struck him.

'Is there an electrics shop near here?' he asked the girl on the till. 'A gaming shop?'

'Don't know.' The girl held out the card reader.

Bisi brought Finn round after his first day back at school, still dressed in his uniform – grey trousers and a white shirt.

'Hello again.' Eden greeted him. 'Remember me?'

Finn nodded. 'Yes.'

'How was school?'

'Why?'

'I'm interested. I bought you a welcome-home present,' said Eden.

'It's my house. Not yours.'

'I know. Go and look in your bedroom,' said Eden.

Finn's room was little more than a cupboard next to the staircase. There was room for a single bed, a wardrobe and a tiny table and chair for homework. Eden had set up the PlayStation and the monitor on it. He had bought a copy of *LEGO Marvel* too.

Finn turned, puzzled. 'What's that doing there?'

'I bought it because you've had a shitty time recently and you deserve something good.'

Finn nodded, his expression serious, as if he was considering what Eden had said.

'Don't you want to play it?' Eden had bought a second controller, a speaker and a SIM card wi-fi router. 'Go ahead. I was thinking we could play it together.'

Finn stared at the PS5 from the bedroom doorway. 'Mum won't like it,' he said.

'Oh, really?'

'She won't let me keep it,' said Finn, 'when she gets home.'

'She isn't keen on games?'

Finn shook his head. 'They're bad for our brains. They stop people talking to each other. They make people angry and they are sexist.'

'Do you think that?'

Finn turned to Eden and looked at him for a while. 'Yes.'

'I guess my brain is ruined, then.' Eden stepped forward into the room and picked up one of the controllers. The monitor came to life. He held the other controller out to Finn. Finn shook his head, stayed standing in the doorway to his bedroom.

Eden started up the machine. The first thing that happened was that it needed an update.

'It looks quite boring actually,' said Finn.

Eden should have done this before Finn had come home. Through the SIM router, the download was slow. When it finally booted up, it took a little while for Eden to register. 'Shall I make you a profile? Do you have an email address?'

'No.'

Eden sighed. This was not going as he imagined it would.

'I'll log in then create a guest account for you. OK? Did your mum not like TV either?'

'Not really.'

Eden sat on Finn's bed, controller in his hands. 'What do your school friends think of that?'

'They don't come round very much,' Finn said.

'Right. I see that.'

Finally, Finn left the doorway, entered his bedroom and lay on the bed that Eden was sitting on the end of. Eden started up the game and started to play. 'Sorry, surfer dude,' said a character's voice. 'You're headed for a wipeout.'

'You want to help me?'

'No.'

'Iron Man. I'm reading an incoming ship. Watch out. It's about to open fire.'

Eden played the game, conscious that Finn was watching him from the bed. Eden was soon fighting Sandman in a New York-like landscape. Prompted by the screen, Eden pressed Y to switch from Iron Man to Hulk. For a while, Hulk floundered around hitting taxis. He jumped off a road ramp but the way was blocked, so Eden started over until he discovered that pressing B meant that Hulk could pick up the bus that had crashed between him and Sandman.

The sound of the fight was tinny on the tiny speaker. Eden had a soundbar on his home system in his flat in Manor

House and it could shake the windows if you turned it up loud.

'It doesn't look anything like the film,' said Finn.

'Because it's *LEGO Marvel*. What football team do you support?' tried Eden.

'Don't like football,' the boy answered.

'I thought all boys liked football.'

'Is my mum dead?' Finn asked.

On the screen Spiderman was riding on the Hulk's shoulders. Eden put down the controller and switched off the machine. The screen turned black. 'I don't know for certain. It's pretty likely though. I'm sorry.'

When he looked round again, Finn was lying on his back looking at the ceiling. 'I've got homework to do,' he said.

'OK. Well. It's there if you want it.'

They sat in silence in the small room. Eden checked his watch. 'Bisi will be here soon to pick you up.'

'I don't want to go.'

'Tomorrow you can stay here,' said Eden. 'Once Bisi has sorted the court order.'

Finn sat up on his elbows. 'Will you still be here?'

'Do you want me to be here?'

'No. I want to be here with my mum.'

'I know. But if I stay here you can come home.'

'How long will you be here for?'

'Until the weekend, at least. Do you want help with your homework?'

'No.'

'What is it?'

'Maths again. Not very hard.'

'You know, you don't have to do your homework if you're feeling sad,' said Eden.

Finn lay down again. 'It's OK. It's just quotients,' he said, as though they were childish.

'I could get you a computer to do your homework on.'

'It's OK, I use Mum's.'

It took Eden a moment to realise what Finn had just said. 'Mum's?' Eden sat up straighter.

'Yes.'

'She has a computer?' He hadn't seen a computer anywhere in the house. He had assumed she was such a Luddite she didn't have one. 'Where is it?'

'In her bedroom.'

Eden paused. 'You sure? I haven't seen one.'

Finn nodded.

'No, there's not.'

'Yes, there is.'

Reluctantly, Finn swung himself off the bed and walked to the room at the front of the house. He pointed at his mother's dressing table. 'That's where it was,' he said.

Except it wasn't there now. The dressing table was covered in pots and tubs of ointments and make-up.

'Where is it?'

'It was there,' said Finn angrily. 'I haven't done anything.'

'There's no computer.'

'It was there. I'm not lying!' Finn shouted. 'I'm not lying!' Finn punched Eden hard in the hip.

'OK. OK. Calm down.'

'I'm not lying!' Finn screamed.

Eden tried to calm him. 'I didn't say you were lying,' he said in a soothing voice. 'I just said . . .'

Finn punched him again, this time in his belly.

'Ow,' said Eden.

'You stole it,' said Finn, furious. 'You stole Mum's computer. It was here. It was right here.'

Eden approached the table. There was a small wicker rubbish bin. In it were strands of his sister's hair, pulled from a brush, an old plastic razor, an empty plastic bag and an empty tube of moisturiser. Spotting the unplugged end of a black lead, he dropped to his knees and picked up the bin. There, behind it, sat a small router, green light blinking. The unplugged power lead lay curled next to it.

'What are you doing?' asked Finn as Eden removed the small plastic bag from the waste-paper bin, put his hand inside it, and used the bag to carefully unplug the lead from the wall.

Fourteen

When Bisi arrived to pick Finn up, Eden was cooking a pan of pasta for him.

'I've got a few more things I need you to sign, Eden.' There wasn't enough space on the work surfaces in the kitchen. Without asking, Bisi began moving the bowls and plates and putting them by the sink.

'Apple had a computer,' said Eden. 'Only it seems to be missing.'

'Maybe the police took it?' Bisi answered vaguely, looking through her papers.

'They wouldn't have done that without letting me know.'

'Wouldn't they? I need you to sign this.' She handed him a sheet.

He looked at the form. It was a document to be submitted for the application for the court order to allow him to look after Finn. 'I feel like I'm sitting an exam,' he said.

She laughed. 'You don't have to sit an exam. They let any idiot bring up a child.'

'Thank you.'

'How is he?'

'Sorry?'

'I asked how Finn was.'

'Well, he hates me,' Eden said.

'You're a police officer. Everyone hates you,' she said.

'Thank you.'

'I'm sure it's not that bad, Eden. You seem a little preoccupied. Is everything all right?'

Why would someone need to take Apple's computer? 'Fine,' he answered. 'We talked a bit about his mother. He asked if I thought she was dead. And when I said I thought she probably was, he got angry.'

She nodded. 'Yep. Because he's angry about it.'

'He didn't get angry about her. He got angry about something completely different.'

She nodded, peered into the pan. 'At least you can cook.'

'This isn't permanent, you know,' he said, lowering his voice. 'They need me back in London at some point.'

She ignored him. 'I brought some information you might find useful.' She produced a couple of leaflets and some typed sheets. 'This is a list of emergency contacts. My number's there, and there's an out-of-hours number too.'

'I'm only going to be letting him down. And he's miserable enough already.'

'How so?'

Eden spread his hands. 'He's going to need to form a long-term relationship with his new family, whoever that is.'

'His new family? Who is that, exactly?'

'I don't know. But that's what you do, isn't it? As a social worker? Find suitable carers for children like Finn.'

'Like you.'

'That's what I'm trying to say. I'm not suitable. I'm a single man. I have a career.' He looked up from the pan. 'What if I find his father?'

'You are welcome to try, obviously.'

Eden looked down again. 'Or what if I find someone who really wants to look after him? I don't know. A family friend, maybe.'

Bisi rubbed the back of her neck. 'I suspect you have some idea about what the outcomes are for a child Finn's age if he's taken into care.'

Eden said quietly, 'Yes. I do.'

'Families looking to adopt are not looking for nine-year-old boys. If you're not looking after him here, in his own home, we'll have to start looking for other options. You saw how hard it is for us to arrange local foster care. The chances are we'll end up looking out of county. I want to ask you a question. Do you remember being Finn's age?' she asked.

'Me? A little.'

'I don't think you had it easy, either.'

Eden frowned. 'Where are you getting that from?'

'You were known to Westminster Social Services after being picked up by police in Paddington,' she pulled out a sheet of paper, 'as an unaccompanied fifteen-year-old. You were in care yourself, weren't you? So you understand what that experience is like.'

Eden was quiet for a minute. 'You found that in my file?'

'Part of our viability check. How come you were living on your own at fifteen?'

He never talked about this. None of his colleagues in the police knew. 'Is this relevant?'

'I don't know. Is it?'

Eden sighed. 'I ran away from my parents. I didn't ever see them again after I was fifteen.'

'What about your sister? You ever see her again?'

'We talked a little when my mother died. I didn't see her. I wish I had now. I don't know where all that time went.'

He looked up to see her squinting at him. 'Why did you run away from home, Eden?'

He drained the pasta. Steam filled the small kitchen. 'Because I didn't like my father very much.'

'Did he abuse you?'

Eden turned to look her in the eye. 'Kind of. Yes. Not sexually. It wasn't anything like that. He saw himself as an adventurer. He took us all travelling with him for years. Greece, Italy, Turkey, Morocco. We lived in vans and on boats. It sounds great, doesn't it?'

'Not if you didn't have a good childhood.'

'He ran the family like a religious cult. You asked about whether I thought Apple suffered from any mental illness. I'm not sure about her, but I think he did, if I'm honest. If you'd have asked me at the time, I would have had no idea, but the more I think about it, the more I think he was ill. But whatever, we had to do what Dad wanted, in exactly the way he wanted. That was the way he ran our family. He thought we were going to show the world how a real family should live away from the corruption of modern life.'

'He was strict?'

'Oh, yes.'

'Did he use physical punishment?'

'Yes.'

She nodded.

'I hated him. I was a boy, I suppose, so it was different for Apple. He wanted me to be like him and I wasn't. So when I was fifteen, things came to a head . . . I figured I was old enough to hitch a ride without anyone asking too many questions. I ran away and didn't see any of them again.'

'Is that the whole story?'

He took some oil and poured it on the pasta. 'It's all you're getting.'

She took the piece of paper he had signed and checked the signature at the bottom. 'I'm sorry you didn't have a good experience of family. Is that what's making you nervous about taking on responsibility for Finn?'

'I've a full-time job. I live in London. I can't just drop everything. I just can't.'

She looked at him for a while, then put the sheet of paper into an envelope. 'Tomorrow morning you can pick him up from Mrs Sullivan's and take him up to school. It'll give you a chance to see how it's done, for them to see who you are. Then, in the evening, you can pick him up from school and bring him back here and spend the night with him. Let's see how it goes from here.'

'I think the computer was stolen from the house,' he said.

'What?'

'I think somebody else has been in this house. Somebody else apart from me and Finn and you – and the police.'

For the first time, Bisi was starting to look worried.

Fifteen

Eden repeated what he had just said.

'Seriously? You really think someone's broken in while you weren't here?' asked Bisi.

'You don't exactly need to break in. The key was right there behind the down pipe.'

'Have you told the police?'

'Not yet. I've only just discovered Apple had one – and it's missing.'

Bisi was on her phone already. 'We can have the locks changed for you. We have people who do that. We need for Finn to be safe.'

'OK.'

'Are you sure you're OK with him coming here?' she asked.

'Do I get a choice?'

'Of course you do,' she said.

Eden added herbs and cheese to the pasta and stirred it.

'Finn? I thought we could eat outside.' Finn was still in his room. 'Before you have to go back to Mrs Sullivan's.'

'Don't want to,' Finn called back.
'Come on. It'll be fun.'
No answer.

Bisi unshouldered her bag and went upstairs. A few minutes later she came down holding his hand.

Eden fetched three folding chairs and set them up on the beach. They ate, bowls on their knees. Eden wondered if that was a mistake; out here on the beach, he felt as if the whole town's eyes were on them. Eden looked around and sure enough, a couple who were drinking rosé wine from plastic glasses seemed to be watching them with special interest. They were staring straight at them. The woman wore a white broderie top with puff sleeves. She put down her glass to rub suntan cream onto the man's muscled shoulders but he carried on looking right at them.

Bisi was watching the boy slowly poking at the pasta. After a few forkfuls, he stopped, put his bowl on the beach and sat down next to it, digging at the sand with his hands. 'Can't you eat some more?' Bisi asked.

'Full up.'

'Come on. One more forkful.'

'I don't like it. It's horrible. I don't like the bits.'

He shouldn't have added the herbs, thought Eden.

'Well, then. Who wants an ice cream?' Bisi said, standing. 'I would love a choc ice.'

'Only if they have vegan ones,' said Finn, quietly.

Eden watched as she disappeared up the beach, towards the pub. He looked down at Finn, and said, 'It'll take her a while. What about a bit more pasta while you're waiting?'

Finn looked up at him, lifted a fistful of red sand and slowly poured it into his bowl of food.

'You're Finn, aren't you?'

Eden looked up to see the toned man was standing in

front of them, the pretty woman in the white top just a pace behind him, looking over the man's shoulder.

Finn squinted up at him.

'Sorry about your mum, mate,' said the man, squatting down in front of Finn. 'You go to school with our boy. We heard it on the news and thought it was, like, really bad. We're getting up a collection for you.'

Eden said, 'Perhaps you can wait for Finn's social worker to come back?'

'A collection of what?' demanded Finn.

'Money, of course,' said the man, with a smile. His teeth were even and white. He turned to Eden. 'Are you the boy's dad? Our son's at the same school as him. Thing is, I do a cabaret spot at the Pavilion. Am-dram, you know? In real life I'm a dentist, but it's a hobby of mine. Stand-up and magic. The wife writes songs. We're planning on doing a special night to raise money for him. Buy a nice holiday somewhere for the lad if we get enough. Tragic, her dying so young.'

Finn picked up another fistful of sand, clutching it tightly. Eden wondered if he was about to throw it at the man.

'I think you should probably go,' said Eden quietly.

The woman added, 'Just telling the boy. Letting him know we're thinking of him and saying sorry about his mum. Everyone is. The whole town. Poor little love.'

'Please go now,' said Eden, more firmly.

'Jesus,' muttered the man. 'Sorry.'

'Just trying to be nice to the boy,' said the young woman resentfully, pulling the man away. 'He needs a bit of love, that's all.'

Finn sat for a while, saying nothing. Then, just as Bisi was returning with her hands full of ice cream cones, he relaxed his hand and let all the second fistful pour in a steady stream into his pasta bowl.

'What did you go and do that for?' demanded Bisi. 'Now it's ruined.'

Finn stood and ran back into the house.

'What happened?' Bisi asked, melting ice cream dripping round her fist.

The man and the woman who had approached them were looking at them again, talking quietly to each other, disapproval on their faces.

The following morning, when Eden arrived, Finn was already standing at the door to Mrs Sullivan's house wearing his school uniform and holding a backpack.

Mrs Sullivan said, 'I've made him a packed lunch. It's in his backpack.' And she leaned down, kissed the top of the boy's head in an easy motion.

'Hello,' said Eden brightly as Finn got into his car. 'Did you finish your homework OK?'

'Yes,' said Finn, buckling up his seatbelt without another word.

'Was everything OK?'

'It was easy.'

The drive to the school was busy with rush-hour traffic, and when they reached the small country lane that the school was on, it was jammed.

Drivers flashed headlights at each other in recognition. The parents looked friendly enough, waving at each other behind their windscreens, but when a parking space came free they drove aggressively into it.

Eden managed to reverse back down the road, found a spot and parked. It was a little after nine by the time they made it to the school gate, but clearly they weren't the only ones turning up late. The head teacher was an athletic-looking man in his forties in a white shirt and tie. He smiled at Finn and then looked up. 'And you must be Finn's uncle Eden.' Another smile. 'Come along, little man,' he said to Finn. 'Miss Killick is waiting to see you.'

Eden was aware of other eyes on him, women depositing their children at the gates, inspecting him from the sides of their eyes. 'Don't you want to say goodbye to your uncle?' asked the head teacher.

'No,' said Finn.

Eden watched the boy walking away. Other children moved aside as he passed, as if fearful of being infected by the misery he radiated.

'Our safeguarding officer called in sick this morning. Such a pity. I know she wanted to meet you, just to say hello,' the head teacher was saying. 'It's important we know who's picking up the boy.'

As Eden reached the pavement and turned to walk back to his car he gave way to a young woman in brightly patterned gym leggings and trainers, pushing a buggy. 'So you're not Finn's dad?' she said.

He looked at her and recognised her from the beach. She had been with the man who had said he was fundraising for Finn. Behind her stood other women, listening.

'No. I'm his uncle.'

'Told you,' said one of the other women. 'He's her brother. Looks a bit like her, doesn't he?'

'We're sorry about what happened to Finn's mum,' said the woman in the leggings. 'I'm Pamela. We seem to have got off on the wrong foot on the beach yesterday. We're only trying to help. Give him something to smile about.'

'I'm Emma,' said another woman. 'Pam's been raising some money. We were going to take him out to the adventure park, if he'd like that.'

A third woman approached, and then a fourth. 'Poor boy. He must be feeling very sad.'

'I was thinking of saying, Finn could come on a play date with my Cyrus if he's feeling down,' said leggings woman – the one who had said her name was Pamela.

'Are they friends?' asked Eden.

'No, but . . .'

'I'm sorry, I have to go,' Eden said, pushing through them. When he reached the corner of the road he was parked on he looked back. They were all huddled, discussing him. Pamela looked back at him, disapproving.

'Stuck up, just like the boy's bloody mother,' she said, loud enough for him to hear.

Sixteen

'I felt like one of those animals on a David Attenborough documentary,' Eden was telling Mike Sweet. 'Once the first predator has picked you off, the rest gather for the kill.'

'It's called community,' Sweet told him, stirring sugar into his tea.

'It's called fuck-you-nosy-bastards.'

Sweet smiled, laid the teaspoon down on the table. 'Good-looking new man turns up at the school gates. You're the entertainment. I know a few who would kill for that kind of attention.'

After the locksmith finished at his sister's house Eden had arranged to meet Sweet on the seafront. The café that Sweet had picked was in the local theatre, big glass windows looking out towards the sea.

'You absolutely sure the computer was stolen?' Sweet asked Eden.

'It's missing, and the lead was still there, plugged into the wall. Finn remembers it being there, so I guess it would have been taken some time between Friday night, when my sister went missing, and midday on Sunday when we let ourselves into the house. Anyone who knew where she kept the key could have got in the house and taken it away.'

'Because the computer contained some kind of evidence, you guess?'

'Maybe she wrote something on it. I've looked for a diary but not found anything. On its own, the computer wouldn't have been worth much if it's like everything else in my sister's place. Why else would you steal it? Something funny is going on.'

Sweet nodded, head tipped slightly to one side, as if still uncertain. 'I'll get someone to come round and pick up the lead so we can check it for prints. That second wine glass?'

'Yes?'

'We picked them both up, like I said we would, checked them over. I said I wasn't going to share anything relating to the investigation, but there's no harm in you knowing that the only fingerprints on them are your sister's.'

'Really?'

'Hundred per cent.'

Eden had been sure the glass had been some kind of clue to someone else's being on the boat. 'You still don't think there's anything suspicious about her disappearance?'

'I've an open mind. You thought there was a third person on the boat, but your nephew says he didn't hear anything. The glass doesn't tell us anything. There's not a lot to go on so far.'

'To be fair, my nephew isn't exactly chatty.'

'You're not his mother.'

'No. I'm not.' Eden was drinking a coffee. It was on the bitter side. He put the cup down.

'You had dealings with my sister before she disappeared, didn't you?'

'Yes.'

'Can I ask what they were?'

Sweet sighed. 'Local police were called to the school about eighteen months ago. Your sister, Apple, was trying to block the entrance to prevent children going in. She was quite distressed and wouldn't move even when the head asked her to. Local plod had to arrest her so that the children could get in.'

'God,' said Eden. 'I had no idea.'

'There's a 5G mast close to the school. Apple was convinced it was going to harm the kids. She became quite distressed, apparently. Teachers said she was upsetting the children. The local officers thought it would be best if they removed her and so she ended up in custody.'

'Was she charged?'

'Obstruction, but that was dropped. She had been on some medication apparently and had come off it against the advice of her GP.'

Eden remembered the packet of pills in the bathroom. He checked his watch. 'Listen, I have to go. I have an appointment.'

'An appointment?'

'Something I need to do before I have to go and pick Finn up from school.'

Before Sweet could ask more, Eden stood and walked away through the theatre lobby to the door at the back of the building. That way, Sweet would not be able to see in which direction he was heading.

He met Molly at the foot of the New Quay. She was standing next to a white rowing dinghy, with a backpack over her shoulder, holding a pair of oars in one hand.

'Thanks for doing this,' he said. 'I'm asking you because I don't know anyone else who has a boat round here – apart from the harbourmaster.'

'I thought you were asking because I was a friend of Apple's.'

'Right,' he said. 'I'm happy to pay for the petrol.'

'Diesel,' she said. 'No need. You're my friend's brother, like I said.'

'I just want to be clear . . .'

'Perfectly clear,' she said.

'And I have to be back at school at three. Can we do it?'

'Better hurry up, then,' she said. 'Get in the back.'

The boat was beached prow-on, so once he was in he had to step past her to the back of the dingy, stepping over the thwart as the boat wobbled beneath him, then grabbing the side to steady himself. When he made it to the seat at the back and turned to sit himself down, he caught sight of Molly grinning at his clumsiness.

'Funny,' he said.

'We are simple country folk. We take our pleasure where we can,' she said. She laid the oars on the rollocks and shoved the boat out into the shallow water, throwing the backpack in, then jumping in after it. As the boat slid back in the water Molly sat calmly on the thwart and took hold of the oars. After a couple of strokes they were out into a deep channel.

The incoming tide took them upriver, towards the boats that were moored off the main docks, close to where *Calliope* sat in the river. Molly headed for a blue tub-like boat with a kind of half-cabin at the front. 'Jump on,' she said, taking hold of the back of the boat.

Eden scrambled in, then held out his hand for Molly to follow. With a small smile, she ignored the hand and hopped aboard with practised ease. On board the bigger boat, she walked the rowing boat round to the bows, tied it onto the mooring line then came back and started up the diesel engine.

Again she went forward and dropped the mooring, let the boat drift back on the tide for a second, then gunned the engine and they were moving against the incoming water.

'We may not get as far as the area where they found your sister's boat, given how long we've got, but water is just water. You'll get the idea.'

When Eden had called Molly to ask her to take him out into the bay she had not asked why, she had just named a time. He had wanted to see where his sister had gone the night she had disappeared.

Standing under the small cuddy roof, Molly steered the boat towards the mouth of the river, pushing the throttle lever forward as the vessel forced its way out against the incoming tide. In the narrow river mouth, the current was at its strongest. Eden stood beside her as they passed under the dark mass of the Ness cliff. It rose above them, steep, rocky and raw. And then they were out into the sea, sailing past a red navigation buoy and the boat began to rock. Molly eased off the throttle and it was suddenly much quieter. Out here, the boat felt very small.

The cuddy they were standing under was made of wood, beautifully varnished. She saw him admiring it. 'Plymouth Pilot. Eighteen feet,' Molly explained. 'Round here they're kind of like Jeeps. Had this one for years. Bought it as a wreck. Did it up myself. Rebuilt the engine. Everything.'

'Can I ask you a question, Molly? What do you think she was doing out here at night with a small child?'

'Well, that's the thing. I mean. What the hell?'

Looking ahead, her eyes on the horizon, she took one hand off the wheel and rubbed her eyes. They motored on for a few more minutes and Eden became accustomed to the chug of the diesel engine. He looked back at the shoreline, the undulating red cliffs topped with green.

'I didn't tell you this, but she rang me, Friday afternoon – the afternoon before the night she disappeared. I didn't pick up. So she left a message.'

'What was the message?'

'She wanted me to look after Finn,' she said. 'Only I didn't.'

Seventeen

Out at sea, the wind had picked up. Molly was staring hard at the water in front of them.

'So she hadn't been going to take Finn with her?'

'I'm sorry. If I'd picked up her call . . . I don't know. Maybe it would have been different.'

'Why? What was she up to?'

'Yeah. I've been asking myself that every bloody minute of the last four days.'

'Did she tell you why she wanted you to look after him?'

Molly shook her head. A gull swooped over the boat, as if checking out what it was doing out here. 'Did you often look after Finn?'

'Sometimes I did. She was on her own, you know. But I couldn't anyway. I was . . . busy.'

'You told her you couldn't look after Finn – so that's why she took him out on the boat?'

'It's worse. I didn't even see the message until later. I was out getting bladdered.'

Eden wished he had brought something warmer to wear. It was colder out here than he had expected.

'The boatyard isn't doing too well. I had a bust-up with my brother. I was in a bar drinking on my own when this hen party came through and I knew a couple of them, so next thing I was clubbing it down the seafront and that was pretty much it. I'm told I can be a bit of a twat sometimes.'

The boat rolled heavily, but she didn't seem to notice.

'So yeah, that's what Finn was doing on the boat, I suppose. Apple couldn't find anyone to look after him. If I'd answered the message and found out what was going through her head, maybe things would have been different.'

'So do you have any idea at all why she wanted to come out here?'

'No bloody idea,' Molly said.

'Don't you find that strange, her sailing out here with a nine-year-old boy?' he asked, looking around. In the far distance to the south there was the dim silhouette of a ship, grey against the horizon.

'Pretty strange,' she said.

He looked at the sea, as if expecting to see something that might explain what had happened. The odds of finding anything in open water were minuscule. He wasn't sure why he had wanted to come out here in the first place.

'Where is your boatyard?'

'Just the other side of the bridge. Used to be my dad's place, only he died and we inherited it. Not supposed to be anything to do with me. I trained as a marine biologist, believe it or not. I was signed up to do a masters. My brother was going to run the yard, but he's barely capable of doing up his own shirt. Last year I took a look at the books and saw he was losing way too much money, so I gave up on my masters and now I'm spending my life scraping barnacles off other people's boats, until the place gets back on track. You don't always get what you want, you know, Eden. You going to adopt him?'

There was a bench seat around the edge of the boat. He sat down. 'You're quite direct, aren't you?'

'So I'm told. Are you?'

'Can I ask you a question? Did you know my sister had issues with her mental health?' he asked.

'Did the police say that?'

'Finn's social worker talked about it. She wanted to know if I had any mental-health issues too.'

'She had a few episodes. She was pretty open about all that. Anxiety. I think she was diagnosed, but she never liked doctors because she was such a bloody hippy. And she went through these periods of thinking the world was against her. She accused the local police of being out to get her after they arrested her at the school – you heard about that?'

'Yes.'

'She thought that they were spying on her. Who knows? Police love sticking their noses into other people's business,' said Molly.

'Are you speaking from personal experience?'

'See what I mean?' Molly muttered.

'Sorry.'

'Yeah. So. Your sister went through these dark times and saw bad stuff all around her. Thinking people were out to get her. Thinking that the government were spying on all of us. Thinking we were being controlled by chem trails in the sky. Some of it was nuts, some of it was perfectly rational. She said our rivers were being poisoned by people chucking sewage and chemicals into them, that the sea was being killed by the amount of plastic we're chucking in there. All that's true.'

'Our father was the same,' said Eden. 'He thought the world was out to get him and it did in the end.'

'Apple said your father was a tricky piece of work.'

'Did she?' He raised his eyebrows.

'She felt sorry for you, you know. She thinks he was tough on you because you were a boy.'

Eden stared at the woman in surprise, wishing that he had had this sort of conversation with his sister. Until now, he had always tried to think about his childhood as little as possible.

'What did you argue about with your brother?' he asked.

'Why do you want to know?' she said defensively.

'Because I do.'

'Money, of course. He always spends too much of it. I caught him taking cash out of the business as,' she lifted her hands off the wheel and drew commas in the air, '"expenses". Always reckons he has some scheme to make it back. That's all.'

'Is that why the police keep an eye on him?'

'Oh. That's why we're here, is it?' Molly said, looking at him with leaden eyes. 'One thing you should know. Frankie got caught up in a bit of stupidity when he was younger. Now anything happens and the police are always up for blaming Frankie. That's how they work around here.'

'You didn't tell me that Frankie used to go out with my sister.'

'Oh, for fuck's sake, Eden. Who told you that?'

Eden said, 'Who do you think? Is it true?'

She throttled down. The sound of the sea seemed to fill the space the engine's noise had been taking up. 'I can't believe this. You said you wanted to see where your sister had disappeared.'

'I'm sorry. I'm just trying to find out what really happened.'

'Yes. They did have a thing. He's a good-looking boy and that's what gets him into trouble half the time. It was over a couple of years ago, OK?' She turned the throttle up again and the boat lurched forward.

'The police think she may have gone overboard deliberately. Is that possible?'

Molly looked into the distance. 'I mean. It's possible. She was pretty dark sometimes. But on the other side of it, she loved Finn. She absolutely adored him. They are saying she locked him in his cabin and jumped overboard? I just find that really hard.'

'Hard to understand, or hard to believe?'

'Both, I suppose.'

'You messaged her. She had a phone on her, then?'

'An old brick. She wouldn't use anything new. Because George Soros, you know . . . Bill Gates . . . whatever. They want to track our thoughts.'

'I couldn't find it anywhere.'

'She must have had it with her when she fell in.'

'That's what you think? She fell in?'

'I mean, she loved Finn so much, she loved him so hard. Whatever the police say, she'd never leave him alone on purpose.'

'Was there anyone else she went sailing with?'

Molly narrowed her eyes. 'Why all these questions?'

'What if there was someone else on the boat with her?'

She frowned. 'What makes you think that? Is that what the police are saying?'

'I don't know what the police are saying,' he said evasively. Sweet had warned him against sharing information with Molly.

She killed the engine and the boat slowed.

'Why do you think there was another person on the boat with her, then?' she asked. 'Did Finn say something?'

'Forget I said it.'

She looked at him oddly. It was quiet except for the noise of the wind and the waves lapping at the sides of the boat. She reached into the backpack and pulled out a Thermos with two mugs. 'Do you take sugar?' she asked.

'No.'

'That's a pity,' she said and poured a mug of tea. It was very sweet, but it was hot at least.

'Out there, about another two miles,' she said, pointing south-west. 'That's where they found the boat.' Now the engine was off, the boat floated side on to the swell, rolling with each wave. It was making Eden feel nauseous.

'She didn't jump,' he said.

'No. I don't think she did either.'

Eden stared into the distance for a while, then looked back at the shore, which seemed a long way away already.

He shivered and looked at his watch. 'Shouldn't we be getting back? I have to pick up Finn.'

'Sorry. Yeah.' She went to switch the engine on. It roared into life – and died almost immediately afterwards.

Molly frowned, pressed the ignition again. 'Shit,' she said.

'Is everything OK?' asked Eden.

She pressed the ignition again. The engine spun without firing. Molly closed her eyes and swore again.

Eighteen

The first thing Molly did was check the fuel. Then she hauled off the casing to the diesel engine and peered at it for a minute.

'Little shitter,' she said.

'What?'

'It's my boat. He's not even supposed to take it out but he does all the time.'

They were adrift in the channel, just like Finn had been. 'Are we in trouble?'

'No. My brother is when I get back, though, the little shitcake. There's moisture in the filter.' She looked up. 'Look in the forward compartment. There's a spare filter in there. It'll be on the right. It'll be called R25P or something.'

Eden did as he was told. There were flares, a torch, ropes and chains and a box labelled exactly as she had said, R25P. He handed it to her.

'I need to be back to pick up Finn,' he said.

'It's a ten-minute job,' she reassured him.

'I can't let Finn down.'

'I know. Don't worry.'

'What did your brother do wrong?'

'Sneaky little bastard has borrowed my boat without telling me. He tried to hide it by topping up the diesel tank but he's always got a tank of dodgy diesel that he hasn't cleaned up. Clogged up the filter. Don't worry. I always carry spares.'

'Don't we need to call the coastguard or something?'

She paused. 'Relax. It's a simple fix. Just give me a minute. Besides, I'd never live it down if you did. "Did your lilo get caught by a strong breeze, Molly?" I'd rather drown.' She realised what she'd said and stopped. 'God. Sorry.'

She screwed the replacement filter into place. 'Pass me that rag, can you?' She took it from him and dabbed it around, soaking up spilt diesel. She stood, switched the fuel line back on and then returned to the wheel.

Molly pressed the ignition again. The starter motor whirred for a while. She glanced over at Eden, smiled, and just as she did so the engine roared back into life. 'The look on your face!' She laughed.

Putting the boat into gear, she swung the wheel around and headed back towards Teignmouth, gunning the motor. The wind was against them and waves broke on the bows, spattering the windshield. It was exhilarating.

As they reached the river mouth, Eden checked his watch for the tenth time.

'It's OK,' she said. 'You'll be fine.'

The tide swept them into the harbour fast. She looped back and turned them into the current and then grounded the boat, bow on, onto the beach. 'Jump,' she said. He did and ran to the house to pick up his car keys.

By the time he reached the school there were still a few women standing there. Pamela was one of them.

When children emerged, mothers leaned down to be

hugged and kissed, children handing over pictures they had drawn to be admired. The small crowd thinned.

Eden watched as two boys slung their arms around each other's shoulders happily, half wrestling. Eden focused on the children's faces, trying to spot Finn.

A woman with short, untidy black hair emerged from the double doors, holding hands with a young girl. 'Are you still waiting for yours?' she asked.

'Yes.'

'You're not here usually, are you?'

'No. First time,' answered Eden.

'And why is Pam over there looking at you like you have horns?' the woman asked.

'I was a bit rude to her this morning,' he said. 'She was probably just trying to be helpful.'

The woman laughed. 'Pam is always trying to be helpful.' The trickle of children coming out of the doors was slowing. 'If by helpful you mean nosy.'

'I have discovered that already.'

'Her husband is a private dentist. He's why all the rich women of Teignbridge have teeth that gleam like new piano keys.'

It was Eden's turn to laugh. Behind him, he could hear the last sound of cars pulling away. At the other side of the gate, Pamela had picked up her boy and had turned away down the street. The playground in front of the school was quiet.

Suddenly it was just him and the woman with dark hair and her daughter standing there.

Why had Finn not come out? Was he being kept in after school?

'I hate school. Can we go home now?' the woman's daughter said.

'Everyone hates school,' the woman answered. 'It's what it's for. We're just waiting to see that this gentleman here is OK.'

Eden was staring at the double doors.

'Looks like yours is going to be the last,' said the woman.

'Maybe he doesn't want to see me?' Eden wondered aloud. Was Finn hiding from him? He had no idea at all if the boy even liked him.

'What's your child's name? Sheena, will you run back in and fetch this man's boy?' She turned back to Eden. 'Whose class is he in?'

'His name's Finn,' said Eden.

Her mouth dropped open. 'Oh, my word,' said the woman. 'That's why Pam was all over you.'

'Yes.'

'You should go in there, then, yourself,' said the woman gently. 'They won't mind. I'll come with you.'

'No point,' said Sheena, tugging at her mother's arm. 'Can we get an ice cream, Mum?'

The woman looked puzzled. 'What do you mean there's no point, love?'

'Finn's already gone,' she said. 'He left in the last lesson.'

'How d'you know?' her mother asked her.

'Someone came to pick him up.'

Eden was already walking through the gate into the hallway. 'Hello?' he called out.

'His classroom is Opal. It's just down the corridor on the left.' He turned. The woman at the gate had followed him inside. 'This way.'

Followed by her child, Sheena, she led him down the wide corridor lined with children's drawings and posters.

'Miss Killick?' the woman called out.

At a low children's table in a bright windowed room, a

woman in a white T-shirt was looking through some written work. She looked up.

'This man is looking for Finn.'

The woman frowned. 'Finn has already gone home.'

'Who picked him up?' asked Eden, puzzled.

'Mrs Sullivan,' answered Miss Killick. 'His foster carer.'

At first he was irritated he had not been told of the change of plan – then he remembered that Mrs Sullivan had said she was going to be away.

'What did she look like?' he demanded.

'What?' The teacher was looking nervous. 'Is something wrong?'

Nineteen

The police took an age to arrive.

Two officers, stepping out of their car at an achingly slow pace. The young man with ginger hair seemed to spend a long time searching for a clean page in his notebook before he asked, 'What did she look like, this woman?'

'Dark hair. Youngish. Tidy. A skirt, I think.' Miss Killick looked terrified. 'She said she was Finn's foster carer. Her name is on the list. And she said something to Finn and Finn walked straight towards her. I had no reason to think she wasn't who she said she was.'

Eden was on the phone to Bisi. 'No. We didn't send anyone to pick him up. We wouldn't have without notifying you. What's wrong?'

'Could Mrs Sullivan have picked him up?'

'She's away. She told us she's away.' And the description Miss Killick was giving the officer sounded nothing like Mrs Sullivan.

'Has anyone else ever picked the lad up?' the officer asked. 'Apart from this carer?'

'No. Just his mother.' Mrs Killick turned to Eden. 'Your sister.'

Eden wanted to get the officer's attention. 'You should be organizing a search.'

The officer turned to Eden, attempting a smile. 'It's probably just a mix-up, sir.'

'It's not a mix-up.' He turned back to Miss Killick. 'Did you see him get into a vehicle?'

She shook her head. 'No. I watched them walk out into the playground. She leaned down and said something to the boy, then took his hand and they walked together to the gate. That was all I saw.'

'You have to treat this as a suspected abduction.' His voice echoed round the half-empty building.

'An abduction?' Miss Killick's eyes were huge.

Eden's call was still connected. 'Eden?' Bisi was saying. 'Talk to me. What's wrong?'

'Don't jump to conclusions, please, sir,' said the officer. 'We are handling this. May I suggest you wait outside?'

'The first few minutes are crucial,' Eden was saying. As an officer working on crime data, he had studied this.

'She walked,' Miss Killick was saying. 'But I think she was holding a set of car keys.'

'Car keys?'

'Yes.'

'I think so,' said the schoolteacher, scrunching up her eyes as if trying to remember. 'After she spoke to him, she swapped them from one hand to the other so she could take hold of Finn.'

'She must have known him,' the officer said. 'If he walked to her like that.'

Eden held the phone to his ear. 'I have to go. I'll call back.'

He ran outside, looking left and right.

* * *

The woman with the black hair was still outside with her daughter. 'God. Is everything OK? Did you find him?'

'No. He's gone. Someone took him. Do you have a car?' Eden demanded.

'Take a breath,' she said.

'What?'

'You need to calm down.'

Eden blinked. 'Sorry. I'm . . .'

'I know,' she said. 'I understand. You think someone took Finn?'

'There was no one else who was supposed to be picking him up and now he's gone with a woman but nobody seems to know who she is.'

She looked down at her daughter. 'Would you like us to stay? Until you know what's happened to Finn?'

'Do you have a car?' he repeated.

'No. We walk to school,' said the woman.

He needed people to be out there looking for Finn. From the data, he knew the most crucial thing immediately after an abduction was to search the local area. 'Can you come with me and drive around and see if—'

'Shouldn't you leave this to the police?'

'No,' he said. 'I need to look. And it's easier if you have someone else in the car because a driver can't look around.'

She hesitated, then said, 'Yes. We can do that, can't we, Sheena?'

Eden set off trotting towards the street where he'd left his Audi. The woman followed.

'Mum, slow down,' Sheena wailed. 'Wait for me.'

Eden clicked the keys, pulled the door open, jumped in and started the engine, but had to wait while the woman strapped her daughter into the back.

'Hurry,' he ordered her.

'I'm going as fast as I can,' she protested.

As soon as they were ready, he backed out of the street and started to drive down the hill. 'Look down any roads or alleyways,' he instructed.

'Shall I look too?' asked Sheena.

'Do you know Finn?' Eden asked.

'He brings packed lunches. He's in Year 5 in Opal class. I'm in Year 4.'

'If you see him, let us know,' said her mother. 'OK, love?'

In the mirror, Eden saw Sheena nod.

He passed a second police car, driving up the hill towards the school.

'It'll probably turn out to be nothing,' the woman said, looking to her left and right.

There was no sign of him so far. At the bottom of the hill Eden turned. 'Let's try again,' he said, 'driving the other way.'

'Maybe some friend's mum had arranged to pick him up.'

Eden was looking left and right, turning back into the road. 'Miss Killick said she was his foster carer. She gave Finn's foster carer's name – but it definitely wasn't her. It was someone pretending to be her. We need to keep trying, just in case.'

'Do we?' The woman sounded anxious now, worried that she had become caught up in something she didn't understand.

From the corner of his eye, Eden saw her checking the time on her phone. 'Please,' he begged. 'My nephew is missing.'

In a few minutes, they were back up at the school. The second police car had parked next to the first. He drew up. The narrow road carried on upwards. 'Where does this lane go?' he asked the woman.

'Up to Haldon. It's a moor on the top. And there's a golf course.'

Without asking the mother or her child whether they wanted to get out, he put the car back in gear and drove on.

'You're really worried, aren't you?' she asked.

He nodded. 'I was supposed to be looking after him.'

'My name is Jackie, by the way.'

The lane was narrow, with high, thick hedges on each side. There was nothing for Jackie and her daughter to see. After only a hundred metres there was a crossroads. Eden paused. If Finn had been taken in a vehicle, they could have gone any of three ways.

He chose the road that ran straight ahead. A little further down, a narrow track led off into some trees. Eden stopped the car and jumped out.

'What?' Jackie was leaning out of the car window.

'Just a minute.'

He looked around.

'Did you see something?' Jackie asked.

'Child abductions in broad daylight tend to be similar. The person taking the child tries to act normally. But if they're in a vehicle, they might have to secure or hide the child somehow.'

'Oh, Jesus,' Jackie said anxiously, looking at her daughter. 'Are you sure about this? You really think this is an abduction?'

The road was quiet. Above them in the trees a crowd of rooks gazed down at them.

Out of the three possible routes the driver might have taken, Eden had chosen this option. The odds were that he was wrong. Though there were patterns to child abductions, there was no guarantee that this one was following any pattern at all.

Jackie got out of the car too, ordering her daughter, 'Stay in the car, love.' When she caught up with Eden she asked, 'How do you know all this stuff?'

'I'm a police officer.'

'And you think this is real?'

'It may be, and I know what happens if people don't react fast if it is.'

'Oh, fuck,' she said. 'You're scaring me now.'

The track he had stopped at was the start of a drive leading to an old house, hidden behind the trees. He walked a little further down the path. Judging by the padlocks on the iron gate, the house was unoccupied.

Though it looked like the kind of location a driver might choose to pull up at, there was no clue that anyone had been here recently.

'I think you should take us bck now,' said Jackie quietly. Eden turned to see that she had followed him into the lane. 'Please. I need to get my daughter home.'

He turned to face her. She looked frightened. She had left her daughter alone in his car.

'Yes,' he said, shoulders slumping. 'I'll take you back.'

'I'm sorry. I really am. I really hope everything is OK.' Jackie turned and Sheena was standing at the top of the lane. 'I told you to stay in the car,' she snapped.

Sheena said, 'You promised me an ice cream.'

'I'm sorry. But we had to try to look for Finn, honey.'

As Eden watched Sheena took a step towards them then stopped, her attention suddenly on a small muddy puddle in the track.

'Oh, God. Don't, Sheena!' Jackie scolded.

Ignoring her mother, the girl reached a hand down into the puddle.

'It's dirty!'

By the time Jackie reached her she had fished something out of the water.

'Put it down, Sheena. It's filthy.'

Eden caught a small glimpse of red.

Sheena held it up.

'Put it down,' echoed Eden quietly.

'Finn has one,' said Sheena. 'I've seen it. Just like this.' In her hand was a red action figure.

Twenty

By the time they made it back to the school, Detective Sergeant Sweet had arrived. He was talking to the head teacher. Eden heard him asking, 'CCTV?'

'Our governors decided it was not appropriate for this school. We've never needed it.'

Sweet turned towards Eden as he approached. 'There you are, Eden. I was kind of worried you'd disappeared too. You OK?'

Eden pointed up the hill. 'They headed up the hill in that direction. We need to issue a Child Rescue Alert.'

The head teacher looked pale. 'Obviously, we will review our safeguarding procedures.'

'And it definitely wasn't Mrs Sullivan?'

'Mrs Sullivan is away. There's a driveway about two hundred metres up the road where the driver stopped before continuing onwards. I want to show you something.' He took Sweet's arm and led him to the Audi, pointing at the dashboard of the car and the red Hulkbuster action figure. 'That toy was Finn's. He must have dropped it, which suggests either the abductor swapped vehicles or Finn was taken out of whatever vehicle he was in and put . . .'

He stopped himself. Sheena was still standing close. He didn't want to say it out loud in front of a young girl – that he believed Finn might have been bundled into the back of a van, or a car boot.

Sweet peered at the toy. 'OK, now. What makes you think it's his?'

'I've seen him playing with it.'

Sweet dug in his jacket pocket for a blue glove, put it on, reached inside the car and picked up the red action figure.

'I found that,' said Sheena.

Sweet turned to see the small child next to him. 'I know you. You're Graeme Pine's little girl, aren't you? You found this?' He held up the toy. 'You're a very clever girl.'

'Hello Mike,' said Jackie. 'We were helping Eden look for Finn. Is it true he's been taken?'

Sweet turned to Eden and gave him a small smile. 'Now, Jackie. Don't go jumping before we know the facts. Mr Driscoll doesn't know where Finn is.'

'You two know each other?' Eden asked.

'I went to school with Mike's sister,' explained Jackie.

Sweet bagged the toy. 'Wait there,' he told Eden.

He got in his unmarked car and spoke on the radio for a couple of minutes, then got out again. 'Eden. I'd like a private conversation,' he said, beckoning to him.

'We should be out looking for Finn,' said Eden. 'There is no time.'

'I've put the word out. Missing child,' said Sweet. 'Everybody's on it now, I promise.' Sweet opened the passenger door for him. 'I'm praying this is all some ghastly misunderstanding,' Sweet said when Eden had closed the door behind him, 'and that some well-meaning parent has taken him home or something – but I promise we are taking this seriously. How are you coping, Eden?' he asked.

'I'm coping fine. It's about how Finn is doing, not me. Someone has taken him.'

'Yeah. Right. And just to confirm, you don't know of anyone else who was supposed to be picking him up?'

'No.'

Sweet wriggled in his seat to free up a notebook from his trouser pocket, and flicked to a page. 'From interviewing his teacher, we think it may be someone he knew. She says Finn walked towards this woman perfectly naturally, without raising the alarm.'

'Maybe, but the boy is traumatised. He's been looked after by one stranger and he's about to be looked after by another one. Mrs Sullivan had taxi drivers picking him up. If someone says they've come to pick him up, I wouldn't be surprised if he just followed her.'

'But why do you believe someone would want to take your nephew? Things like this don't just happen without good reason.'

'Perhaps because he knows something. Perhaps because he was on the boat when Apple vanished,' said Eden.

'We've been there already. Your nephew told you he didn't hear anyone get on the boat.'

'I'm sorry, Mike. I don't believe it's as simple as my sister just falling overboard. She's been on boats all her life.'

Sweet looked sympathetic. 'OK.' He looked around. 'Well, you will be assured, we are treating this as an abduction as of right now. There will be eyes looking out for him all over the county. Look, if it means anything at all, I'm sorry for what you're going through. If there's anything I can do to help, just let me know, OK?' He leaned past Eden and opened the door. 'For now, just go home. Best thing you can do. Wait there. I promise as soon as I hear anything, you'll be the first to know.'

Getting out of the car, Eden heard him on the radio, checking in. Eden looked around for Jackie and Sheena – to thank them for all their help – but he couldn't see them. He guessed they had already gone home.

He stood for a while, observing the scene. The head teacher was standing at the door of the school, looking as if he wished he were a million miles away. An officer had her arm around Miss Killick, and it looked to Eden, from the redness of her eyes, that the teacher had been crying.

Sweet called him at four-thirty. 'Nothing?'

'No.' Eden had done as he was told. He was back at home, drinking coffee, sitting by the beach door.

There was a long pause. 'Shit,' said Sweet. 'Nor us. I'm sorry, mate.'

The beach outside the back door seemed to carry on as if nothing had happened. Some children played in the water; others were peering over the edge of the stone docks with crabbing lines in their hands.

Eden could do nothing. He was a stranger here. He didn't know the area. Sweet was right. The best thing for him to do was nothing – to stay here and wait for news, so he went upstairs to Finn's small bedroom and sat on his bed.

As a child, Apple had never had a proper bedroom of her own. If they had a room at all, rather than a tent or a mattress in the van or boat, she had always shared with Eden, even when they were too old for that. Apple had given her son a space of his own, however cramped.

At around five, he heard cars pulling up behind the house, footsteps coming down the alleyway. When he opened the door there was a young officer, red-faced and sweaty in his tactical vest. He didn't have Finn with him.

Eden's heart sank. 'Oh, shit,' he said. 'What?'

'God. Sorry!' the man exclaimed. 'No. It's not that. You were probably thinking the worst. I should have called in advance. I've come for the computer lead.'

'Has there been any news?'

'Not that I've heard.'

A heavy-looking woman in her forties – whom Eden presumed must be a forensics officer – appeared behind him. Glad of something to do, Eden handed her the plastic bag with the lead he had recovered, then led her up to the bedroom where the computer had been and watched her dusting the area for prints.

'You're the boy's uncle?' She looked up from her work.

'Yes.'

'Sorry. It was on the radio on the way over.'

Eden took out his phone and found it on the BBC site: *The nine-year-old boy is the son of missing local yachtswoman Apple Driscoll.*

'Do you have a list of names of the people you know who have been in the house?' the officer asked.

Eden looked up from his phone. The police officer had his notebook out.

'Finn Driscoll, obviously, my nephew—'

'The boy who's missing?'

'Yes. Detective Sergeant Sweet. Bisi Smith, who's Finn's social worker . . .' The officer noted the names in his book. Eden tried to remember if there was anyone else. 'And a woman called Molly Hawkins, who came in for a drink.'

'Molly Hawkins?' The man looked up from his notebook.

'That's right. She was a friend of my sister's.'

'Frankie Hawkins' sister?'

'That's right.'

'Molly Hawkins. Was she alone in the house at all?'

Eden tried to think. 'No. I don't think so. Why? You think she . . . ?'

The officer licked his thumb and turned a page in his notebook. As he did so, Eden heard his Airwave radio crackle. 'Sierra Four One. This is Mike Whisky. Urgent call. Are you with Mr Driscoll now?'

The forensics woman, kneeling on the floor, was just packing up her gear.

'Yeah, Mike Whisky. What's up?'

'Tell Mr Driscoll he needs to get down to Teignmouth Pier. Right away.'

'Hear that?' said the officer. 'I'll drive you. Shift your car,' he ordered the forensics officer. 'I need to get out of here.'

The forensics officer looked at her kit. 'Hell, mate. Give me a minute,' she said.

'Jesus,' said the officer.

Eden wasn't going to wait. He was out of the beach door, running, past startled day-trippers on the beach, past the queue of people waiting for the ferry, up the lane to the lifeboat house, heading through the car park, dodging a Range Rover reversing too fast out of its space, and onto the promenade, running as fast as he could towards the pier.

Twenty-One

Running onto the wide green expanse of The Den, Eden could see the pier still far off, lit in the evening's grey by flashing blue lights. He sprinted across lawns and down pathways, past a startled dog walker.

As he approached, he spotted Finn sitting on a silver metal chair next to the ice cream stall. There was something big and white on his lap. A uniformed woman was sitting next to him, holding Finn's hand. As Eden got closer, he saw Finn rubbing his eyes with the back of his hand. He was crying.

'Finn!' shouted Eden. Finn looked up, spotted Eden running towards him.

Sweet turned too. He was already on the scene, speaking on his phone, but ended the call the moment he saw Eden and held out his hands to slow him.

'Where was he?' demanded Eden, panting.

'The lad was in the amusement arcade by himself. He'd been there the last couple of hours apparently.'

Eden stared at the boy. 'He just stayed there? On his own?'

'Totally unharmed. Not a scratch on him. Loads of kids

in there. I guess nobody's going to notice another one. One of the mums found him crying about fifteen minutes ago, asked him who he was and he wouldn't tell her. She recognised him from the alert on social media.'

'Finn?' called Eden. 'What happened? Are you OK?'

'Where's Mum?' Finn shouted back at him angrily. 'Where's my mum?'

For the first time, Eden noticed that the white thing on his lap was a furry nylon monkey. 'He keeps asking for his mother,' said Sweet. 'We've been holding off interviewing him until you arrived. We wanted an adult he knew to be present.'

Eden approached the boy, squatted down next to him. 'You're OK, Finn. Everything is going to be OK.'

'No, I'm not,' said the boy. 'No, I'm not.'

'Who picked you up from school, Finn?' asked Eden. 'Where is she?'

The monkey on Finn's lap had a surprised expression on its face and nylon fur that was brushed upwards into a peak. It was cheap and ridiculous.

Eden kneeled next to his chair. 'Did someone give you that monkey?'

'The staff on the pier say he won it,' said Sweet.

'I did. I won it. It took me ages.'

'We were worried about you,' Eden told the boy.

Finn looked at him furiously. 'She promised me.'

'Who promised you?' asked Eden, standing to pull up a chair.

'The lady promised me my mum would meet me here if I stayed here and didn't speak to anyone and now you've spoiled it.'

'Oh,' said Eden. That was why he had stayed. That was why he had not come home. 'What lady?'

'The lady. The lady who picked me up from school.'

Eden exchanged a glance with Sweet, who stepped forward and pulled up another chair, next to Eden. Sweet leaned forward. 'Who was it who picked you up, son?'

'A lady. She said she was taking me to meet my mum.' Eden understood now. That was why he had gone to her so readily. She had told the boy he was going to meet his mother.

'What lady, Finn?' asked Eden gently. 'Did she have a name?'

Finn thought for a little while. 'She didn't tell me.'

Sweet took over asking the questions. 'The woman who picked you up from school this afternoon?'

Finn nodded.

There was a small crowd gathered around them now. Sweet smiled at the uniformed officer who had been comforting Finn and said in a low voice, 'Can you get this lot to give us a bit of privacy, love?'

'Right.' The woman stood and began asking the onlookers to move back.

'Think carefully,' asked Sweet. 'Had you ever seen this woman who picked you up from school before?'

Finn shook his head.

'Why did you go with her if you'd never seen her before?'

'Because she said she would take me to meet Mum,' Finn said exasperatedly.

'She said that to you?'

'Yes. She said my mum was waiting for me.' Finn wiped his eyes with the back of his arm.

'She drove you away in a car. Do you remember anything about it?'

'Why?'

'It was a bad thing to do, to take you away from school like that. Your uncle here was very worried.'

Finn frowned at Eden disbelievingly.

'Do you remember the car?'

'It was sort of silver.'

'Grey? Or silver?'

'I don't really remember. There was a cat in the car.'

'A cat?'

'A plastic cat. In front of the steering wheel. It moved.'

'A toy cat?'

'Real cats don't like going in cars,' said Finn. 'It waved a hand like this.' He raised one arm stiffly up and down.

'It sounds like a *maneki neko*,' said Eden. 'It's a Japanese thing. It's supposed to bring good luck.'

'That so?' said Sweet. He turned back to Finn. 'Do you know what make of car?'

Finn shook his head.

'And she didn't tell you her name?'

'No. She knew mine though. She called me Finn.'

'And this woman. What did she look like?'

'I don't know. Just like a woman.'

'Tell me everything that happened.' Sweet was squatting low now, his eyes at the same level as Finn's. 'Everything you remember.'

'She drove quite fast and was a bit annoyed at me when I said I needed to go to the toilet. So she pulled over and I went for a wee and then I got back in the car and we drove some more and she was angry with me because I said I'd lost my toy and wanted to go back but she wouldn't and then she went into a wood and parked there.'

'You lost your Hulkbuster toy,' interrupted Eden.

'How did you know?' Finn frowned at Eden.

'Because a girl found it.'

'Can I have it back?'

'The police have it. They'll give it back soon. Shall I take you home?'

'I can't go home,' wailed Finn. 'I'm supposed to stay here and meet Mum.'

Eden looked up at Sweet, then back down again, meeting Finn's eyes. 'I'm sorry, Finn,' said Eden gently. 'I think that woman tricked you. Mum isn't going to be here.'

Finn wailed even louder.

Sweet leaned forward a little closer. 'This woman in the car. She drove you to a car park. What happened there? Did she do anything to you?'

'She just talked to me.'

Sweet said, 'What about?'

'About the boat trip with Mum. She asked me the same thing he did.' He pointed angrily at Eden.

'And what was that?' Sweet's voice was low, his tone curious and friendly.

'Whether I saw anyone else on the boat.'

'That's what she wanted to know?' Sweet asked.

'And she asked me where Mum's special hiding place was.'

Eden looked at Sweet. 'What do you mean?' Eden asked.

'She said Mum wanted something she had hidden there. She couldn't go to the house herself because of bad people. She said Mum had told her to fetch it for her, so I had to tell her where it was.'

'What thing?'

'I don't know. If she had something she wanted to keep safe, Mum hid it in her room. Under the floor.'

'Under the floorboards?'

Finn nodded.

'Did you tell the woman that?'

Again, Finn nodded. 'She was being nice to me. She said my mum wanted to know and she'd meet me here afterwards to say a big thank you.'

Eden asked gently, 'What was it that your mother hid? What do you think it might have been?'

'I don't know,' Finn answered angrily. 'I don't know I don't know I don't know. And I told her I wanted to see Mum because she said she was going to take me to her, and she drove me back down to Teignmouth and she put on glasses and a scarf around her head and we walked to the pier and she gave me twenty pounds and said I could play there and not tell anyone who I was and if I was still there in an hour, my mum would come and get me only I wasn't supposed to talk to anyone and it's been ages and ages. And I won this monkey to give to Mum as a present.' He held out the white toy.

Sweet looked stricken. 'She said if you waited there on your own, your mum would come?'

'But she hasn't.'

Sweet crouched closer and put his arm around the boy. 'I'm so sorry, Finn. I'm so very, very sorry. Like your uncle said, I think the woman was lying to you.'

'About my mum?'

'I think she just wanted to get away – to escape – without you telling anyone.'

Finn looked at Sweet for a while, then let out a loud, high scream. The white monkey fell to the tarmac and Finn started hitting himself on the side of his head with his fist over and over.

Eden grabbed the boy's hand. 'Don't,' he said. 'It's not your fault. None of this is your fault. I'm so sorry this happened to you, Finn.'

Finn wailed louder, his feet kicking out at Eden as Eden put his arms around the boy. It was the first time he had given him a proper hug.

* * *

By the time Eden reached the house the police were already inside.

'I'm sorry,' said the officer guarding the kitchen door at the back of the house. 'Bit of a bloody mess.'

'Oh, Jesus.' Eden examined the door frame. There was a long crack in the wood from where someone had forced the back door. It looked like they'd used a crowbar. Hidden down the short alleyway, the back door was not overlooked by neighbours.

Eden went upstairs.

'We already looked,' the officer called up to him. 'Some bastard's had the floorboards up.'

Whoever it was had guessed Eden would leave the house to collect Finn. They knew where they were going. They would have been in and out in a couple of minutes. Whoever had stolen the computer, Eden supposed, had not been able to find something else that was hidden in the house. That was why they had had to trick Finn to reveal where it was hidden.

Finn was sitting in the back of a police car parked in the road behind the house on the beach when Bisi arrived.

'I want to go into my house,' he wailed, punching the seat in front of him. 'I want to go into my house.'

'We can't.' Eden sat next to him, trying to explain. Neighbours were peering out of windows. 'The police need to search it to see if they can find any clues to whoever it was that broke in,' said Eden.

'It's my house!'

'Can I just have a word with your uncle, Finn?' asked Bisi, leaning against the car door.

Eden left Finn in the back seat. 'Oh, God,' Bisi whispered when Eden explained what had happened. 'The absolute bitch. I hope she rots in hell. What's happening now?'

'They're waiting for a forensics team to return.'

'Will they be finished soon? Finn needs a meal. He needs to get to bed.' Bisi peered at the boy.

'Being honest, I very much doubt it.'

Sweet joined them in the small street behind the house. 'Callous bastard,' he said.

'I'll try and explain that he'll have to sleep somewhere else tonight.' Bisi got into the car next to Finn and put her big arms around him.

'Any ideas who she was, this woman?' asked Eden.

'We're checking as much CCTV as we can get our hands on. She was wearing dark glasses and a scarf, which doesn't help. If we can find out which car she was driving, that would be something. I'm guessing she parked it somewhere and walked to the pier.'

There were small car parks dotted around the town. Because there was nowhere to park in Teign View Place, Eden had taken to parking his car in one of them – a car park behind the beach huts on the Back Beach.

'She knew Mrs Sullivan's name,' said Eden. 'She knew exactly what to say when she got to the school.'

'Someone in Social Services?' suggested Sweet. They looked at Bisi, sat in the car, chatting to Finn.

'Or someone in the school.'

'Jesus,' said Sweet. 'And they're the ones who should be looking after him.'

Bisi called Eden over. 'The police will be all over this place for hours. It's settled. You're both going to sleep at my place tonight.'

Twenty-Two

The boy wakes scared. Something is wrong. It is all his fault.

'Mum?' he whispers into the night. The sadness is bigger than the darkness and the darkness is so black he cannot make out where he is.

The night his mother had said she was going to take him out on *Calliope* he had shouted at her, because he didn't want to go out on the stupid boat.

'Please, darling,' she had pleaded with him. 'This is something I have to do.'

And he had screamed at her and slapped her. 'Why can't you be like all the other mums? Why do you always have to be so fucking weird?'

It was bad to hit her. 'Fucking' was a bad word to say. She had been upset.

It was the other kids at school who had called his mum weird.

'Your mum is fucking weird.'

Now in the black room awake and frightened, he calls out for her. 'Mum?'

There is no answer.

He gets up and fumbles in the dark. He is not in the right place. This is not his room. The floorboards are cold and uneven. Now he is really scared. He can hear his own heart beating. In the dark, he cracks his foot against something hard and wails.

Floorboards creak. He finds a wall and inches along it until he finds what he thinks is a door. It rattles as his hands push on it. But it's not a proper door. A door would have a handle. When he feels for one, it's not there. A door with no handle, he thinks, and that is a scary thing too. There is no way out of this room.

He stands still, bangs on the door with his hands and he screams as loud as he can: 'Mum!'

Twenty-Three

Eden woke when the banging started. At first he thought it was coming from downstairs but it wasn't; it was coming from the room Bisi had given Finn, next to his one.

In old-fashioned pyjamas borrowed from Bisi's husband, Eden lifted the latch on the bedroom door and opened it to find Finn crying, fists bunched from where he had been hitting the bedroom door.

In the dark corridor, Eden put his arms around the boy. 'She didn't come,' Finn said quietly.

'No,' said Eden. 'But I'm here.'

'I banged on my door and it was locked and she didn't come.'

Eden held the boy and felt each feathery judder. 'It wasn't locked. It was just on the latch.'

'I waited for ages and ages,' Finn whispered.

'You poor boy,' said Eden.

Bisi arrived, bowling down the stairs from the top floor. 'What happened?'

'He had a nightmare,' explained Eden.

'The door was locked,' complained Finn, still half asleep. 'I couldn't escape.'

'Oh,' gasped Bisi. She squatted down and hugged him. 'I'm sorry. I was stupid. I shouldn't have closed your bedroom door. I didn't think.'

Eden led Finn back to his bed and sat there with him as the boy cried. Bisi brought up a mug of sweet tea. 'No milk,' she said. 'You're vegan.'

Bisi and Eden sat with him until he settled, then went downstairs to the big warm kitchen because neither of them felt like sleeping.

Bisi lived in a large, solid Victorian farmhouse in the middle of Dartmoor, at the end of a granite-walled lane. The house was surrounded by wind-shaped beech trees that had rustled and swayed as Eden had carried Finn through the front door.

Now he was tucked up in bed again, and the door to his bedroom was propped open, Eden and Bisi sat in the kitchen, next to a huge cream-coloured Aga, drinking weak fruit tea. It was three in the morning. The rest of the house was quiet.

'I just hadn't expected you to live all the way out here, in a place like – like this.' Eden looked around at the solid farmhouse furniture.

'Because you're a racist?' she said, smiling.

'Clearly,' he said.

She laughed loudly. He liked Bisi.

Her husband was a big ex-military man called Peter, whose voice was plummy and English. 'Bisi has plans for you, I gather.' He had cooked Finn beans on toast. They had seventeen-year-old twin girls who obviously got their height from Peter. They towered over Bisi. One of them had given up her bedroom for Finn.

It was a nice house. Chintzy curtains and paintings of rural scenes on the walls. A mess of books on the shelves. The kind of place a real family would live.

'Why did they break into the house?' Bisi asked. 'And will they do it again?'

Eden had been thinking about this. 'If my sister's dead, I don't think it was an accident. I think somebody killed her.'

'Oh, Christ. Why aren't the police saying that, then?'

'I believe that – whoever it was – they stole my sister's computer because there was something on it that might explain what really happened, something that might implicate them. Well . . . maybe there was something else in the house they were worried about. Something they couldn't find the day they stole the computer. They needed Finn to tell them where it was hidden.'

Bisi put her mug down on the scrubbed pine table. 'What I really meant when I asked the question was, is the house a safe place for Finn?'

'Right,' said Eden. 'Well, I think they found it, whatever it was. So they don't need to come back.'

Bisi looked sceptical. 'Eden. Finn was put in a terrible, terrible situation yesterday. If there's any risk that he's still in any danger, or that any of this is going to blow up into something that can affect him adversely, I'm going to have to take him away and put him somewhere safe. You understand that, don't you?'

Eden cradled his mug. 'Yes.'

'I need you to be honest. If you see anything at all that concerns you, you need to tell me about it. OK?'

In the morning the twins made a fuss of Finn and cooked him fried banana sandwiches, before their dad bundled them into an old Subaru to drive them to sixth-form college in Ashburton.

Sweet phoned a little after ten. 'You can go home now. The forensics team are done.'

'Did you figure out why someone broke in?' asked Eden. 'What they were looking for?'

'We're not sure. And the lad has no idea what she kept there?'

'Any prints? Any idea who did it?'

'You know I wouldn't share that with you, even if we had?'

'I know,' Eden said.

'How is he?'

Finn was in Bisi's big overgrown garden playing on a rusty swing. 'He's scared.'

'Poor bloody kid,' said Sweet.

The street door had been patched up and made secure, but inside the house was a mess. There was fingerprint powder on all the door handles and on the table surfaces. The kitchen drawers had been left half-open.

'It's dirty,' said Finn.

'Don't worry. I'll clean it,' Eden said gently.

In the living room, Finn's red action figure stood on the dining table. 'It's back,' he said, picking it up.

There was a note: *Thought you'd want this. Mike (the policeman)*.

Finn went up to his bedroom and Eden took a cloth and started wiping the place down. When he'd finished the knobs and surfaces, he took out the kitchen drawer and dumped the contents on the tabletop.

There were some Euro coins, the pack of tobacco that Molly had filled a roll-up with, a loose battery, a USB lead, a couple of keys and a pencil sharpener. The rest was documents and papers. He started to pick through them.

The leaflets were old, mostly political: a couple from Extinction Rebellion, another, titled 'Wake Up Your Neighbours', advertising a newspaper called *The Light*; there was one headlined 'Facts about masks: it's not about health it's about CONTROL'.

Under a spiral-bound notebook, there were three brown A4 envelopes. One was marked 'House', another 'Boat', and the third 'Car'. He looked at the last envelope in surprise. That was something he hadn't considered. His sister had a car. So where was it?

The one marked 'House' was stuffed with bills. Some had 'Paid' written on them in his sister's hand. The more recent ones were red. There was one from South West Water threatening to pass her bill to a debt recovery agent. A letter from the Halifax Building Society warning her that if she did not agree to a debt repayment plan, they would take her to court and this might lead to the repossession of her house. Another from NPower advising her to contact Citizens Advice. He would need to settle them. He set them aside to deal with later.

Apple had been broke. She had needed money.

The one marked 'Car' included some recent garage bills and an insurance cover document. He had seen no car keys around the house or in the boat. He looked again for a hook somewhere. Perhaps they had been in a pocket when she went overboard. Leafing through, he found a receipt for a parking permit.

'What are you doing?'

He looked up. Finn was standing in the kitchen doorway. He looked pale and hollow-eyed.

'That's Mum's stuff. Leave it alone.'

Twenty-Four

'OK,' said Eden. Watched by the boy, he piled the papers on top of each other.

'You're not allowed to touch all that,' said Finn, angrily.

'I'm sorry.'

Before putting it back into the drawer, Eden held up the USB cable. 'Do you know what this was for?' It was a short one. A standard USB at one end and a mini-socket at the other.

'No.'

'Did she use it with her phone?'

'I don't think so. Her phone was rubbish.'

Eden replaced it in the drawer. 'Are you OK?'

Finn didn't answer.

'What about a snack? What do you like?'

He was missing school today. After what had happened yesterday, that was no bad thing. 'I'm not very hungry,' he said.

'How's about some hot chocolate?'

Finn thought about this for a little while. 'OK,' he answered.

Eden put a pan of oat milk on the stove. 'Does your mum have a car?'

'Yes. It's green,' said Finn.

'Where is it? I was looking for the keys.'

'It's not your car. It's hers.'

Eden whisked a bit of cocoa into the milk, then added sugar.

'There,' he said, taking a mug to Finn, who was sitting in the small armchair in the living room now. He had wrapped a blanket around himself, though the day outside was already bright and warm.

When Finn had taken a few sips, Eden said, 'I don't want her car. I've got my own. I just wanted to make sure it was OK. Do you know where it is?'

Finn shook his head.

'Where did she keep the key?'

'I don't know,' Finn said irritatedly.

Eden realised he had been talking about Apple again. Everything he did reminded the boy that she was not there any more.

Eden returned to the kitchen and replaced the drawer in the table. When he returned to the living room, Finn's eyes were shut. Eden uncurled Finn's fingers from the handle and put the half-drunk cup onto the table.

He sat for a while, watching the even rise and fall of the boy's hands across his chest.

Eden woke to a buzzing in his pocket. His phone.

It had been an interrupted night. He was exhausted and had dozed off on the couch. He got up and let himself quietly out of the glass door onto a beach that was already busy.

'They found him, I heard.' It was Molly.

'Yes. He's OK.'

'Thank Christ. Some nutcase kidnapped him from school – that right?'

'I'm not sure who they were,' said Eden.

'At least the boy's safe.'

'Yes. He's asleep now. He was up in the night. A nightmare, I think.'

'He's home? Listen. If you need any help, just call. I know I let Apple down, but I promise I won't let that happen again.'

'Thanks,' Eden said warily. 'I'll be fine.'

'You sure? You sound stressed.'

'Do I?'

'Hardly a surprise. It must have been awful, losing him like that, even if he turned up again. Jesus. You must have been terrified. You want me to come round?'

'No,' he repeated, more firmly. 'I'm fine.'

'OK. Suit yourself. Just offering.'

He had been warned off her and he had ignored the warning. It had occurred to him that when Molly's boat had broken down at sea, she had blamed her brother. But the delay meant that he arrived at the school well after Eden had already gone missing. And only when he arrived at the school, asking where Finn was, had people realised that the boy had been taken. It might have only been an extra ten minutes, but it had allowed the abductor to get well away from the school before the alarm was raised. So no, he did not trust her.

'Police were on your sister's boat yesterday,' she said.

'I know.'

'Saw them going out with the harbourmaster. Did they find anything?'

'They wouldn't tell me if they had,' he said – which was true. Sweet had only told him the results because they hadn't found anything.

'Nightmare,' Molly said. 'There are enough rumours flying round about what happened to your sister already.'

'Are there?'

She dropped her voice. 'Sorry. Yes. There are.'

'Like what?'

She hesitated. 'Talk. You know. Round these parts, if something happens people jump to all sorts of conclusions. She came across people smugglers at sea, that kind of garbage.'

It was something he had already considered himself.

'Listen. I wanted to ask you something,' Eden interrupted. 'There is one thing you could help me with. You know my sister owned a car?'

'Yes. She did. Shitty little thing.'

'Where did she park it?'

'On the Den. It's just a couple of minutes from where you are. It's right on the front. I kept telling her it's the worst place to leave it. Saltwater wrecks the brakes.'

'What make is it?'

'An old Toyota Corolla. It's green. At least where it's not rust, it's green. Why?'

He hesitated. 'I'll go and take a look for it.'

'You won't find it.'

'Why not?'

'It's in the garage.'

'Why?'

'Somebody totally rear-ended her last week. I told her she should junk it, but she's taken it to have a new rear bumper fitted.'

'That's why I couldn't find a key. What happened?'

'I'm not sure,' Molly said. 'I asked her, because, as you have probably already worked out, I'm pretty nosy, but she wouldn't tell me.'

'She wouldn't tell you?'

'No. She was quite weird about it.'

The beach was already filling up. To his left, the ferry was pulling its way off the beach, loaded with passengers. The breeze brought the sound of laughter across the water. A perfect day in early summer.

'I'm rowing later on. Maybe I'll drop by,' she said.

'I'm not sure if it's a good idea. Finn's pretty shaken.'

She ignored him. 'I'm his mate. He likes me. I'll see you later, then.'

'Wait,' he said, before she rang off. 'Maybe she just reversed into something and didn't want to admit it?'

'Doubt it. Your sister had no front at all. Nothing between her and the world. She never lied to cover up things. She was a straight person. I liked that about her. It's pretty refreshing.'

Molly was pushy and loud. He didn't like her at all. But at least she talked about his sister. He was pleased to hear how much Apple loved Finn – and that she was honest. It was Molly's own honesty he found harder to believe in.

Twenty-Five

Though it was sunny when he finally woke, Finn said he didn't want to go outside onto the beach.

Eden made a lunch of soup and bread and Finn ate it silently at the small table in the living room. It was a fine day. The water outside was full of activity. Eden opened the door.

'What do you want to do?' Eden asked him. 'We could catch a ferry to the zoo on the other side of the river?'

Finn shook his head. 'I want to stay here.'

'We could play a game?' Eden had no idea what sort of game a nine-year-old would want to play.

'What about a film?'

Finn shrugged. On his laptop, Eden searched through his streaming subscriptions for children's films. He looked for something from the Marvel Universe, but they all looked too violent or too grown-up for Finn and he hadn't heard of the others.

'What about this?' He pointed to the Indiana Jones film *Raiders of the Lost Ark*. Eden remembered watching it as a child in a tourist cinema somewhere on Kos.

Finn looked at the film and said, 'It looks really ancient.'

'Try it,' said Eden, offering Finn his earbuds.

The earbuds were a novelty. Finn put them in his ears and Eden pressed Play. 'Is it loud enough?'

Finn nodded. He sat with the laptop on his knees, watching the film.

'I'll just be out here,' Eden said. He pulled a chair out onto the beach and sat outside by the back door watching the world go by.

It was a good spot. The house was impossibly small, but Molly had been right; it was situated in a unique location. From the beach at its back door, you got a view of everything that was going on in the estuary. Ships unloading timber at the docks. Trawlermen loading their lobster pots. A family was taking turns at pumping up a paddleboard. Some teenagers were sitting on the beach passing a guitar around, strumming it.

He yearned to be back in the grubby anonymity of London, to be back at work.

By the afternoon, Finn was still holed up in the small house. The sun was hot, shining on the back wall, heating the living room.

Eden watched as a boat with two women sitting side by side approached the shoreline. The oars moved with practised ease.

When the boat reached the land, both women stepped out and tugged it a little way up the beach. They were both dressed in T-shirts, baseball caps and Lycra shorts.

'Oi, Eden. Give us a hand, will you?' When the woman who had called out took off her cap, he recognised Molly, who seemed determined not to leave them alone today. 'Come on.' She beckoned to him.

He looked back. Inside, Finn was engrossed in the film.

He walked cautiously down towards them.

'Lift it,' said Molly. 'On three.'

She counted aloud and the three of them marched up the sand carrying the fibreglass dinghy she had been rowing in.

'I thought you might want to know, the cops have bloody gone and impounded the *Calliope*,' she said. 'Down,' she ordered and, together, they lowered the heavy boat onto the sand.

'What?'

'Told us we can't go near it.' She reached down and pulled a plastic Co-op bag out of the boat, handing it to Eden. 'To replace what I downed the other night,' she said.

He peered in. There was a bottle of white wine in the bag.

The other woman hugged Molly goodbye and disappeared up towards the beach huts. 'What was it you were saying about the boat?' asked Eden.

'They've put tape all over it. "Do not cross". Like on *Vera* or something. When I saw them doing it, I took the boat out and said, "What do you think you're doing?" The bloke said he was a crime scene officer. Does that mean they think something bad happened to Apple?'

Eden held his finger up to his lips, nodded towards the house.

'Is he OK?' whispered Molly. 'Has he talked any about what happened yesterday?'

'He's very sad. The woman who took him promised she was taking him to see his mum. He believed her.'

She looked genuinely shocked. 'Oh, God. That's so horrible.'

Finn's two skinny legs appeared in the doorway.

'Finn?' Molly called up the beach. 'Will you come down here?'

And to Eden's surprise, Finn, who hadn't ventured out all day, came running down the sand and threw his arms around Molly, squeezing her hard.

'Oh, you poor little bug,' she said. 'Is he even feeding you?'

Eden watched his nephew hug the woman in a way that Finn had yet to hug him. He liked her. Molly looked down at Finn, hair in front of her eyes, and when Finn finally let her go, she raised her hand and wiped her eyes with her sleeve. 'Shit,' she muttered as she saw the smear of make-up on her shirt.

She looked up. 'Well, if you think I look bad, you should take a look at yourself,' she told Eden, undoing the popper of her left rowing glove, then peeling it off.

'Thanks a bunch.'

'You look like you could do with some of that wine.'

'It's three in the afternoon,' Eden protested.

'It's three on a Friday afternoon,' replied Molly, removing the other glove.

Eden shook his head. 'I don't really drink during the day.'

'That's the whole point of the seaside.' She went into the house and returned with two glasses, filled them up close to the brim and then returned to put the bottle in the fridge. 'You know your fridge light isn't working,' she said, fetching a second chair.

'Want to join us, Finn?'

'I'm watching a film.'

'Suit yourself.'

The way Finn had thrown his arms around her. She wasn't lying, at least, when she had said she had been a good friend of his sister's.

'Did my sister drink?'

'When the mood took.'

Out on the beach, Molly seemed to know half the people

who wandered past. Some stopped and chattered to her, eyeing Eden with curiosity.

'You're the boy's uncle?' one young lad said.

'Yes.'

'They've raised two grand for him, I heard. And he ran off from school yesterday.'

'He didn't run away. Someone took him.'

'Who do you think it was?' asked Molly, when the boy had gone.

'I don't know.' He watched her face closely as he spoke. 'Somebody trying to find out information.'

'Like who?' she asked. When he didn't answer, she stood and walked all the way down to the waterline, spent a while peering at the debris that had washed up. She returned with a thin shell, about ten centimetres long.

'It's still alive,' she said, turning it over in her hands. 'Washed up though.' It looked like a long brown toenail.

'Put it back, then,' said Finn, emerging from the house, squinting in the afternoon light.

'Oh. Film finished, then?'

He nodded.

'Any good?'

'OK,' he said.

Molly held up the shell. 'A lot of these have been washing up on the coast recently, mostly dead. Starfish too.'

'What is it?' Finn asked.

'A razor fish. *Ensis magnus*. That's its foot, see?' She pointed. 'It uses that to burrow deep into the sand.'

'Can I see?'

She handed Finn the shell and went to the kitchen and returned with the wine bottle to top up their glasses.

'That's enough of it being out of the water. Will you put it back in the sea for me, Finn?' she asked when she was back.

'Is this one going to be all right?' he asked, a sad look on his face.

'Of course,' she said, with false brightness. 'Of course it will be all right.'

They both watched him go down to the shoreline with the shell.

'You're not a very good liar, are you?' Eden said.

'Why? Did you think I would be?' She looked at him, eyebrows up.

Eden gave a tiny shrug. As a matter of fact, he had done.

'But he's had a bad enough time already without having to worry about bi-valve die-offs. They're very sensitive to changes in the environment.' She changed the subject. 'Why do you think they impounded your sister's boat? You really think something shady is going on around here?'

He had been wondering exactly the same thing. What had they found out about his sister's disappearance that they weren't telling him yet? But he still wasn't sure about Molly, so he just answered, 'It's not my job to think anything. I'm not a copper when I'm down here.'

She drank faster than he did and was better at it. By the time the bottle was empty his head was fuzzy. 'Why is the sand here so red?' he asked.

'It's got iron in it,' she answered. 'Iron oxide.'

'Like blood.'

'I suppose so. Aren't you going to invite me to stay for dinner?' Molly asked. 'Finn would like that, wouldn't you?'

'Yes,' said Finn.

'No,' said Eden.

'Well, that's handsome,' she said, standing. She leaned down to kiss Finn on the forehead.

That night Eden sat on Finn's bed.

'Not tired,' said Finn.

It was almost midnight. Finn was still not asleep. Eden looked around the room. The PS5 was still untouched.

'You like Molly, don't you?'

'Don't you?' asked Finn.

'No.'

Finn frowned. 'Why not?'

'Because she's loud and barges her way in without really asking. And because I don't really know if I trust her.'

'That's silly.'

'Is it? What does your mum normally do to help you go to sleep?' Eden asked.

'Stories,' said Finn.

There were a few books propped in the corner of the room, but mostly picture books for a younger child. 'What kind of stories?'

'Mum tells me stories or I listen to them on my Yoto.'

'On my what?'

'My Yoto. Except I left it on the boat.'

'Oh. Wait,' said Eden. 'I forgot.' He went downstairs and returned with the orange and white headphones he had found on the boat. 'You mean these?'

'Yes. 'Cept those are just the headphones. It's no use without the rest of it.'

'The rest?'

'The Yoto. It plays stories. When I can't get to sleep, I listen to stories.'

'What sort of stories?'

'Harry Potter, mostly. Percy Jackson.'

Eden stood by the bed looking at the headphones. There on the side were the letters 'Yoto'. 'So what . . . you put these headphones on at night and you listen to stories?'

'That's what I said, wasn't it?'

'And you were listening to stories with them when you were on the boat?'

'But they're no good without the Yoto.'

'What stories did your mum tell you?'

'She made them up.'

'What kind of stories?'

'All sorts. About anything.'

Eden sat on the bed. When they were young, their mother had never told them stories; their father certainly hadn't.

'Maybe try telling yourself a story?' suggested Eden.

'That's stupid,' said Finn, turning his back on Eden.

Eden went downstairs to the living room. There were still people outside on the beach, drinking. When Eden checked his phone there was a message from DS Sweet. *Sorry. Have some news. Can I come to you first thing tomorrow?*

Twenty-Six

'The body of a woman has been found,' said Sweet when he came to visit the next morning. 'We're pretty certain it's your sister's.'

Eden was surprised how relieved he felt at the news being confirmed. With bodies lost at sea, there was always a chance that they were never retrieved. He had believed Apple must be dead and she was.

'Where . . . ?'

'A tourist boat spotted a body yesterday afternoon off Truro, apparently. They called out the coastguard, who recovered her at around five p.m.'

It was seven-thirty in the morning. Finn was still upstairs in bed. Sweet was the sort of copper who still put on a newly ironed shirt and tie, even though it was a Saturday morning. 'Sorry, mate,' Sweet said. 'Wanted to tell you before you heard it on the news.'

Eden looked around the tiny living room in the house that his sister had made her home. 'I see. Thank you. Any sign of foul play?'

'She's been in the sea a week. Apparently, that makes it pretty hard to tell anything.'

'Yes, of course.'

'We have her DNA, obviously, because she probably doesn't look much like your sister any more. Are you OK?'

'Me? Yes.' He was going to have to tell Finn though.

'If there's anything at all you need,' said Sweet. 'Anything.'

'Thanks for bringing his Hulkbuster toy back.'

'No prints. So I thought it best to give it him.'

'It was thoughtful.'

'Yeah. Well,' Sweet said. 'You know. Tough on the boy.'

'He had his headphones on,' Eden blurted.

Sweet blinked. 'What?'

'When he was on the boat, Finn was wearing his headphones.' He ploughed on. 'He was listening to stories. That's how he goes to sleep. Do you see? If there had been a third person on the sailing boat, Finn might not have heard him. Just because Finn said he didn't hear anyone doesn't prove anything.'

Sweet went quiet. He closed his eyes and scratched his forehead and when he opened his eyes again eventually he said, 'OK. I'll add that to the notes, if you like.'

'You don't think it's important?'

Sweet looked as if he didn't. 'Maybe it is, maybe it isn't. Like I said, I'll make a note.' He met Eden's eye. There was something uncomfortable in his look. 'And while we're on that topic, I have a question I want to ask you. I was going to save it for another time but . . .'

Eden held his gaze. 'Yes?'

'It's a little awkward.'

'Go on.'

Sweet spoke slowly. 'When I let you onto the boat, you went to the boy's cabin.'

'Right.'

'I think you were looking for something.'

'Do you?' said Eden.

'When I looked in, you had lifted up one of the mattresses and were looking underneath it. What were you looking for?'

Eden understood why Sweet was watching his expression so closely now. He answered, 'Nothing.'

'Nothing? You just happened to lift up that mattress and look underneath it?'

'I was just looking around.'

Sweet waited for what seemed like an age, perhaps to let Eden explain, but he didn't. 'OK.' Sweet nodded. 'You were just looking around.'

'You've impounded the boat, I heard.'

'You heard from Molly, I expect. She's been round again, hasn't she?' Sweet finally broke his stare and looked out of the open back door, almost as if he was expecting her to be there. Eden didn't answer, so Sweet carried on. 'We just wanted to take another look to make sure we hadn't missed anything.'

'And had you?'

'You tell me, Eden. You tell me.'

From upstairs, Eden heard the sound of the toilet flushing. Finn was awake.

'Are you sure there's nothing you want to share with me, Eden, before things get complicated? I'm on your side. I promise.'

Which meant they had found something on the boat. 'No.' Eden shook his head. 'Nothing.'

Sweet breathed out loudly. 'Right you are, then,' he said. He stood in the kitchen, leaving space for Eden to say something more. When he didn't, Sweet turned to leave. 'I'll be in touch, I expect,' he said. 'Listen. However this turns out, I'm sorry about your sister.'

'What shall I tell Finn?'

'The truth, obviously,' answered Bisi. 'You want me to come over?'

Eden was on the phone to her. 'I should be able to tell him. I've knocked on doors often enough bringing bad news.' Eden could hear the twins in the background, the noise of a radio.

'You know,' Eden continued, 'I once had to tell a dad that his wife and daughter had been shot by the daughter's boyfriend. The poor guy had no idea. I had to get to him before he heard it on the news. He was playing five-a-side football in Leytonstone. I remember watching him running up and down on the Astroturf, not a care in the world, knowing I was going to step in and tell him something awful that would change his life forever.'

'I can't imagine. That must have been very hard for you.'

'So I can do this, can't I?' said Eden.

'Maybe take him out somewhere, somewhere the two of you can talk?' Bisi suggested.

'Good idea. Yes.' He thought of the boy, lying on his bed crying in the dark room, and sighed. 'I'll do that.'

When he ended the call he went up to Finn's bedroom and sat next to him on his bed.

'Shall we go for a walk? It's a nice day. We could go up to Dartmoor. I've never been.'

'I don't think so,' said the boy.

'We could go for a drive, then – maybe go to Exeter and buy you some clothes. Go for a meal. Do you like Mexican food?'

'I don't really want any clothes,' said Finn.

'A film, then?'

'Could I bring a friend?'

'I was thinking just me and you.'

Finn sniffed. 'My friends are all pretty weird at the moment anyway. They don't know what to say to me. And people who have never been my friends are trying to sit next to me at break.'

'I expect they feel sorry for what happened to you,' said Eden.

'I just think they're a bit nosy.'

'Probably that too.'

'So shall we just stay at home? I don't want to go out anywhere.' And then Finn looked down at the floor and asked in a perfectly normal voice, 'Is it about Mum? Is she really dead?'

Eden was so unprepared for the question, he simply answered, 'Yes. I'm afraid she is. They found her.'

'I thought so,' Finn said, and he picked up the red action figure and held it up for a few seconds.

'How does that make you feel?'

'Everybody knew and nobody wanted to tell me. That makes me feel stupid.'

'It's not quite like that. We weren't certain until now, that's all. But now we are. We didn't want to tell you something that might not be true, but it is. That's what the police officer came to tell me. They found a body and they think it's your mum.'

Finn sighed. He moved the action figure's arms back and forward. 'What's going to happen to me now?'

'Well . . . I'm here,' said Eden.

And they sat together on the bed for what seemed like an age.

* * *

It wasn't until the evening that Finn started crying.

Eden had cooked spaghetti and they had both sat on the small sofa watching *Indiana Jones and the Temple of Doom* when it started. First it was just a trickle of tears, then he was gulping air.

Eden put his bowl down on the floor and put his arm around Finn and said, 'It's all right to cry.' He paused the film and got some tissues and handed one to Finn.

'It's my bag,' Finn wailed.

Eden was confused. 'What bag?'

'My school bag. I left it in the woman's car.'

'Don't worry about the bag, Finn. I'll buy you a new one.'

Finn just carried on crying harder.

'It's got my homework in it. We're supposed to hand it in on Monday.'

'Oh, that's not important,' said Eden with a smile. 'Miss Killick won't mind you not doing your homework. I promise.'

Finn threw his bowl on the floor, spraying pasta everywhere. 'It is important!' he shouted, enraged. And he started to punch Eden on his arm and on the side of his chest, small fists pummelling him over and over.

'Your homework?'

'Mum says I always have to do my homework!' he continued to shout. 'My homework was in the bag!' He was crying so hard now, he could barely talk. 'If I haven't got my bag I can't do my homework.' He hit Eden again, harder this time.

'Oh, Finn,' said Eden, catching hold of his fist. 'I'm sorry. I didn't understand. Of course it's important.'

'My bag,' he said.

'I'll sort it. I promise,' said Eden.

When he'd stopped crying, Eden took him up to bed.

Eden was learning to dread this time. Finn didn't seem capable of going to sleep without his mother, without her telling him a story. He lay there, red-eyed, staring at Eden.

'Why don't you tell me a story?' Finn demanded.

He switched off the bedside light, leaving the landing door open. 'I don't know how.'

'Just try,' whined Finn.

Eden racked his brain, trying to think of a story he knew well enough to tell. He wondered how Apple had managed this when there had never been stories when they were children.

Finn rolled over onto his side, eyes still wide.

'OK. There were once four children. Their names were . . . Lucy, Edmund . . . I can't remember the other two.'

'Is this a true story?'

'No. When I was a child, we travelled everywhere.'

'Was that with my mum?'

'Yes. She was there too. We were living in this van. Not a camper van, just an ordinary van. Me and your sister slept in the back of it. Mum and Dad used to stay in a bell tent. We stayed in this campsite once in Portugal and this woman there felt sorry for me, I think. Your sister was older than me. I think she coped better. I was lonely. The woman read me this book once, but I can't remember all the names properly.'

'Make them up, then.'

'OK. There were once four children. Their names were Lucy, Edmund . . . John and Jane. And they were sent away for the holidays to stay with some relation in the countryside who lived in a big house. I think he was a professor or something, and he wasn't interested in looking after children, so they were free to play all day in the house. Anyway. One of them – I think it was Lucy – found this old wardrobe. I think they were playing hide-and-seek – and when she opened the door and went inside to hide it was snowing.'

'It was snowing? In the wardrobe?'

'Yes.'

'And?'

Eden had stopped talking. He was thinking about the old Fiat van that he and Apple had used to sleep in, on an old mattress that lay in the back.

'What happened next?'

Eden racked his brains. 'I'm afraid I don't really remember.'

Finn rolled over so that Eden could no longer see if his eyes were open or not. After a few minutes, Eden stood and crept slowly out of the room. 'Don't forget about my bag,' said Finn, still wide-awake.

Twenty-Seven

On Sunday the rain came back. A low grey drizzle descended and an east wind chilled the air. On clear days, you could see from here all the way up to Dartmoor, Eden realised. On days like this, the world seemed to close in. Beyond the bridge across the river, the world turned hazy and grey. The beach, which had been full on Saturday, was silent. The red sand turned darker. The darkness below Finn's pale eyes was deeper too. Eden was not sure if the boy had slept at all last night.

Bisi called back while they were having a fried breakfast, Finn pushing mushrooms and tomatoes around his plate without much enthusiasm. 'OK. I've sorted it,' she announced. 'There will be someone at the school at eleven today to get you the worksheets that Finn was given on Thursday. Why don't you come around to mine for a meal afterwards? A bit of lunch?'

'Still checking up on me?'

'Always working, Eden. You should know that by now.'

Eden and Finn left the house at twenty to eleven, walking along the boardwalk to the car park at the end of the spit, where Eden had left his Audi.

He spotted the unmarked police car easily. It was two rows away, but as they walked past it Eden could tell it wasn't a civilian model from the matrix display on the back shelf. The man inside, watching something on his phone, was unmistakably a plain-clothes officer.

As he pulled out of the car park Eden saw it start up, following him at an approved distance.

Outside the school, Eden parked on the zigzag lines. 'I'll be a minute,' he told Finn. The school gate was locked when he got there, but there was an intercom. 'I'll come and let you in,' said a woman's voice.

Eden was surprised to see that the woman coming out to see him was Jackie, the mother who had helped him hunt for Finn on Friday. 'What are you doing here?'

'I volunteer here. I'm planning on becoming a teaching assistant next year, now Sheena is old enough to cope with it. So I have keys and I only live down the road. Miss Killick lives in Torquay, so she asked me if I could come in. And she wanted to know how Finn is.'

Finn was sitting in the car, watching them. 'They found his mother's body yesterday,' he said. 'He's getting used to it, I suppose.'

'Jesus. Poor boy.'

'I never got a chance to thank you for helping me last week,' said Eden. 'By the time I'd finished talking to the police you'd gone.'

'I'm just glad he turned up unharmed,' said Jackie, unpadlocking the gate to let him in. 'This way.' She led him across the tarmac. Shoulder at the swing door to push it open, she said. 'Miss Killick is totally distraught. I think that's half the reason she wanted me to do this. She's embarrassed. She knows what a huge mistake she made. Ofsted are going to kill them for this. It's a shame, because it's a great school.'

He followed Jackie down a wide corridor whose walls were covered in pictures of fish and dolphins. Each drawing had a child's name written in big letters underneath. He paused to try and see if there was anything Finn had drawn.

'Good, aren't they? I love looking at them. Year 4 is doing a project on the sea.'

Finn was Year 5. There wouldn't be a picture by him here, Eden realised, but he spotted one of a man on a blue boat with a red cabin. It was very carefully coloured in. The man had fair hair, a blue shirt and a big smile on his face. Underneath was written: 'MY DAD BY SHEENA.'

Eden pointed. 'This must be your daughter's?'

The boat had what looked like a fishing net behind it crammed with fish. Jackie, who was almost at the classroom door, came back and stood next to him. 'Yes.' She smiled proudly.

'She's good.'

'Obviously I think she's a genius.' She disappeared into Miss Killick's classroom and by the time he joined her she was standing at a table at the back of the classroom, leafing through a tray of papers. 'She said it was in here – yes. Is this it? "Abstract noun poem. Choose one of the abstract nouns below and write a poem about it."' She held up a sheet.

'I think so.'

'OK. Is that all?'

'Do you help Sheena, when she has homework like this?'

'If she asks for help, yes. If she doesn't, I leave her to it.'

He read out the nouns: '"Hope, anger, love, illness, happiness, war, fear." Jesus,' he said. 'Pray to God he doesn't ask for help.'

'I know.' At the gate, after he had thanked her, she said, 'Look after yourself, will you? You look worried.'

* * *

He drove on up the lane afterwards, to the track where Sheena had found the action figure. 'This is where the lady let me have a wee.'

'I thought so. Do you remember anything else about the car, or about her?'

'No.'

There were remains of blue and white tape tied to a hawthorn. Eden was relieved to see it. It meant that local police had searched the place properly, at least.

When he drove back into the lane heading away from Teignmouth, the police car that had been surveilling them had turned and was facing them, expecting to be following Eden back down the hill.

It had to reverse backwards for about thirty metres to find a spot where it was wide enough for both cars to pass. Eden gave the driver a little wave.

The police car followed them all the way up to the moor, down twisting lanes, and over cattle grids. They dipped into valleys and rose again onto hills covered in green bracken, slowing for sheep that scattered off the tarmac at the sight of the car.

Bisi's house still looked improbable. In daylight he noticed how the window frames needed painting and how some of the slates on the roof had cracked and needed fixing.

'You got your homework?' said Bisi, opening the big wooden front door.

'Yes,' said Finn. 'I have to write a poem.'

Bisi leaned down and kissed Finn on the head and ushered him inside. 'That's nice. Peter is out with the twins. They're traipsing all over the moor. It's Ten Tors next weekend so they're doing a practice hike. I told them to be back by now so they could meet Finn again.'

'Ten Tors?'

They followed her into the kitchen. 'You not heard of it? I hadn't either until I came down here. It's a bloody nightmare weekend, if you ask me. You know what a tor is? Those lumps of stone on top of the hills out there. It's a giant hike they do, from tor to tor. The kicker is it's only teenagers who do it. The shortest route is about 35 miles. My kids are doing the 45-mile hike. It takes two days, usually in pouring rain.'

'I thought you were in Child Protection.'

She laughed. 'They say they love it. The girls take after my husband, not bloody me. Here he is now.'

She pointed out of the sash window where their silver Subaru was pulling in, splashing in the puddles.

Bisi was pouring tea into a huge pot when the two girls pushed through the door in muddy hiking gear and went to hug their mother.

'Get off me,' pleaded Bisi. 'You're filthy and you smell. You remember Finn.'

'We need cake,' one of the girls pleaded.

'You need a shower,' answered Bisi.

'Hello Finn.'

He smiled up at them. Peter walked in carrying a heavy-looking backpack.

'Go. Wash.' Bisi ordered the girls away.

She had cooked a vegan stew with mashed potatoes. The six of them sat around the kitchen table and ate it while Peter pushed dishes aside to unfold Ordnance Survey maps.

'Eden isn't interested,' said Bisi.

'Of course he is,' replied Peter. He traced his finger over the route the girls – and thousands of others – would be taking next weekend.

'All these kids on the moor.' Peter beamed. 'It's a beautiful thing.'

'Sometimes people die,' said one of the twins.

'That hasn't happened for years,' said her dad.

'Shut up now, Peter,' ordered Bisi. 'You're boring our guests.'

Peter took no notice. He looked over at Finn. 'I bet you'd like to do it, Finn, when you're big enough.'

'No, I don't think so,' said Finn.

The girls laughed, delighted. The meal was loud, messy and chaotic. The food had too much salt in it and the leeks were still hard and inedible. Bisi was a terrible cook.

Eden looked at the big map spread out in front of him, the dark brown of the high moor, the pale contours that wound close together. 'If there are thousands of people doing it, isn't it awfully crowded?'

'No,' said one of the twins. 'There are loads of different routes. They work it out so everyone's spread out.'

At one point Eden glanced at Finn, who was sitting in his chair talking to one of the twins. He was smiling. This was family life, Eden realised. Finn loved it.

He called Sweet when they were back home. 'I'm happy to tell you where I am and where I'm going,' said Eden. 'You don't need to waste your resources on surveillance.'

'You just can't get the staff these days,' tutted Sweet. 'To be fair, we're as interested in keeping the boy safe as we are in knowing what you're up to. It's just a friendly eye, for your own safety, understand?'

Eden took the reassurance with a pinch of salt. 'So. What did you find on the boat that's made you so interested in me all of a sudden?'

'You know I'm not going to tell you that, Eden.' He heard a woman's voice in the background. 'Look after yourself, Eden. Look after the boy. Keep your head down.' Sweet ended the call.

* * *

That afternoon Eden sat with Finn at the living room table as he did his homework. '"Choose one of the abstract nouns below and write a poem about it." Which word are you going to choose?' Eden asked Finn. He watched Finn scan the words, weighing up each one.

'What about hope?'

Finn shook his head. Eden had met him exactly a week ago. He felt like he didn't know him at all.

He looked at the photograph of Finn on the wall in his school uniform. 'Love?'

Another shake of the head. 'Anger,' Finn decided.

'OK,' said Eden. 'Bold choice. Who took that photo of you in your school uniform?'

'Mum did.'

'On her phone?'

'She didn't have a camera on her phone.'

'Of course she didn't,' said Eden. She didn't trust modern technology. 'So how did she take this photograph?'

'On her camera.'

He thought of the USB lead he had found in the drawer. He hadn't seen a camera anywhere in the house.

Twenty-Eight

Finn sat at the table, curling his arm around the paper so Eden couldn't see what he was doing. He worked for about ten minutes, occasionally looking up and chewing thoughtfully on his lip. 'Finished,' he declared, and put down his pen.

'That didn't take long.'

'No.'

'Can I see it?' asked Eden.

Finn turned the paper over. 'No.'

'OK. Fair.'

At around four-thirty that afternoon, Molly returned. Again, Finn ran to her and gave her an enormous hug. She was carrying a plastic bag full of clothes. 'I'll just change in the bathroom, if that's OK?'

'Not really. No.'

'Your sister used to let me,' she said, moving past him, up the stairs. When she came down she was wearing running shorts and her hair was jammed into her baseball cap.

At the door, he could see the other women, similarly dressed, preparing the boat in the grey drizzle, carrying down the oars easily.

'Is that a gig?'

'No. Gigs are the big ones,' said Finn.

'Is that right?' Eden said.

'Gigs were pilot boats,' continued Finn, as if repeating something his mother had once told him.

'OK.'

Molly grinned. 'That's a seine boat. Originally it would have been a net fishing boat. They were designed to carry the weight of a catch. Gigs were made for speed. When a ship appeared off the harbour here, the local lads would race to be the first one there in the gigs to offer their services as pilots. It's always been a tricky bit of water here, because of the current and the sandbanks. Every now and then, a ship still attempts to come in on their own without a pilot and they usually get stuck somewhere on The Salty – that's the sandbank in the middle. You can't see it now because it's submerged. Whenever that happens, everyone turns out on the beach to have a good giggle. Anyway. That's what gigs were for.'

'Are you giving me a lesson here, you two?'

'Yes,' said Finn earnestly.

'See that one – the one we're going to go out on?' Molly pointed at the white boat the women were preparing. 'That boat there is fibreglass, but it's moulded on a wooden seine boat built for this river by a local family. The family used to live in the house right next door to you.' She pointed to the north side of the house. 'That's what this place was. It was a workplace. Look over there.' She pointed out of the window to a rusty piece of machinery on the stone quay. 'That was the winch the guy who lived next door used. Still there. My dad was a boat builder too, and my granddad. That's why I ended up with the bloody boatyard. There used to be a big old shipyard where those hideous flats are now.'

She pointed further down towards the estuary mouth. 'Used to be known all over the world. They used to build classic sailing boats, lifeboats, motor launches and all that stuff and send them everywhere. Beautiful boats. Really beautiful ones. My granddad used to work there. There was a lot of fishing here, too, back in the day. Numbers crashed, quotas changed. And the docks are struggling for work because no one wants to use small ships any more. There's a couple of boats do whelks and lobster pots these days and that's about it. Looks pretty enough, but round here a lot of people are just holding on.'

'Like my sister was?'

'Yep. Like your sister was.' Molly nodded, then trotted down the beach and joined the others pulling the seine boat down to the water, while Finn and Eden stood at the door watching. When it was mostly in the water, Molly got in with the others and grabbed her oar, just before the last woman in pushed it off.

'Did you used to watch your mum doing this?' Eden asked Finn.

'Yes, I did.'

The four long oars began to work together, digging in the water, and the boat moved off fast to the mouth of the estuary, disappearing out to sea.

An hour later, when Molly came back, soaked to the skin, she asked if she could shower – 'Apple used to let me.'

Before he stood aside to let her up the stairs, Eden said, 'Something I wanted to ask. What was the name of the garage Apple took her car to?'

On Monday morning, as Eden was getting ready to take Finn to school, a young man in cargo pants and a sweatshirt knocked at the door, holding a blue backpack.

'Bisi sent me,' the man told Eden. 'I work with her. She thought Finn might want this to replace the stolen one. She put a packed lunch in there.'

'Did she?' Eden had already made cheese sandwiches with vegan cheese, bought from a local deli.

'There's a drink in there too.'

'Right,' Eden said. He hadn't thought of a drink.

He watched as Finn searched through the bag. There was a chocolate bar as well. Nice touch. Finn took the folded piece of paper he'd written the poem on, put it into the bag, then zipped it up, without letting Eden see.

He dropped Finn off, keeping an eye out for Jackie, but she wasn't there. Pam and her son deliberately steered a path clear of him, which he was grateful for.

Instead of going home, Eden drove to the garage Molly had told him about, checking in his rear-view mirror on the way. If the police officer was still following him, he was being more subtle about it today.

The industrial estate was in a valley, warehouses dotted round the steep side. The garage he had been looking for was on a bend in the road that rose up the slope.

Outside the workshop, a squat mechanic was wheeling a tyre across the tarmac towards the workshop. He eyed Eden as he parked.

'Can I help you, sir?' Eden guessed from his accent he might be Turkish.

Eden explained he had come to pay for the work on his sister's car.

'You're the brother?'

'That's right.'

He disappeared into the garage and returned a minute later. 'No. We don't have the car. The police came and took it away last week. I have the bill, though.' He held a piece of paper.

'The police?'

'That's right.'

'What day was this?'

'Let me see. Come this way.' He led Eden back past the inspection pit to a small office and flicked the pages in a large desk diary. 'Wednesday,' he said.

'They took it away on a truck?'

'I don't know. I wasn't here. You'd have to ask the boss. He's back later maybe.'

'Wednesday. You're absolutely sure?'

'Of course I am sure. We made a note.'

'Do you have the paperwork? The police must have given you something.'

The man shrugged. 'You have to come back and talk to the boss about it.'

Wednesday. That was odd. As far as Eden knew, on the Wednesday of last week, local police were still not publicly regarding Apple's disappearance as anything other than an accident. Nobody had mentioned to him that they had impounded her car, but if they had impounded it, someone must have been thinking even back then that there was something about Apple's disappearance that wasn't straightforward.

'You remember the officer's name?'

'As I told you, I wasn't here. Speak to my boss. You going to pay the bill?'

Back in his own car, Eden called Sweet. Sweet's line was busy. 'Something strange has come up,' Eden said, leaving a message. 'Can you call me back?'

Twenty-Nine

When he returned to school that afternoon to pick up Finn, Eden spotted the unmarked car again, in amongst the family vehicles. Eden parked his own car and he was in the throng at the gate waiting for the children to emerge when Jackie hailed him. 'You need to come in. Something's happened.'

'What's wrong?' Eden's heart was suddenly fast in his chest.

'Nothing like last time. But I'm afraid the head needs a word with you. There was an incident.'

'An incident? What?'

'Finn bit a child today during the lunch break.'

'God,' said Eden. 'He bit someone?'

Jackie looked sympathetic. 'I'm sure it's nothing. I'll show you where to go.'

Finn was sitting on a soft chair outside the office with the new blue bag on his lap.

'You bit another child?'

Finn didn't have time to answer before the head teacher opened the door. 'Oh, there you are, Mr Driscoll. Come on in. Both of you. Sit down, sit down.'

It was a small office, neat. There were two plastic chairs arranged in front of his desk.

The head spoke briskly. 'So, Finn. You got annoyed with another pupil today, didn't you?'

Finn sat stone-faced, his hands on his knees.

'We understand it was a swap that went a bit wrong.' He addressed Eden. 'Another child wanted to exchange something in his lunchbox for something Eden had. We discourage swapping because it can lead to unhappiness, but we have a very firm policy on hurting each other, don't we?'

Finn stared straight ahead.

'Obviously, Finn, we know you've had a very difficult time, so we do understand if you might find it hard to control your emotions right now. But we have a zero-tolerance policy for things like this.'

Eden nodded.

'And when we lose our temper,' continued the head teacher in a gentle voice, 'it's good if we can find a way to say sorry.'

'Did you say sorry, Finn?' asked Eden.

Finn turned and looked at Eden and shook his head.

'Are you going to apologise?'

Finn looked down.

'That's a really bad thing to do, Finn,' said Eden. 'Biting someone.'

'We've asked Finn to fill in a Reflection Sheet so he can think about what he did and decide what he could have done better next time, haven't we, Finn?'

Finn remained silent.

'Perhaps you can help him with that, Mr Driscoll?'

Eden looked at the boy. It was as if he wasn't even listening.

'Don't take it too seriously,' said the head teacher. 'He's

had a terrible time. But it's our policy to always meet with parents if this kind of thing happens.'

'Is the other child all right?' asked Eden.

'He's a bit sore, but,' the head teacher did his best to sound reassuring, 'I'm sure he'll be OK.'

Outside, in the corridor, Finn walked on ahead. 'Wait.' Eden reached out and took his shoulder to stop him. 'What did he do?'

'He was annoying. He tried to steal my chocolate. The one in my lunchbox.'

'But biting,' said Eden. 'You can't do that.'

Jackie was out in the corridor, her expression sympathetic. 'It'll all blow over,' she told Eden. 'It probably didn't help that it was Cyrus that he bit.'

Finn walked on ahead again, towards the double doors at the end of the corridor.

'Cyrus?'

Jackie pulled a comical face. 'Pam's son.'

'Pamela's son? Oh, Christ. That's not funny.'

She laughed. 'You'll have to get used to it. It comes with the territory.'

'God – the politics of it. And you're planning on getting deeper into all this, becoming a schoolteacher?' he asked her.

'A teaching assistant.'

'Why the hell would you do that? Are you mad?'

He meant the question to sound light, but Jackie answered seriously, 'We need the money, that's why, and there's not much else you can do without having to get someone to look after your child. Listen. I'll keep an eye out for Finn, I promise. All the teachers are looking out for him. He's a good boy. They understand it's not easy for him right now.'

Eden caught up with Finn and they walked in silence back to Eden's Audi.

When they got in, Eden looked in the rear-view mirror at Finn buckling himself up. 'It's OK to be angry,' said Eden. 'But it's not OK to hurt people.'

Finn looked sideways, out of the window, pretending not to have heard.

'You called. What now?' On the phone, Sweet's voice was terse.

'Last week, as far as I could see – before Finn was abducted – you weren't treating my sister's disappearance as a serious crime.'

'Of course we were taking it seriously, Eden. I hope you don't think for a second that we weren't.'

'That's not what I meant. As far as I could see, you were treating it as a death by misadventure.'

'That's true,' said Sweet.

'So why did you impound her car?'

There was a pause.

'What did you say?'

'I went to pick up Apple's Toyota from the garage up at the Broadmeadow Industrial Estate. Apparently you beat me to it.'

Another silence. Then: 'I have no idea at all what you're talking about, Eden.'

Eden was puzzled too now. 'The mechanic said . . .' Eden heard Sweet tapping at a keyboard.

'I've just checked. The only reason we would have impounded it was if it was part of our investigation. There's nothing about anyone requesting your sister's car for any reason. Which garage did you say your sister left her car at?'

Alarm bells ringing loudly now, Eden ended the call. Whoever had picked up the vehicle had shown the garage a document of some kind. Either someone impersonating a police officer had picked up the car – or worse, an actual police officer had.

When the phone rang again later, after Finn was in bed, Eden was relieved to see DI Kadakia's name on the screen. He was sitting on the small sofa with a can of beer, looking forward to a chat with his boss and a chance to talk about the world he understood.

But Sammy's voice was brusque. 'I have bad news. Hasina Hossein is refusing to testify against Ronan Pan,' he said.

Thirty

'What happened?' Eden asked his boss.

'She changed her mind.'

This was a blow. Without her evidence, there was no case against Pan. 'How did he get to her? It must have been him, right?'

'I don't know how,' said Sammy. 'But she's stopped talking to us. You're right. She's frightened of something.'

'I should have been there.' Eden had worked so hard to win Hasina's trust, to keep her whereabouts a secret. If Eden had stayed in London he would have been able to keep his eye on her – and her relations. He should have guessed how Pan would operate, but he had been distracted.

'You couldn't be here, Eden. You have other stuff going on. But there's something else too.' He could hear the hesitation in Sammy's voice. 'He's made a complaint to the IOPC.'

'What? Ronan Pan has made a complaint to the Independent Office for Police Conduct?'

'A complaint about you. Pan claims you assaulted him.'

Eden remembered the look that had been on the young

officer's face when she told him 'you were hitting him pretty hard.'

'I have to ask this, Eden. Did you assault him?' asked Sammy.

Eden blinked. 'I was worried he was going to assault PC Ali. Why is this being taken seriously?'

'Because the IOPC say there is an officer who is willing to testify that they saw you hitting Ronan Pan.'

That was another bombshell. DC Ali had said she would not put it in her report, but she had obviously changed her mind.

'Don't you have anything to say?'

'Is this an investigation already, Sammy?'

He could hear Sammy's unease. 'I'm asking because I'm worried about you.'

'Right,' said Eden. He looked around the room, at the child's drawings on the wall. 'I did hit him, yes. And it's possible that I may have used too much force.'

Sammy took an audible breath. 'I see.' And then another. 'Thank you for being honest. You know what will happen if they find against you.'

'Yes, I do.'

'It's a ploy by his lawyer, obviously. But . . .'

'We drop the case against him, he drops the case against us?'

'Something like that,' said Sammy. 'Anyway. That's our problem, not yours right now. I don't want you to worry about this. You have enough on your plate. How are you doing?'

'Something's off here. I can't figure it out. And the boy hates me.'

Bedtime with Finn had not gone well. Eden had bought a couple of children's books from the Oxfam shop in the middle of the town and had tried reading them to Finn, but Finn had not been interested. 'They are rubbish,' he had said.

'He's struggling to control his emotions. And I feel like telling the children's team that I am struggling to look after him.'

'Steady,' said Sammy. 'Don't burn your bridges yet, Eden.'

There was a noise behind him. He turned to see Finn standing at the bottom of the stairs. He was glaring at Eden.

'None of it is ever easy,' Sammy was saying. 'I saw on the news that they had found your sister's body. I'm sorry.'

'Hold on. I have to go,' Eden interrupted, wondering how much of that Finn had heard.

'Phone me back when you can, OK?'

Eden ended the call. 'Couldn't you sleep?' he asked the boy.

Dressed in a T-shirt and a pair of sleeping shorts, Finn shook his head.

'Do you want me to take you back upstairs?'

Finn looked up at Eden. 'Do I have to say sorry to Cyrus?'

Eden stood. 'Do you not want to say sorry to him?'

Again, the shake of the head.

'No,' he said. 'You don't have to if you're not sorry. But you should say sorry to the head teacher maybe for what you did. It's never good to bite people, Finn.'

'You're a policeman. Don't you ever hurt people?'

Stung, Eden wondered how much of the conversation he'd heard. 'I don't bite them. I might have to restrain them.'

'Same thing,' said Finn, still standing at the bottom of the steep staircase.

'Well . . . no. Not really. Restraining someone is holding them back from doing something.'

'I was restraining Cyrus from stealing my chocolate.'

'Right.' Eden suddenly felt exhausted. First someone was

muddying the trail of evidence around his sister's disappearance and now, after all the work he had put in in London, Ronan Pan was going to walk away a free man. 'I'm sorry. It's good you stood up for yourself. That's important. But try and do it with less biting.'

'OK.'

'Back up to bed, then.'

'Not tired.' Finn sat down on the bottom stair.

Eden felt lost. He did not know how to handle children. He was no good at this.

'Who's going to look after me next?'

'What do you mean, next?'

'When you've gone? Who's going to look after me then?'

Eden took a sip from his can of beer. 'Wouldn't you like to be part of a real family, a proper one, maybe with brothers and sisters?'

Finn thought about that for a while. 'Would that mean I have to go somewhere different?'

'Would you like that?'

'No.'

'How would you know?'

Finn's face hardened. Eden didn't know what to do, except put his drink down, sit on the stair next to the boy, nudging him aside to make space, and put his arm around him. To his surprise, the boy leaned into him, just a fraction. The two of them sat like that, together, for what seemed like a long time.

On Tuesday at the school gate, Eden said to Finn, 'I've put two chocolate bars in your backpack. If you want to you can give one to Cyrus.'

'Can I have it myself?'

'If you like. Just don't bite him again.'

'I'll put poison in it and give it to him,' Finn said, his face perfectly straight.

'OK.'

Walking back to his car, Eden was surprised to see that there were two police officers in the car that had been surveilling him – and one of them was Sweet.

'Hello, Mike,' Eden greeted him, leaning down to the open window.

'Nice weather, now the rain has finally stopped,' said Sweet.

'Is it?' answered Eden.

'We'd like to ask you a few questions,' Sweet continued.

'What kind of questions?'

'The sort of questions people ask at a police station,' answered Sweet with a note of apology in his voice.

A formal on-the-record interview. Eden nodded. 'I'm happy to do that, obviously.'

'Good. Good.' Sweet rubbed his hands together. 'Well, let's get this done so we can all get on with our happy little lives. This officer can show you the way.'

The officer Eden didn't recognise behind the wheel got out. 'I'll direct you to the station,' he explained.

'I can probably find it myself,' said Eden.

'Easier this way,' replied the officer.

Yesterday had been bad enough with the news about Ronan Pan. Today was already worse.

'Excuse me,' said Sweet, opening his car door a little. Eden stood back to let him get out. Sweet walked round the car and took the other officer's place behind the wheel.

'What have you got that you're not telling me?' asked Eden, but Sweet already had the engine whirring and was indicating to pull out.

'Sir?' said the officer. 'Your car, then. Shall we go?'

Thirty-One

By the station, DS Sweet meant the HQ in Exeter. The police officer sat in Eden's passenger seat as he drove down dual carriageways and around roundabouts.

It was a shiny new police headquarters, a modern block, big and very square, a bit like an Amazon warehouse, with none of the gravitas of the old red-brick HQ Eden guessed it would have replaced. Eden wondered if its big alternating vertical stripes of black and white were supposed to remind visitors of the black and white pattern on a police hat.

'*In Auxilium Omnium*,' read Eden, looking at the motto on the giant crest printed on the glass next to the front door.

'Helping everyone,' explained the copper.

'I thought it might mean, "You're going to need all the help you can get."'

'Sorry?' The policeman didn't crack a smile.

After they'd checked him in at the front desk, the officer led Eden down corridors and into a lift where they stood awkwardly together until he delivered Eden into a bland meeting room with brightly coloured chairs. 'Sergeant Sweet will be with you shortly,' he said and disappeared.

Sweet arrived a few minutes later, two other officers by his side, a plastic folder in his hands. He introduced them and they shook hands. It was all very dry and formal.

'Well?' Eden asked.

Sweet gave a little smile. 'During the course of our investigations a couple of things have come up. We need to discuss them.'

'A couple of things?'

'Do you mind coming this way?' one of the other men asked, opening the door wide.

Eden was marched down the corridor, through a security door, towards the custody suite. The interview room was much like any other he had worked in: a table, chairs, microphone on the table and an IP camera mounted on the ceiling.

'Water? Tea?' asked Sweet.

'No, thanks.'

'Have a seat.' Sweet placed the folder he had been carrying down on the desk, reached forward and turned the recording device on and identified everyone in the room, including the two detective constables. He settled into a chair opposite and pulled it closer to the table.

'I don't think I need to explain the need for this to you, do I?' He waved at the recording device.

'We have those too. In London.'

'Of course you do,' said Sweet. 'Eden Driscoll. Thank you for voluntarily agreeing to this interview today. As you know, we have some concern over the circumstances surrounding your sister's death. We are talking to people who might be able to help us.'

'Excellent,' said Eden.

'OK. Ready to begin?' Eyebrows raised. 'First question. When did you last see your sister?'

'April 2010.'

'So. Fifteen years ago?'

'Yes. In Portugal.'

'Not seen her since?'

'No.'

'Or had any other contact or communication with Miss Apple Driscoll?'

'Only when my mother died. We spoke on the phone. Why?'

'Can you explain that? I mean, most of us don't always get on with our siblings, but we don't cut them out of our lives.'

OK. This was going to be a wide-ranging interview – to start with at least. Eden settled back in his chair. 'Mine was not a typical family. I loved my sister, but I felt I needed to get away from them. My father was a very overbearing man.' It was not the whole truth, but.

'You're thirty. So you haven't seen her since you were—?'

Eden did the maths for him. 'Fifteen.'

'Harsh.'

'Is this therapy?'

Sweet laughed gently. 'So you said you spoke just the once, when your mother died?'

'My dad had already died at this point. I had written to my mother a few times. Mostly because I needed to get something signed – when I went to university and needed to sign on for housing benefit – that kind of thing. She was living in Portugal. The last time I contacted her I think it was to ask her for a copy of my birth certificate – because I was joining the police. So Apple knew that. But after that we fell out of touch. Then a couple of years later I got a letter from Apple. All it said on the envelope was, *Eden Driscoll, Metropolitan Police, London*. Literally that. She was writing to tell me that my mum was dying of cervical cancer. It took three weeks to reach me from Greece, by which time my mother was already dead. So we spoke that time on the phone. There was some stuff we needed to do. My mum left her estate to both of us – I told her I didn't want it. She could have the lot.'

'Why was that?'

'Because she had stayed. I had run away. She deserved it. She was the better person.'

'And you are sure that was the last time you spoke to her? And you had no idea she had made a life for herself here?'

'No idea at all. I didn't even know she had a son. Until you phoned me.'

'No contact at all?'

'None whatsoever.' Eden sat back in his chair. 'You haven't even told me whether you have identified the body recovered from the water as my sister's yet.'

'You arrived in Teignmouth on Sunday May . . .' Sweet checked his notebook for the date '. . . eighteenth.'

'Well. Have you?'

'We expect the DNA confirmation shortly. On the day following your arrival, you requested to go aboard your sister's yacht with myself and the Teignmouth harbourmaster. Can I ask why you put forward that request?'

Put forward that request. Eden smiled at the older cop's language. 'Because my sister's life had ended on the boat. I wanted to see if there was anything on board that explained why.'

Sweet nodded. The other two officers' faces were giving nothing away. 'You made a thorough inspection of the boat. Is that right?'

Eden was trying to work out where he was coming from. He had an inkling. 'I wouldn't say thorough. I looked through drawers to see if she had left any notes that explained her state of mind.'

'Did you remove anything from the boat?'

'I picked up something that belonged to my nephew – a pair of headphones. I cleared that with you.'

'Was there anything else taken from the boat?'

'Only a bag of rubbish. I discovered a note in that which I shared with you.'

'Right. When you boarded the boat, were you expecting to find anything?'

Eden knew where he was heading. 'I was looking. I wasn't expecting anything.'

Sweet leaned forward a millimetre or two. 'Tell me about your search of the cabin at the front of the boat.'

Eden looked him in the eye. 'I looked in the cabin. I saw that Finn had slept in the starboard bunk and that he'd left those headphones there.'

'And?'

Sweet had obviously seen him lifting the other mattress and the board beneath it, so there was no point denying it. 'And I checked the compartment on the port side of the boat.'

'Why?'

Eden paused. 'You haven't told me anything about my sister's post-mortem,' he said.

'Are you avoiding the question, Mr Driscoll?'

'Was there any sign of trauma to my sister's body?'

Sweet took a big breath and exhaled. 'The preliminary report discusses some pre-mortem bruising consistent with a fall from a boat.'

'To her head? To her arms? Her abdomen?'

'We will share the report with you as soon as it's completed, Mr Driscoll. Why did you check the compartment in the cabin at the front of the boat?'

Eden nodded slowly. 'I was looking for something that might have been hidden there.'

'Oh. You were looking for something? Like what?'

This was much more than general fact-finding, Eden realised. He found himself crossing his arms across his chest and knew from experience that made him look like someone with something to hide, so he uncrossed them again. 'I sailed on that boat when I was a child. My father built a compartment beneath the bunk as a place to conceal things. Valuables, for instance. I was wondering if Apple had used it to hide anything.'

'And had she?'

'I don't know. I didn't see.'

'Because I interrupted you?'

Eden kept his face as blank as he could. 'I couldn't see. That's all.'

'You sure about that?'

'Yes.'

'And you didn't tell me that's what you were doing at the time . . .'

'No. I didn't feel it was relevant.'

Another nod. Sweet looked down at his typewritten notes, then met Eden's eye again. 'You mentioned that your father used it as a place deliberately constructed to conceal valuables. What kind of valuables?'

'Money. Passports. Boats were often robbed, especially in some of the shadier ports in Portugal and Spain, or in North Africa.'

'Any other kind of valuables, Mr Driscoll?'

He remembered how hot that cabin had been when he

and his sister had slept in it under sheets, sweating. 'I'm not sure what you mean.'

'No?' Sweet leaned forward another degree. He even sounded a little sad when he asked, 'For the record, Sergeant Driscoll, can you account for the fact that we found traces of controlled substances in the compartment?'

Thirty-Two

Eden realised he should have expressed shock at that point. It would have looked better in the video.

Instead, he asked, 'You're saying the forensics officers found traces of a controlled substance in the compartment below the port water tank?'

'Can you account for it?' Sweet asked again.

'What sort of controlled substance?'

Sweet smiled. 'I'll ask a third time, Mr Driscoll. Can you account for the presence of controlled substances on your sister's boat?'

This time, when Eden crossed his arms, he left them that way. He looked up at the camera. 'No. I can't.'

'I also want to ask once more why you were so keen to check that particular compartment.'

'As I said, it was the kind of place my sister would have hidden something. If she had something to hide.'

Sweet leaned forward and made a note. 'It's where she would have hidden something if she had something to hide,' he repeated slowly. 'And why do you think your sister was hiding controlled substances on that boat?'

'Was she?'

'Please answer the question. Why was your sister hiding controlled substances on the boat?'

'I can't comment on that,' said Eden. 'You think she was involved in smuggling?'

'Do you?'

'I hadn't spoken to her for years. I know as much about her life as you do. Probably less.'

'Right.'

Eden was calculating now, trying to imagine how they were seeing this. Any officer working on serious crime knew that the National Crime Agency was reporting that gangs were bringing large quantities of narcotics across the Atlantic in container ships. The difficult part was bringing them into Europe. One route was to distribute the drugs onto smaller boats in the Bay of Biscay – or even further out at sea. This cargo would be distributed to even smaller boats again – boats like his sister's – each one another link in the chain.

Sweet tilted his weight back in the chair, looked down at his notes. One of the detective constables spoke for the first time. 'OK. We'll come back to the boat later. That wasn't the only hiding place she had, was it? There was a place that she used to conceal items beneath her floorboards. What was she hiding there, Mr Driscoll?'

'As you are aware, I don't know.'

'Was she also concealing drugs there?'

'I don't believe so. No.'

'You sure about that? We applied for a warrant to investigate your sister's bank account.'

Which meant they definitely suspected that Apple was involved in criminal activity, thought Eden.

'This is a copy of her most recent bank statement. As you will see, a week before her death, £5,000 appeared in her bank account,' said the detective. 'Can you think of any reason why someone would have sent your sister £5,000?'

Eden looked at the statement that Sweet pushed across the table. This time he was shocked – and he hoped that showed on the video. 'No. As far as I know, my sister was broke.'

'It arrived from a pre-paid credit card, intended to be used as a gift card,' said the officer.

'Oh.' Eden was becoming worried.

'Oh,' repeated Sweet. 'So you understand why we were interested in this particular transaction.'

'Because pre-paid gift cards are used a lot in fraud and money laundering,' said Eden.

'Exactly. Money laundering. Drug dealing. People use them to hide the identity of a payee. So you can guess that any sum of money that large being paid through one of these cards is not exactly clean. Again, any bright ideas?'

Eden shook his head. 'No. Really. I don't have any. You said there was bruising on my sister's body that was consistent with a fall from a boat. Have you ruled out the idea that it might have been caused in a struggle?'

'We haven't ruled out anything at all.' Sweet stared straight at him. 'However unpalatable it might be.' Lowering his gaze, Sweet looked over his notes again. 'You contacted me last week to say that you believed your sister's computer had gone missing.'

'That's right. I believe someone came in and took it away. Were there any prints on the cable?'

'Only your sister's.'

'So did you have my sister's fingerprints on record? Or did you recover them from her body?'

'As it happens, we had them on record. She had been arrested for obstruction a couple of years ago, but had been bound over to keep the peace. There was also a charge of criminal damage.'

'Criminal damage to what?'

'To telecommunications equipment.'

'A 5G mast?'

'I believe so. She had some interesting beliefs. But her computer, which might confirm who she had been in contact with, is missing. And you have no idea where that might be?'

'No, why would I? It was me who told you the computer was missing.'

'Indeed you did. You did tell us it was missing.' He looked up and met Eden's eye.

'You think I was doing that to cover my own back?'

'I don't know. Did you?'

'Of course not. You know how easy it was to get into Apple's house. Anyone could have done it. But I think whoever it was didn't get everything they wanted. That's why they came back to search Apple's house again. That's why they kidnapped Finn.'

'Possibly. Moving on,' Sweet said, 'on several occasions recently Miss Molly Hawkins has been a visitor to your sister's house.'

'You've been keeping a very close eye on me.'

'We are looking into the death of a woman, the abduction of her child and suspected drug trafficking. Understandably we are taking this investigation seriously. How well do you know Molly Hawkins?'

'Not well at all.'

'Really?' Raised eyebrows. 'You drink on the beach with her though?'

'She doesn't need an invitation.' He sighed. 'She's not a friend of mine. She was a friend of my sister's. She has been very kind to Finn. He seems to respond to her in a way that he doesn't to me. You think she was involved with whatever happened to my sister?'

'Have you been in contact with her brother, Francis Hawkins, known as Frankie Hawkins?'

'No. I don't know him. We've never met. Can you share why you are concerned about Frankie Hawkins? What has he done?'

Sweet ignored the question, lifted one sheet of paper and put it underneath another one. 'OK, then. Your sister owned a 2001 green Toyota Corolla.'

'Yes. It's missing. According to the mechanic I spoke to it was seized as evidence by the police.'

Sweet raised his eyebrows a little further. He turned the piece of paper around so that it was facing Eden. 'Really?'

'Yes,' said Eden. 'I spoke to the guy in the workshop. I informed you of the fact.'

'You did. However, how do you explain this?'

Eden looked down at the form Sweet had put in front of him. It was a document addressed to the owner of Kara's Garage, of Broadmeadow Industrial Estate, Teignmouth, permitting the bearer to carry out the seizure of the Toyota under the Police and Criminal Evidence Act 1984.

It was just as the garage hand had said. His sister's car had been taken away by the police.

'I don't understand,' said Eden.

'Then look at the signature.'

He looked at the paper and this time his heart missed a beat. There it was. *Name: Eden Driscoll.* His rank and warrant number were written beneath it.

'That's totally impossible,' said Eden, looking up.

Thirty-Three

Eden stared at the document Sweet had just given him. 'That's not my handwriting!'

'Curious. Your name though.'

Eden frowned at the photocopy. 'I didn't write that. And I didn't collect the car. It wasn't me. Someone was pretending to be me.'

Sweet's voice was calm and controlled. 'Can you explain why they would do that?'

'Look.' Eden pulled out his wallet and pulled out his driving licence with his signature on it, passing it across the table. 'That's me.'

Sweet held it up and squinted, then handed it back to him.

'First her computer,' said Eden. 'Then the space under the floorboards. And now her car. Somebody is removing evidence.'

Sweet seemed to spend a little time thinking. 'Yes. The question is who?' And he looked at Eden and smiled.

'Finn's mother was smuggling drugs?' Bisi looked horrified.

Eden took a while to respond. He was still thinking it all

through. The thing that worried him most was the unidentified deposit into his sister's account.

'Possibly,' he said eventually. 'It seems to be what the police think.'

'Why did she do it? Was she desperate for money?'

It was early afternoon and the rain had given way to a muggy afternoon. Bisi and Eden were on the beach by the house. Bisi had come to find out how things were going and found Eden sitting outside the house on the gunnels of a boat that lay lopsidedly on the beach.

'She certainly had bills to pay.'

'But – smuggling drugs? And with a child.'

'I don't believe it. I don't think she would be involved in anything like that.'

'But the police think otherwise,' said Bisi.

Sitting there, Eden noticed for the first time that the trawler tied up at the side of the quay was called *Sheena*. It had a blue hull with a red cabin, just like in the drawing. He smiled.

'What a shitshow,' Bisi said.

'There's something else you need to know.' A tern bobbed on the tide.

'What?'

'It's possible that they think I'm involved somehow, too.'

Bisi frowned at him. 'But you're not, are you? Tell me you're not.'

'No. Of course I'm not. But it's possible that someone wants to make it look like I am.'

She looked at him, alarmed. 'They want to make it look like you are?'

He thought about the person who had given his name when they picked up Apple's car. 'From what people have told me, my sister felt the world was out to get her. Same as my father.'

'And you think the world is out to get you?'

'No. I think someone may be trying to muddy the waters around what really happened with my sister, though. Somebody used my name to collect Apple's car from the garage. The car has disappeared. It makes it look like I was trying to destroy evidence.'

'Holy shit,' muttered Bisi.

'You look worried.'

'Is it hot?' she said. 'I'm sweating like a dog. Shall we get a drink?'

Having made it to the walkway at the top of the beach, she sat down at one of the tables outside The Ship Inn. 'Coke,' she said. 'Diet.'

At the bar, an elderly man with an even more elderly dog was nursing a pint. Sitting on the window seat, a man was holding a copy of the local paper, the *Express and Echo*. The headline was 'Dead Sea Creatures Wash Up on Beach'.

Eden returned with a glass of sparkling water for himself and a Diet Coke for Bisi.

'This is a difficult situation,' Bisi said, picking up the Coke. 'There are a lot of red flags. You have to understand that my only responsibility is to Finn, right?' She sucked at the straw and then put the glass down on the table. 'If this blows up into something bad, if there's a hint that they suspect you're involved in drug smuggling – not even that but that someone is trying to get at you in some way, threaten you or implicate you in some kind of criminality – then you know I've no choice but to take him away and put him back into care?'

'And that would mean him moving out of the area?'

'Out-of-county? I'm afraid so. We're struggling with places for boys of his age.'

'I'm just not the ideal person for this situation. I'm cocking up at work because I'm down here, not paying attention to my own life.'

She stared at him. 'Don't be so self-centred. You're a relative. You have an income. Believe me, that makes you ideal.'

'I just can't see how I fit Finn into my life.' He paused. 'Which is, I suppose, self-centred, isn't it?' He looked at the light beneath the cloud and the way the wind made little waves on the water. 'He doesn't even like me.'

'He's angry that you're there instead of his mum. And he hasn't yet found a way to tell you how grateful he is that you are.'

He thought about the two of them sitting on the stairs last night. He was silent for a while, before he said, 'Ouch.'

'Arsehole,' she said.

'So, what? I stay here until we know what's best for Finn?'

'If you want to do the right thing, yes. Absolutely.'

'And if the police find that my sister was involved in drugs, somehow . . . ?'

'That isn't a problem. The problem is if they think that you were involved. You are his chance at some stability. And he deserves that.'

Eden thought for a while. 'I'm not involved, obviously.'

'As long as they believe that, then we're fine,' Bisi said. 'But as I already told you, I can't let Finn stay with you if there's any risk to him. Or if they suspect you're involved in anything illegal.'

Eden thought some more. 'I'm not. I promise. Though I may need a little time to prove to them that's the case,' he said.

'You will find that time is quite a scarce commodity when you're looking after a child.'

'So I am discovering.'

'On that particular point, don't forget. School pick-up in,' she checked the screen of her phone, 'just over an hour.'

* * *

He had just over an hour. There was something he needed to do. If he took his car, he would be followed, so he walked instead.

Thirty-Four

Eden set off using his phone to navigate. He returned to the road at the back of the house and headed parallel to the river until he found a smaller pedestrianised street that took him to the docks. There was a service road that ran along the top of the quays, with a walkway alongside it. He walked past the empty docks, past the large blue warehouses. The place seemed quiet.

Further along, the docks gave way to a less formal quayside. Small sailing boats were piled alongside each other; there was a lock-up full of kayaks. A couple of camper vans were parked by the edge, looking out over the estuary. A woman who looked to be in her seventies was sitting in a folding chair next to one of them, doing a crossword.

'Can I walk up the river this way?'

'At this tide, you can,' she answered. 'There are steps down to the riverbank at the end of the quay. Walk along the shoreline and there's a tunnel under the bridge a little further along. Just be careful of the tide coming back in, otherwise you'll end up stuck.'

He thanked her and discovered she was right. There were

concrete steps at the end which led down to the tidal riverbed. Setting off over the mussel shells, stones, fragments of pottery and mud, he realised he should have worn more suitable shoes. This terrain was going to trash his trainers.

Crows pecked at something dark at the high tide line. He walked on, hopping across stones over a small stream that emerged from a dark outflow in the red stone river wall. Sure enough, just as the woman had told him, there was a stone arch under the shore end of the road bridge. He made his way through it and walked on, past a small headland, learning to keep to the stonier ground. The mud was colloidal, glutinous. It looked firmer than it was and his shoes sank deep into it.

As he rounded the corner he saw the next promontory, a low-lying, grassy headland crammed with boats, all hauled out of the water onto the hard standing.

Molly had said her boatyard was further up the river. This, he guessed, must be it. He checked his watch. It was after a quarter past two. He would need to be at school soon.

He walked on a little way to be sure of himself. Sure enough, by the time he'd tramped on a little he could make out a sign: *Hawkins Marine. M&F Hawkins. Boat Repairs.*

The boatyard was further than he had calculated and the uneven shore made the going slower than he had hoped. By the time he got close, it was almost time to turn back. But he had made it this far.

The hard standing had been shored up against erosion with rubble. He clambered over uneven bricks and rocks until he made it up to the top of the slope, where motor boats were lined up against each other, some on trailers, others on cradles, or propped upright with timbers. The place seemed deserted at first, but he could hear the sound of a radio.

'Hello?'

Nobody answered. Eden walked on, and, rounding the prow of a cabin cruiser, he saw the silhouetted outline of a man sitting in a battered Toyota Hilux pickup, door open.

'Hello,' he called again.

The man in the truck didn't hear him until he was close; he leaned across to the radio and switched down Ariana Grande.

'I'm looking for Frankie Hawkins,' said Eden when he was close enough.

The man had deep-set eyes, sun-leathered skin and thick dark hair swept back from his forehead. He looked Eden up and down and made a show of pretending not to recognise the name. 'Not here,' said the man. He turned the music back up.

'When you see Frankie, can you ask him a question for me?'

'What question?'

'Just over a week ago he borrowed his sister's Plymouth Pilot. He must have gone quite a way in it because he had to refill the diesel tank. So I'm guessing he probably took it out to sea.'

The man flicked a lighter. 'I don't know what the fuck you're on about, bud.'

'Will you ask him which night of the week that was. Was it on the Friday?'

There was a long pause. 'If I see him,' said the man.

'OK. Thank you.'

Eden turned to go. 'Bud? What did you say your name was?' the man called.

'Eden Driscoll. I'm Apple's brother,' he called. 'See you, Frankie.'

It was a guess, that the man he had been talking to was Molly's brother, but he reckoned a good one. The man didn't contradict him, and he hadn't contradicted him that the boat had been taken out at night, either.

Eden headed back the way he had come. Before he disappeared among the boats, he looked back. The man in the truck had turned in his seat and was watching him.

He was going to be late, so Eden picked up his pace, moving faster over the uneven shoreline, splashing his trousers as he walked.

Startled, a heron flapped into the air just ahead. Eden made the mistake of looking up just as the stones gave way to a patch of mud. His left leg sank into it, catching his foot so he fell forward, tumbling onto the stones beyond.

'Bollocks.'

The mud had sucked the running shoe right off his foot. His sock was brown and sodden.

'Bollocks bollocks bollocks.'

He retrieved the shoe, wiped the worst of the mud from it and then replaced it on his foot, setting off again, more carefully this time, one foot soggy with mud, trying to make up for lost time.

Finally, he made it back to the short tunnel that ran under the bridge. He slowed in the cool dark air to catch his breath. Ahead were the docks and the steps he had come down twenty minutes earlier.

He was just emerging into the sunlight when the man who had been hiding around the corner hit him hard in the belly with a large wooden stick.

Eden fell backwards into the tunnel, doubling up, winded. He tried to shout for help but there was no breath in him.

Thirty-Five

Before Eden could figure out what had happened, the man had pressed the thick stick he had knocked him over with against his neck, pinning him down. It was a piece of builder's timber, Eden realised; wide and heavy. It would take a strong man to swing it with that force. The weight of it was choking him.

Eden reached a hand up to try to grab the wood and the man pressed it down once as a warning. One sharp jab and he would do serious damage to Eden's throat and his neck.

'Lie still,' the man said, his voice gruff.

Eden squinted up, trying to see who it was who had attacked him. He was large, dressed in black motorbike leathers, and was wearing a navy blue balaclava.

'Shoes,' ordered the man.

'What?' Choked by the weight of the wood on his neck, Eden's voice emerged as a croak.

'You heard what I said. Give me your shoes.'

Eden looked down. 'My trainers?'

The wood twitched a second time.

Cautiously, Eden bent a knee, raised a foot to where he could reach it, unlaced his shoe and held it up. The man grabbed it with his free hand and dropped it onto the ground beside Eden.

'Other one.'

'Oh, for God's sake.' Eden repeated the action. When both shoes were off, the man relaxed the stick and Eden could move his head finally.

Before he understood what was going on, the man had bent down, picked up both shoes and thrown them, one at a time, as far as he could. One arced up, landed in mud with a dead squelch. The other made it to the other side of the low-water line, landing in the shallows with a splash.

'Now fuck off!' shouted the man. 'Go back home to London. Leave us alone. You're not welcome here.'

He threw down the piece of timber and trotted past Eden, back down into the tunnel Eden had just emerged from.

Eden jumped up to head after him and realised exactly why the man had stolen the shoes. He took a few paces across the stones and yelped. There was no way he could chase after anyone on this rocky ground.

He moved slowly, each footstep painful.

By the time he emerged from the other side of the tunnel, the man in the balaclava had long disappeared.

It took almost ten minutes to retrace his route through the tunnel and then make it back to the quayside, carefully picking his way across the uneven ground. When Eden got to the top of the steps he sat down, took off his muddy socks and examined his feet. His right foot was bleeding from where glass – or a broken mussel shell – had pierced it.

The woman doing a crossword by her camper van watched him as he walked past her, leaving damp footprints on the tarmac. He paused. 'Did you see a man in motorbike gear walk by?'

The woman shook her head and looked back down at her crossword.

When he finally made it to the school, Jackie was at the main doors, beckoning him inside. 'Oh, God.' She raised her hand to her mouth. 'What happened to you? That wasn't Pam getting her own back, was it?'

'Stupid. I tripped. Down on the beach.' His voice sounded sandpapery still.

'You tripped?' She sounded sceptical. 'How?'

'Never mind. Where's Finn?'

He had managed to go home and wash his wounded foot and change before heading to the car but there was a large bruise on his neck where his assailant had jammed the wood, and the skin there was scratched and raw. His hands were covered in cuts from where he had fallen.

'He's with Miss Killick.' Jackie pointed down the corridor.

In the classroom, Finn was crouched over a desk, drawing. Miss Killick was at another table, looking through a pile of worksheets.

'I'm sorry,' he said. 'I've kept you late.'

'It's fine,' she said. 'Honestly.' After what had happened with Finn, she was not going to complain about his being late. She looked up and saw the state of him. 'Are you OK, Mr Driscoll?'

'I fell. On the beach. It was stupid.'

Finn looked at him, eyes wide. He must look scary to the boy, he realised.

'Honestly. Looks worse than it is,' he said, trying to make his voice sound normal.

'It's OK,' said Miss Killick nervously, picking up her work bag. 'Try not to make a habit of it.'

* * *

That night, again, Eden struggled to put Finn to bed, attempting to read from the books he'd bought.

'Why don't you make up a story?' complained Finn. 'That's what Mum used to do.'

'I don't know how to make up stories,' said Eden, trying to return to the book.

'Tell me a real story, then.'

'I can't.'

'Please,' the boy whined.

'What do you mean, a real story?'

'Like you said about you and Mum living in a van.'

Eden thought for a bit. He took a breath. 'OK. I could try.' The boy looked exhausted. Finn needed sleep. Eden wondered where he should start and decided on the thing that he had always hated most about his father. 'Our dad wanted our family to be special.'

'What do you mean, special?'

'These days I realise you would call it coercive control.'

'What's that?'

'Ssh. Try to close your eyes and listen.'

'I can't close my eyes. They keep wanting to stay open,' said the boy.

'Try at least.' Eden closed his own eyes and saw the inside of the white van they had lived in that time they went island hopping in Greece. He took a breath.

'The thing about our dad was he thought he was better than everyone else and wanted us to go along with that. I don't remember when we left England. I was too young. It was like he was always looking for something but didn't really know what it was. We travelled around everywhere. We never seemed to have much money. Sometimes Mum and Dad did jobs, like fruit picking or working on camp sites. It was never for very long. Dad always had an argument with somebody and then we had to go. I don't know how Mum put up with it.'

He realised he wasn't telling a story, but Finn seemed to be listening.

'So we lived in a van for years. Different vans. He bought and sold them. Dad always wanted to find a place where he could set up a commune. It would be his community. He really liked telling other people how they should live and what they should do. He always had some big idea. Some big plan. Once, we were on this little island in Greece. I must have been around twelve, thirteen. Dad found an abandoned farmhouse and started doing it up. He said it was a really special place with spiritual energy. We were going to make it our home.'

He saw the farmhouse in his head. The rich honey-coloured stone. The heavy lintels above the doors and windows. The terracotta tiles. It had been beautiful, he realised now.

'Mum was really happy at first, I suppose, because she was tired of always being on the move. The farmhouse was just stone walls really, and a roof that leaked when it rained, and it had scorpions in it, I remember, but it was nice to live in a real house for a change. And then a young American woman joined us. She was into yoga and we all started to do yoga in the field every morning.'

Eden opened his eyes; Finn's were still open. He showed no sign of going to sleep.

'The American girl was pretty nice. She didn't seem to be so in awe of Dad. I can't remember her name. She was younger than Mum. Mum used to complain that she walked around everywhere in her underwear, but Dad didn't mind. Apple really liked her too. I don't suppose she was much older than Apple and I think she liked having another woman around, apart from Mum. Dad dreamed up these big plans to open a yoga retreat. It was kind of the happiest we had ever been, I think. Mum cooked these big suppers and Dad made a table outside from an old door and some trestles. We used to sit and eat dinner together in the old farmyard as the sun went down and the stars came out.'

Finn was listening to everything.

'I think Dad saw this woman as the start of his big community. It was like he thought he could absorb her into the family. He started taking over the yoga, telling her what to do, and you could tell he was annoying her, but he didn't seem to notice. And then one night we were all sitting around that table – he made her sit next to him at one end – and I remember the American girl got up suddenly and slapped Dad right in the face. I never knew what happened. She called him creepy, out loud, in front of all of us. I was shocked. We all were. Nobody had ever stood up to Dad like that.'

Eden went quiet, trying to remember. A church bell was ringing ten o'clock somewhere. He didn't know what had happened between the American and their dad, but he could guess.

'What happened next?'

'Ssh. Close your eyes. In the morning the American woman was gone. I don't know if Dad threw her out or whether she just left. But that was the end of his plans for setting up a yoga retreat, and it was the end of the farm too. I think my mum was pleased she was gone, but that meant it was just us again and we were alone. I was really sad about it. Apple was too. I think. And right after that, a bunch of local people came up with sticks – one had an axe – and they started breaking up everything we had done to the place. They said we had no right to be there on the farm. They smashed our van's windows too. It was really scary. Apple and I ran off into the olive trees and watched it all happening. Dad always reckoned the American had told the villagers to throw us out. I don't know if that's true but he blamed her. Called her a crazy, vindictive cow. But we drove straight out of there and caught a ferry off the island the next morning. Dad said he'd been mistaken about the place. It didn't have the right energy at all.'

Finn's eyes were still shining in the darkness.

'I'm going to go downstairs now,' said Eden.

'Will you tell me more?'

'Maybe another time.' Eden didn't think about those times much. He had never talked about it with anyone. He had never wanted to.

Downstairs, there was another message from Sammy: 'Call me.'

It would be something about Ronan Pan, he thought. But he was wrong.

'Might be nothing,' said Sammy, when he called back. 'A letter arrived for you at work. A bit of an odd one. Normally I'd think nothing of it, but, given the circumstances . . . It took a few days to get to your desk because there were only three lines on the envelope. It was addressed to *Eden Driscoll, The Metropolitan Police, London.*'

Thirty-Six

'Handwritten address. Female hand, by the look. "Urgent" written on it in big letters. I can forward it if you like.'

'Can you open it?'

'Haven't got it now. It's on my desk at work. Should have brought it home, but I'm not in my office until later. Can it wait?'

It was the same address his sister had used when she wrote to him before, when their mother was ill. So she had been trying to get in touch with him before she had disappeared.

'Can you open it and photograph it, as soon as you can? Send it on to me?' In London he didn't drink during the week, but here he was, rooting around in the kitchen for a wine glass. 'Know what, Sammy? Someone assaulted me today. Out of the blue. Told me to get out of Dodge, basically.'

'Jesus. Were you hurt?'

'No. Not really. A bruise, that's all. And I lost a pair of trainers.' Eden put the phone down and unscrewed the cap off a bottle of red and picked up the phone again.

'What did the local police say?'

'Haven't told them. It was hardly worth it,' said Eden. 'Just a few scratches.'

'Really?' He could hear the tone of reproach in Sammy's voice. 'What's going on that someone wants to take a pop at you?'

'Local police are starting to think my sister's death isn't so straightforward. I don't know. I think maybe it's stirring things up a bit around here.'

'They're thinking your sister's death is suspicious now? God. I'm sorry,' said Sammy. 'And you haven't reported the assault, Eden? Don't you think it might be a teensy bit relevant?'

There were lights shining on the water outside. Eden went to the back door to look out. 'I don't think it was anything, honestly. Thing is, if I tell the police, the social worker will find out that someone attacked me. I'm supposed to be the one keeping my nephew safe. If they think I'm attracting trouble, they'll have to take him away. And right now I seem to be all he has got.'

'There was I, thinking you didn't want to look after the boy anyway.'

It was almost a high tide. A trawler had tied up on the end of the stone quay. It was the one with the red cabin.

'Yeah. Well,' said Eden.

'Tell the police, Eden. Just do it.'

'I just wanted to think it through, I suppose.'

'Well, you know what to do now, don't you? First thing in the morning, you need to call them up and tell them that somebody jumped you. You have to. The more information they have, the better.'

'Right,' Eden said and he took a swig of the wine, watching a man working on the trawler outside. 'Of course I will. First thing.'

* * *

But he didn't. At a quarter to eight in the morning, Eden realised he needed ingredients for Finn's lunchbox, so he called upstairs, 'Finn? I need to go out to the shops for two minutes. Will you be OK?'

The local Co-Op opened early but seemed full by the time Eden got there. He dashed around filling a hand basket with bread, crisps, cheese and bananas and was in the queue when he realised he had forgotten the chocolate bars. He abandoned his place in the queue to find that a man in a red mobility scooter was looking through the newspapers, blocking the confectionary aisle. There was no easy way of trying to squeeze past, so Eden went down the next aisle to approach from the other end, but by the time he had got there, the mobility scooter had travelled down to that end, blocking that way instead. 'Could I get through, please? I'm in a hurry.'

By the time Eden had reached the chocolate bar multi-packs the checkout queue had grown and he had to stand in line while people fussed over which lottery tickets to buy. He had told Finn he would just be two minutes. To pass the time, he picked up a local paper to look through – the same one the man had been reading in the pub yesterday. For a second day, the lead story was about the thousands of dead crabs and starfish washing up on a beach near by. One expert blamed climate change. Another blamed pollution.

'Woman killed in hit-and-run', said the headline at the bottom of the page. He browsed through the paper, and was meaning to put it back as the queue moved, but he still had it in his hands when he finally made it to the till, so, rather than abandon the queue again to put it back, he added it to his shopping.

Heading home, he walked briskly, only partly because he

needed to get Finn dressed and fed – and make up the lunch-box. He had left Finn on his own; what he had promised would be two minutes had become fifteen.

Breaking into a run, he jumped off the thin pavement to avoid a woman with a buggy, and a cyclist who had to brake hard to avoid him called him an idiot.

The bin lorry had parked across the top of the narrow street that led down to his sister's house. He tried to nip between it and the wall, but a man was coming towards him dragging a large green bin. Eden had no choice but to back up until he had passed. When the way was clear, he ran on down the narrow street and finally skidded left into the road that led to the back of the house.

He crashed in through the back door. The house was quiet.

'Finn?' he yelled.

Finn was in the front room, dressed, sitting at the dining table, calmly eating a bowl of muesli.

Returning to the kitchen, Eden put the kettle on for coffee and started making sandwiches with vegan cheese slices.

He made the coffee and joined Finn at the table with the newspaper he had just bought. The main photograph was of pinky orange starfish, lifeless on red sand.

'Is there going to be a funeral for Mum?' Finn asked.

Eden said, 'Yes. Of course. But it will be a few days before we can plan that. Why?'

'What are you supposed to do?'

Eden put the newspaper down again.

'Well. People who loved your mum talk a little about her and if she had favourite songs, you sing them. Did she have favourite songs?'

'She liked "Barbie Dreams" by Nicki Minaj.'

'Did she? OK,' said Eden.

'We used to sing it in the kitchen.' Finn got up and said, 'Can we go to school now?'

'Put your bowl and your glass in the sink first, please.'

Finn ignored him and went to pick up his bag.

'Didn't your mum make you put your dirty dishes in the sink?'

'Yes, but you're not my mum.'

'Come on, then,' Eden said, giving up. He went to check he had locked the back door, then returned to the front room and opened the door. 'Well?'

Finn was standing at the table looking at the local newspaper. 'That's her,' he said.

'Come on,' Eden said again, irritated.

Finn was still looking at the newspaper, pointing at a photograph on the front page. 'Is she dead?'

'Yes. She was hit by a car. The driver drove away without helping her.' Eden had read the article. A tragic hit-and-run on a quiet country lane. 'Put it down, please. We need to get to school.'

They walked along the boardwalk, past the flats that had been built on the site of the boatyard, along to the beach where people queued to catch the ferry. The car park was at the end of the small headland, next to the beach and the narrow neck of the estuary.

It was only when he was taking out the keys that Eden paused. 'What did you mean,' he asked, '"That's her"?'

Finn looked at him and said in a matter-of-fact voice, 'The woman who picked me up from school.'

Thirty-Seven

'Tell the sergeant what you said to me earlier,' said Eden. He held up the copy of the *Express and Echo*.

'It's the woman,' said Finn. 'There in the newspaper.'

Eden had called the school to tell them they would be in later.

'Are you absolutely sure about this?' Sweet asked. 'Take another look.'

Along with a copy of the picture that had been published in the newspaper, Sweet had brought two other photos of the dead woman. He laid them on the living-room table. One looked as if it had been culled from social media – a woman at a dining table with friends on either side – the other from a posed group, maybe removed from a picture frame found at the woman's house.

Finn nodded. 'Yes.'

'You didn't see her for very long,' Eden reminded him.

'But it is her,' insisted Finn. He looked up at Eden. 'Is she dead too?'

Eden answered, 'I'm afraid it looks very much like it.'

In the newspaper, the woman had been named as Elaine

Pritchard. She was single, thirty-eight years old. Her body had been found in the ditch of a lane close to a village called Combeinteignhead. She had been hit by a speeding vehicle – and what seemed to make it even worse, her body had lain undiscovered for two or three hours.

'We're going to show you pictures of three cars now, Finn,' said Sweet quietly. He pulled out two pictures of cars in driveways. 'Do you remember which one the woman drove you in?'

Police would have gone to the dead woman's house, so they would know which car she drove. One of the photos would be her actual car, Eden guessed.

'That one,' said Finn straight away. He pointed to a silver Hyundai i20. 'It has a cat in the front of it.' He raised his arm and waved it up and down, just like he had done before.

Eden saw the expression on Sweet's face. Finn had picked the right one. So it wasn't just someone who looked a bit like the woman who had abducted him. It was her.

'Was there anything suspicious about the hit-and-run?' Eden asked.

'There you go again,' said Sweet. 'Our job, not yours, my friend.'

'Bit of a coincidence, though,' Eden said. 'Could it have been a motorbike?' He thought of the man in motorbike leathers who had attacked him under the bridge.

'What? Why are you asking a stupid question like that?'

'A motorbike could kill someone.'

'Our job,' repeated Sweet. 'Not yours. What's up with your neck?'

Eden put his hand up and covered it. The bruise was bluer today.

'He fell down on the beach,' said Finn.

'Did he, the silly old fool?' said Sweet.

Finn giggled.

Eden turned to Finn. 'Shall we get you up to school, then? I'll catch you up.'

'Doesn't really look like that Japanese cat brought her much luck,' said Sweet.

'Do you think it was deliberate?'

'Open mind,' said Sweet. 'Bit of a coincidence, though, as you say. Like that nasty bruise on your neck.'

'I tripped on the beach, as Finn told you,' answered Eden.

'As you like.' Sweet pulled his car keys from his pocket. 'I may be a yokel, Eden, but I'm not an idiot. You can tell me what really happened in your own time, I suppose. Have you told the social worker?'

Eden showed him to the door. 'I have to get this boy to school now.'

'Right,' said Sweet. 'Of course you do.'

He dropped Finn at school, then returned home. Bored of his own company, he headed back out for lunch. The small town was full of old pubs. A few doors away from the house he found one called The Jolly Sailor that served food. He scanned the menu for a while and eventually ordered mussels.

A tall woman with dark hair was waiting to be served at the bar. 'Double vodka tonic,' she asked of the girl. Her voice was deep. 'Not so much ice,' scolded the woman.

The girl had her back to the woman now and was pressing the glass up against the bar on the optic when a barman came across and whispered something to the girl.

'What's wrong?' said the woman loudly.

'I'm sorry, Mary,' said the man gently. 'Your husband has asked us not to serve you in here.'

'Oh, for God's sake,' said the woman. 'Long live the patriarchy. You do everything he says, do you?'

The face of the young woman behind the bar was scarlet.

'I'm calling your daughter, Mary,' he said. 'She'll be along to take you home in a minute.'

'I don't want to bloody go home.' The woman turned to leave and caught sight of Eden watching the scene. 'And what the bollocks are you looking at?' she shouted at him as she walked past, leaving the door wide open.

Back at the bar, the barman was telling the young woman, 'It's not your fault. You weren't to know.'

Fifteen minutes later, Eden was eating the mussels when a teenage girl came in, her face flushed. He recognised her as the girl with the dyed blonde braid he had sat opposite on his first night in the town. She walked straight to the bar.

'Sorry she's bothering you,' the girl said to the barman. 'Where is she?'

'She's already gone, lovely,' the barman replied. 'Maybe try The King William. She might have headed up there. I'm sorry for all your trouble.'

'It's OK.' The girl turned to leave the pub and paused, spotting Eden. She frowned, as if trying to remember where she recognised him from.

Eden was wiping his mouth on a napkin, the bowl of shells in front of him, when his phone buzzed. It was an email from Sammy Kadakia: *Here you are. Hope it's useful. And again, so sorry for your loss.* Attached there was a single JPG. Eden opened it.

It showed the envelope:

Constable Eden Driscoll
Metropolitan Police
London

And next to it, the letter. Sammy Kadakia had laid the page on his office desk and photographed it, alongside the envelope.

> Hi baby bro.
> I hope this reaches you ok.

The letter had been written in blue biro in Apple's big, rounded script, on a sheet of lined paper torn from a notebook. He recognised it as the same paper he had taken out of the bin on *Calliope*.

> Not sure where you are these days but guessing you're still in the The Old Bill. I am living in Devon now and have a son called Finn who is 9. He's a sweetheart and reminds me very much of you when you were little.

He was reading a letter from a dead person.

> I'm sorry I have not tried to be in contact much.
> I need to talk to you urgently. If you get this please get in touch.

She had written the address of the little cottage in Teign View Place and signed the letter,

> Apple and Finn x
> PS sorry no email etc. don't trust it. Please please come.
> PS miss you

Thirty-Eight

He sat on the sea wall on the front, watching the waves beneath his feet.

His sister had been trying to get in touch with him. Urgently.

Someone had broken into his sister's house to remove her computer. They had kidnapped a child to learn the whereabouts of something else she had hidden.

Someone didn't want him here. Someone didn't want him looking into whatever it was his sister had been doing, and was making life difficult for the investigation by messing with the evidence. Presumably the same someone who had assaulted him under the bridge. They had threatened him. Told him to go home.

He shouldn't even have been here in Devon in the first place. He stared at his phone for a while before deciding to make the call.

'Hello?' answered a woman's voice. In the background he could hear the familiar hubbub of a police station office, phones and the constant drone of busy voices. He missed it.

'Is that Constable Lisa Ali?' he asked.

'God,' said Lisa. 'Eden bloody Driscoll. I heard about your sister. I couldn't believe it. I'm so sorry.'

'Thanks,' said Eden tersely. 'And did you also hear about Ronan Pan?'

'I did. I wept when I heard they were going to drop the charges. Hasina Hossein trusted you. I think she freaked out that you weren't here.'

That's what he thought too. It didn't make him feel any better.

'And did you know that Ronan Pan made a complaint about me too?' he asked. 'And that he has testimony from a police officer backing him up?'

'What? No, I didn't hear that. Who the fuck?'

The police constable's surprise sounded genuine enough.

'Oh, shitting hell!' exclaimed Lisa. 'You think it was me, don't you? You think it was me who made the complaint?'

He could hear the clattering of keyboards in the background. 'Well? Was it?' he asked her.

'No, it sodding wasn't. I didn't like what you did, but it wasn't me who reported you.'

'I was calling to say it was fine – if you had. Like I told you in the pub after, if that's what you saw, you should have reported it. So, you don't have to pretend it wasn't you—'

'You're not listening, Eden. It wasn't me. Swear on my mother's life.'

He thought for a minute. 'Who, then, if not you?'

'An officer. One of us who was there?' she asked.

'It can't have been anyone else. The only other person who was there was the person Bailey mistook for Ronan Pan, but he was face down all the time.'

In the background of the call he could hear the sound of

laughter now. Police officers laughed all the time at work. You had to or you'd go crazy – so they said.

'But.'

'But what?' asked Eden.

'But it can't have been. They were all the other side of the wall, remember? I was the only one who saw.'

Far out at sea a gannet plunged into the water. 'You sure about that?'

'Yes. You were there too. Think about it.'

Eden replayed the scene. She was right. Eden let that settle for a minute. 'OK. Do you think you can do something for me, then?' he asked. And he thought for a minute, then he told her want he wanted of her.

Finn was waiting at the school gate, bag over one shoulder. When he saw Eden he asked, 'Can I bring a friend home?'

'A friend?' said Eden, pleased to know that Finn had friends. 'Yes, of course. Who is it?'

'His name is Cyrus.'

It took Eden a second. 'Isn't that the boy you bit?'

Finn nodded.

'Really? Are you sure?' asked Eden.

'Yes.'

'OK,' said Eden warily. 'If that's what you really want. Where is he?'

'He's still in there. Can you ask his mum if he can come home with me?'

'Right. OK.'

Eden looked around just in time to see Cyrus's mum, Pamela, arriving in Sweaty Bettys and trainers. Her hair and make-up were perfect. She didn't much look as if she had been exercising. He took a breath and approached her. 'Hello, Pamela.'

She folded her arms in front of her, head tilted slightly to one side. 'What now?'

'Finn just asked me if Cyrus could come around to play with him today.'

'You're kidding me!' exclaimed Pam.

'Yes. I don't know if that's such a good idea after what happened . . .'

Pam looked as puzzled as Eden felt about it. 'Maybe they've got over whatever argument they had. Cyrus can be a very generous boy.'

Eden didn't want to say that it had been Cyrus who had wanted to take Finn's chocolate bar.

'Cyrus,' Pam called. 'Is that right? You want to go and play at Finn's house?'

Eden turned to see Cyrus standing with Finn. Cyrus looked so much bigger than his nephew.

'He's got a new PS5,' explained Cyrus.

Pam looked at Eden, smiling. 'Well, I suppose—'

'It's fine,' said Eden. 'It would be good for Finn.'

''Course it would.'

'I'll pick him up about five, then?' Pam suggested.

'Six, Mum,' said Cyrus.

'Six is fine. I should probably feed them, I suppose,' said Eden, unsure of the protocol. 'I'll give you my address.'

'I know your address. Saw you there the other day, on the beach, when you got the hump with us.' She smiled at Eden. 'Don't worry. That's all water under the bridge now, isn't it? If you're feeding him, Cyrus doesn't like salad. Or peas,' said Pam.

'Right.'

'Anything green, really. Here's my number.' She held out her phone with the screen showing.

'One thing,' he asked as he took down her number. 'Your husband doesn't ride a motorbike, does he?'

Pam's laugh was high and loud. 'God, no. I wouldn't let him.'

'Is that your car?' Cyrus was asking, looking at Eden's Audi. 'Cool.'

Once he'd added Pamela's number to his contacts, Eden messaged her his. He felt awkward; it all felt a little too much like a hook-up. Other parents paused in their chatter, watched them knowingly.

'See you later, Cyrus. Give Mum a kiss.' She leaned down and let Cyrus kiss her on the cheek, then turned and walked down the hill.

While Finn was upstairs, Eden made a coffee and started searching a site called Marine Traffic. He zoomed in on Teignmouth Harbour, trying to figure how much it could show. Right now there was a yacht out at sea, off the Ness, which showed up as an arrow, and a dot in the harbour which seemed to be a boat at anchor. Most of the boats – including *Calliope* – didn't show up at all. He guessed that there had to be something switched on aboard ship before it would show up on the website.

A shadow fell over the screen. 'What are you doing?'

Eden looked up and saw Finn standing next to him; he closed the laptop.

'What's up? Aren't you playing with Cyrus any more?'

'It's OK.' Finn shrugged. 'He doesn't really like me. He just wanted to play on the PS5.'

'I figured,' said Eden. 'Are you disappointed?'

'No. I don't like him very much either, but maybe he'll be nicer to me now.'

'Good thinking. Better than biting.'

'Maybe.'

'You don't mind that he lied?'

Finn shook his head.

'Is he OK playing on his own?'

Finn nodded and sat down on the sofa. 'What are you making for supper?'

'I was thinking maybe peas and a salad.'

Finn giggled. It was the first time he had laughed at something Eden had said. Then he stopped abruptly. 'You're not really going to, though, are you? You should probably make him burger and chips. He'd like that.'

Eden looked at him. 'Do you get bullied a lot at school, Finn?'

'Sometimes.'

'Is it because your mother was a bit different?'

Finn seemed to think about this for a second. 'Yes.'

'What if we just get some sausages and chips from the chippy around the corner?' suggested Eden.

'Yes,' said Finn. 'He'd like that.'

Thirty-Nine

They were sitting eating chips on the beach when Pam came to collect Cyrus. Eden had bought a veggie sausage for Finn.

'Well, this looks nice,' she said. 'Have you two been playing nicely together?'

'Yes,' said Cyrus.

'Yes,' said Finn.

Pam had changed clothes. She was wearing a white pair of gym shorts and pink trainers. Cyrus went inside to fetch his jacket and Finn followed him in.

'He's a very special boy, my Cyrus. He doesn't hold a grudge, even though Finn bit him.'

'Can I ask you something about my sister?' said Eden.

'Poor girl,' said Pam. 'A tragedy, really. We're all so upset.'

'She wasn't very popular at school, was she?'

Pam made a sympathetic face. 'Not when she made all the fuss and tried to stop our kids going into the school. They had to call the police, you know. But we made an effort with her, just like Cyrus did with your boy now. Her heart was in the right place, but she'd always go off on one and start telling us how we should live our lives. Not to speak ill of the dead, but it was a bit annoying. Thing is, it shows no respect for the rest of us, does it?'

'I guess she just believed in different things.'

'Exactly,' said Pam, sounding as if she'd proved some kind of point.

Finn hadn't finished his chips. Eden wrapped them up to take them inside just as Cyrus emerged again.

'I know we got off on the wrong foot, you and me, but you're new round here,' Pam said. 'Maybe me and the girls should take you out one night, show you the lights?'

'I can't really,' Eden excused himself. 'I have to look after Finn.'

'Don't be scared.' She grinned. 'There are things called babysitters, you know. I have a list. I can get you one, if you like. Come on, Cy.' She held out her hand to her child. 'Say thank you.'

With the boy at her side, she walked east down the walkway towards the road. At the corner, by The Ship Inn, she turned and waved.

'Ooh la la,' said a voice behind him. He turned to see Molly there, dressed in her rowing gear, holding a backpack. 'Making friends with the locals, I see.'

'It was a play date,' said Eden.

'I'm sure it was,' observed Molly. She took off her rowing cap and wiped a line of sweat from under her brow with the back of her glove. 'Just finished a beginners' rowing session. You should join us next time.'

He shook his head. 'You're all right.'

She held up the backpack. 'OK if I use your shower? Apple used to let me.'

It had been Molly's fault he had not made it back to school in time. 'What if Apple wasn't in?'

Leaning down, she pulled a towel from the backpack and

put it around her neck. 'Some of the people with the beach huts let me change in there.'

'Did you ever let yourself into Apple's house?'

'Why you asking?'

'You knew where the keys were?'

''Course I did. Round by the drain.'

'And did your brother?'

'Jesus, Eden,' muttered Molly. 'What is this? Are you trying to say my brother was involved in your sister's death?'

'I'm just trying to understand. You knew Apple's boat pretty well, didn't you?'

She frowned. 'I serviced the engine a couple of times. Took her out of the water over winter. Yeah. I knew the yacht pretty well.'

'Yet you never figured out that there was something strange about the boat?'

'What are you on about, Eden?'

'You're a boat expert.'

'What? What is this? What do you mean, strange?'

'We should go inside,' said Eden.

'You're being weird.'

He took Molly's arm and guided her into the living room, lowering his voice. He had been told not to trust her with any information about his sister's death, but he was beginning to tire of doing as he had been told by the local police. It was getting him nowhere and he was starting to wonder if they were the ones he couldn't trust. Molly was loud and intrusive, but she had never shown herself to be dishonest, whatever the police said. 'The police took me in for questioning yesterday. They found traces of drugs on the boat. They think Apple was involved in something.'

'You're kidding!' Molly blurted. He watched her face; her shock looked genuine enough.

'Molly?' Finn's voice came from upstairs.

Eden raised his finger to his lips. Next thing, Finn was down with them, hugging Molly tightly. He loved her unconditionally. He had total confidence in her, even if Eden didn't.

'We'll talk more in a minute,' said Molly.

'What about?' demanded Finn.

'None of your business, nosey,' Molly told him, untangling herself from his grasp. Eden went to put the kettle on to make coffee, and a few moments later heard the noise of the shower starting.

There was a loud bang on the beach door. Finn squealed.

When Eden looked around the kitchen door, he saw Sweet standing on the other side of the glass door, looking thunderous.

Eden leaned down and put his arms around the boy. 'Go upstairs to your room for a minute, Finn.'

'Why?'

'Just do it, please.'

When he finally opened the door to Sweet he said, 'What's wrong with you? You scared the boy.'

'You're holding something back from me, Eden,' Sweet said. 'It's disrespectful. I just wish you'd talk to me about it.'

'About what?'

'What are you involved in, Eden? I'm trying to give you as much rope as I can here.'

'I don't understand.'

Sweet glared. 'Just had a scene of crime report back from the killing of Elaine Pritchard. They found traces of car paint in the hedge and on her body and it was an easy one to match apparently. Not a very common car.'

Eden suddenly knew what was coming.

Sweet continued, 'Green Toyota Corolla dated between 1997 and 2002.'

Eden said it: 'My sister's car.'

'Which was signed for in your name. We're going to need to question you again now, because frankly, none of this looks good for you.'

The room suddenly felt darker. 'Someone is trying to stitch me up, Mike,' said Eden.

Sweet nodded. 'Maybe. Or maybe not. But it would really, really help if you were being more honest with me.'

'You don't actually believe any of this, do you?'

'Well, if there is someone out there trying to make you look bad, it looks like they're doing a pretty good job of it.'

Which was just when Molly Hawkins clattered down the stairs, hair wet, with just a towel around her, saying, 'What's wrong?'

'Oh, for God's sake,' muttered Sweet, looking her up and down. 'And you're doing a pretty good job of it yourself.'

Forty

'I'm in trouble, Molly,' said Eden when Sweet had gone. 'I think someone's trying to frame me and if I end up a suspect, they'll take Finn away from me. That's why I have to know what happened the night my sister disappeared.'

Sweet had gone and the two of them were sitting together on the red sand down on the beach between the quays.

Molly's voice was disbelieving. 'You sound like your sister, thinking the world was out to get her.'

'But it did get her.'

'Besides, why would anybody be trying to frame you?'

'I don't know.'

'OK,' said Molly slowly. 'So?'

Eden lowered his voice. 'I'm pretty sure the police think my sister was caught up in something to do with smuggling drugs. They found traces of drugs on the boat, and a load of money just turned up in my sister's bank account.' Still watching her carefully, he told her about the green Toyota, and how his name had been used to make the car disappear. 'And I think they suspect your brother was involved somehow, too.'

'Frankie? Fuck's sake. That's why you were asking about him? You think that's true?'

'I don't know.'

'They're always trying to put something on him.'

'But is it possible?'

'No. I mean. Yes, but . . .' Molly squinted into the low sun. 'He's always up to some shit, but even if he's a knob, he liked your sister. He'd never do nothing to hurt her.'

Eden thought for a while. There was someone on the trawler that was named after Sheena, moored at the far side of the quay. Eden recognised him as the man with straw-coloured hair he had seen on the day he arrived. That must be Jackie's husband.

'Something else,' he said.

'Oh, God. What?'

'Somebody attacked me yesterday. Came at me with a sodding great lump of wood.'

'Jesus, Eden. Why?'

'I don't know. At least . . .' I'm not sure I know. At first I thought it was because they were trying to scare me. But I wonder if it's the opposite. If they actually want me to go running to the police.'

She looked at him, puzzled. 'And you didn't? Why didn't you?'

'Because if I tell the police, they'll tell Bisi. And if Bisi thinks I'm a target – for whatever reason – they'll have to take Finn away from me.'

'Oh, Jesus, Eden. Why would they want that?'

'I don't know. I can't figure it out. Maybe because if I don't get custody of Finn then there's no point me being here. Maybe to stop me sticking my nose into Apple's business. Either way, someone doesn't want me around.'

Molly was watching the man on the trawler, too. When he looked up, she gave him a wave. He waved back.

'You know him? Who's that?'

'Graeme. He does lobster pots. Stinky old job. You know him?'

'I know his wife.'

''Course you do. You been here five minutes and you know all the ladies.'

Eden ignored the remark. 'Stinky job?'

'Best way to catch them is old fish. They use the stuff the other trawlers chuck away. Mostly smooth-hound, round here. Best if it's gone off a bit. Stick it in a barrel full of brine for a couple of days and it'll stink to high hell.'

'What about your boat? You reckon your brother took it out to sea. Could he have been out at sea in it the night my sister disappeared?'

Her mouth dropped open. 'Oh, Jesus, Eden. This is all bollocks. I bawled him out about taking out the Plymouth Pilot without my permission. He said he was just having a bit of fun. He's an arsehole, but he's harmless, Eden. It has to be bollocks.'

'I know. It may be. But if I don't find out what happened, I think they'll take Finn away.'

'Just, please, don't go dragging my brother into this.'

'I'm sorry. But I think he is involved.'

'Fuck. He's stupid, I know . . .'

'I wanted to ask, does he wear motorcycle leathers?'

'No! What are you asking that for?'

'OK. Can you arrange for me to talk to him?'

'Why? You're really bugging me now, Eden.'

'Because he clearly doesn't tell you everything he's up to, does he? Maybe if I speak to him and explain how serious my situation is, he'll tell me what he was doing with your boat. If you don't think he's involved in anything shady, let him rule himself out.'

She shrugged. 'If it'll shut you up thinking he's involved in all this, I can ask.'

Eden pulled out his phone and showed her the photograph of the letter from Apple.

She took it from his hand and stared. 'She sent you this? "I need to talk to you urgently." What's that about?'

'I don't know. It only just arrived in London. She had something on her mind though. Do you have any idea why she wanted to talk to me?'

She shook her head slowly. 'When did she post this?'

'I don't know. There was no date and the Post Office don't postmark stuff any more.'

'Jesus.'

'Another thing.'

'What now? I didn't realise this was a grilling, Eden.'

'Did you ever see her camera?'

'Oh, yeah. Stupid old thing. She didn't have one on her phone so she had one of those old-fashioned ones with a card in the side. Why?'

'Because I can't find it anywhere.' Eden thought of the space where Apple had hidden things under the bedroom floor and wondered if it had been there – and if it had been, why she would have wanted to hide it. What had she seen? 'Something else I wanted to ask you about.'

'I thought you were done.'

'I was looking at that app that shows where boats are.'

'Marine Traffic?'

'Could we check it to see if your boat went out that night?'

Molly shook her head. 'No. The Pilot won't show up on that. It doesn't have AIS.'

240

'And you don't have to have it on a boat?'

'Not if it's a pleasure boat.'

'A pleasure boat? That sounds very Nineteenth Century. So. My sister didn't have to have this kit on her boat?'

'No. But she did. Nearly all yachts do unless the owners are stupid.' She took a pack of tobacco from her backpack. 'The sea is a dangerous place. It's useful that people know where you are.'

'Apparently, there's a way you can see the data from the night my sister went missing.'

'If you pay, yes. There are companies that store the data, if you know what to ask them.'

'So if we look at it, we would be able to track *Calliope* on the night my sister disappeared? And see if any other boats were out there?'

She thought for a while. 'OK. I can do that.'

'Can you?'

'For the same reasons as you. Most of all, I want Finn to be OK.' She had put a cigarette paper on her thigh and was filling it with tobacco.

He considered for a minute and then decided that he didn't have much option other than to trust her. 'What about this? There was a note in the waste-paper basket on *Calliope*.' He took out his phone and scrolled until he found a photo of the scrap of paper that he'd given to Sweet, then pinched in. '15W E14,' he said. He watched her eyes carefully as he handed her the phone, hoping to learn something from her reaction. 'Is it a location? Does it mean anything to you? Would you know where that is?'

Molly finished making the cigarette. She stared at the screen for a while, then burst out laughing. She laughed with her chest shaking, until she had to wipe tears away with the back of her hand.

'What?'

Fighting for breath, she said, 'Call yourself a copper?'

'Sorry?'

She managed to finally control her breathing. '15 watts. E14 screw.'

'I don't—'

'A light bulb. Probably for her fridge. You know? The light is broken on it.'

'Oh,' said Eden, deflated. 'Right.'

Molly was laughing again. 'You're such an idiot.' She stopped when she saw he wasn't joining in. 'I'm sorry. Now I've offended you.'

'No.' He shook his head, embarrassed. 'It's fine.'

She dropped her voice again. 'I know you're trying to find out something that explains why Apple went missing. It's just too crazy. It sounds like the mad stuff she used to go on about.'

The river was busy. A sailing dinghy was tacking across the water. The harbourmaster's launch sped past on its way inland.

'OK. I was wrong about the bulb, but I'm not wrong about someone pretending to be me picking up the car. Why would somebody attack me on the shore by the tunnel?'

Molly stood up. 'I just find it so hard to believe. What the hell was your sister doing with drugs on the boat? She would never, ever mess with people like that.'

'Well . . . I think there might be an explanation for that.'

'You're kidding me . . .'

'Long story,' said Eden.

'So Sweet was right? You do know something?' She stood looking at him, curious, then pulled out a lighter and lit her thin cigarette.

'I'll tell you about it some time. I promise,' he said.

Forty-One

'Has Molly gone?' asked Finn, disappointed.

'I'm afraid so.'

'Is it time for bed?'

'Yes.'

'Are you going to tell me another story tonight?'

'Really?' Eden was exhausted. All he wanted to do was sit downstairs and watch some box set on his laptop, maybe open a can of beer.

Finn went upstairs and brushed his teeth. 'I'm ready,' he called.

Reluctantly, Eden went upstairs and sat on the edge of his nephew's bed again.

'A story. What do you want me to talk to you about?'

'Anything.'

'I don't know where to begin,' said Eden.

'What happened after you had to leave that island?'

'The island we were chased away from?'

'Yes.'

'Didn't your mum ever tell you about all this?'

'No. She just told me that something bad had gone on, that's all. She never said what.'

'She didn't say it was all my fault?'

'What was all your fault?'

Eden smiled. 'Never mind. Did she tell you how we got *Calliope*?'

Finn shook his head on the pillow.

'OK. That was after the island. After we lost the farm, Mum was really down, really depressed that we had nowhere permanent to live. She stopped cooking and cleaning. Apple and I had to do everything. I guess she was sick of us just moving all the time.'

Eden had always resented his mother for not protecting Apple and him from their father. For the first time he was starting to realise she had been the first of his victims. He ground people down.

'So Dad persuaded her to write to her mother and ask her for some money. Your great-grandmother. She was quite well-off. She's dead now.'

Finn curled up next to Eden.

'Your great-grandmother hated our dad. She thought he had stolen her daughter away from her. But she thought if she gave Mum some money it might help her get her own life, so she sent her ten thousand pounds, which was like a fortune in those days.

'We were still in Greece. Mum had her heart set on some nice old house in one of those harbour towns. She found one she liked on the island we had run away to. It was a place called Mykonos.'

'Mykonos,' murmured Finn.

'She took us to see it. It had three floors and a roof you could sit on and see the port. Me and Apple would have our own rooms. Using the money Gran had sent us, she was going to get a mortgage and then get a job to pay off the rest. It was going to be great. But Dad insisted it was going to cost too much, and he could persuade the owner to lower the price, so he disappeared to have a drink with him down in the town.

'We were camped up in the van. I remember he didn't come back that evening. Me and Apple went to sleep, all excited because we were going to get a house to live in.

'Only next morning there was this really weird atmosphere. Me and Apple couldn't work out what was wrong. Apple asked Dad, "So, can we go and see the house, then?" And Dad grinned and told her, "No. Because we're going to live somewhere much better." And we couldn't work out why our mum wasn't as excited as he was. Then he said, "We're going to live on a boat." Instead of getting a mortgage on the house, which he said we could never really afford, he had spent all our mum's money on a yacht. He'd found someone down at the port who was selling it and apparently it was a real bargain. And that was *Calliope*.

'It was mad. He didn't really know how to sail or anything. None of us did.'

He looked down. Finn had closed his eyes. Eden started to stand, but Finn said, 'Go on,' without opening them.

Eden sat back down again. 'Dad said the van was no good anyway. It was old and always breaking down, plus it was all smashed up now too. So we started living on the boat. I hated it – so did our mum. But Dad liked it and it turned out Apple did too. We sailed all over the Mediterranean. It sounds great, but it wasn't. It was small, cramped and hot. He bought a big old army tent, and sometimes we lived in that too, close to whatever place we were moored in. The problem was, one thing led to another. Boats are expensive to keep. You have to maintain all the gear. You have to pay mooring fees, if you stay in a proper port, anyhow. I think Dad thought having a boat would mean freedom. I'm not sure it did. Mum was having to take cleaning jobs in some of the places we stayed. Dad kept asking her to ask Gran for more money.

'One day, we were staying in this place in Portugal. It was called Tavira. We were up in this campsite above the port, staying in our tent. I loved the campsites. There were sometimes other children there you could play with. In this one it was mostly old people in camper vans, but they were nice to us kids. They gave us sweets and cakes and looked after us.

'This black minivan came onto the campsite one day. It was a hearse, with big windows on the back. That's what the hearses were like there. I thought one of the old people had died, but these three guys got out. They were all wearing those shiny dark glasses.

'I was playing cards with this old woman. I can't remember her name now, but one of the men in dark glasses came straight up to me and asked, *"Onde está seu pai?"* Where is your father?

'And when I pointed towards the tent, where he was having a siesta, I remember the old woman looking at the men in dark glasses and muttering, "There's trouble." And she was right.'

Finn was breathing evenly now. Eden got up as gingerly as he could. He had almost made it to the door when Finn opened his eyes and said, 'What happened then?'

'I'll tell you next time,' said Eden. 'Go to sleep.'

Forty-Two

Bisi had been right. Having a child meant that there was less time for everything.

On Monday, when Eden dropped Finn at the school gate, he asked again, 'What happened next? The men in the hearse. What did they do?'

'I'll tell you tonight,' said Eden.

'He looks good,' said Jackie, watching him walk in through the front door. 'Doesn't he?'

'What do you mean?' Eden turned to her.

'I don't know. Just a little more confident than he's been. A little more like himself again.'

'Really?' By the time he looked back at the school, Finn had disappeared inside.

A police car was still tailing him. Eden had watched it hanging back, parking a little further down the hill. Once in his own car, he pulled out his phone and read a message from Molly: *Frankie says OK. Can u come see me? Have stuff to show u.*

The next message was her address. It was on the other side of the river, in the village that ran across the opposite shore.

I'll catch the ferry, he replied.

She answered with a laughing emoticon. *U've gone native.*

When he returned to the car park on the spit, he got out and headed off in the direction of home, conscious he was still being watched by the man who remained seated in his car, waiting for him. Instead of going home though, Eden joined the small group of people waiting on the back beach for the ferry to arrive from the far side. There was no reason to let Sweet know where he was going.

The ferry was a low black boat, with a white chequerboard pattern on the side that Eden presumed was supposed to look like cannon ports. A single string of weathered bunting hung between two poles.

When it arrived, the ferryman slung a plank down so that people could get on or off. Eden followed the others up it and took a seat on the varnished bench on one side, and soon they were churning across the estuary, salt wind in his face.

When he had let Molly know he was coming on foot, she had told him to find the alley to the right of the Ferryboat Inn. It was a narrow alley, with the pub right above it, giving it a low ceiling which seemed to get lower as he walked down it. By the time he reached the end, Eden was being forced to stoop to prevent his head from hitting the painted board above him.

He emerged on the other side into a narrow, typical Devon street of oddly shaped, Hobbity little houses, all angles and oddly placed windows. According to the message, Molly's place was 'Just to the left of the thatched one in the square'. It wasn't really a square at all, just a jumble of old fishermen's cottages.

Molly answered the door with a piece of toast in her hand. 'I spoke to Frankie earlier. He says he'll meet you at the boatyard at two. Come on in.'

She stepped back. It was similar to Apple's house, only darker, even less square, and even less tidy. Downstairs was a kitchen-living room and a small staircase, with books piled on one side of the steps. A computer was on the table, surrounded by bills and letters.

'I'll tell Frankie two is OK, shall I?'

'Great. So you've got the marine traffic report?' he asked.

'You're not going to like it.'

'Really? Why not?'

She went to the kitchen to put the kettle on, dropping teabags into grubby mugs.

'Do you have coffee?' he asked.

'No,' she replied.

When she'd handed him the tea she sat down in front of the computer and showed him printouts of the files she had received.

'Right, then. Take a look at the top page.' She pointed. 'You can see *Calliope* at her mooring at five p.m.'

The first sheet of A4 was a printed map which showed the river mouth and the open sea. There were a couple of arrow-shaped icons and a single circle. Molly had drawn a ring around the circle and labelled it in biro: '*Calliope* @ 5 p.m.'

'Your sister would be on board by this time. She'd have switched on the electrics and the VHF radio, but she's not moving yet. The AIS comes on automatically with the radio.'

He turned the page.

'There,' she said. 'That's confirmation.'

The boat's info was given: '*Calliope*. GB TNM. Speed 0kt'. There was a photograph of the boat too, taken on a sunny day out at sea. 'All this information is recorded, then? On the radio?'

'Kind of. Each boat's transmitter has a unique signal that brings up its maritime records. Next page. There she is setting sail.' This time the icon was shaped like an arrowhead, circled and labelled '*Calliope*' again.

'Carry on,' she said.

Eden flicked through all the pages. From the time code, he could see they represented a snapshot of her activity every thirty minutes. They showed *Calliope* moving further and further out in the bay that swept in a big curve from Lyme Regis down towards Plymouth.

Then she disappeared.

Eden flicked between the pages. One moment *Calliope* was there, the next she had completely vanished.

'She's gone?'

'Exactly. For some reason the boat went dark. Either there was an equipment failure or, more likely, your sister deliberately turned off the AIS.'

Eden stared at the blank spot where his sister's boat had been. 'Why would she do that?'

'You tell me, Mr Eden Driscoll of the Metropolitan Police.'

'So, say she was out there to meet another boat – if the other boat didn't show up on satellite or radar, like your Plymouth Pilot, there's no way of telling who she met?'

'Pretty much. If you're trying to use this to prove her innocence, it's not looking too good for her, is it?' She leaned across, turned a few more pages and pointed to a marker. 'That's a trawler called the Bright Dawn. It's the one that first spotted your sister's boat drifting and called in the coastguard. So we know *Calliope* was somewhere in that area at around 2.15 a.m.'

The Bright Dawn's marker was a good distance southwest from where *Calliope* had been when her AIS had gone offline. It was true. There were about twenty nautical miles of her journey missing.

A couple of sheets later there was a further boat approaching. 'That's the *Mullen Glover*. The Plymouth lifeboat that picked up Finn.'

He flicked backwards and forwards between the Bright Dawn arriving on the scene and the *Mullen Glover* reaching the same place. It had taken the *Mullen Glover* a further forty minutes to arrive and all that time – and for maybe hours before that – Finn had been alone on the boat, trying to get out of the cabin.

'So she could have met another dark boat, and there could have been someone else getting onto *Calliope* with her?'

'But we don't have a Scooby-Doo who that would be,' said Molly. 'So the police will be looking at this too. She goes out to sea, disappears and then they find traces of drugs on her boat. Whatever she was doing out there, it's looking pretty shady. It would explain why Elaine Pritchard abducted Finn and why she ended up dead. Maybe whoever killed her didn't know there was a boy aboard at the time, and they needed to know how much Finn knew.'

Eden went through the pages, one by one, again. 'Can I keep them?'

Molly walked him back to the beach. The sky was dark. It was going to rain again soon. Eden wished he had brought a waterproof.

They stood together on Shaldon Beach. As the ferry worked its way across the water towards them, he held up the printed sheets and said, 'So this doesn't prove that Apple met someone who killed her out there – but it doesn't prove that she didn't.'

'I guess so,' said Molly. 'Listen. I want to ask you to do something for me. Don't jump down Frankie's throat when you see him, will you? Even if he's an idiot – even if he's done something unbelievably stupid – he's still my brother. And whatever Apple did, she's still your sister.'

On the ferry back Eden checked his watch. It was still early. There was time to do one thing before his meeting with Frankie.

Forty-Three

The Wild Goose in Combeinteignhead was just opening. Eden ordered a low alcohol beer and asked the young man at the bar which house Elaine Pritchard had lived in.

'I'm not from the village. I don't know.'

It was an old, thick-walled pub, all prints and horse brasses, quiet on a weekday. Eden waited as the barman went to fetch a woman who helped in the kitchen.

The woman who emerged a few moments later frowned at him across the bar, suspicious, wiping her hands on a dishcloth. 'Why do you want to know where Elaine Pritchard lived?'

'Long story. I'm a police officer, based in London. I was down here when she was killed, though, and I just wanted to take a look.' It wasn't the entire truth, but it wasn't a lie, and he hoped it was enough.

The woman was in her fifties, hair dyed an unlikely black. 'Poor Elaine. Never the happiest of women. Just her luck.'

'You knew her?'

'Only a little. She came in here sometimes for a lunch,

always by herself. Sat on that table by the garden. We had a chat though. Unlucky in love.'

'Unlucky in a lot of things,' said Eden.

''Xactly. Came down here after a divorce. Was always on the dating apps. No point looking for a good man round here, I told her. Ones that aren't no good are all spoken for. Tell you that for free, love.'

'So she met men?'

'String of them. All useless. Tried it myself, love. Half the ones you find online are already wed, trying it on. Gave up long ago. I warned her about that, but she was the needy type, you know? Always falling for the next one, then coming back here and sitting on her own, all tragic.'

'Which house?'

She hung the dishcloth from her apron and put her hands on her hips. 'You really a copper?'

'I really am.' Eden reached in his pocket and pulled out his warrant card, though he had no right at all to be flashing it around here.

She peered at it across the bar. 'Rosemary Cottage. Little place down on the corner of the Shaldon road. Blue door.'

'And do you know where she was hit by the car?' He took out his phone and opened a map, and she pointed to a lane about half a mile south of the village.

'Terrifying. Walk my dog there sometimes. Drivers round here are insane. Got to run, darling. Come back and have lunch, if you like.'

The village nestled in on the far side of the river from Teignmouth, low land surrounded by the roll of Devon hills. When he had finished his drink, Eden walked down the road and found the cottage easily. It was small, low and dark. He peered in the windows at chintzy armchairs and bookshelves full of novels.

He found the place where Elaine had died easily as well. There were still tiny traces of white tape on the blackthorn hedges and, when he got out of the car to look closer, he saw old footprints and signs of trampled grass still showing around the muddy ditch where her body must have lain, and where the forensics officers must have worked.

Eden stepped back and looked up and down the narrow road, tarmac stained mud-red. Considering how twisty the lanes were, this was a relatively straight section. She would have had time to hear the car speeding towards her, to see the person behind the wheel, to know what was going to happen to her. The driver would have had plenty of time to see her, too.

The traffic on the low bridge across the estuary was slow. A long lorry was having trouble negotiating the sharp turn at the end. Looking right towards the docks, Eden saw the familiar shape of *Calliope* lying in the shallow channel. It would be Finn's boat now, he supposed. He wondered, when all this was over, if anyone would ever want to buy such an old boat. Maybe Molly would help him sell it.

He checked the rear-view mirror. The police car that had been following him all day was far behind now.

The rain had started again by the time he made it back up to the lights. He turned left, towards Newton Abbot. A short way out of the town, there was a track running down to a boatyard. There was a sign there, just as there had been on the riverside: M&F Hawkins.

As Eden turned into the track he almost hit a motorcycle racing up the road towards him. The rider braked too, but skidded on the wet surface, bike sideways. He careened into the metal fence, hitting it wheels first.

Eden unbuckled his seatbelt and jumped out of the car, but the rider was already up, picking up his motorbike.

'You OK?'

The rider, in a full-face helmet, didn't answer. Instead, he jumped onto the bike and restarted it.

'Wait!' called Eden. The man was in black leathers, just like the man on the shoreline who had assaulted him. Eden stepped into the middle of the track and held his arms wide in front of the motorbike.

The bike roared. The man put it into gear and it lurched towards Eden. For one brief second, before he jumped to one side to avoid being hit by the biker, Eden saw his own reflection in the mirrored visor.

At the top of the track, the bike turned left into the traffic, narrowly missing a car whose driver pressed the horn in anger.

Eden watched him disappear, roaring up the road.

His instinct was that he should follow him, but he paused. Instead, he leaped back into his car and drove fast, down into the boatyard, where boats rested on giant trestles and trailers. Beyond the yard lay the broadest part of the estuary. The tide was out and the dark mud was dotted with squabbling birds. He looked round. In front of a rust-red shipping container was the notice, *Hawkins Marine*.

The container doors were open. In front of the container, a man lay on his back. It was the man he had seen here the first time he'd visited. Blood stained the stony ground around his head.

Forty-Four

If he had been on duty, the first thing Eden would have been obliged to do was stop and check for signs of life, even though Frankie Hawkins was clearly dead. But he wasn't on duty.

Instead, he jumped back into his car, started up and tore up the track, buckling up as he reached the road and turning left to follow the motorbike.

He quickly reached a tailback of cars. The motorbike would find roads like this much easier. Oddly, though, there was no oncoming traffic.

Eden took a risk, put his flashers on, and moved into the right-hand lane to overtake all the stationary cars. The reason there was no traffic heading the other way soon became obvious. At the start of the next village, there were roadworks. The temporary traffic light facing him was red and the queue of oncoming vehicles had started to move in his direction.

The line of traffic to his left was gridlocked, leaving him no place to duck into. The car coming straight for him in the same lane was flashing its lights angrily. Eden spotted a turning to the right ahead. Instead of slowing, he speeded up, and, just as the oncoming car started blowing its horn, he turned up the hill, slowing down as he entered another village.

'Damn,' he said loudly.

The chances of catching up with the motorbike had never been high. Now they were zero. It would have skirted round the stopped traffic easily. It could be a mile away already. The road Eden was on wove past an ancient red-stone church, a squat square tower surrounded by huge trees, dark in the morning rain.

At the top of the hill was a pub. He should stop and call the police – tell Molly the awful news. He drove on past the pub, up a narrow lane, past houses raised above the road by a stone walkway, looking for somewhere to park.

A little way further, the road seemed to be blocked again. A man in green trousers and a checked shirt was directing traffic while a woman raced around, picking up something from the tarmac.

As the man held up his palm to Eden to stop him, Eden realised what he was seeing.

The road was full of potatoes. Dozens and dozens of them.

It was a comical sight, strange, after the horror he had just witnessed at the boatyard. A couple of potatoes rolled down the hill towards him, past the man, who chased after them too.

'What happened?' Eden asked, leaning out of his window.

'Idiot on a motorbike just came past. There was a car parked outside, with someone collecting their groceries, so the bugger just mounted the pavement, hit all our displays, knocking our vegetables bloody everywhere.'

'Just now?'

'Turned right up the hill. Can still hear him.'

'Get out of the way!' shouted Eden.

'I beg your pardon?'

'Please. Out of the way. This is urgent.' He revved the engine and the man and the woman jumped back. Eden accelerated past a small grocery shop, bumping over loose potatoes, past the furious man, turning hard right up a narrow lane and then left up into the high-hedged countryside beyond.

At the first junction he took a left, guessing that the motorbike was heading away from the scene of the crime, but these lanes were full of turnings. Fifty metres on, there was a choice between continuing straight ahead and another turning that headed up towards Haldon.

He stopped and turned off the engine. The man had been right. You could still hear the bike. Above the birdsong, he could hear the whine of an engine, but it was distant and difficult to tell in which direction it was coming from.

Eden got out and tried to pinpoint the sound. It was impossible.

And then the engine slowed and stopped.

A few seconds later Eden noticed a black smudge rising on the skyline above him. It was smoke.

He jumped back into his car and turned up the hill, speeding in the direction of the dark cloud, but the lane was narrow. He had only gone a quarter of a mile up the steep lane when his way was blocked by a truck coming the other way.

One of them would have to give way. Eden hadn't had time to notice any gates or passing points. He had been in too much of a hurry.

But the driver flashed his lights and reversed slowly up the hill behind him, into a narrow passing place.

Eden stopped alongside the driver's window. 'Did you see a motorbike?'

The man behind the wheel was ruddy-faced, with cropped ginger hair. 'Fuckin' nuts!' he exclaimed. 'Motorbike was on fire and the guy was just standing there. I asked the bastard if he needed help and he just ran off into the woods. Just called the fire brigade now.'

There was no time to talk more, but Eden made a mental note of the truck so he could tell the police about the witness. It was owned by a company called Teign Valley Environmental Services. There was a phone number, but he had no time to take it down.

Eden sped on and found a right turn towards the fire. When he reached it, the bike was on its stand and the fire had already burned itself out, blackening the surrounding ground.

He peered into the woods to work out where the rider might have disappeared. There were tracks heading into the woods in two directions.

He picked one and set off, running in the rain into the undergrowth. The big trees above him were swaying in the wind.

The wood was used by walkers, so it was hard to make out fresh footprints. He was wasting time. After twenty minutes, he gave up and trudged back to the motorbike.

By the time he reached it, the motorbike was surrounded by blue and white tape. Sweet was there, stony-faced.

'And just where have you sprung from?' he demanded.

'I was in the woods. Looking for the guy who killed Frankie Hawkins.'

'And how, exactly, did you know that Frankie Hawkins had even been murdered?'

'You should know that, Mike. Ask your boys. Your man was following me. I saw a bike come out of the yard, so I followed him. Witness said he set fire to the bike and ran off into the woods.'

'What witness?'

'He was driving a truck. He told me he saw the motorbike rider disappear into the woods. Listen. I was supposed to be meeting Frankie Hawkins. He was dead when I got there.'

'That so?' said Sweet. 'Our man surveilling you followed you to Hawkins' yard. When he got there, he found poor Frankie Hawkins, half his head blown off. And you'd been there, so as far as I'm concerned, you're the last person to see him alive. You need to come with us.'

'I swear to God, this was the gunman's motorbike.' Eden pointed to the burned-out machine. 'I chased him in my car and lost him. Witness told me he ran into the woods.'

'What were you even doing talking to Frankie Hawkins, Sergeant?' demanded Sweet.

Eden opened his mouth, closed it again.

Sweet began reciting a caution. 'You do not have to say anything. But it may harm your defence if you do not mention when questioned something . . .'

Eden checked his watch. 'I have a boy to pick up from school in half an hour.'

'Well, I suggest you get someone else to do it.'

He ran through a list of the people he could ask. Bisi would find out soon enough that he was being taken in for questioning again, but he didn't want to draw her attention to anything that would make life harder for Finn. Molly was Finn's favourite, but her brother had just been murdered. He couldn't ask her to look after the boy right now. She would be in pieces as soon as she heard. He had no option but to dial Pam. 'Give me one minute.'

'Oh, my God!' the woman said breathlessly, before he had a chance to say anything. 'Have you heard? Man was shot dead in Teignmouth just now. They're saying it's a gangland assassination. Something about drugs. Do you know anything about it – you being a copper?'

'I don't, Pam,' lied Eden, trying to keep his voice even. 'But I do have something work-related to do this afternoon and I wonder if you could look after Finn for an hour or two after school?'

'Of course, love,' she said, like they were the oldest friends in the world. 'Maybe you could join us for a bite later.'

'You know he's a vegan?' he said.

'Is he?' Pam answered sympathetically. 'Poor little darling.'

He felt guilty for making Finn go to Cyrus's house, but he had little choice. He called the school to let them know of the change of plan, Sweet standing there impatiently, tapping his foot on the verge.

From overhead came the sound of a police helicopter, scouring the rough land on top of the hill.

Forty-Five

The police drove Eden back to the police station in Exeter. They kept him waiting there for an hour, then questioned him for over an hour and a half, going over and over the same questions. Why was he talking to Frankie Hawkins? What was his involvement in the shooting of Frankie Hawkins?

'There is CCTV. It'll show that Frankie was already dead by the time I got there.'

What did he know about Frankie's activities? What was Eden's sister doing with drugs on her boat? How could he account for the paint on Elaine Pritchard's body matching that of the car that he claimed he didn't sign out from the garage?

'What do you know about her?' Eden asked.

'This is an interview, not an information exchange,' said Sweet.

'She was single, because nobody reported her missing. She was on dating apps. Have you checked the men she was going out with?'

'I can make this last all evening if you like, Eden.'

They went over the slightest detail. What time was it exactly when he'd arrived at the boatyard?

Some time after six, a constable entered the interview room and asked for a word with Sweet.

Eden took the chance to drink some water. He wondered how Molly was doing. She would have been told about the murder of her brother by now.

When Sweet returned to the interview room there was something different about him. He looked less certain of himself. 'Turns out you're right. There is CCTV of the motorcyclist shooting the victim. And it's a minute before you get there.'

'Thank you,' said Eden.

'However, you left him lying there without checking he was dead,' said Sweet.

'He was dead. I didn't need to check.'

'And how did you know which way to chase the killer?'

'I didn't. I literally took that road through the village because the A381 was blocked. It was pure fluke.'

Sweet appeared determinedly sceptical about his answers, exasperated by how little sense it was all making.

'Do you think this was some kind of gangland execution?' Eden asked him. 'It's what it looks like.'

'Don't even start!' replied Sweet tersely.

'Or maybe that's just what it's supposed to look like?'

'Oh, Jesus, Eden. Will you listen to yourself?'

'I was assaulted on the shore last week. By a man in motorbike leathers. He told me to get out of town. I think it was the same man who killed Frankie.'

Sweet exhaled. 'And why am I just hearing about this assault now?'

'I didn't think it was important at the time.' A lie.

'Thanks, Eden. Thanks for the confidence you have in

me,' Sweet said archly. 'And this van and the driver you met coming the other way, the one who said he had seen the rider disappearing into the woods. Can you describe him again?'

'You haven't found him, then, either?'

'Just answer the question.'

'Like I said, it wasn't a van, it was a pickup truck. The driver had short, reddish hair. Round face. Forties maybe. Can I go now?'

Sweet looked at his colleague, then at his watch.

'You've got nothing to hold me on. I was a witness. I've told you what I saw. I need to go and pick up Finn.'

Sweet sighed. 'Yeah. I suppose so. Interview terminated at 5.55 p.m. Go on, then. But Eden?'

'I know what you're going to say.'

'Stay in the neighbourhood, won't you? Don't even think about going anywhere.'

In the police station car park, waiting for a taxi to take him back to his car on Haldon, he called Molly.

'They said you were there,' she said. Her voice sounded raw.

'I must have arrived just after it happened.'

'Oh, Jesus Christ. You saw him?'

'Yes. I did. I'm so sorry, Molly.'

She was crying again. 'What the hell did he get himself involved with, Eden?'

'I don't know.'

'First your sister, now my brother. They're saying it's drug gangs. They want to know if my brother has received any money recently, like Apple did. It's crazy. He never had anything, and anything he had he spent straight away. Drug gangs, for fuck's sake. I don't understand any of it. My brother wasn't involved in any drug gang.'

'The police are looking into it. They'll have some answers soon.'

'You really believe that?' She snorted.

'I'm just so sorry, Molly.'

'Yeah. I know,' she said.

She cried some more when he told her he had to go to pick Finn up. 'I'll call you after. OK?' he promised.

Pam turned out to live in a mock-Tudor new-build with a double garage on the east side of Teignmouth. She opened the door and beamed.

'Hi, love. We just had spaghetti alla Norma. Quick glass of vino before you take the lad home? You absolutely look like you need one, darling.'

'Ah, no. I need to get home. It's been a pretty shitty day.'

'Oh, you poor dear,' she said.

'Finn?' he called through the open door.

'Good as gold,' said Pam. 'Never heard a peep from either of them. I think they're pals now. Absolutely sure you won't come in?'

Finn appeared at the door, pale and silent. 'Sorry,' said Eden. 'I had to do something really important. One thing, Pam. You said you had the name of a babysitter?'

She smiled. 'You going out on the town?'

'Just in case.'

'Hold on,' she said. She pulled her phone out of the back pocket of her jeans and scrolled through. 'There you go. Ella Sweet. And she is sweet too. She's excellent. I'll message you her number now.'

'Sweet? Is she a relation of Mike Sweet's? The police officer?'

'Yeah. That's the one. She's his daughter. Lovely girl.'

'Small town,' he said.

'Isn't it? Don't be a stranger, Eden.' She leaned forward, presenting her blushered cheek, to be kissed.

At the car park at the seafront, Finn still hadn't said a word.

'What's wrong?' Eden asked him.

The boy didn't answer. Eden took his hand as they walked home in the drizzle along the sand, past the ferry, to the small house on the back beach.

It wasn't until he had brushed his teeth and was lying in bed that Finn finally spoke.

'Cyrus says that Mum jumped off the boat on purpose,' he said.

'Oh, Finn.' Eden leaned toward the boy and put his arms around him. 'It's not true. That's not what happened.'

'But how do you know?' asked Finn quietly. 'How do you actually know that?'

'Because I knew her.'

'No, you didn't.'

'Not as well as you did,' said Eden. 'No.'

'The night she went, I was cross with her. I shouted at her.'

Eden still had his arms around him. 'She loved you, Finn. You know that, don't you?'

'No one was there. I was angry. I was the only one who was there and I didn't help her. You keep saying she didn't jump in, but how do you know that if you weren't there?'

It was a question Eden couldn't answer.

Forty-Six

Eden and Finn sat together on the bed for a while, side by side, then Eden tried to cheer Finn up by saying, 'Shall I tell you more stories about your mum and the boat?'

Finn nodded.

'Where shall I start?'

'Those men with the dark glasses.'

'The ones in the hearse?'

'OK. Get into bed, then.'

Eden thought for a while in silence, trying to work out how to tell this story. Finn seemed content with this. Eventually Eden said, 'So the men in dark glasses, they took Dad away in the hearse.'

Finn settled back.

'It was quite weird. I mean, a hearse is like a car for dead people. But Dad came back later in the evening and our mum asked him why they had wanted to talk to him. He said he was just doing some business. He had this plastic bag with him and I saw him stash it away in the tent.'

'What was in it?'

'Ssh,' said Eden.

'Was it money?'

'Go to sleep.'

'Only if you carry on with the story.'

'OK. Anyway, after that we started sailing long-distance a lot more. We got pretty good at sailing, I suppose. Dad and Apple at least. These were the days before GPS. You know? Before you could find out where you were, just by looking at your phone. You had to do it all by looking at paper maps, and working out how far you'd come by looking at the stars. There were so many of them.'

'How do you tell where you are by looking at the stars?'

'There's one star that doesn't move,' said Eden. 'If you find that one, you know where North is. Now, close your eyes and let me speak.'

For once, Finn did as he was told.

'So we carried on doing that. We used to sail to Morocco and Algeria. Not all the time. Just every now and again. Mum said she wanted to be left behind. She hated it. But Dad insisted she came. It looked better that way. Just a happy family, sailing on their boat. So this is really a story about the last time I ever sailed on the *Calliope*. It was the trip we did to a place called El Jebha in Morocco.

'We all took turns sailing. We would have two hours at the wheel on our own, day or night. I hated it. I remember that time, sailing over to Morocco, I fell asleep in the night and we drifted way off course. Dad was absolutely furious. He made me do another watch as punishment, so it was four hours instead of two. I was so tired.

'He went back down to the bunk he and Mum had in the galley and left me out on my own again. I was just angry with him. It was so unfair. We used to go to these beaches and there would be other kids just having fun, having normal lives. We had to do all these stupid things because of our dad.

'El Jebha was this little fishing port nestling at the edge of mountains. There were always a few other yachts there but Dad insisted, like he always did, that we moor well away from them. And Dad also insisted we empty the water tanks when we got to places like that. It was a weird thing he always did when we arrived in Africa. He said the water would be stale if we didn't. It's funny how we just used to believe him when he said stuff like that. And then, the second night, he would always put us up in a hotel, which me and Apple used to love.

'That time we had a room on the top floor of this hotel with four dark wood beds lined up in a row against the wall opposite a balcony that looked out over the port. Clean white sheets. Dad ordered dinner in French and the woman from the hotel kept telling him how beautiful his daughter was. He meant your mum.'

Eden looked down at Finn. He looked as though he was asleep, but Eden carried on with the story, all the same.

'When the food came, I remember how Dad sniffed at the plates suspiciously and told us in English which ones we could eat and which ones we couldn't because there was probably meat in some of them. When the meal was finished, Dad stood up and told us he'd see us all in the morning, and he set off down the hill to the port. We were way up on this hill above. He said someone needed to stay and look after the boat, like he was some kind of hero. It was always the same.

'That night I was still angry with him for making me take a double watch. I think that's why I forced myself to stay awake. I just needed to understand something. I remember getting up and walking to the balcony and sitting in this chair and watching the docks. There were cafés by the waterfront where the old men used to sit and play chess and drink tea.

Some time after the lights went out, I remember seeing this dark shape on the water . . . and little ripples left by the oars of a boat. I could see the glow of cigarettes too, I remember. This boat going back and forth to *Calliope*.

'And then in the morning, when I went back and looked, Apple's bunk was all tidily made up and the water tank underneath it was full again.'

Eden leaned forward and kissed the boy on the forehead, feeling bleak. There was more of the story that he wanted to tell to Finn, but he was not sure if there was going to be time.

When he went downstairs there was a message from Bisi: *We need to talk.*

It was brusque and to the point. She would have heard that he had been witness to the murder of Frankie Hawkins. She might even have heard that he had been taken into custody. Though he had not been charged with anything, she would probably be thinking that he was not safe for Finn to be around any more. It would be the end soon. They would be taking the boy away.

He messaged Molly – *Are you OK?* – then waited for a reply. Sitting at the table, Eden made notes for himself on his laptop about everything that had happened that day, from the conversation with Molly in the morning, to his arrival at the boatyard and what he had seen there, right up to running through the woods looking for the gunman. He noted that the man on the motorcycle was around the same build as the man who had assaulted him on the shore.

In a notebook, he doodled the logo of the truck that had been in his way as he had tried to make it up the hill and remembered that there had been four words.

It came to him. Teign Valley Environmental . . . something.

He picked up his phone and searched for it on the web and there it was. Teign Valley Environmental Services. The logo was green, just like the one he had seen on the side of the truck.

He stared at it, puzzled, trying to figure out why it was ringing a loud bell in his head.

His phone buzzed. It was a message from Molly: *You still awake?*

Yes

Don't think I'm going to be able to sleep

Shall I call you?

He waited for an answer, but it didn't come. Looking back at the screen a second time, he blinked. TVES. He switched to his photos app and scrolled back until he found the photo he had shown Molly just that morning.

'15W E14' and below that, the letters 'TVES'.

Forty-Seven

Teign Valley Environmental Services' website contained little information. It was a company that offered waste-disposal services to local industries and farms. It was based on an estate on the outskirts of Newton Abbot, not far away.

It was too late to find out more. On his way to bed he looked in on Finn again. The boy was fast asleep, for which he was grateful.

That night, in his dead sister's bed, he dreamed he was at sea in a boat all on his own. The deck was a tangle of ropes he didn't understand, and when he turned the wheel it spun uselessly. His father was there too, with a frying pan in his hand. He held out the pan to Eden to show him what was in it – the overcooked remains of a fish, bloody flesh flaking off the bones.

The noise of a car woke him and he tried to work out where he was. It took a minute to remember. The noise hadn't even been that loud; back in London he wouldn't have even noticed it.

The window was open, and a freshening wind was flapping at the blind. When he got up to close the window, he saw that a vehicle of some sort had driven onto the quay to the right of the house. It must have been that that had woken him. Looking out, he saw that the tide was high, and it wasn't a car – it was an old Land Rover pickup, and Jackie's husband was unloading a blue barrel off the back of it and rolling it towards the trawler.

When he gave Finn his clothes that morning, Eden realised he had given him his last clean school shirt.

There was no washing machine in the house – the kitchen was too small. Instead, there was a launderette nearby and he took a bag full of clothes over there. The machines were all coin-only, and Eden had no change. He was used to only ever using his phone to pay for things.

He went to the bank, took out cash, then went to the Co-op and asked for change. When he was back in the launderette, he called Molly.

'Not great,' she answered, when he asked. 'What are you doing?'

'I'm in the launderette watching Finn's clothes go round and round.'

'Police came to question me. That's why I never got back to you. They wanted to know about what Frankie had got himself involved with. Truth is, I don't know. I really don't know.'

The slow rotation of the drier was hypnotic. He stared at it as she talked.

'They've frozen our bank account and everything. They tore my house apart. Now they're turning over the whole boatyard. There are so many people down there. They won't let me near it. I keep telling them there's nothing there to find, but what if there is?'

'I have been thinking. I have a hunch there won't be,' said Eden.

The drier stopped, began turning the other way. Molly continued, 'You didn't know what your sister was up to. What if I didn't know what Frankie was really up to all this time?'

With the phone tucked under his chin, he folded the clothes and put them back in the bag he had brought them in.

'What if someone is making it look like Frankie was in a drug gang?' Eden asked.

'What do you mean?'

'I'm not sure.'

'You think someone executed my brother to make it look like he was guilty? That's insane.'

'You're the one who says he wasn't like that. And the only evidence that he was that I can see is that someone killed him.'

'I can't think about this. It's too much. Can I come over tonight?' she asked. 'I don't think I want to be on my own. My house is a mess.'

Eden didn't answer immediately. He sat in the warmth of the launderette, trying to figure things out.

'Just as a friend,' she added. 'Your sister has a blow-up bed in that cupboard under the stairs.'

'OK,' he said. 'Listen. I have to go. I have a few things to do today.'

'Of course,' she said quietly. 'Right.'

He folded the last shirt, zipped up the bag and left.

Teign Valley Environmental Services was based in an industrial unit, between a tyre warehouse and a trade plumbing-supplies retailer. The sign above the office doorway said Total Waste Management.

Through the glass door, Eden could see an empty desk. When he opened it he heard a buzzing sound somewhere deeper inside the building.

A man in his forties, wearing a light blue shirt and chinos, appeared, smiling. 'Can I help you?'

'I have a weird question. There was a guy I saw driving a flatbed truck of yours yesterday up on Haldon.'

The smile stayed fixed. 'Was there?'

'Yes. There was a bit of an incident.'

'With our vehicle? I didn't hear of anything.'

'No. But your driver was witness to the incident. The driver had ginger hair.'

'What's the matter? Is there a problem? Is this a complaint of some kind?' The man raised his eyebrows.

'No. Nothing like that. I just wanted a chat,' said Eden.

'A chat?'

'A conversation.'

The man eyed him. 'Only me here today, I'm afraid, mate. Not a lot of time for chatting. That all?'

'OK,' said Eden. He looked around. The office was bland. It gave no clue as to the business being done in the warehouse behind. 'What kind of stuff do you do here?'

'What have you got?'

'A big old fibreglass boat.'

'Yeah. We could help you with that. We do glass fibre. Not cheap to dispose of, though. What kind of size?'

'What about cars?'

'Cars?' said the man, puzzled.

'I have an old banger I need to get rid of. I saw your sign. Total Waste Management.'

'No, mate. Just waste. Industrial and domestic waste. Try Ogwell Salvage and Spares. They'll give you a decent price for scrap. You done?'

'Right. One more thing. Do you know this woman?' Eden reached in his pocket, pulled out his phone and started flicking through his photographs.

'What is this? I thought you were asking about a boat?'

'Give me a minute.' Eden didn't look up from the phone until he found the photograph of his sister that they had used on the BBC News. 'Did this woman ever get in touch with you?'

When he looked up, the man's expression had hardened, his eyebrows moving a little closer.

'Do you recognise her?' Eden asked.

'No. I don't recognise her,' said the man blandly. 'Why would I?'

Eden smiled. 'OK. Well. Sorry to bother you, then. Thank you for your time.'

He turned and left the office, returning to his car.

The man had lied about recognizing her, he was sure of that. It had shown in his expression. Besides, his sister's face had been all over the news almost a fortnight ago. It didn't mean a lot, but it made Eden curious.

There was another message from Bisi. *Where are you? Need to talk. Urgent.*

He drove away, up to a mini-roundabout, but instead of heading home he drove round it and headed straight back to the industrial estate, parking a little way off, the far side of the plumbing supplies company.

Dipping low in the seat, he called Bisi.

'There you are,' she said. 'I called round to your house. We need to meet. Are you avoiding me?'

He came straight out with it. 'Are you going to take the boy away from me?'

She hesitated. 'We heard you were a witness to a shooting yesterday.'

'I didn't see it, but I was there just afterwards, yes. It was just a coincidence, Bisi. I had nothing to do with it.'

'I have to tell you, Eden. We can't do this. We have to put him in safe hands. It's our job. I appreciate what you've done. I've seen you with him. You would be a good parent. But not now.'

It was what he had been afraid of.

'We will be round tomorrow to take him back into emergency care. Mrs Sullivan is back from looking after her mother. She can take him for a few days. She's a good woman.'

'I'm sure she is,' said Eden.

'After that, I don't know. We will have to consider our options. Most of the time, I really enjoy this job, believe me. Normally I think we make things better, not worse.'

'I suppose it's for the best,' said Eden, eyes still fixed on the front of Teign Valley Environmental Services. 'All in all.'

'If you want my opinion, I think you'd have made a really good dad, Eden. I really do. But it looks like you got what you wanted in the end.'

'Not really,' said Eden. 'Not really at all.'

Time was running out. At around midday, the roller on the company's big door opened and a truck drove out. It was the same one that had blocked his way on the way up to Haldon yesterday. And Eden had been right. The man in the offices had been lying. The driver was the man he had seen yesterday: the one with the red hair.

Eden waited until the truck was out on the main road

before he followed it, out over the mini-roundabout again, and through the outskirts of the next village.

A black Audi was a good car to follow someone in. It was like a thousand others on the road. Keeping his eyes on the GPS, Eden hung back, only driving closer when the vehicle ahead approached a junction. Soon they were on an empty B road, winding through open country into lush valleys. Huge trees overhung the road he was driving along, turning it into a tunnel of green-lit leaves. When the trees parted he caught glimpses of the fringes of Dartmoor up ahead, hills thick with spring bracken.

He had been on the road for ten minutes when the truck slowed and indicated left, bumping down a single-track road. Eden drove past until he found a farm entrance he could turn in, then headed back down the lane slowly, trying to figure out where the truck had gone.

It didn't take long. The track turned into a farmyard. There was a small hand-painted sign, nailed to a tree. A white arrow with *Car parts* written in red paint.

Eden reversed a little way down the road, parked the car in a passing place, out of sight of the farmyard, and walked back, up a rise and through the farm gate. The truck he had followed was near the farmhouse. There didn't seem to be anyone around. Between the gate and the main house, there were about twenty cars in various states of disrepair lined up alongside the side of one of the barns. Most looked as if they had been in some kind of accident, bonnets buckled, windows smashed, bumpers torn away.

He walked towards the line of cars and peered into the barn. 'Hello?' he said quietly, and got no reply, so he took a step inside.

The vehicles inside were being dismantled, their parts separated, organised into dozens of boxes.

The only car that was different from all the others was the one covered by a red tarpaulin, weighted down by lumps of metal.

He heard a step behind him and before he could turn, a voice said, 'Can I help you?'

Forty-Eight

Eden turned.

A woman in a checked shirt and khaki trousers stood behind him.

He had no authority to be here; he didn't have the power to search the place. If they suspected he was interested in what was under that tarp – and if he was right – then he was in a lot of trouble.

'I'm looking for Jordan's house,' he improvised. 'I think I'm lost.'

'Jordan?'

'Jordan Blackburn?' A name plucked from thin air. Smiling, he looked around. 'School friend. Farms goats?'

'Goats?' She was looking at him, puzzled.

'It's OK. I'm in the wrong place. Don't worry.'

He turned on his feet and began walking back to the entrance.

'Wait,' the woman in the checked shirt called.

He continued walking. 'It's OK. Won't trouble you.'

He could hear other voices too now – men's voices, asking the woman who she was talking to, whether anything was wrong. Eden knew that if he was right, he was in danger if they figured out who he really was.

Yesterday, the man in the truck had said he had seen the biker setting fire to the motorbike, then had watched him running off into the woods. If Eden's guess was right, that had been a lie, just like the lie he had been told at the Teign Valley Environmental Services office about the man with the red hair not being at work.

'He was asking about some farmer who keeps goats.'

The gunman must have been in the truck. He had not run off into the woods. That was how he had got away. He may have been lying in the back, or ducking down out of sight in the front seat. Eden quickened his pace, hoping that the truck driver was not among them, and that he would not recognise him as he strode away.

When he reached the road, he broke into a run. His car was parked out of sight. By the time he reached it he was sweating. He had not been to a gym in two weeks, but it was more than that: if he was right, these people were killers.

About ten metres from the car, he took his key fob from his pocket and pressed it, unlocking the doors. Jumping inside, he started the engine and turned the car round in the passing place. Only when he was back out on the B-road, at a safe distance, did he call Sweet.

Sweet picked up straight away. 'What now?' he asked.

'I think I might know where you'll find my sister's car,' he said.

'Really?' His voice sounded more interested now.

Eden sent him a location pin from his phone.

'One more thing,' said Sweet. 'I was going to come round to tell you. We have the results of the DNA test on the body.'

Eden could tell from the tone of his voice. 'It's my sister, isn't it?'

'I'm sorry,' said Sweet. 'Go home now. Look after your boy. Leave this to me.'

When he ended the call, Eden realised how fast his heart was still beating. He had needed to get away fast. If it was the Toyota under that tarp, a murder weapon that linked those people to the murder of Elaine Pritchard, it was important that he was nowhere near it. Good policing was about keeping the evidence uncontaminated. But it was more than just procedural prudence. He had been scared.

Sweet had told him to go home, but he didn't.

The first thing he did was drive to Exeter and buy an iPad, a pair of headphones and some wrapping paper.

Back home, he approached Apple's house cautiously, letting himself in at the kitchen door. He looked around, trying to imagine her here, greeting him, showing him round, offering him a cup of some disgusting herbal tea. She was dead. He had known it all along, but now it was confirmed.

He wished he had come here when she was still alive. Upstairs, he went into Finn's room, and looked around that too: the small bed, the piles of clothes, the PS5 he had shown no interest in. Noticed a piece of paper folded on his desk. Curious, Eden reached out and picked it up.

It was a poem, titled 'The Red Rock'.

Eden read it:

Sometimes I am so angry
I can't help it
sometimes I feel so angry
that if I get any angrier
I will explode into a million million pieces
and they will cut into anyone who is close to me
Into pieces

Or I will flood all over you
Like a big wave
I won't be able to stop it happening
Or I will mash you like a red rock
A big one
Falling down a cliff
Right on top of you
And your squishy head
So don't make me angry

In Miss Killick's neat red biro: 'This is very good indeed, Finn. Well done.'

Eden folded the paper and put it back on the table by Finn's bed. Downstairs, he plugged in the new iPad and registered it to Finn Driscoll. Sitting at the small table, looking out at the low tide, he opened the Voice Notes app and started to record.

'I know you like listening to stories. I've bought you a subscription to an audiobook thing, where you can listen to all sorts. It'll work on this machine. Ask a grown-up to show you how to do it. You can choose any books you want. I hope the stories will help you sleep. And there are some headphones you can use too.'

He pressed pause and thought for a while, looking through the glass door, then continued.

'And now, because I'm not sure how long it would be before I got the chance to do it in person, I'm going to tell you the rest of the story about me and your mum, and the bad thing that happened. I don't know if you'll understand this, or if you'll understand what I did, but you wanted me to tell you the story . . . and I owe you it, so here it is.'

He took a breath and continued.

'So we were on the last trip I ever had on the *Calliope*. We set off from El Jebha, heading north. I made a point of taking a shower, even though Dad had told us to use the showers in the hotel. You know the shower in *Calliope*. It's probably the same. It's tiny and it uses a lot of water. When he discovered what I was doing, it made Dad really angry. And then Apple made a stupid joke about teenage boys taking showers and that made him angrier still. By then I think we'd all figured out what he was doing, why we were sailing to North Africa so much, but nobody admitted it. Nobody said anything. I hated that. But all through the crossing back to Europe, I kept using as much water as I could, doing the washing-up, everything like that. I left the tap running and when he went to put the night-sailing lights on, Dad couldn't work out why the boat's battery had gone flat and he had to charge it again by running the engine, which he hated to do.

'By the time we reached Portugal and moored below the cliffs near this place called Albufeira, the tank was pretty much empty. We always moored up somewhere no other boats could see us. It's what happened each time.'

And Eden paused again and thought about what he had just said, and something occurred to him. He took out the printouts that Molly had given him and stared at them for a long while before continuing the story he was recording for Finn.

'So now I'm going to tell you how it ends. You have to remember there were no mobile phones in those days. Maybe there were, but we didn't have them. Just a radio on board. When the boat was moored, back on the Portuguese side of the sea, Dad used the radio to give a signal to the men with the hearse that he was back. And then we would all get in the tender – you know what a tender is, don't you? The little boat you row to shore on. We would all get in the tender and he would take Mum, me and Apple onto the shore . . .'

He talked for another twenty minutes as the day moved into the afternoon. A couple of times he stopped, edited the file, re-recorded a minute or two, and then continued. When he'd finished, he labelled the file 'Story for Finn' and added a shortcut to the home screen so he would find it. Then he paired the headphones with the iPad, put the device back into its box, carefully wrapped it in paper and put it on the dining table, ready to give to Finn when the time was right.

It was almost three in the afternoon. It would be time to pick his nephew up from school soon, for the last time.

Back downstairs, he flicked through the pages of the printout again, looking at the sweep of the bay, from Lyme Regis to Start Point, and all the vessels in it.

The symbols on the A4 sheets were small, mostly clustered in places like Exmouth and Dartmouth. He turned over the pages, watching *Calliope* make her way out of the harbour before her symbol disappeared, turning them back, reversing time to watch her retreat into port.

He stopped. He had not noticed it before and there was no time to look at it properly now – he had to go and pick up Finn – but before *Calliope* had set sail, there had been two dots inside the estuary at Teignmouth. Two hours after *Calliope* left her mooring, the second dot made its way out of the estuary mouth, into open water.

Forty-Nine

He let Molly in by the beach door. 'My stupid brother,' she said. 'What was he doing?'

Eden reached out and put his arms around her, pulling her out of the rain. 'Thanks for coming round.'

'Where's Finn?'

'He's upstairs in bed,' said Eden.

It was nine-thirty and dark outside. He sat Molly down at the table and gave her one of Apple's beach towels from the cupboard to dry her wet hair with.

'You know what?' he said. 'I was beginning to think your brother was involved in something bad. I was thinking Apple was too. But I called you over because I wanted to show you something.' He took out one of the sheets of A4 and pointed to the arrow that left the port an hour after Apple had. 'What's that boat?'

'I don't know. You can't tell from the printout. I'd have to look at it on a browser.'

'Can you do that?'

'Yes. If I log into my account.'

'Wait a minute.' He went upstairs and returned with his

laptop and opened it up for her. 'I've done a lot of thinking, and I believe the police have got everything completely wrong,' said Eden. 'About my sister – and about your brother.'

'And you think this proves something?'

'It doesn't prove anything. It's just something we hadn't spotted before.'

She leaned forward, staring at the screen until she'd found the right files. 'What time are you looking at?'

'Around 10 p.m.,' said Eden. 'Can you find that?'

She put her finger on the mouse pad and clicked a couple of times. 'Is that it?'

'There.' Eden pointed at the small arrow leaving the mouth of the River Teign for open sea. 'What's the name of that boat?'

She clicked on the symbol, then turned to him, mouth open. '*Sheena*,' she said. When you clicked on it, the photo popped up. Blue hull, red cabin.

'I thought it might be. Do you fish for lobsters at night?' he asked Molly.

Her eyebrows moved closer together. 'You could, I suppose.'

'They were loading up with those barrels of bait last night at some crazy hour.'

'Barrels?'

'Four of them.'

'That's a lot of bait.'

'I think we've been looking at this all wrong,' said Eden. He pointed to the printed pages again. 'That's my sister's boat, leaving Teignmouth on the Friday evening she disappeared.' Eden pointed to the arrow on the map and followed it through the next three sheets. 'You can see her heading out to sea and then she disappears.'

'Because she switched off her transmitter.'

'But I don't think it was because she was doing something illegal. It was because she didn't want to be seen, sure, but what if she was trying to hide from someone else?'

'Who?'

'Look.' He pointed to the sheet on which *Calliope* had vanished. *Calliope* disappeared just as *Sheena* emerged from Teignmouth Docks.

Jackie's husband had been loading it with something last night. Apple could have spotted him doing it, just as Eden had.

'You think Apple turned off her AIS to hide from *Sheena*?'

'Maybe Apple wanted to figure out what *Sheena* was doing out there. She reckoned that if she didn't have AIS on she might be able to get close enough to see?'

'*Sheena* has radar. It would be able to make out boats coming close.'

'I don't know. Maybe she just wanted to hide who she was, then. Get close enough to see then run for it without anyone knowing who she was. Either way, she wanted to go off grid. She had seen something that was wrong and she had gone to find out what it was, or to figure out how she could stop it.' He hesitated. 'I need to make a call.' He pulled out his phone and dialled Sweet. When he answered, Eden asked straight away, 'Did you find the car?'

It sounded as though Sweet was watching the TV. 'What time of day do you call this, Eden? I have a life.'

'Sorry.'

He heard Sweet leave the room, closing the door behind him. 'No, I haven't found the car yet,' the detective sergeant said. 'We are doing this by the book. We have to. I have applied for a warrant to search the premises.'

'By which time they might have got rid of the vehicle.'

'By the book, Eden. That's the way we do things down here, to build a case that won't fall apart. You probably do things differently in London.'

Eden wondered if he had heard about the Ronan Pan debacle. Word seemed to get around. 'Fair enough,' he said. 'Something else. Your daughter does babysitting, doesn't she?'

'How the hell do you know that?'

'Parent at the primary school told me. Is she free tonight?'

'What? Why?'

'I was going to go out somewhere with Molly,' Eden said.

'What?' mouthed Molly.

'Really?' Sweet said. He lowered his voice. 'Is that a good idea right now? You two together? Her brother just got killed, almost certainly in a hit.'

If he told Sweet the real reason he wanted to go out, he doubted he would agree to let his daughter babysit. 'It may not be a good idea, but Mike, we both need a break for different reasons. Molly needs some support right now. But if I'm taking her out, I need someone to look after Finn for a while. Tell her I'll give her twice what she usually charges.'

'This time of night? It's late already.'

'Please. I've just put Finn to bed. It's easy money for her.'

Sweet went quiet for a while. 'OK,' he said. 'I'll ask her.' They heard him shout, 'Ella!' Sweet muted the phone while the conversation took place. He was back after a few seconds. 'She can do it, but she has college in the morning, so don't make it too late.'

'OK,' said Eden. 'I'll put her in a taxi.'

'I hope you know what you're doing,' said Sweet.

'I hope so too.'

'I'll drop her down there myself.'

'What the hell?' said Molly when he had ended the call. 'We're going out?'

'Look out of the door,' said Eden. 'What do you see?'

Molly moved to the door. 'I don't understand.'

'*Sheena* isn't there. She set sail thirty minutes ago. Around the same time that she disappeared two weeks ago. Last night she was loading up with what looked like bait. Tonight she's gone. Don't you want to know what she's doing out there?'

'What? You think she's gone to pick up drugs?'

'No. I don't. I think she's taken something out there in those bait barrels, but I don't know what.'

She frowned. 'Seriously?'

He thought of the car under the tarp. 'Police round here take their time doing everything. I'm pretty sure I found Apple's car today, but Sweet hasn't done anything about it yet. We can't afford to wait for the evidence to disappear. If we want to find out what that boat is doing, we're going to have to take a look for ourselves.'

'Jesus.' Molly was shaking her head slowly from side to side, trying to take this in.

'Ella Sweet will be here in just a few minutes. She's going to look after Finn. Can you go and fetch the Plymouth Pilot? You said you always had her ready to go.'

'You really want to follow *Sheena* out there?'

'Exactly.'

She was still moving her head slowly, as if processing this. 'If you're right, these people killed your sister.'

'If I'm right, they killed your brother, too.'

'Oh, God.' She took out her phone and opened up an app. 'It'll be blowy. There's an easterly.'

Eden hadn't thought of that. It was one thing to be out there on a trawler, but quite another on a much smaller boat. 'Too much?'

'No. Not too much. How are your sea legs?'

'We don't have a lot of time,' he said, opening the beach door.

In fact, Sweet was there less than a minute after Eden had ushered Molly out of the door and closed it, and looked Eden up and down. 'Aren't you going to dress up a bit if you're going out?'

Eden looked down at his jeans.

And then Sweet's daughter stepped out of the darkness of the alley behind him and Eden recognised her straight away.

'This is Ella,' announced Sweet.

Sweet's daughter was the young woman he had sat opposite outside The Ship Inn that first night in Teignmouth – the woman he had seen in another pub, looking for her mother.

'Pleased to meet you,' said Ella. If she did recognise him – and she must do – she was trying not to show it. She was a copper's daughter. She would probably be hoping he did not remember her, talking to the lad as she had been about illegal parties, drugs and drinking.

At the time, rushing to show her where Finn's room was and writing down his number for her, trying to get out of the house to the boat with Molly so that they could chase the trawler, Eden was too busy to think any more about it or what it might mean, that it was Sweet's daughter he was showing around his sister's house.

Fifty

Harbour lights reflected on a rippling tide that was higher than Eden had ever seen it.

While Eden was sorting out Ella, Molly had taken oars and rollocks from the rowing club lock-up and rowed a dinghy up to the Pilot's moorings, then brought the boat back, beaching her bows-first in the sand.

'Get on board,' ordered Molly above the chug of the engine.

The bows of the boat were much higher than that of a dinghy, too high to clamber up. Instead, Eden had to step into the water to get in. He was in the wrong clothes for this.

'Hurry,' she said. She was buzzing now, as eager to get going as he was.

He hauled himself up and swung his legs over the side of the boat, jeans dripping wet.

She gunned the engine in reverse and the bows pulled back from the beach.

As Molly roared the boat out into the deep water of the main channel, heading for the river's mouth, the easterly wind hit them. 'Can you pull the fenders inboard?' she asked.

He remembered this from his days on *Calliope*. In port, you hung fenders over the side to protect a boat. When you were under sail, you pulled them back inside.

The tide had turned already, pushing them along with it. Spotlights shone on the red face of the Ness cliff, making the unlit rock look craggier, stranger. Eden watched as a wave broke at the Ness's base, sending spray high in the air. Molly had been right. It was going to be windy.

When they had passed the cliff they were suddenly in open sea, waves coming at them from the east. As each crest approached, the boat seemed to tilt upwards, then slam down again as it passed. Water sprayed against the small windows at the front of the cuddy.

'Life jacket,' Molly called, pointing at the locker at the front of the boat.

Eden reached out and found one, handing another to Molly. Rain had started to come down harder. They were sheltered by the half-cabin, but it poured into the boat, down into the bilges.

In his pocket he felt his phone buzz. He lifted it out. It was a message from Constable Lisa Ali: *Can we talk?*

Later? Did you find out what I asked?

She answered with a name. *Billy Bailey*. Detective Constable Bailey of the Major Incident Team he worked with back in London.

Definitely him? Eden typed.

100%. Why?????? Explain pls!

Later. No time now, he replied and put away the phone.

'Who was that?' asked Molly.

'A colleague. From London.'

Molly had switched on a screen and was peering at it. 'There,' she said. On unsteady feet, Eden edged towards her. The boat rose and crashed down again. The screen was some kind of navigation chart, but it also showed other shipping. She was pointing at an icon. When she tapped on it, a small window popped up on the screen. It read: '*Sheena*.' Though her boat didn't appear on AIS, that didn't stop Molly from using it.

'How far is that?'

'About two nautical miles. She's moving slowly for some reason, so half an hour away with this wind, or less, if we keep up a decent speed.'

They had already passed the blinking navigation buoys at the estuary entrance. Ahead of them was rain and darkness. 'What do you think he's doing out there?' Eden shouted.

'No idea. But if we're lucky, we're going to find out.'

'That's what my sister thought.'

Molly stared into the nothingness ahead of them. 'Admit it. You actually thought she was bringing in drugs, didn't you?'

'Yes. I did. I didn't want to, but I saw her bank account and I thought, maybe she had done it.'

'Her bank account?'

'Someone paid five grand into her account about a week before she died.'

'I knew her. I knew she wouldn't do anything like that, not even because she was skint.'

'She wouldn't?'

'No. She wasn't that kind of person at all.'

'I'm glad,' he said.

Behind, the lights of the shore got smaller. In daylight, a few days earlier, this part of the sea hadn't seemed so vast.

The small light on top of the cuddy was illuminating a small circle of sea around them. In the black night, it was as if they were travelling along in their own ball of rain. The constant motion of the boat was making Eden feel disorientated and nauseous.

'You know Jackie?' asked Eden. 'Graeme's wife? She works up at the school.'

'A bit,' said Molly.

'The day Elaine Pritchard came to pick up Finn from school, Elaine Pritchard knew exactly what to say. She even knew the safeguarding officer wasn't there that day.'

'Oh, God,' said Molly.

'Yeah. I know. It's been bugging me. It was either someone in Social Services, or it was someone in the school who had told her. I think it may have been Jackie. She made this show of helping me look for Finn. I thought she was being nice.'

The boat laboured on through the water.

'We should be able to see Graeme soon.' The front windscreen was spattered with water. 'Can you see a light?'

Eden stepped out of the shelter of the small roof, into the falling rain. Hands on the side of the boat, he leaned a little way out to see past the windscreen. There was nothing out there that wasn't black, and certainly not the light of another boat.

She leaned forward and flicked a switch. The red and green navigation lights on either side of the boat went dark. So did the white light above the cabin. Now the only light was coming from the depth finder and the plotter.

'They'll see us coming otherwise,' she said, though Eden had already understood what she was doing. Apple would have done the same. She had tried to become invisible.

For a moment he thought he was going to be sick, then a wave smacked against the side of the boat, soaking him. The cold water helped. He returned to the shelter of the cuddy, hair matted to his forehead, salt water dripping into his eyes. He shook his head. 'Nothing.'

'We should be on her in . . . maybe ten minutes,' she said.

He stepped back and peered out of the boat again. Still nothing.

'They don't want to be seen either,' she told him.

'So they have their navigation lights off too?'

She nodded and slowed the engine.

'Are they close?'

She looked at the screen. 'Pretty close. I don't want them to hear us though. From the look of it, they're drifting. If their engine's off, they'll hear our motor unless we're quiet.'

'Won't they see us on radar?'

'Not if they're not looking.'

Eden thought for a second that he saw something off the port side. He peered into the night, wondering if he had just imagined it.

'How are you doing?' Molly asked.

He had come out without proper gear and was soaked through. 'Wet,' he said, not looking round, trying to accustom his eyes to the darkness.

He blinked, wiped the water from his face and stared hard. There seemed to be a smear of light, a kind of interruption in the blackness.

'There,' said Eden, first uncertainly, then a second time, more confidently. A dim orange light was showing through the rain.

Molly throttled down a second time. No longer moving, the Plymouth Pilot drifted side-on to the waves and began to roll. Accustomed to these conditions, Molly looked unconcerned, but Eden had to fight the urge to vomit.

And then, unmistakably, carried on the wind, came the sound of banging. Someone was working on the deck.

'Is there another boat here?' he asked. 'Are they transferring the barrels to someone else?'

'If it is, I can't see it.' She went to check the radar. 'Might be something small. The weather means there's a lot of clutter on the screen.'

Eden stood beside her. The screen was dotted with white spots. 'You think they can hear us?'

'I don't know. Wind's coming from their direction, so we'll probably catch them better than they hear us.' She pushed the throttle forward again, only a little, but enough to turn the boat into the waves, bringing the bow towards where Eden had seen the light.

They chugged slowly into the wind, engine low, letting *Sheena* drift towards them.

'Look,' he said. The light showed again, coming into view. It was a cabin light.

'Is this exactly what Apple was doing?'

'Maybe,' answered Molly, looking back at him anxiously.

And then, with the speed with which the wind was pushing the trawler towards them, they were close enough now to make out her shape.

There was a second light playing on the working deck. Eden could make out a figure moving around, dressed in yellow oilskins.

'Can you see what he's doing?' asked Eden.

Molly joined him at the side of the boat. 'No. He's still too far away.'

'Is he waiting for someone?'

She looked around for navigation lights, then returned to the cuddy to look at the plotter. 'I can't see any other boats. But if it was a small one—'

'Like us?'

'—we wouldn't be able to see them until they were on us.'

'Can we get closer to figure out what they are doing?'

'Not without him seeing us.'

'OK. I guess we should back off, then. Let the police know what we've found out.'

She looked at him. 'You're bloody kidding, aren't you?' she said.

Fifty-One

He was a police officer. Police procedure was not to take unnecessary risks, especially when a civilian was present. 'We can alert the police as soon as we can, and they will pick up *Sheena* the moment it gets back to the dock.'

'But you don't want to do that, do you?' said Molly.

The lights of the shore were just a smudge in the darkness. 'No. But obviously I should.'

There was a brief lull in the rain.

'What is he doing?' asked Molly. 'Aren't you wondering that? C'mon, Eden. We still haven't seen. At least we need to try to figure out what he's actually up to out there.'

As he hesitated, there was a dull splash in the water. 'Jesus. Did someone just fall in?' He thought of his sister.

'Or did they just throw something overboard?'

'Throw something overboard?' Eden blinked into the rain.

'Oh, fuck's sake. They're not taking something out here for another boat. They're dropping something off into the water.'

Eden was trying to think it through.

'Maybe it's for another boat to come by and pick up later,' suggested Molly.

He had heard of that. Packages with locator beacons, being dropped off at sea for other boats to collect. But what made no sense was that *Sheena* had come with her load from Teignmouth. Smuggling went in the other direction.

'TVES,' he said aloud. 'That's why Apple was keeping an eye on them. It wasn't about drugs at all. They're not dropping off, they're dumping.'

'Dumping what?'

'I don't know. What stuff would you want to get rid of out here?'

'Oh, for pity's sake,' said Molly. 'Chemicals or something?'

Graeme had already disposed of at least one object – whatever it was. If they allowed the *Sheena* to return to port, there might not be anything left on board to incriminate her.

The diesel had been quietly ticking over in neutral. Molly put the boat gently into gear and turned her into the wind slowly.

'You sure about this?' he asked her.

'Of course I am. The trawler will start drifting towards us. Keep a look-out.'

His sister would have used her camera. There might have been photos taken from her bedroom window of Graeme loading up the boat. If so they would have been on her computer. That was why someone had come back, to find the SD card – or the camera itself, if they hadn't already found it on *Calliope*. Eden took out his phone to record any evidence, noting that there were still two bars. He was going to call the police and let them know what was going on the moment they were sure of what they were looking at. If they got close enough, he would get photos too.

The lights from *Sheena* were becoming clearer, the shape

more defined, the red glow of the bridge showing. Molly's Pilot would be visible too, but whoever was on *Sheena* was too busy doing whatever they were doing to notice.

They were that close now Eden could see that Graeme had his arms around one of the blue barrels, the ones he supposedly kept fish bait in, and was trying to move it across the working deck. Eden started taking photos.

'Christ,' said Molly. 'That's what all this was about. You're right. They're fly-tipping. Apple caught them dumping waste out here. That's what she was on about. Not just fly-tipping up on Haldon. She had figured out they're getting rid of stuff out here.'

As she spoke, they both heard the gentle plomp as the second barrel fell off the low back of the trawler into the sea. Eden had seen Graeme loading four.

'Bastard,' said Molly quietly.

Incongruously, over the water, came the sound of 'Ain't No Particular Way' by Shania Twain.

The song ended abruptly. 'What now?' snapped an angry voice.

It had been a ringtone. Someone had just phoned Graeme. They could hear Graeme talking but couldn't make out the words.

'OK. We need to get out of here,' Eden said, but it was already too late.

Before the call, Graeme had been peering over the side of the boat, watching the weighted barrel sink slowly into the water. Now he was looking right in their direction, phone at his ear.

'Which boat is faster?' asked Eden.

'Theirs.' Molly was thinking the same thing as he was. It must have been Graeme who had killed Apple out here when she had discovered what was going on.

Maybe, that night, Graeme had come on board *Calliope* to try to persuade her not to tell the police. Maybe he had thought he could reason with her. Maybe they had drunk a glass of wine together before he had realised that she was never going to change her mind.

They heard the trawler's engines roar into life.

'Is he making a run for it?' shouted Eden. He needed to call the police.

'No, he's bloody not. Hold on.' Molly revved the engine hard.

Out of the drizzle the *Sheena*'s bow was suddenly shooting towards them, giving Molly little time to turn away.

'Shit. He's going to try to bloody sink us.' Eden grabbed the side of the boat with his free hand, the one without his phone.

They had drifted too close. It was easy for Graeme.

The trawler's bows, big, blue and rusty, were much higher than the Plymouth Pilot. They crashed straight into the side of their boat, smashing the port side of the cuddy, crunching fibreglass, ramming hard into them.

Fifty-Two

At some time in the night, Finn wakes, foggy with sleep.

This might be another dream. He is not sure.

He can't see anything. The blackness is thick – except for a thin line on the floor. It is a door.

He gets up carefully and walks towards the light, finds the door handle and it turns with a squeak. But the door isn't open.

'Mum?'

He tries again, tugging it harder.

'Mum!' Louder this time. Still no reply.

Yes, he has been dreaming, he remembers. He had been sitting on the Ness beach, the one that faced the sea. There were notices all along the bottom of the cliff: *Danger. Falling Rocks*. The beach scared him.

He looks around, trying to work out where he is. Only his toes are lit at the bottom of the door. The rest is black.

Something is wrong but he does not know what it is. The night is a dangerous place where bad things happen.

'Mum?' More quietly this time. He called but she never came.

Then he bangs on the door with his fist, punching it. The noise he made shocks him.

'Please. Please come. Please.'

That feeling of being at the bottom of a cliff, knowing that something is going to happen, something big and dark, rolling downwards.

Bang bang bang go his small hands on the door.

'Don't leave me here. Please, Mum.'

He fills his lungs and screams as loud as he can. No one comes.

The door will not budge. He sits down on the floor next to the bed he has been sleeping in, puts his chin on his chest and he weeps.

'I'm scared,' he says as much to himself, because there is no one there apart from himself. He wipes his eyes with his pyjama sleeve. 'Please, Eden. Help me. I'm really, really scared,' he says.

It is some time before he hears steps. He can make out a shadow in the line of light below the door. Now he is fully awake, he knows it is not his mother, and that it will never be her. The steps are heavy. He doesn't recognise them.

It's not Eden, either.

Fifty-Three

Flung off his feet, Eden felt his head crash into the side of the boat. Cold water broke over him.

For a moment, dazed by the blow, Eden expected the force of the collision to tip them both over into the sea, but the Plymouth Pilot wobbled back upright.

It took him a second to get his bearings. He was on his back at the bottom of the boat. When he turned his head, he saw Molly scrabbling to her feet. She had been knocked down by the impact too. The port side of the cuddy was in bits – wood and splinters of glass everywhere.

Eden needed to call the emergency services; he should have done this minutes ago when there was still time. He had been holding his phone when the trawler had collided with them – part of the reason he had not been holding on with both hands. Now he realised he no longer had it. He must have dropped it when he had fallen. He looked around. The bottom of the boat was awash with debris.

Molly had somehow tucked herself under the remaining half of the cuddy roof and was revving the engine, trying to turn the boat away into the darkness. 'Fuck,' she said, looking back over her shoulder. 'Fuck. Where've they gone?'

The boat that had hit them had disappeared into the gloom.

Eden stood and joined her under the wrecked cuddy roof. Wind blew through the smashed glass. She reached over to the VHF radio above her head, tuned it to Channel 16 and grabbed the handset on the end of the curly wire. 'Pan-pan, pan-pan, pan-pan,' she called into the handset. 'This is Plymouth Pilot. Plymouth Pilot. Location . . .' she peered at the plotter. 'Keep a look-out!' she shouted at Eden.

'You think they're coming back?'

'Graeme has radar. They'll be able to see exactly where we are. We're an easy target. Location fifty degrees twenty-seven minutes north . . .'

He heard the trawler before he saw it.

'Look out!' shouted Eden.

Sheena was approaching fast off the port side again, this time straight on.

Molly thrust the engine into reverse. Instead of hitting them in the middle of the side, which Eden guessed would have cracked the hull wide open, the steel trawler hit the bows, shoving the Pilot to the right. There was a loud cracking sound.

'Three degrees twelve minutes west. Now a mayday. Urgent assistance required.'

The trawler scraped along their port side, roaring past. Eden got a glimpse of Graeme standing at the wheel, looking down at them.

'Mayday, mayday, mayday. We have been struck by a trawler . . . Shit.' Molly threw down the handheld mic and reached up to the VHF set again. Twisted a knob. Swore and turned to Eden. 'No signal. Useless. Can you see the aerial?'

Eden took a step back so he could see. The left-hand side of the roof had been dislodged completely and was hanging down. Though there was still a small black aerial attached to it, it was hard to see where its wires led in the darkness.

'Did they hear any of that?' he asked.

'Don't think so. He must have buggered up the wiring first time he hit us. Use your phone. Call 999,' she ordered.

Eden looked around the bottom of the boat, trying to see under the dark water at his feet. 'Lost it. Where's yours?'

'Shit shit shit. Mine's in the forward compartment in a bag. Get it for me.'

Yanking a piece of wood that had once been part of the cuddy out of the way of the door, he peered inside. It was black in there. He felt for a light switch.

'Brace!' shouted Molly. He heard the engine roar into reverse.

A third time the trawler hit them, this time closer to the stern, bouncing the boat around so that it ran alongside the trawler again. Eden jolted sideways, the edge of the narrow doorway punching him in the ribs.

'This is insane!' shouted Eden.

'Find it?'

'No. It's going to come back,' he said. Even if they found a phone, by the time the emergency services responded with help, Graeme would have sunk them. His boat was bigger, faster, stronger. 'We have to have a plan.'

'He'll say it was a collision in the dark. We weren't showing lights.'

'What do we do?'

Graeme was chasing them, coming up behind the Pilot.

'Get a rope,' ordered Molly. 'There are a couple in the cabin, right at the back.'

'Rope?' Again, on his knees, he scrabbled into the dark

space, feeling around with his hands. The diesel was at full throttle, the noise deafening, but even louder was the sound of waves smashing into the fibreglass bows.

His fingers found a rope, a long loop, neatly coiled. He backed out of the small cabin with it.

'Good.' Molly grabbed it. 'Now take the wheel. Keep it straight.'

Pushing past her, he grabbed the small wheel. 'What are you doing?'

She didn't answer. She was undoing the small piece of rope that held one of the rubber fenders. 'He'll catch up with us very soon. Just hold the course.'

Now she was attaching the white fender to the end of the rope Eden had fetched for her. When she was done, she weighed the fender in her hands. 'Too light!' she shouted. 'How good are you at throwing?'

'OK, I guess.'

She looked around. 'To your right. Pass me the mallet.'

There were some tools tucked into an open canvas pocket that hung to the right of where he was standing. He reached in and pulled out a heavy metal mallet.

'How far do you reckon you can throw that?'

He lifted it, judged it. 'Twenty-five feet, maybe? Thirty?'

'OK. That's good.'

She set about measuring the rope quickly, yanking it through her hands. When she had paid out enough of it, she tied it to the mallet and to the fender in a configuration he didn't understand. When she was done, one loose end of the rope lay on the deck. The other she wound round a cleat on the side of the Pilot.

'What are you doing?'

'You ever hear of a Highwayman's Hitch?'

'No.'

'Doesn't matter. Never tried it before. Hope it works. I'm going to let Graeme come up alongside us. I'm going to get really close to him. All you have to do is stand here and, when I tell you, throw the mallet as far as you can across his bows.'

'Why?'

'Not over them, right across the front of them. When it reaches about twenty feet, that rope is going to tighten, and when it does, the tension is supposed to undo the knot. The mallet will drop off and sink, leaving the rope just with the fender on the end. I want the rope to go right under the trawler, as close to the keel as possible.'

Eden looked round. The trawler had switched a lamp on now, casting light on the rain-pocked sea ahead of it. It was gaining on them so fast there was little time to think. 'I don't understand.'

He watched her as she wrapped the other end of the rope around a second cleat. 'No time to explain. Come and stand here. Take care not to stand on any of the ropes, OK?'

They swapped places.

'When I say, throw it in that direction. Try and throw it so it lands in the water over there so that the rope runs right under where the trawler is about to go.' She pointed with one hand.

Sheena was gaining on them. Her bow was almost at their stern and Graeme was turning her away, preparing to loop around on their port side to take a third shot at ramming them side-on, to swamp them properly this time.

Instead of veering away, Molly turned to port. The trawler turned further to port too, presumably because Graeme didn't just want to slide alongside the *Pilot* again, he wanted to ram her, to have the full force of the trawler's speed hitting them amidships. Whatever he had wanted, though, the two boats were coming alongside each other.

Sheena's bows were going to nudge them at an oblique angle about halfway along the Pilot, with all the force taken out of the collision by Molly's manoeuvre.

'Now!' she shouted.

Eden threw the mallet as far as he could. The rope played out over the side of the Pilot. It was a good throw. Eden watched the mallet arc into the air in the floodlight, then splash down the far side of the other boat just before the bows cut through it. The fender was full of air, so while the mallet sank, it – and the rope tied to it – would stay on the surface.

'Now pull!' shouted Molly, leaving the wheel. She grabbed the other end of the rope, tossed it round a cleat, and started to yank on it, fist over fist as the two boats ground alongside each other.

Eden joined her, pulling it in. He understood now. The fender was holding the rope up. When they pulled it, the rope was running right under the keel.

Looking up, Eden caught sight of Graeme in his wheel-house, puzzled, trying to work out what was happening.

There was a sudden loud crack and then a scream, and the rope was tugged from Eden's grasp. The cleat they had been running the rope around had been ripped off the side of the boat.

Dimly, Eden realised it was Molly who had screamed.

Fifty-Four

Eden looked back towards Molly and she was staring down at her hand. It was covered in blood. She must have been gripping the rope more firmly than he had been. When it had wrapped around the *Sheena*'s propellor – just as Molly had intended – it had jerked the rope right out of their hands, tearing flesh from her right palm.

'Take the wheel!' she screamed, holding her wounded arm to her chest.

She leaned past him and put the throttle up higher.

They were racing away from the trawler now.

'Ha,' she said, looking back. 'Ha! Aren't I queen of the sea? It fucking worked.'

'What?'

'That rope. We fouled their propellor when he ran over it. He's not going anywhere for a while.'

'You're a genius.'

The trawler had fallen far behind now. Eden slowed the boat.

'Are you OK?' he asked.

'Lost some skin. Stupid,' she said, wincing. She clutched

the hand to her chest. Eden could see the blood dripping down onto her shirt. 'What now? We leave them there?'

'We need to get you to a doctor.'

'It's just skin. We need to fix the aerial to call the coastguard to come and pick them up. We can put lights on now, right?'

She leaned past him and flicked two switches on the dashboard. On the broken cuddy roof, hidden under debris, a red and green light came on. There was a small wooden pole, too, that had been knocked askew. The white light on top of that shone out.

For the first time since the collision Eden could see the damage the trawler had caused. There was wood, fibreglass and broken glass scattered at his feet. He caught sight of his phone, face down near the back of the boat, and left the wheel for a second to pick it up.

The screen was cracked.

He held the phone up to try and use facial recognition to open it, but the camera didn't seem to work and it was asking for a PIN. Either the screen was too wet or the glass was too cracked for him to be able to enter one. He rubbed the screen on his trousers and tried again. It was dead.

'If the boat is immobilised,' he said, 'it's safe to go nearer, right? If he's dumping something we need to know what, because by the time the coastguard gets here he'll have probably got rid of everything. Can we clean up the wound and take a look at whatever he was trying to do?'

'Graeme fucked my boat up,' said Molly. 'Yes. OK. Turn round. Wouldn't mind seeing the look on his stupid face.'

'We sure about this?' Eden looked at the blood on her shirt, where she was holding her damaged hand against it.

'Absolutely. Abso-bloody-lutely.'

Eden grinned at her, turned the boat round and began to

retrace their own wake. The rain was finally thinning and there was a little more visibility now. It was a minute before they saw the lights away to starboard. Eden nosed the boat towards them.

As they got closer, Molly pulled a large lamp from the forward locker, plugged it, one-handed, into a socket and shone its beam onto the trawler. Graeme was standing at the back, struggling with a blue barrel.

'I don't know what's in those barrels but I bet it's not good.'

Eden took his phone again and wiped the screen.

'Are you filming this?' Molly asked.

'Can't. It's busted.'

'Fuck you!' shouted Graeme, catching sight of them. He abandoned the barrel and strode towards the wheelhouse. Diesel fumes puffed from the exhaust at the rear of the boat.

'What's he doing? The propellor's out of action, isn't it?' said Eden.

'Think so.'

But the trawler's engine roared into life and the boat suddenly lurched forward, speeding away from them, turning hard to starboard so that it seemed to tip in the water.

'What the hell?' demanded Eden. The trawler was tracing a tight curve. It would be heading back towards them soon. 'I thought you said—'

'Shit!' shouted Molly. 'This was a mistake. The propellor's got free. We have to get out of here.'

Eden pushed past Molly to take the wheel.

He gunned the boat's engine and turned away to port, conscious they were now heading away from the coast and from potential rescue, not towards it.

'I guess the rope didn't bloody hold! she shouted. 'Shit. Shit. Shit. We shouldn't have come back.'

Graeme was furious, determined to finish the job.

The rain had stopped now and an early crack of light had appeared along the eastern horizon to their left. Eden was concentrating on keeping the boat as straight as possible, running into the waves.

'How long before he catches up with us?'

'A minute.'

'Can you try and find your phone?'

She was scrabbling on all fours in the forward cabin when *Sheena* loomed out of the darkness, roaring towards them, this time from behind.

'What should I do?'

She gave up on the phone and stood. 'Wait till he's close, then turn hard to port. We can't stop him hitting us but we can take the energy out of the blow.'

The trawler was already so close Eden could see the blue of the hull in the darkness. In a few seconds the bow was looming over them.

'Now!' shouted Molly, and he swung the boat away from colliding with the trawler. The smaller boat seemed to take an age to turn.

It was a mirror of their very first encounter. The curve of the trawler's hull scraped alongside the Pilot, tilting their boat towards the metal hull, scraping alongside, splintering what was left of the cuddy. Eden stepped back, ducking away to avoid the flying debris.

And then the trawler was past them again, turning back in a circle.

The right side of the roof was smashed to bits now, too. Too late, Eden realised that it had come down on top of the wheel. The Pilot was still circling round to port. He needed to aim her away from the trawler.

'Jesus. I can't steer.' He started tearing at the pieces of

wood that had come down, trying to jettison them overboard or yank them behind him, but though they were cracked and bent, they were still attached to something.

'Turn the boat again,' implored Molly desperately.

'I'm trying!' he shouted. 'I can't get at the wheel.'

They were on a tight anticlockwise circle, engine at full speed, tilting as they went. Instead of turning away from the trawler, they were coming straight back to face her.

Tugging as hard as he could on the wet wood, Eden managed to shift a large sheet of the cuddy's marine-ply roof, exposing the top of the wheel, but when he tried to turn the wheel, it was still jammed.

'Brace! Brace!' shouted Molly. 'Fucker's going to hit us again!'

Too late, Eden saw that one of the uprights had fallen into the spokes of the wheel and was jamming it. Eden reached behind the wheel, grabbed the square piece of timber and started to yank at it.

He looked round. *Sheena* was heading straight for their bows as they came back to complete the circle.

This time there was no chance of turning away.

Sheena hit hard. Eden crashed into the steering gear. Instead of pushing the boat down into the water like last time, the angle of the collision seemed to force the Pilot's bows upwards. Eden heard a crack – louder than the last one – and then the trawler was past them and they tipped forwards again, bow dipping into the waves.

Eden hauled himself upwards. 'What happened?' he asked.

Molly was lying on the floor of the boat.

Something sounded wrong. Their engine was still roaring but they didn't seem to be moving at all.

'I think the shaft has gone.'

This meant nothing to Eden. The Plymouth Pilot was lying at a funny angle, tipping to the left.

Eden looked. The trawler was turning again to come in for the kill.

'We're going down,' said Molly.

'What?'

'Look.' There was water pooling around her. 'I think he cracked the hull.'

Eden had no time to process that.

'He's coming back to kill us,' said Molly.

Sure enough, the trawler was already in its slow arc, veering back again.

Fifty-Five

Molly looked defeated. Her boat was sinking. 'What do we do?' Eden asked her.

'Stay with the boat – or what's left of it – if we can. It's our best chance,' Molly said. She was on all fours now. 'Trouble is, once we're in the water, he can pick us off easily.'

The Plymouth Pilot seemed to be taking on water fast, its weight tipping the boat to one side. Eden was having to grab onto the starboard side of the boat to stay upright. It was only a matter of a couple of minutes, he guessed.

The sky was a fraction lighter and Eden could make out the silhouette of the trawler against the sky, even with its lights full on as it continued to turn slowly towards them again.

It was coming in for the kill this time. Molly reached out and grabbed hold of Eden. The Pilot was leaning over hard now. 'Fuck,' she said. 'Here goes.'

Everything seemed to slow down. He felt the nails of her left hand digging into his shoulder. He reached around and held her.

In the boat as a child, he had always been terrified of

Calliope sinking, of what it would feel like to be sucked under.

He thought of Finn, who had lost his mother and now was going to lose the only other relation he had in the same sea.

The bows of the trawler, still turning, would soon straighten and then it would be heading directly for them. All it needed now was a nudge and they would be under the steel hull, being dragged towards that propellor.

'I'm sorry,' he said. They clung to each other as the world slowed.

And then there was a dull sound – crump – and the sky was suddenly full of light, and even from ten metres away Eden felt the heat of an explosion.

Flames went skyward from the rear of the trawler. Something on board the *Sheena* had burst into flames.

'What in Jesus . . . ?' said Molly's voice in his ear.

Instead of straightening to plough into them, the trawler carried on turning.

It scraped past them, barely nudging their stricken hull. Still clinging onto Molly, Eden scanned the flames for any sign of Graeme.

Sheena's stern had just passed them when there was a second blast, as strong as the first, and then, above the roar of the trawler's engine, he heard a man screaming.

They paused and listened. It was an inhuman noise, shrill and limitless, stopping for a second as he took in breath, then recommenced screaming. Molly reached out and killed the throttle, putting the Pilot into neutral. 'What happened?'

'I don't know.'

'A fucking bomb?'

The scream continued. Lit up by the fire, the smoke

looked orange at first. Then Eden realised the colour was in the smoke itself. 'Looks like a chemical fire of some kind,' he said. 'Was it the stuff he was dumping?'

'Like an industrial accident of some kind?' The man's screams were weakening.

'Poor guy,' Eden said.

'Poor guy who was trying to kill us.'

'Yeah. All the same.'

'Your phone working yet?' asked Molly.

'I can't raise anyone.'

'Wouldn't worry now. They're going to see this for bloody miles around.'

The trawler's rudder was hard down. It circled uselessly around them as it burned, and still the man somewhere aboard it screamed.

'Jesus,' said Molly.

Eden said, 'We should do something. Can we get close?'

'Why?'

'Because we should try and save him.'

She stared at him. 'He's the guy who killed your sister. Maybe my brother too.'

'Doesn't matter.'

'It's not like we could get close anyway. It's moving too fast. Our boat's dead in the water.'

They were in the middle of the circle, the trawler moving around them.

She was right. The speed *Sheena* was travelling, there was no way to get on board. In fact, the danger was as much to them, that they would drift into the path of the revolving trawler and be hit one last time before the Pilot sank.

And then there was another flare of heat from the boat.

'That's the diesel going up,' she said.

It must have been the main tank because the trawler's

engine cut out and the boat finally slowed. Without the engine noise, the sea suddenly seemed strangely quiet, apart from the gentle clanking of chains and the repeated thump of waves against their hull.

'Shit,' said Molly. 'I suppose I have to do this now.'

She reached over the side of the sinking Pilot and pulled in the rope they had tried to use to disable the *Sheena*'s propellor. When she got to the frayed end she said, 'Tie it onto my belt. I can't. My hand's a mess.'

He leaned forward and lifted her life jacket, then tied it round the belt.

'What about the chemicals? What if there's another explosion?'

She looked down as he worked. 'Call that a knot?'

'It's the best I can do.'

She tugged on it with her good hand and said, 'Have to do.' Then she reached her arms up and dived into the rolling water.

Even in a life jacket, Molly looked at ease in the water. The trawler had drifted to a standstill upwind of them. It seemed to be slowly being pushed towards them.

She reached it in a couple of minutes. The back of the trawler, the bit off which Graeme had been jettisoning the chemicals, was low. It would have been easy enough to climb onto if Molly could use both hands, but she was only using one of them. Eden watched her struggling to pull herself out of the water with her left hand, but eventually she did it.

'Now you!' she shouted.

He jumped rather than dived and was shocked at how cold the water was. His head went under and he surfaced, gasping for breath. His swimming was not as elegant as hers, but it helped that she was pulling the rope with her left arm, yanking him towards the burning trawler.

When he reached it, he hauled himself out and scanned the scene. Lit by deck lights, the back of the boat was black from the explosion. A fire still burned at the rear of the trawler, but the fierceness of the flames had died down.

Looking around, Eden saw no sign of the blue barrels. He guessed there had been two left on board before the explosion. When the first of them had gone up, the second one must have followed soon after.

At the front of the deck, close to the wheelhouse, lay a dark shape. He didn't want to look.

The windows at the back of the wheelhouse had blown out in the blast and, when he climbed the gangway up to it and stepped inside, there were fragments of glass spread evenly across the metal floor.

He found a fire extinguisher to one side of the doorway. The label read 'Powder'.

Holding it in one hand, clutching the handrail with the other, he returned to the deck. This time he looked.

Graeme was on his back, head against a bulkhead. There was blood on the metal deck around him.

His waterproofs had melted onto him. Where it showed, the skin on his chest and face was black, cracked with red. Eden leaned down. There was a bubble of snot on his lips that grew and burst. He was breathing.

With one arm around his face, sheltering it, Eden approached the flames at the tail of the boat. The barrels had been near the low back deck, ready to be jettisoned. There was nothing left of them but a pile of smouldering residue. Something had made them explode.

He broke the seal, pulled out the pin and started spraying the extinguisher at the flames. The extinguisher emptied fast.

When the cloud of powder disappeared, Eden had beaten the fire back a little, but it was still burning.

Molly had already found a bucket with a rope tied on and was lowering it over the side of the boat with one hand.

Once it was filled, she approached the prostrate boat-owner with it and said, 'This is going to hurt, but it's all we've got.'

Eden took the bucket from her and began to pour the water over Graeme's head and over the fried skin of his chest.

Graeme was beyond caring about pain. His body twitched a little as the water flowed over it.

'You should be using this for the fire,' Molly said. 'Not for him.'

'You don't know what kind of chemicals were in the barrel. I wouldn't be surprised if it was water that set them off.'

'Just going to let it burn?'

'Unless you can find another extinguisher.'

While Eden refilled a second bucket, then a third, Molly went to the wheelhouse. 'Mayday. Mayday. Mayday,' he heard her voice calling.

It had only been around fifteen minutes since *Sheena* had first tried to ram them, maybe less, but it felt like hours.

The rain had stopped. Light was gathering strength in the east. The wind had subsided and the waves seemed less daunting in this big boat, however stricken it was.

Eden continued soaking the fisherman with water to try to cool his roasted body.

A nylon rope tied to a rail had started to burn, sending thick black smoke over the side of the boat, stinging Eden's eyes. 'Do you think they'll be long?' Eden asked.

Graeme had been ramming them. The barrels which had been secured had been loosened so that he could drop them over the back. Eden imagined one of them tumbling sideways in a collision.

Now the rain had cleared, they could see an orange glow that would be Torquay, and, to its left, Plymouth.

It felt like an age before Molly said, 'Look,' pointing.

Out of the dark northwest sky, a point of light was moving towards them. It was the first of the helicopters to arrive.

Fifty-Six

The prow of the Plymouth Pilot disappeared below the waves shortly before the first helicopter arrived, its pale shape sliding into darkness.

Now the wind of the helicopter's rotors was flattening the waves around the trawler. From it, men dropped onto the deck. They were brisk, working with a kind of efficiency Eden recognised. Eden pointed at Graeme and they nodded, set to work methodically, lifting him onto a solid stretcher. The second helicopter arrived just as Graeme was being raised into the air, spinning gently as he rose.

They winched up Molly next. By the time the harness was lowered for Eden, he could see the lifeboat approaching them, lights blazing on the water.

In the belly of the helicopter, Molly sat opposite him while they gave her painkillers and dressed her hand.

She shouted something at him, but it was impossible to hear above the noise of the engine.

'What the hell was in those barrels?' She shouted louder this time.

He shook his head. Mouthed, 'No idea.'

'Bastard tried to kill us.'

Eden nodded. Graeme had killed his sister to cover up what he was doing. But that didn't explain the deaths of Molly's brother and Elaine Pritchard. Eden was exhausted, but his brain was still racing. He had left Finn with the babysitter. That would be another black mark against him as far as Bisi was concerned.

At least he would be able to tell Finn part of the story. None of this had been the boy's fault. He could tell him that for certain now. His mother had died trying to stop something terrible.

It was impossible to converse in the noise, so he looked down, out of the side window. High in the air in the rising sun, the sea his sister had disappeared into looked huge and black. His clothes were still damp with seawater; the interior of the helicopter was hot and stuffy.

The helicopters took them to Plymouth. There was a burns unit in the hospital there, apparently. They landed on tarmac by the car park and were immediately surrounded by medics and police officers. After the long wait at sea, everything seemed to happen fast.

As Eden emerged from the machine, he saw they were already wheeling Graeme away, medics running beside the gurney holding drips and monitors. Blue lights were flashing everywhere.

Back on land, Eden found his legs were shaky. One of the helicopter crew led him to a group of people. Nearby, Molly, blood on her shirt, was protesting, 'No, I'm fine,' but a woman in scrubs insisted on walking her to the emergency department so they could examine her hand.

'We need to take a look at you too,' said a paramedic, a woman in green, taking Eden's arm.

'I'll come for you!' Eden shouted at Molly's retreating figure.

'You bloody better!' Molly called back.

'Walk this way, if you don't mind,' said the paramedic. 'Are you OK on your feet or do you need a wheelchair?'

'I'm sorry. I have to go,' Eden told her, pulling away. 'I have to get back home. It's urgent.' Finn would be wondering what had happened. Eden had not meant to leave him alone all night.

'It's important we give you the once-over.'

But now there was a uniformed officer striding over to him. 'Are you Mr Driscoll?'

'Yes. Is everything all right?'

'Got someone on the phone for you,' said the police officer. He was holding out a handset.

'It'll take a minute,' the paramedic was saying.

The police officer handed over his phone and Eden pressed it to his ear. 'Eden?' Mike Sweet's voice. 'What's happening?'

'How is Finn?' demanded Eden.

There was a long pause, and during it Eden felt the world shifting under his feet. He heard Sweet saying, 'He's fine. And he will stay that way if you do everything I tell you to do.'

'It was you all along,' said Eden. 'Wasn't it?'

Fifty-Seven

'Don't talk,' said Sweet evenly. 'Don't end this call. Don't do anything apart from listen to me, or I will hurt the boy.'

'Don't. Please.'

'Then do as I say.'

'Right.' Eden was thinking hard. 'You thought I was dead, didn't you?'

'I fucked up,' said Sweet. 'I fucked up really bad. Everything's got a bit out of control. I'm just asking you to help me.'

'What?'

'One copper to another. I just need a little time. Just a little time to get away. And I want you to help me. And if you don't, I can't promise anything.'

The officer who had given him the phone was in earshot, waiting to get his handset back. 'Just a minute,' Eden told him, and walked a few paces away.

Molly had disappeared into the hospital now. The paramedic was still waiting for Eden, hands on her hips.

'You've got Finn?' Eden asked.

'Yes.'

Eden had given Finn to Sweet's daughter to babysit; he had practically handed the boy over to Sweet. 'Where?'

'With me. At his house.'

Eden was trying to take this in. 'And I'll get him back safely?'

'Everything will be fine, I promise. Just give me a chance.'

'Your wife. She was the one who hit Apple's car from behind, because she was drunk.'

'Ssh,' said Sweet. 'I just need you to help me.'

'How do I know he's OK?'

'Don't start pretending you give a cuss now, Eden Driscoll,' said Sweet angrily. 'You were all happy to head straight back up to London, first time I met you.'

Eden was tired, but he had to see Finn, to know he was OK. He hadn't slept all night: his trousers were still damp, his hair matted with salt, his shirt felt filthy, but he needed to keep Sweet talking, even if there was no one besides himself listening, just so he could figure out his next step. 'Must be hard, everyone knowing your wife is an alcoholic,' Eden said.

'What's that?'

'That deposit into my sister's bank account. It was you who paid Apple the money to keep her quiet about your wife running into the back of her car when she was drunk.'

'Married life,' said Sweet. 'You should try it some day.'

'No, thanks,' said Eden.

'She's my wife. I stick up for her. I'm proud to do it. I'm proud of everything I do to keep them safe.'

'And you took it to Teign Valley Environmental Services, because . . . I'm guessing you had something on them, too, didn't you? You asked them to get rid of the car, no questions asked.'

'Are you done? We need to sort this out. If you help me, I can help you.'

Eden looked at the officer who was waiting for his phone. Dawn was breaking behind him. 'Jesus.' Eden banged his skull with his fist as it occurred to him.

Graeme had been dumping stuff for Teign Valley Environmental Services. Sweet had taken his sister's car there to be disposed of. The car that had been used to kill Elaine Pritchard. All of this was connected.

'Are you OK?' said Sweet. 'You're going to need to be OK.'
'Not really.'

He had shown Sweet his sister's note, right at the start, the one with 'TVES' written on it, letting Sweet know that he was following the trail his sister had started on. That was why Sweet needed to get him out of the way and back to London so badly.

'Pull yourself together, mate,' said Sweet, as though they were somehow in this together. 'If you want to see the boy again, you need to keep quiet.'

Eden's head was spinning. It had been Sweet who had stolen the computer. All that stuff about pretending to need permission to enter the house was pure theatre.

'Oh, Jesus. You killed Frankie Hawkins. Or had him killed somehow.'

'Calm down, Eden. Please. I need you to be calm right now. For the boy's sake. For your information, Frankie Hawkins was a little shitbag who dealt drugs to all the kids around here. Threw nice little beach parties to sell them all whizz and smokes. For all I know, he and your sister were in cahoots. Your sister wasn't exactly an angel. We found traces of cocaine on her boat.' Sweet stopped talking abruptly. 'What's so funny? Are you laughing at me?'

'No. Nothing is funny. Just tell me what I need to do.'

'You can't laugh at me. You left Finn in my daughter's care. And you went off in the bloody boat. When she didn't come home in time, I called her up – and I have to admit, I was pretty angry with you. She has college, you see.'

'You're a model father.'

'Don't get funny!' Sweet shouted. 'I'm ten times the parent you'll ever be.'

The officer standing on the tarmac was looking bored. He picked a dandelion clock from the verge and blew at it, sending little parachute seeds up into the pink morning air. 'All OK, mate?' he mouthed.

Eden nodded, put his thumb up.

'My daughter was stuck babysitting your boy so I had to go there. I drove over, sent her home in a cab and stayed there instead. You'd left your printouts on the table. It didn't take me long to figure out what you were doing.' So it had been Sweet last night on the phone, calling Graeme up, telling him to be on the look-out for Molly's boat.

He'd told Graeme to kill them. It must have been a surprise to find out that he and Molly were still alive.

'What do you want?'

'I called your phone. You didn't answer.'

'My phone went down with Molly's boat.'

'Good.' Sweet seemed to think about this for a second. 'If you're lying, I'll kill the boy. I swear to God. I've got my back against the wall, Eden. You know that. That makes me dangerous.'

'I've seen that already.'

'Not a word to anybody. I just want to find a way to end this. OK?'

'OK,' said Eden as evenly as he could.

'Don't even think of calling the police.'

He wasn't going to. Sweet was police, after all. Eden was no longer sure who was on his side around here, and who was not.

* * *

The police officer drove Eden to the seafront in Teignmouth.

'I can drive you right to your house if you like?' he said.

'This is fine,' said Eden. Sweet had made it clear. The first sign of a police officer near the house and he would kill Finn.

It was Saturday morning. The Den looked so ordinary. The empty bowls lawn and the terrace of Victorian guest houses. People going about their early morning business. A jogger running along the seafront, above the sea wall. An elderly man smoking a cigarette while waiting for his Yorkie to pee against a lamp post.

He hadn't liked this place much when he had arrived here.

He set off, towards the small street where his sister's house was. When he reached it, as instructed, he knocked on the back door, the one in the alleyway where he had met Sweet for the first time, what seemed like an age ago.

Sweet opened the door a crack and peered out. When he was assured that Eden had come alone, he pulled the door back another couple of inches. 'Get inside,' he said.

Eden stepped into the small kitchen. Sweet was holding a gun. Eden guessed it was the one that had killed Frankie Hawkins.

Fifty-Eight

'Clothes off,' said Sweet, pointing the gun at Eden.

'Where's Finn?'

'All your clothes. Off. Now.'

They stood in the kitchen. Sweet looked rough. He was unshaven. Eden probably looked no better. They had both been awake all night.

'I don't mind killing you,' he said. 'I'm in deep enough.'

'Yes, you are.' Eden unbuttoned his shirt and removed it.

'Trousers,' said Sweet.

'If I do this, Finn will be OK?'

'What do you take me for?' he said, but Eden noticed he was wearing black gloves.

'I'm not wearing a wire, if that's what you want to know. I don't have a phone on me. Nothing like that.'

'Trousers,' Sweet said again. The gun looked like a converted starting pistol – the sort of thing criminal gangs used all the time these days. Easy enough to get hold of if you knew the right criminal.

The gloves were not a good sign.

'Finn?' Eden called. 'Are you there?'

There was no answer.

'Finn?' Eden's eyes widened. He looked at Sweet. 'You told me he was OK.'

'He is. He's locked in his room.'

'Why can't I hear him, then?'

'Trousers. Give me your trousers.'

Eden unzipped his trousers and lowered them. He stepped out of them and held them up. Sweet grabbed them with his left hand, gave them a shake, threw the legs over his shoulder and patted them down to check that he was not carrying a phone.

'Happy? If you've done anything to hurt the boy . . .'

Sweet threw the trousers at him. 'Put them back on. Where are your car keys?'

'In the drawer behind you,' said Eden, hoping that he would reach for them. That might give him a chance to jump him.

'Get them, then,' said Sweet. 'And a screwdriver.'

'What?'

'Stop fucking about,' said Sweet angrily. 'We have to move fast.'

'I'm not doing anything until I see Finn,' Eden said quietly. He leaned to pull his trousers up; picked up his shirt and put it back on.

'Get the key. And the screwdriver. Then we get the boy.'

Eden buttoned his shirt as slowly as he dared.

There was a big black key in the lock in Finn's door. 'Open it,' said Sweet.

Eden did as he was told. He opened the door and was relieved to see that Finn was alive, at least. The boy was tied to the bed, with belts around each wrist. Apple's purple scarf had been tied tight around his mouth. His eyes were wide and red from crying.

'Oh, God.'

'Undo him,' ordered Sweet.

The first thing Eden removed was the scarf around his mouth. Finn gulped breath. When he released the second belt, Finn sat up and put his thin arms around Eden. 'I thought you were dead too,' Finn said.

'I'm sorry,' said Eden. 'I'm so, so sorry.'

'Put some clothes on him.'

Finn's clean clothes were still in the plastic bin bag Eden had brought back in from the launderette. He dug out a shirt, some pants and socks, some trousers. With Sweet's gun on them both, Finn put on what Eden gave him. Eden helped him get his legs into his trousers.

'Put the rest back in the bag,' said Sweet.

'What?'

'Put them in the bag.'

'Why?'

'Just do it!' Sweet muttered. Eden stuffed the mix of school uniform and ordinary clothes back into the bag.

'Give up, Mike. Police will be here soon to interview me about what happened on the boat. They'll be wondering where you are.'

Eden watched Mike looking carefully around the room. He spotted Eden's red action figure on his bedside table and put it in his pocket. 'Get the boy's toothbrush,' he said.

That puzzled Eden, but he did as he was told.

'Downstairs,' Sweet said. 'Bring the bag with you.' Sweet grabbed a dark blue puffer jacket off the couch and laid it over the gun, concealing it, then moved towards the beach door, glancing out. He looked around the small living room one last time. Reaching out, he snatched the photograph of Apple and Finn off the wall and stuffed that into his pocket with the action figure almost as an afterthought. 'What's that?' Sweet nodded at the parcel wrapped on the table.

'It's a present for Finn.'

'Take it,' he ordered, then returned to the door. When he was sure no one out there was watching them, he turned the key and kicked open the UPVC door. The air outside was fresh and clean. There was a tang of salt.

'Walk in front of me. Talk to nobody. Don't say a word.'

It was early still. Eden took Finn's hand and they walked outside into the light. The ferry hadn't yet started crossing the estuary. The sand was wet from last night's rain still, and the grey clouds over Dartmoor meant that more was on the way.

The beach was deserted until they reached the hard standing by the car park, where a woman in a red apron was unlocking a horse box that served as a food stall.

Sweet turned his back to her so she wouldn't recognise him as she opened up. 'Hurry,' he ordered.

Eden clutched Finn's hand tightly, feeling him tremble, calculating the distance to the nearest cars he could hide behind. On his own, he would have risked it. With Finn it was different.

'Where's your fucking car?' Sweet muttered and pressed the fob.

About ten metres away, lights flashed.

Hand in hand still, Eden and Finn approached the Audi. Its shiny paintwork was dulled by a salty layer of dust.

'He's in the back with me. You're in the front, driving.'

Eden did as instructed. He got into the driver's seat of the car that he had arrived in two weeks earlier, tossing Finn's present onto the passenger seat.

'You,' Sweet ordered Finn. 'In the back with me.'

Finn sat behind the passenger seat. The man with the gun sat right behind Eden.

'Go,' said Sweet.

'Where?'

'Where I tell you to go.'

So Eden pressed the start button and put the car into gear. 'Up the hill,' said Sweet.

Eden looked in the rear-view mirror as he left the car park onto the seafront road. Sweet was lying down across the back seat, hidden from view.

'Just drive. I've got the gun on your boy. Anything happens, he gets it first, you second.'

They drove up the road Eden had driven such a short time ago to arrive at the town. It was a Saturday morning and everything was still quiet.

Soon they were up in the high land above the town, the road that led up onto Haldon.

'Now slow,' Sweet said. Eden released his foot from the accelerator. 'Turn down that track on the right.'

It was a small rutted track into the forest, muddy puddles on either side of a line of thin grass.

Eden did as he was told. They were off the road soon. As soon as they were out of sight, among the dark firs, Sweet sat up straight in the back of the car. There would be no witnesses if he killed them here, thought Eden.

'That's far enough,' Sweet announced.

Instead of a bullet, Sweet gave him the screwdriver with the red handle, passing it over his shoulder to him.

'Get out,' he said.

Fifty-Nine

The screwdriver, it turned out, was for removing the Audi's number plates. No number plates would make it harder to trace the car's movements. Up to this point his car would have pinged every number recognition camera on the route. When the police started looking for him, they would be able to trace his journey heading out of Teignmouth. From now on, they would be less visible.

'Back in the car and drive,' said Sweet.

Eden reversed onto the road. 'Head north,' said Sweet.

'Where are we going?'

'Just drive.' And he lowered himself down onto the back seat again. 'And turn the radio on. Find a local station.'

Eden flicked through the radio channels on the screen until he came to BBC Radio Devon. It was still early. The announcer was listing traffic issues on routes into Exeter and tailbacks on the A303.

Eden drove at a slow speed, trying to remember the roads. Sweet did not want witnesses. He would kill them at some point, he was pretty sure, but he would need somewhere more isolated to be able to get away with it. If any eyewitnesses remembered seeing the car, they would remember the boy in the back and the car being driven by a single man. Eden was being set up.

'How are you doing, Finn?' Eden asked.

'I'm scared,' he said.

'So am I,' said Eden. 'But it'll be OK.' He was not at all sure it would be.

They drove onto the dual carriageway across Haldon, but after a mile, Sweet directed them off the main road and they were soon on smaller ones, lined by conifers and birches whose leaves were dripping in the thin drizzle.

Sweet had not killed them earlier when they had stopped by the side of the road nearer Teignmouth, so Eden supposed he had another plan in mind. He kept trying to think of what it would be.

They emerged into typical Devon lanes, high hedges and hills, winding descents into deep valleys and out again, heading north-west, towards Dartmoor. 'Turn right here,' ordered Sweet.

Another lane, bounded by greenness. Sweet was sticking to roads where they would not be seen. Eden was trying to remember the odd names of places they passed through: Dunchideock, Doddiscombsleigh and Lustleigh.

'Turn it up,' said Sweet.

Eden did as he was told and reached for the radio.

The news bulletin was all about an accident in the Channel off Plymouth. Three people had been air-lifted to safety. One was in a critical condition in the burns unit of Derriford Hospital. There were no other details yet.

'Right,' said Sweet. 'Then left.'

Eden drove through the hilly farmland east of Dartmoor, trying to glimpse Sweet's face in the rear-view mirror, trying to figure out what he was planning for them. Finn sat, pale and tense, staring straight ahead.

They emerged onto moorland, still sticking to the smaller roads. They seemed to have been driving for hours, but it was only maybe thirty or forty minutes. Sweet clearly had a destination in mind, Eden was sure of it.

Rounding a bend, a white Range Rover blocked their path on the single-track road.

Sweet slid down out of view. 'Don't say anything. Don't even fucking try.'

The driver of the bigger car was a man who expected Eden to make way for him. Eden reversed into a gateway and the Range Rover moved slowly forward.

The cars passed inches apart. The man was on the other side, so close Eden could have rolled down his window and touched him. All he could do was turn to the other driver and mouth, 'Help!' but the man – in a tweed cap and jacket – had his eyes fixed ahead on the gap in front of him, anxious to avoid any scrapes to the expensive paintwork.

'Good boy,' said Sweet. The Range Rover roared away. Eden motored on too.

The lane narrowed again, stunted oaks to the right. Then Eden caught a glimpse of a large body of water beyond them.

'Turn here.'

Then they were on a rutted track descending towards where Eden figured the lake would be.

They emerged out of the trees onto a narrow track leading down to a dark wooden shed. Eden realised that Sweet had brought them to a reservoir. A large one.

Everything was starting to make sense now and none of it was good. The winter had been a wet one. The reservoir was deep. Eden imagined the steep sides disappearing under the black surface. How easy it would be to sink the car in that water.

Eden braked.

'Why have you stopped? Keep going,' Sweet ordered. They were out in the open, where anyone could see them. Only a green path ahead, leading down to the trees surrounding the reservoir. Eden looked around. It was still early, and there was no one there to see them, anyway.

'How are you doing, Finn?' he asked again, keeping his voice calm and as reassuring as he could.

'I'm thirsty,' Finn answered. 'And I'm hungry.'

'Drive on. Or I swear I'll do it,' said Sweet.

It had crept up on him, this feeling for the boy. He had not expected to feel so much. He wished he had recognised this obscure sense of purpose – before it had been way too late to be of any use.

The stupid pop music on the radio was interrupted by another news bulletin. It took Eden a second to realise what the announcer was talking about. 'The injured man was taken by helicopter to Derriford Hospital in Plymouth and is reported to be in a serious condition. In what appears to be an unrelated incident, police have asked the public to be on the look-out for nine-year-old Finn Driscoll, the child who was found alone on board a yacht in the English Channel a fortnight ago. The young boy was reported missing from his home in Teignmouth this morning. Police are also asking members of the public to be on the look-out for a thirty-year-old man, believed to be in a black Audi A8.' There was a number to report any sightings to.

Bisi would have gone to the house this morning to collect the boy. She would have found the house empty, Finn's clothes missing, photos taken from the wall. Sweet had a genius for confusion, for obscuring the facts. He had made it look as though Eden had absconded with the boy. Bisi had done what she had to do – raise the alarm. A vulnerable child was missing, abducted by his uncle. If they disappeared now, people would assume that Eden had taken him.

Eden began to understand how things were going to play out now. In the back of the car, Sweet had sat up. There was a smile on his face. Everything was going to plan. He could make the boy and the uncle disappear.

Eden expected the bullet at any second.

'Drive on. Slowly now.'

Of course, Sweet wanted the car to be down at the water's edge. If he killed them here in the open, it would be messy.

The trees at the bottom of the track were dense. No light made it through beneath their green canopy. This was the place he had brought them to die.

Sixty

'I'm sorry, Finn,' said Eden again. He leaned forward and turned the GPS screen on. 'Hold on.'

Finn looked back at him in the mirror, puzzled.

Before Sweet could process what was going on, Eden floored the accelerator. The car lurched forward as tyres skidded on loose dirt.

'What the hell are you—?'

'Hold tight, Finn,' Eden called out.

He swung the wheel round and they were back on the thinly tarmacked road. The Audi sped up fast, bouncing over potholes.

'Stop the car or I shoot the boy!' shouted Sweet.

'And what then?'

The Audi had power. It was moving at fifty already, much too fast for this tiny track. Eden's eyes flicked from the road ahead to the GPS screen on his left, giving him little time to judge the turns in the road ahead. There was no chance of dragging his eyes up to look in the rear-view mirror to see the expression on Sweet's face.

'And what then, Mike?' Eden shouted again.

'And then I kill you.'

Eden pressed the pedal down a little further. 'At this speed? What do you think will happen to you if you kill me?'

The track was tiny, narrow, trees and ditches on both sides. Sweet would be calculating what would happen if the car came off the road now. There was no telling what it would hit.

'Slow down. Slow bloody down.'

Eden ignored him, bouncing over a junction. As long as he was heading west, he was heading into the moor. He slewed round a corner, swinging to the right and then the left. The back of the car spun round. Finn screamed.

Accelerating hard to regain control of the steering, Eden glanced at the GPS screen again. The blue line he had been driving along came to a dead end. The road he was on simply disappeared.

He would have no choice but to keep driving as fast as he could forward into the moor. If he stopped, he would be shot and so would Finn.

The road dipped down again and there was a clear view of two gates blocking the road ahead. One was straight, leading into a green field. The other – a sharp left turn – blocked a track that was heading up into the higher moorland. He had run out of road.

He braked hard, swinging the wheel to the left as he did so, so that the rear of the car skidded around. For a moment the car was almost stationary, but Eden kept it moving. He couldn't afford for them to stop.

'Fucking stop!' screamed Sweet.

Eden floored the accelerator once more and the car gathered speed again. They were in open moorland now, bouncing on bare land, on what looked like an ordinary footpath.

Right hand on the wheel, he pressed on the horn with his left. Inside the car, engine roaring, in this huge, open landscape, it sounded such a pathetic noise. He was pressing as hard as he could, as if that would make the horn louder.

In that second he glimpsed Sweet sitting up behind him, raising the gun towards the back of his head.

The first bang was the car hitting the steel gate, bursting it open with a jolt, bouncing over the uneven ground. The second was the gun.

Eden felt the tug at his left shoulder as the bullet smashed into it. The noise of the horn stopped abruptly.

The gun had been aiming for the back of his head. Only the jolt of the car had stopped the first bullet from killing him, jerking Sweet's arm downwards, making him hit Eden's body instead.

The pain was instantaneous, a white light, obliterating his vision, making thought impossible.

The car was still shooting forwards, faster again now, up the hill. Eden shook himself, trying to break through the agony, trying to concentrate, keeping his foot on the pedal. It was hard. The seconds felt like hours and his strength was pouring out of him. The boy was crying and there was nothing he could do. He knew the second bullet would come soon.

And before he could collect his thoughts, it did.

The car must have been doing around sixty when it left the moorland path.

It bounded to the right, across uneven land, into bracken and smashed hard into a single block of granite that protruded from a clump of gorse.

The roar of the engine died. The horn blared.

A group of rooks took to the air, heading east towards the woods around Fernworthy Reservoir.

The horn continued its single note in the still landscape.

For a while, nothing.

And then, above that blare, from inside the crashed car, came the sound of a man screaming.

The first of the hikers appeared over Sittaford Tor. About half a dozen of them, dressed in brightly coloured rain gear. When they saw the car, skewed, bonnet crumpled, they dropped their immense packs and broke into a run down the tussocky hillside.

More walkers appeared over Hew Down. Like the others they had dropped their backpacks and were running as hard as their aching legs would allow them, towards the ruined vehicle.

Still more appeared from the east, emerging from the forestry path. Thirty or forty, running towards the source of the noise. They seemed to emerge from every point of the compass.

The nearest were about ten metres away when the rear door opened and a man fell out of the car onto his knees.

To their horror, they saw the man was covered in blood. It ran down his white shirt onto his trousers. The blood seemed to be coming from the middle of his face, pouring into his mouth and down his chin.

The hikers were teenagers, youngsters, unused to this much carnage, but they still ran on towards him.

The bloody man steadied himself, looked around. 'Get back!' he shouted. And to their horror they saw he was holding a gun.

But there were more and more of them now, pouring down the slopes, surrounding him. They were girls and boys, waterproofs drenched, muddy from the walking, faces dirty, hair matted or under sodden woollen hats. They had abandoned their hike to come to help. The man stood, turned slowly, gun in his hand, blood still streaming from his wound, and stared into their appalled faces.

'Do you need help?' a young woman asked.

Another stepped out, arms out, gently waving her hands palm downward to try and calm him. Behind her the rest inched forwards.

There would not be enough bullets for all of them.

He fell to his knees on the hard ground, and the gun bounced away from him.

Sixty-One

'So now I'm going to tell you how it ends. You have to remember there were no mobile phones in those days. Maybe there were, but we didn't have them. Just a radio on board. When the boat was moored, back on the Portuguese side, Dad used the radio to give a signal to the men with the hearse that he was back. And then we would all get in the tender and he would take Mum, me and Apple onto the shore. He would always give us some money to have a meal there, while he returned to the boat and waited.

'You're a bit young to hear this story, I suppose, Finn, but I want to tell you the truth. I've never told anybody the truth about what happened. I've been too ashamed of my part in it. I may not get another chance to tell you about it.'

Finn listens to the story in bed, with the headphones on. He is in a different bedroom now, not at home. This is Mrs Sullivan's house.

'Anyway. This time we got into the tender, just like we always had done. Except I thought Apple was looking at me funnily, as if she knew something was up. I was wearing my backpack, I remember. That might have given it away.

'Dad looked jumpy too, but then he always was nervous at this stage, because if the police caught us it would be the end of everything. We always moored quite a way from other people so that nobody would see what was happening on the boat, so it took a long time to make it to the beach. I remember, we were moored the far side of a rocky headland, but when we rounded it we saw we were at this huge tourist beach. One of those with umbrellas and beach bars, and loads of people lying on the sand.

'Dad went a little way up the beach to one of the bars and then dropped us. He gave our mum the notes to pay for the supper. He always controlled the money. Dad always controlled everything.

'"I'll be back later," he said. And we got out. We all knew what he was doing. The men would come by in a fishing boat or something. We weren't supposed to know it, but I think we all did. We just never talked about it. It was business. We brought the stuff over from Morocco or Algeria and nobody stopped us, or searched us, because we were just a happy family on a pretty sailing boat. That's why the men in the hearse wanted us. We were a family, with children. We could get away with it.

'Apple and me adored those beach bars. For one evening, we could pretend we were normal. They were full of people who spoke English. Quite often there would be families there, on holiday, and we could act as if we were just like them. They'd serve fish and chips and burgers for the tourists, and I thought that was the best food in the world, except we weren't allowed to eat them because we were vegetarians. I used to sit there looking at them enviously.

'Seriously. It was heaven. In the bars, they would play music on the radio and we would listen to every song, 'cause Dad didn't allow us to listen to pop music. He said it was all rubbish. Your mum would sing along. *"Better off Alone"*, *"Barbie Girl"*. I don't know how she managed to learn all the words, but she knew them and she would go all starry-eyed singing along.

'Listening to those cheesy little songs. It was a kind of freedom.

'I remember that night we sat out at a table in front of the bar, looking at all the lights. It was beautiful. Apple started talking to some German boys at the next table. Mum ordered wine, which she never did if Dad was there. Apple wanted a glass and Mum normally said no, but it was strange that night. It was as if we all knew something was wrong.

'Mum always used to try to order something local, like roasted peppers or caldo verde, but there was not much you could eat if you were a vegetarian really, besides chips.

'That night I said out loud I wanted a burger. I told Mum I didn't want to be a vegetarian any more. In our family, it was like saying I didn't believe in any of it any more. And I didn't. That was the point. I wanted to give up on it all.

'Amazingly, Mum said I could have a burger if we promised not to tell Dad. She actually laughed. It was that kind of night. Nothing was normal. It was probably the first time I'd ever eaten meat. I remember biting in and thinking it was really strange. It wasn't at all like I imagined. I remember finding the texture really repulsive, but when Apple asked me what it was like I said it was delicious.

'Mum got drunk. So did Apple, I think. Anyway. We waited for Dad to come back, and we waited, and we waited.

'"Maybe it's taking longer than usual," Mum said.

'"Maybe what's taking longer than usual?" Apple asked. She was teasing Mum, I think, because we all knew what Dad was doing but we never, ever talked about it. It was kind of a taboo. If we admitted what Dad did, then we weren't a special family, like Dad said we were, living a charmed life, better than all the tourists and the locals, sailing around the Mediterranean on our boat.

'There was a toilet at the side of the restaurant. I remember going to it at some point with my backpack, late in the night, and taking out the packages I had taken from underneath the water tank – the ones my father had hidden there that night in Morocco – and putting them on top of the toilet cistern.

'I'm thinking now, maybe I had spilled some of it in the boat. I don't know, but it would make sense if I had.

'Why had I stolen them? I ask myself that all the time. What did I think I was doing? Really I just wanted to get back at Dad somehow, I suppose.

'But Dad just didn't come back and Mum started to get scared. She kept asking the Germans what the time was. Some time around one in the morning the restaurant owner started switching off the lights and we paid the bill. Mum took the remainder of the bottle of wine with her and we sat on the beach, waiting for the boat that never arrived, and Apple and I fell asleep next to each other.

'Some time in the early morning we saw the crowd of people gathering a little further down from us, and then police arrived and began shooing everyone away. They said they were closing the beach and we didn't know what happened. When we asked, they told us the body of a man had washed up and we had to leave. I think we all knew who it was right then.

'I never meant for it to happen. I promise. I hated him but I never meant for it to happen.

'Later, the police told us that somebody had tried to rob our boat and had beaten Dad and thrown him overboard. In the papers it said he had been hit with something blunt over a hundred times. It was reported as a robbery. There was no mention of anything else.

'We knew it was the men in the hearse, but we were too scared to say anything. They obviously thought Dad had stolen some of the drugs. People do terrible things to each other because they are greedy.

'I had been so angry with him, I just thought he would get into a bit of trouble and that was it. I really didn't know how serious it all was. I never heard what happened to the stuff I had left at the restaurant. Maybe the people who owned the restaurant found the packets and sold them, or just flushed them away.

'The thing is, Mum and Apple never found out it was my fault. I knew it was. It was my fault he was dead and that he'd died a violent death.

'Mum was completely lost without him. It was crazy. He had controlled her, he had abused her, he had stolen her money and spent it on stupid things, but she was like a ghost after he died. It was as if she had forgotten everything bad that he had done.

'I hated my dad, but I couldn't stop thinking what it must have been like, them beating him to death. I couldn't stand the guilt of it. I couldn't stand Apple and Mum being so sad. And because we had no money and nowhere else to go, we had no choice but to carry on living on the boat Dad had given us. That was too much for me.

'One day, I told Apple I was leaving. She was upset, but she didn't do anything to stop me. And I knew that I was leaving her on her own, and she'd have to look after Mum. I knew what I was doing to her but I couldn't stand it any longer. And so I hitchhiked to England on my own and turned up in London. A copper found me sleeping in St James's Park. Dad had taught us to be afraid of policemen, so I tried running away from him but he found me again the next day. "I bet you're hungry," he said. He was kind. He bought me some food, got Social Services involved. Never asked me my story. I ended up in a children's home. Hated it, but it was only until I was sixteen, and then they put me in a flat with other kids. And I went to real schools for the first time and I just tried to be as normal as I possibly could be.

'Like I said, I've never told anyone else about this. Only you.

'So if you're listening, I'm sorry, Finn. And I'm sorry I'm not there any more when you need me. It's like I left your sister once and now I'm doing it all over again. And I loved your mother. And I love you. And I'm really glad to have met you. You don't know how much that has meant to me. I'm sorry that I'm not very good at showing that. Basically, I'm sorry for everything.

'That's all I have to say.'

Sixty-Two

Finn does not really like Mrs Sullivan's house, but at least she is nice to him. Although it has only been two nights so far, Bisi has told him that he will probably be here for a while.

He misses living in the house he lived in with his mum – and also for a little while with his uncle Eden. He misses the sound of the river and the gulls on the roof. This house is too tidy. The toilet smells of stuff that is supposed to smell like lemons, but doesn't.

Angela isn't bad. She's sure to always leave the bedroom door open for him.

Mr Sullivan has been to the house on the back beach to collect a few things. He has set up the PS5 Finn's uncle gave him in his bedroom. Finn has had a go at playing it. It is easier than he imagined it would be. He thinks he could be good at it, probably beat Cyrus if he really tries, but whenever he plays it he feels that his mum is going to come in at some point and she will be disappointed.

There is a ring on the front doorbell. Mr Sullivan lets Bisi into the house.

'How's the best boy?' she booms. 'How are your bruises doing, my multicoloured marvel?'

She is so loud. Mr and Mrs Sullivan are so quiet, he loves that Bisi is here, being so noisy, filling the whole house, greeting Angela, asking how his night was.

They had looked at the bruises in the ambulance, put some stuff on them. The bruises fascinate him. He looked at them in the living room mirror. They are marking time on his face. Some of the purple is already turning yellow.

Bisi has brought some shopping – as promised – because Mrs Sullivan complains that she can't find vegan food in her local supermarket. Bisi has picked a few bits up at the Morrison's on the way. He can hear them talking about what she has brought.

'Tofu burgers?' Angela was saying, as if she was being asked to cook something Martian.

'Oh, there you are!' Bisi calls out, discovering Finn listening in the living room. 'I've got a visitor for you, Finn,' she announces.

And when Molly walks into the Sullivans' living room, hand covered in a bandage, Finn runs up and gives her one of his famous hugs.

'You were so brave,' says Molly. 'So, so brave. Like your mum was.'

Finn nods. She reaches out to touch the discoloured skin on the side of Finn's face, but he flinches backwards.

'Sorry,' she says.

The arrest of a local police detective on charges of kidnapping, assault and murder has been all over the news since yesterday morning. It was even on *BBC Breakfast*.

'Are you ready?' Bisi asks.

Finn nods.

'Come here,' orders Angela and she runs her hand through

his hair to straighten it, then kisses him like everyone always does, on the top of his head. 'Supper at five. Vegan burgers, chips and peas. You're very welcome to join us, obviously,' she says to Molly.

Molly smiles.

Upstairs, in Mr and Mrs Sullivan's bedroom, there is a table crowded with pictures of boys and girls, each in their own frame. Finn wonders if his picture will be there one day. He doesn't know what is going to happen to him next.

They get into Bisi's car: Finn in the back and Molly in the passenger seat next to Bisi. It is a mess of sweet packets and folders from work, which Bisi has to move to make space for all three of them. She finds some Fruit Pastilles in the glove compartment and offers them around. 'Take two,' she orders Finn.

It is another bright day. The summer is getting underway. The rain seems to have gone completely now. The back beach will be packed.

'Have you thought about going back to school next week?' Bisi asks when they are on the main road, looking in the rear-view mirror.

Finn is looking out of the window and he says nothing, so Bisi leaves the question for another time.

Sixty-Three

The three police officers had waited in the corridor for what felt like hours. The round-faced man was nervous in hospitals despite his years in the police. There was a younger woman, with straw-coloured hair and a habit of biting her nails, and a second woman who was even younger still, with long, straight black hair.

They watched people entering and leaving the hospital room, hoping, each time, that they would be the next to be allowed in. There was a coffee machine on the next floor and they had taken turns to go up to it in the lift.

They exchanged polite chit-chat about the job while they sat, waiting.

'OK,' said a man in blue eventually. 'You three can go in now.'

It was a small, plain room, with a single bed and a window. There was a clock on the wall at the foot of the bed, and a vase full of freesias on the bedside table.

'Sammy?' said Eden, with a lopsided grin. Since coming round, Eden had got used to his own voice. It was still thin, an old man's croak.

Sammy stepped forward and squeezed Eden's good hand; the one above the covers. 'Hello, Eden. I just wanted to come and see how you were.'

'Bloody hell,' said Eden, seeing who had stepped out from behind Sammy.

PC Lisa Ali was there too. 'Hello, Eden,' she said.

DI Sammy Kadakia introduced the third person there. She was a detective from Devon and Cornwall Police.

Eden tried to push himself up a little on his pillows, but pain exploded from his shoulder.

'Don't,' said Sammy.

'Oh, God,' said Lisa. 'You look shit.'

'I asked Inspector Rachel Eason to come along to update you about the investigation into the death of your sister,' said Sammy. 'I figured you needed to know. And Lisa has some news too.'

Rachel from Devon and Cornwall Police spoke: 'I'm afraid that the man whose life you attempted to save on the trawler two nights ago didn't make it,' she said. 'He died of his injuries this morning.'

'Graeme,' said Eden.

'Yes. Graeme Pine. We have been interviewing his wife about what she knew. She claims to have been totally ignorant of all his activities.'

Sammy smiled. 'Surprise surprise.'

'Which,' continued the woman, 'seems highly unlikely as we are ninety-nine per cent certain that it was his wife—'

'Jackie,' said Eden.

'Yes, Jackie Pine, who would have informed him that not only was your nephew's carer away, but also that the school safeguarding officer was off sick, on the day that your nephew was abducted. That allowed Graeme Pine to arrange for the boy to be taken. We haven't charged Jackie yet, but we will,' said the woman.

'I think it must have been her,' said Eden.

'Only a matter of time. We have also discovered that Graeme turns out to have had several dating accounts on his phone. One of which connects him to . . .' The woman looked at her notebook.

Eden's head had been fuzzy from the painkillers all morning, but the name of the woman appeared from nowhere. 'Elaine Pritchard,' he said.

'Correct.' Inspector Eason smiled at him. 'Locals confirm that they had seen a man who looked like Graeme Pine visiting her on a couple of occasions. We had the description, of course, but didn't link it to Graeme Pine until he turned up on that burning trawler. We think Graeme persuaded her to take the boy out of school and ask him a few questions. He needed to know if the boy—'

'Finn.'

'—Finn Driscoll. He needed to know if Finn had heard him board the yacht and whether his mother had ever talked about what they were up to on the trawler. Whether Elaine got cold feet about having abducted the child, or whether Graeme just didn't want her blabbing about it, we are working on the assumption that it was him who killed her, driving your sister's car.'

'I think it may have been Sweet, pulling the strings,' said Eden. 'He had already taken the computer.'

'We found that,' said Inspector Eason. 'At least, we found the remains of the hard drive in Sweet's garage. There were photographs taken from Finn's house of Graeme Pine's trawler being loaded.'

'I was right,' said Eden. 'When Sweet realised they were on there, he figured out there still might be an SD card with duplicates on it too – and maybe others. He needed Finn to tell him where it would be hidden.'

'It's possible, I suppose,' said Eason. 'We will be pursuing that as a line of enquiry. It's obviously been a big shock to our force. We're pretty sure it was Graeme Pine who also carried out the killing of Frankie Hawkins with a handgun. We have recovered a set of motorbike leathers and they are with the forensics team now. We believe that Mike Sweet supplied the weapon. He was one of ours. It's a difficult time for all of us.'

'Are you OK, listening to all of this?' asked Sammy. 'It's a lot.'

'Yes. I'm fine, actually,' said Eden.

'Some of this is still pure speculation,' said Eason. 'We know that Sweet's wife is a problem drinker. It's no secret that Mike Sweet had asked all the local pubs not to serve her. We believe she was driving drunk the day she rear-ended your sister's car. Sweet bribed your sister not to report it. Paid five thousand pounds into her account using an untraceable gift card.'

'My sister was scared of the police, too, I think,' interrupted Eden. 'She didn't trust them. That's why she wrote to me. It turned out she was right not to. Mike Sweet was corrupt – willing to pay her money to cover up a crime. I think she was worried that if she got on the wrong side of the police, Social Services would get involved again. She believed they were spying on her. I think that's why she wrote to me when she first began to suspect that Graeme Pine was using his trawler to dump chemicals.'

'Maybe I should take notes?' suggested Eason.

'There will be time for that later,' Sammy told her. 'Now it's just about filling in the gaps for Eden. He's had a time of it. It'll help him if he knows.'

'Is there any evidence that Frankie Hawkins was actually dealing drugs, the way Sweet says he was?' Eden asked.

'He's been known for it. Turns out he was running raves round at Labrador Bay,' the inspector said. 'It's this spot you need a boat to get to – just along the coast, past the Ness. Using that to deal a bit of E and stuff, but nothing major. Nothing of the scale that would mean anyone wanting to kill him. But enough for mud to stick when Sweet flung it. It looks like the longer you stayed around here, the more Sweet was panicking that you were on to him – or that you would be soon. If he could make people believe that your sister was involved in some kind of drug-running operation with Frankie, they'd stop looking for the real reason your sister died.'

'And the more likely I'd lose custody of Finn,' said Eden. 'So that's what Frankie was using Molly's boat for on the night my sister disappeared,' said Eden. 'A rave.'

'What?' asked Eason, puzzled.

'Nothing. It's not important. Carry on.'

'One thing is still a puzzle. There really were traces of cocaine on the boat. Initially we believed Mike Sweet might have planted them but one of the scientists says that they may have been there some time. Apparently cocaine is a,' she looked down at her notes, 'persistent chemical.' She looked up again. 'It may have been there for years. I don't suppose you have any idea how it got there?'

Eden shook his head. 'No,' he lied. 'No idea at all.'

'Ah, well. A mystery. On to Teign Valley Environmental Services,' she said, flicking onto another page. 'They had been struggling for years. It appears they had been cutting corners by dumping illicit materials, instead of processing them correctly, and then faking records. Sweet had been on to them for ages. They're looking at all the accounts now, but it looks like they might have been paying Sweet off for some time. He was extorting them, we believe, to keep quiet about the scale of their illegal operation. Which only made things worse for them financially, and of course the worse it got, the more corners they cut. And that included paying Graham Pine a bit to dump toxic materials at sea at night. Something your sister must have cottoned on to.'

A nurse popped her head around the door. 'Everything OK? There are some more people outside waiting to see you. You're quite the celebrity.'

Eden told her that everything was fine and the nurse retreated.

Lisa picked up a card on the bedside table and looked at it. It was from Molly and signed with a big X. 'Finn sends love,' the note said.

'Our guess,' continued the officer, 'is that when your sister followed Graeme Pine out to sea, she couldn't find anyone to look after Finn, so she felt she had no choice but to take Finn along. And when Graeme realised she had seen him dumping materials, he came aboard *Calliope* to reason with her. That's when she put the latch on the cabin door. She didn't want anybody knowing there was a young boy aboard. She locked him in to keep him safe.'

'Sweet said there weren't any prints on the second glass on the boat,' Eden said.

'What second glass?' she asked, puzzled.

Of course, Eden thought. Sweet never sent the glass to Forensics because he knew they might find someone else's prints on it. 'Never mind. Go on.'

'We think he argued with her, pushed her overboard, perhaps. We may never know exactly what happened. After that, things began to spin out of control. Once your sister was dead, we reckon Michael Sweet started to panic about

Teign Valley Environmental and all the money he'd taken from them over the years and set about trying to cover things up. Graeme Pine was panicking too, because he had unaccounted-for chemicals on his site and needed to get rid of them before anyone started asking.

'From the traces that the forensics officers found on the trawler, we're pretty sure Graeme Pine was dumping Class 2 oxidisers.' She read from a list. 'Bromates, chlorates, peroxides, nitrates . . . Industrial and farm waste. Usually costs a bit to dispose of, so there's money in it. Stable if they're kept separately in sealed containers, but if the water gets at them, they're often highly flammable. That's what blew up the warehouses in Beirut a few years ago. Killed a couple of hundred people that time.'

'So one of the barrels exploded,' suggested Eden. 'Maybe tipped over and bust its seal before he could get it overboard?'

'Serves him right,' said Eason.

They went quiet for a little while. Sammy said, 'And you . . . are you OK?'

'I'm getting there, I think. There's a bit of damage to my shoulder.'

'Take your time, obviously,' said Sammy.

'We're charging Sweet with your attempted murder,' the woman said.

'He was going to kill Finn as well, wasn't he?'

'He's not talked at all so far, but yes, we assume so.'

'And it turns out that you're not the only force with a dodgy copper in it,' said Sammy to the woman from the Devon and Cornwall police.

Lisa Ali had been silent all the while.

'Tell him, Lisa.'

She pulled her chair forward. It squeaked on the hospital floor.

'You asked me to look into who had taken over visiting Hasina Hossein after you'd gone.'

'Bailey,' said Eden.

'Yes. You were right. I arranged to meet him for a drink after work. I know he fancied me,' she said.

'Against police protocol obviously,' said Sammy.

'I'm not listening,' said Eason, holding up her palms.

'I did it off my own bat. And I told him I'd seen you hitting Ronan Pan. He encouraged me to complain about your conduct to the IOPC. When I asked why, he told me he already had. It would back up his testimony.'

'It was him.'

Sammy took over. 'Turns out Ronan Pan is back in the frame, this time for attempting to pervert the course of justice. He appears to have offered Bailey a very fat bung to fabricate the evidence, and to scare the hell out of Hasina Hossein. Pan is claiming that Bailey extorted him, but it's enough. We're hoping Hasina will change her mind and testify against him now.'

'Sammy has asked me to visit Hasina,' said Lisa. 'We're getting on OK.' She smiled.

Sammy reached out towards him and laid his hand on Eden's good arm. 'I'll obviously find you a more suitable role in London, mate, if they decide to let you stay with the boy. Something with regular hours so you can look after him.'

He looked down the bed towards Sammy's hand. 'I don't know,' he said noncommittally. 'I'll see.'

'Vacancy here, obviously,' said the woman, meaning it as a joke.

The clock at the end of the bed ticked.

'Well. You don't have to decide anything yet, of course,' said Sammy.

The clock ticked some more.

'Can I have a little word with Eden on my own?' Sammy said eventually.

'Right.' The woman from Devon and Cornwall stood up. 'Hope to see you very soon,' she said.

Lisa raised an eyebrow. 'See you, Eden,' she said.

'Out,' said Sammy.

When they'd gone, and the door was closed, he said, 'You know you almost lost us the chance to convict Ronan Pan.'

'I know. I was an idiot. I lost my temper and did something stupid.'

Sammy nodded.

'I'm working on it, I promise. I'm seeing an expert who knows a thing or two about anger,' said Eden.

Sixty-Four

Finn, Bisi and Molly park in the hospital car park, before riding up in the lift, following the directions the man on reception has given them.

When the doors open, a man and two women stand by the open door, waiting to take the lift down.

The man is saying, 'Give Eden a week. I promise he'll be begging to come back to work at the Met. I know him. He's a city boy.'

They step back to let the two women and the boy pass.

There is a nurse in the corridor holding a clipboard, who points Bisi in the right direction – 'second door on the left' – and then Bisi is knocking on the door and cautiously pulling it open.

'Oh, my God!' exclaims Molly, who is last to enter the room but the first to speak. 'Look at you.'

Eden smiles. 'Finn,' he croaks.

'Hello,' says Finn shyly.

Eden tries again to push himself up on his elbows but it hurts too much, so Bisi takes his good arm and raises him up a little and presses buttons to raise the bedhead. 'How are you?' Eden asks Finn.

'Not bad. I played your PS5 this morning. It's OK.'

'I think you saved my life,' says Eden.

Finn looks grave. 'Yes, I did.'

Eden's smile broadens. 'Thank you.'

While Bisi arranges Eden's pillows, Finn takes a space on the edge of his bed.

'Go careful,' warns Bisi. 'Your uncle's been very ill.'

'It's fine,' says Eden, putting his good hand on top of Finn's. 'And I hear you've been biting again.'

Finn nods. 'His nose,' he says, 'just there,' pointing to Eden's nose.

'You must have bitten him quite hard,' suggests Eden.

'Really hard,' agrees Finn.

Molly makes a face. Eden tries to imagine it.

'He shot you. And he was going to shoot you again. I was angry. So I bit him. And he missed because I bit him.'

Just like that.

'He screamed?'

'Really loud. Really, really loud.'

'How did that feel?'

'Horrible,' says Finn. 'I hurt him really badly.'

Eden nods back at him. 'Did he hurt you?' Eden asks.

'No. All the people came because of the noise and because of all his screaming and they stood around him and they stopped him from hurting you any more.'

Molly asks Eden, 'Was it just luck, or did you know there would be a lot of hikers there?'

Eden thinks about it for a little while. 'It was a lot of luck. A bit of guesswork too. I didn't know for sure. Bisi's husband, Peter, had shown me the map of the route the Ten

Tors hikers were taking and I'd seen the reservoir on it and knew that one of the routes ran just to the west of it. He'd said there were thousands of people who do it every year, in groups, and how they spread them out so they don't all walk together, so it was all I could think of.'

The army helicopter had arrived within minutes of the hikers finding the car. At first they had assumed that Sweet had been injured in the accident until they looked in the car and saw a second man, also bleeding heavily, slumped against the airbag on the steering wheel and heard the pale boy begging them to help him.

In a few days there will be funerals for Apple and for Frankie. There will be a lot of crying to do.

'Did you listen to my story, Finn?' asks Eden.

Finn says, 'Yes. I finished it.'

'What story?' asks Bisi, intrigued.

'Eden made a story for me. On my iPad.'

'That's nice,' says Bisi, pleased.

'What did you think of it?' Eden asks.

'It was quite sad, wasn't it?'

'Yes. It was,' answers Eden.

'But I liked the boy in the story.'

'Did you?'

'What story is this?' Bisi interrupts.

'Just something that Uncle Eden made up,' says Finn, looking right at Eden, as if daring him to defy him.

'I'd like to hear it some day,' Bisi says. 'It sounds amazing.'

'I don't think so.' Finn shakes his head. 'It's a story for me.'

'Aren't you the lucky one?' says Bisi.

'Yes,' replies Finn.

'You'll need physio, I expect.' Bisi looks at Eden now. 'In a little while at least.'

The bullet had missed his subclavian artery by millimetres.

He would need another operation soon, but he had still been lucky.

'I hear rowing is good for shoulders,' says Bisi. 'I also know that Molly is a good teacher.'

'Get lost,' Eden tells her.

Molly laughs. Eden tries not to because when he does it hurts.

There will be a lot of paperwork to get through about Apple's estate and the house. He will have plenty of time. And Eden will have to decide what he wants. Finn too.

For now, though, Eden lies as still as he can so he doesn't aggravate his shoulder, listening to the laughter of the two women, and feeling the weight and the warmth of the boy who has pushed his way onto the bed next to him.

And Finn is leaning down across Eden's chest now, listening to the beat of his uncle's heart.

Acknowledgements

Thanks to Jane Casey, who held my hand through a lot of the process of making this book happen, and to my pal Elly Griffiths who also helped more than she knows. Thanks, too, to Ann Cleeves for her support. Adrian Driscoll has held my hand reassuringly through much of my publishing journey. I repay him now by stealing his name. Also, thanks, Graham Bartlett, Neil Stewart of Envirogreen, Christopher Shaw, Lisa Pash, Vic Bailey, Lucy Sampson, Colin Scott, Corrie Corfield, Fiona Erskine and the staff of Emilie's in Glenbeigh for the best coffee and a chair. Deep gratitude to Jon Riley for his generosity, to Karolina Sutton for her wisdom and support and to Julia Wisdom for inviting me to bring Eden Driscoll to Hemlock. As always, thanks to Jane McMorrow.